BLEACHER GIRL

*

Blue Collar Press

Shirley Johnson

COPYRIGHT 2022 SHIRLEY JOHNSON
COVER ART DONE BY BENJAMIN RUPPERT, SAPPER_SPY ART
COPYRIGHT 2022

ISBN 979-8-9859456-0-7

BLUE COLLAR PRESS

To my Twitter family who supported me the entire way.

Especially,

Mike, Ken, Steven, & Sam

Thank you for all the input!

Shirley Johnson

Chapter One

She was high maintenance. I could tell that the moment she stepped out of the car. And what a car it was. 1987 Buick Regal. Right off the lot. Whoever she was with was bringing the bank to maintain her and I looked to see if I could take him or if I could take her from him.

But the him was another girl. Yeah. It was like that and I let the smile spread across my face because she was gorgeous. And she was someone I had never seen before. She had those fancy jeans you got at the mall at the County Seat store. Her thin black shirt covered two perfect little boobs. Padded bra. That made me laugh. But tits were tits. They were all good.

"That girl is high maintenance," I told Jeff and Shane as I eyed her huge blonde hair that didn't move in the wind. That'd be a girl you'd have to be careful smoking around. I'd dated plenty of those girls with the huge hair and the even bigger shoulder pads.

"That's one of Jennifer's friends," Shane said to me and grinned.

"What? Is she your date?"

"Naw, man, your date if you want. There's three of them and three of us."

The smile was back, wide across my face. A teeth-and-all kind of smile that lights the eyes and dazzles the girls, even if your eyes are plain brown like mine. Even if the girl was high maintenance like this one clearly was. She probably took two hours to get all that make-up on and all that hair teased up. She would be a lot of work. But if you put in the effort, even a plain guy like me could charm a high maintenance one.

"She could be your date. She's here with Jennifer and Jeff

has called dibs on Jennifer already," Shane laughed and elbowed Jeff.

"She's gonna be work," I told the boys.

"Worth it though," Shane laughed and then added, "I'd do her."

We watched as another girl pulled herself out of the backseat of the Buick. A silky sheet of long straight honey hair came out first as she slowly emerged.

"Oh, I like this one even better," I said, a little startled at the sight of her.

I couldn't help but lick my lips. This one drew my interest so completely I forgot the high maintenance one right away. I'd never seen silky long straight hair like that, like it was 1970 instead of 1987.

This one had on a short brown skirt that hit her mid-thigh and buttoned up the middle. It was like fucking Christmas. This one had on a dark red top with tiny short sleeves over her pale arms and as the wind rippled the thin material and I saw all of her, I gulped. She was all tits. I had to blink my eyes several times to make sure I was seeing right.

"My God," I said to Jeff and Shane who were staring with their mouths open.

"That's the Bleacher Girl," Shane told me.

"The Bleacher Girl?" I asked, my voice cracking in excitement.

I looked at her again. She was clear across the back lot of the Sears Store. But after I quit looking at her short skirt and her huge rack, I saw she had a black walking cast on her leg and a huge white cast on her right arm.

"That's who fell through the bleachers?" I asked, my voice dry.

"Yup."

"She must have landed on those jugs or she would be dead falling that far." My eyes popped at the beauty of her.

Everyone had heard of the Bleacher Girl who tripped at the Opening Game over at Sand Creek and fell between the top seats on the aluminum bleachers. The whole game had stopped. She somehow missed the struts and cables all the way forty feet to the ground. It was the talk of four counties. It was a miracle she lived without breaking her neck. It was a miracle none of her hair got yanked out on the way down, I thought to myself as I saw all of her golden honey brown hair cascading down her back and rippling in the wind.

"Goddamn, that's Bleacher Girl?" I rubbed my eyes and looked some more.

"Yup."

"She's fucking stacked!"

Shane and Jeff laughed at me.

"She high maintenance?" I asked them and swallowed hard.

"Nope. Band girl."

"Band girl? My God. Is she taken?"

"No man. Like I said, band girl, ha," Shane laughed. I eyeballed him.

"Serious. She's all yours."

I sighed. I couldn't take my eyes off her. I watched her as she struggled with her crutches in the October wind. She was tiny.

"Fuck me," I said under my breath but Jeff and Shane both heard me.

"If you're lucky!" They both said and laughed.

"Hey! Where you going?" Jeff called after me as I set off running across the wet pavement of the black parking lot.

"Gonna go help her."

"We'll lose our spot in line," Jeff hollered and gestured behind them at the long snaking line to the JayCees Haunted House where hundreds of teens were waiting to go in on opening night, two weeks before Halloween.

"That's ok," I told him and grinned before turning around and running to the girls by the Buick.

**

The girl driving the Buick had parked far away. She parked clear over in the back lot of Sears and Roebuck. Thank God it had stopped raining but it was still too far for Bleacher Girl to walk in the huge black boot brace, plus the blacktop was slippery wet.

I had watched and seen how the two other girls didn't help her get out of the backseat. By the time Bleacher Girl climbed out of the car, those two other girls were halfway across the lot. They left Bleacher Girl to hobble across the dark lot alone.
What bitches.

I ran past them and heard them say, *Hayyy*. I flashed them a quick glance, and kept on running and skidded to stop right in front of Bleacher Girl.

"Hi," I said and flashed her a huge smile. It was exciting to be so close to her. My God, she was sexy.

She didn't answer. She stood there trying to balance on one crutch with her left arm. She was incredibly tiny and just barely 5 ft tall.

"Hi," I said again, "I'm Mike, Jeff and Shane's friend and you're the Bleacher Girl," I blurted and felt like an asshole.

"Faith," she said and bit her bottom lip and looked down at her feet.

"Faith," I echoed. A good girl name. My God this was going to be a lot of work but so worth it.

A shiver ran through me and I rolled my shoulders and popped my neck twice and tried to relax. She was winding me all up.

"Hi," she said and peeked up at me from where she leaned on her crutch with one arm and let the other arm hang limp and heavy in its cast next to her short skirt.

"I like your socks and your skirt," I told her as I eyeballed what had to be the world's tallest socks pulled up over her knees. They had tan and bright pink stripes and were like nothing I had ever seen. "Where did you find such long socks?" I asked and could not stop looking at them.

"Ahem."

She cleared her throat and I peeled my eyes away from her knees and looked her in the face. Only then did she answer me.

"I got them in St. Louis at the Benetton Store. I dress weird. I know," she said and studied my face for a reaction.

Benetton. Maybe she was high maintenance. That place was high. We didn't have one anywhere near here, nor in this state. I ran my fingers through my hair to stall for time. A rich girl. I'd never dated a rich girl or a band girl, or a good girl. A stacked girl. I was out of my league and I loved it there.

"I like them," I said but looked at the skirt. "You get your skirt there too?" I asked and that smile was back. I couldn't help it even if I felt like the world's biggest dickhead with it. Her skirt was mesmerizing. I couldn't look away from it unless it was to look at her tits. Her entire body was killing me and I forced myself to look at her face but my eyes kept dropping. And dropping.

"No, I had it. It's an old one I haven't worn in a long time. But I didn't want to cut the legs off all my jeans, so I've been wearing skirts but it's getting too cold," she explained and pulled at the tops of her socks with her one good hand and then dropped her crutch accidentally.

I picked it up before she could even try to do it. I didn't want her to fall over. I didn't want her to bend over in that skirt. My heart couldn't take it.

"You're not bringing this with you, are you?" I asked as I tested out the crutch. It was too short for me but it brought back the memories like the time I broke my ankle falling out of the golf cart when Dad flipped it going too fast and the other time when I crushed my foot when Dad ran it over when he was drunk.

"I don't know how else I'll walk over there."

"It's just the black-top is slippery." I gestured to the shiny black parking lot.

I put my weight on the crutch to show her how much it slid

around on the slippery pavement. She would surely fall if she tried to use it to get across the lot. It might as well have been ice.

"I can carry you," I told her and felt like an idiot. No girl would let some guy carry her across a parking lot. Not a good girl like this girl. Maybe those other two would, I thought, and looked over my shoulder to see that the other two girls, the ones with the huge hair, had joined up with Shane and Jeff in the line, lighting smokes in the wind, and were moving closer to the door of the Haunted House.

Meanwhile, Faith was staring at me like I was crazy. But I wasn't smiling now. I was serious. I'd carry her all the way, all she had to do was say the words, and I wouldn't try to cop a feel or anything. I'd be a gentleman.

"That won't be necessary," she said and paused as if trying to remember something.

"Mike," I offered and nodded and smiled.

"Mike," she said and smiled back up at me and made my insides flip-flop.

"Be no problem. It's a long way. Look, your friends are near the door. I'm real strong. I mean," I trailed off as she began to giggle. "Really. I was in wrestling before I got kicked out of school. I can pick you up and carry you there."

"I'm not going if I can't walk there. But there's no way I can get there before they go in. They're not even waiting for me."

We both looked across the parking lot and could see the two girls linking arms with Jeff and Shane as they got closer to the doors. The girls were fanning their huge hair and fluffing it and looked like idiots in their matching zipper-covered jeans and matching black tops as they simpered next to the guys.

"If I carried you, I could get you to the door in time to go with your friends." I was ready to run with her if I had to, if that's what would make her happy.

"I can walk but I have to go slow."

She took the crutch from me and started to open the door to

the Buick but it was locked.

"Here."

I took the crutch from her and laid it under the car while she watched. She looked at me like I'd taken a puppy from her and put it down there.

"No one will see it down there and take it. Just don't forget it when you drive off."

"Thanks."

"I'll walk slow with you," I assured her. There was no way in hell I was leaving her. Not only that, but I was really glad we would be going in the Haunted House without her friends. Without mine too.

She began to hobble along slowly next to me and I felt bad for her because she looked cold. My God her whole body had to be freezing with what she wearing. I ached to hold her close and crush her into me.

"I'll carry you there though, if your leg hurts or anything or if you get tired." I flashed her that huge smile and I saw it working on her as she stopped walking and smiled back at up me. Flip-flop went my guts again.

Yes. I was working on her and I smiled even bigger down at her as she hobbled next to me and she looked up at me and gave me another one right back.

Yes. Maybe she wasn't going to be that much work after all. And besides, it wasn't work. It was glorious.

I began to walk on the balls of my feet, brimming with excitement from being right next to her. I could have run twelve miles carrying her in my arms at that moment.

"How do you know Jennifer and Allison?" she asked me and I had to blink a couple of times before answering her.

I couldn't remember who Jennifer and Allison were for a moment. I couldn't stop watching her swing that broken leg and take a teetering step. I was waiting for her to wipe out any second and I was ready to catch her but I couldn't stop smiling at how determined she was to go on her own. I was mesmerized by her swaying tits pressing against her shirt. I was breathing hard and when I saw her nipples poking against the thin cloth, I stopped breathing completely.

"Oh. I don't. Shane does," I finally choked out and pointed to the winding line where our friends were now almost to the door. "We're not going to get to go through with them."

"Oh."
She stopped walking and looked at the line.

"That's ok. We go in together. Me and you," I told her and tried my best to look harmless.

"I won't be able to walk fast in there. Maybe I shouldn't go in. Maybe I'll wait by the exit for them to come out."
There was no way in hell I was letting her bail on the Haunted House.

"What's the matter? You tired?" I asked and cocked my head in concern. I couldn't help but flash her an encouraging smile. She lit me up in all the right spots. She was so good to look at but she wouldn't look at me.

"I can still carry you. Just the rest of the way."
Still no answer.

"You cold?" I asked her as the wind blew her hair and rippled her thin shirt.

She looked very cold. No padding there. No padding needed for her. Hers were all her. I bet they each weighed four pounds. I was gonna have blue balls the rest of my life if we never made it across this parking lot. I was gonna put her off if I didn't stop staring at her boobs. She was gonna think I was a letch and she was gonna be right. I licked my lips and looked away for one second but her jiggling up and down pulled me right back.

"I forgot my jacket in the car," she said and glanced back at the Buick as her hair fell loose in front of her face.

No Aquanet for her. No smoking for her either, I was 100% sure of that. I was pretty sure the only thing she'd ever had in her mouth was a straw. And the thought of that made me lick my lips again. When did I become so depraved?

"It's locked or I'd run back and get your jacket for you. You want mine? It's clean."

I had on my gray Members Only jacket over a red Nascar tshirt.

"No, I can't take your jacket, then you won't have one."
I was already out of my jacket and helping her get her good arm in the sleeve. My fingers around her tiny wrist made me shut my eyes a second. Her wrist made me think of a sparrow I had held once in my hand before putting him back in the nest in the backyard. I didn't want to force her cast into the other sleeve. I was scared to death of hurting her even though I'd had casts before and it never stopped me from skateboarding or sledding or running buck wild with one on my arm and I never got hurt. But she was tiny except in the tits and here I was staring at them again as the back of my hand came dangerously close to the side of one as I helped her get the jacket on.

She made me weak.

"I'm beginning to think this is a bad idea," she said as she wrapped my jacket around herself and covered her chest up from my sight.

"Why so?" I asked and tried to sound innocent, tried to sound like a good guy.

"I won't be able to go fast in there."

"So, we'll go slow."

She looked up at me and was quiet so long I gulped. Finally, she began to walk again and as she did my jacket slipped off her shoulder and blew behind her with all her shiny hair trailing behind her in the wind and I lost my breath. I'd never seen a girl in real life look like her. I was gonna mess up my shorts I was sure.

I looked forward to being in the dark haunted house with her where she couldn't see my face because I was sure if she rubbed against me in the dark, even a tiny graze of her tits against me in the dark on my arm or any part of my body and I was gonna lose my load. There was no way I was going to let her back out of going in that haunted house with me.

"I get really scared in these things," she confessed to me and bit her bottom lip and glanced up at me.

Every part of me wanted this girl.

My brain was pumping the brakes on me all over my body to keep me from grabbing her. My brain knew she was a good girl. She wasn't just the Bleacher Girl, the flute playing, (my God) Band Girl who fell forty feet through aluminum bleachers and lived. This girl was a good girl. A good girl with long shiny, honey colored hair and big dark eyes and huge boobs that were wider than her tiny shoulders. And now they were rising and falling with her frightened breathing.

You had to go slow with a good girl or they'd close up shop and you'd never get another chance and you'd always wonder about her. You'd jerk off to her for the rest of your days fantasizing about those tits and wondering what her nipples, that were poking against her shirt, were like.

But she was Bleacher Girl. She was injured and didn't have both arms to fight you off her. And with a name like Faith, you knew she was the best good girl. Never touched.
I gulped again and took her uninjured hand.

"I'll go slow and I'll be there with you. It'll be fun. It'll be fine. You can close your eyes if you get too scared."

Her hand was tiny inside mine and I wanted to be inside of her right then, pumping her hard.

Her face blazed red as if she read my mind and I had to look away.

Chapter Two

"What happened to you and Bleacher Girl with the huge gazongas?" Jeff asked me.

I wanted to punch the smirk right off his face. Bust out a few of his teeth and bloody his mouth and shut him up.

It'd been a long day. A long day of counting down the minutes till class was over. Geology and stupid Mr. Cargill and his yellow teeth and his yellow mustache and his fucking yellow ridged fingernails talking about rocks and their cleavages. Every time he said it the class snickered collectively. Everyone but me. I had fucking wood every time I thought of her. I didn't want to think of her cleavage too.

Fucking Cargill. Jesus. He whistled on the end of every word. He was another one whose teeth I wanted to bust loose. Fucking perverted asshole. I was so glad she didn't go to this retread school. A school for losers like me. Losers like Mr. Cargill. Geology. How would this even come in handy as an adult?

Cargill liked to say cleavage and wait for the laughter. He probably had old man wood. Gross. Wonder whose cleavage he thought about? I glanced around the room to check out the tits on the girls in that class but they were all A cup. Or they were fat girls. Or they were padded. I could tell who was padding. They stood out like tennis balls.

Not Faith's. Ugh. Thinking of her in class nearly killed me. Hers looked heavy. Like fucking melons. Now I knew where that term came from. Faith. My God. I had to squint my eyes and stop seeing her in my mind, stop thinking about her all day at school. I only had Geology, typing, and PE this semester. Fucking stupid, all of them.

I skipped typing but not before sticking around to swipe the pink attendance slip the teacher stuck to the door to let the office know I was truant. I swiped that on my way out of the building and went home to my little apartment with plans of rubbing one out before going to work. But I rubbed out two right in a row and could have had a third but even I wasn't that depraved.

Faith. My God, she was going to kill me.

Frying donuts for Kahmir all afternoon and part of the evening took my mind off her. Or at least Kahmir's nonstop talking about buying a Burger King franchise for his sister, did.

But now here I was sitting on the hood of Jeff's Skylark wagon in the McDonald's parking lot eating fries and drinking a can of Bud when he had to bring her up.

"So, did you fuck her?"

"Fuck off."

"Did you titty fuck her?"

I didn't answer.

"Were you banging her all night or what? Was it hard to do that with her broken leg or was it easy to squeeze her tits without her stopping you because her broken arm?"

"Go fuck yourself, I'll break your fuckin' arm."

I threw the packet of fries into the chainlink fence and exploded fries and ketchup into the yard of the peely grey house behind the McDonalds.

"Spill the details. Or are you waiting for Shane so you don't have to tell it twice? So we don't catch you telling some bullshit."

I glared at Jeff but it didn't faze him. He looked at me with his hungry eyes, dreaming of the details he was sure I was going to give him about what me and Faith did after the Haunted House.

But there was no after the Haunted House. Not really. Because she had asked me to take her home. She could have ridden with her friends but she asked me. I was so dumbfounded I had forgotten to ask for her number. My God that girl nearly killed me IN the Haunted House. Ten minutes in there felt like a night of wild screwing in the backseat and yet nothing had happened. She had

my heart going so hard from barely nothing that I wasn't sure I'd
live through a night with her but I had to find out.

My ears felt hot remembering the evening. I had to find her
tonight.

I turned to Jeff with the biggest smile; my Saturday night,
let's get some girls drunk, smile.

"Oh yes!" Jeff exclaimed. "There's that smile!"

"No," I said and laughed and ran my fingers through my
hair and spiked it up. "But," I continued and could hardly talk for
smiling, "If you help me find her tonight, I'll tell you everything
tomorrow."

"Fuck. Yes. Where's Shane?" Jeff asked and unzipped his
bright red vinyl jacket.

Jeff was the type of guy who would beat-off to someone
else's sex stories, so you had to be careful what you shared with him
and I planned on telling him nothing ever about Faith, that is if I
ever found her again and ever did anything worth sharing.

"How do we find her?" I asked both guys when Shane
finally got off work and came out the back door smelling like fries
and Polo cologne.

"Jesus, you reek," Jeff told him.

Shane pulled his polyester uniform shirt away from his chest
and sniffed and shrugged.

They were in no hurry to get going and I felt like a pussy for
wanting to find her right away. I had to put the brakes on my
eagerness or they'd fuck with me all night and we'd never find her.

I lit a cigarette and popped open another beer and leaned
against the hood of the station wagon and waited for them to get
their shit together and start the night.

"I gotta change, bro" Shane said and unlocked his mom's 78
Chevy Malibu. "Tell me where you're going and I'll meet up with
you there. I gotta shower."

"I'll say you do."

I agreed with Jeff; I could smell Shane over my smoke and

didn't want to be stuck in a car all night with his stink.

"Less Polo, you smell like a whore," I added.

"That's funny, your mom liked it!"

"Fuck you! My mom IS a whore!" I yelled at him as he got in his car and turned it on. Aerosmith blasted out the speakers and drowned me out.

My mom was a whore but no one else was allowed to say it. Shane knew to not push too much with me when it came to my mom and he shut up. I needed to find Faith and get away from these bozos.

"Hey," Shane leaned out his window as he inched past us in the car, "where you gonna be at?"

"We cruising, looking for Bleacher Girl," Jeff answered with his hands in his jacket pockets as he flicked his head my way.

"Boob Girl?"

"Yeah."

"Screw you guys," I muttered.
I was ready to go off on my own.

"Let's go find her because that Allison is hot and I'd like another go at her," Shane said and licked his lips.

"We'll cruise by the school, see if the football game is over and go from there," Jeff told him.

"Cool," Shane said and tried to do a burnout in his mom's Malibu but didn't quite get there.
**

"You don't think she's up in those bleachers, do you?" I asked Jeff as we sat in the parking lot of the Sand Creek High School looking right at the maroon Buick Regal.

"You sound like someone's mom, dude."

"Screw you. I can hear the band. Listen."

"So?"

"So, she shouldn't be up in those bleachers after falling through them."

"What are you gonna do?" he called to me as I got out of the car.

"Get her."

The Marching Band was on the field. It was half-time. But where was my Bleacher Girl? I ached, probably from having wood all damn day, and I ached with fear at the idea of finding her at the top of the bleachers, sitting out the show, and I ached at knowing I was close to her but unable to find her.

I stared at all the goofy fresh-faced Sand Creek kids with their pink cheeks and their expensive braces on their teeth and I wanted a cigarette.

I hated all of them.

But I had to look at every single one of them for Faith as the Marching Band played on behind me. I scanned the top row, ready to kill whoever had helped her get up there. But she wasn't there. It was all douche-faced guys, with douche haircuts, and douche braces on their ugly mouths. My teeth were pretty straight on top. No one ever saw the bottom ones. Braces were for rich kids.

The seats where the band sat next to the Pep Squad was also empty and no Faith. Maybe she wasn't here at all. I spun around to watch the Marching Band one more time to see if she was out there, maybe standing still, playing her flute, while others marched and twirled and honked out their song.

"Sit down, buddy!" Someone yelled behind me.

"Make me!" I yelled back up at the crowd.

"Hey," I heard from next to me and yanked my arm away as someone tugged on my sleeve.

"Hi Mike."

It was her. My Bleacher Girl.

I couldn't even speak. I stood there smiling like an asshole.

"Hi," she said up to me again as she wobbled to balance on her broken leg.

Now she had a white plaster cast and it looked huge on her and too heavy for her. She had all her hair tucked up in a ridiculous black and gold Marching Band hat with a tall ostrich feather on top that fluttered at every little move of her head. But she wasn't wearing the rest of the uniform. She had on a little red hoodie cut up one arm and a pair of faded jeans with the leg cut up one side. I couldn't stop smiling down at her and I balled both my fists up and shoved them in the pockets of my jacket to keep from touching her.

"Hi," I finally spoke to her and could not quit grinning.

"Who are you here with?" she asked and her voice sounded so small in the crowd, I wanted to squeeze her tight to me like she had done when we went through the haunted house. I wanted her small and soft and squished up against my ribs and in my arms. I wanted her wrapped around me tight again.

The time in the Haunted House had been the best ten minutes of my life. I'd take her back to that Haunted House again if I had to but I'd much rather go someplace quiet with less shrieking. How she had shrieked and buried her face in my shirt and my chest. I never knew a girl could shriek that loud. I wanted to make her shriek that loud again. When I wrapped my arms around her, she had wrapped her one good arm around me tight and squeezed right into me.

I lost my breath when she pressed those knockers into my ribs and tucked her head under my chin. She hid her face against my shirt and shrieked and trembled and my knees nearly buckled. It had taken us forever to get through that Haunted House because she wouldn't look up and she wouldn't budge. Part of it was her broken leg but I think even if she'd had two good legs she would have still stood there, frozen in fear.

I could have stayed in that shrieking, flashing, annoying Haunted House forever with her pressed up against me but I was losing control over myself and I knew I was going to kiss her right there in the noise and it was not a good place to do that. I didn't want our first kiss to be in there. I wanted it to be alone and uninterrupted. I wrapped my arm around her side and hoisted her up a little and carried her out of there. My God the heavy underside of her breast on my hand made me dizzy. I'd do anything to get her in my arms again.

"I'm not here with anyone," I told her now and looked out at the field as the Marching Band filed off, their routine over with.

"Did you come here to find me?"
I gulped. I was sticking my neck out here.

"Yes." It was all I could get out.
She bit her lips and looked down and nearly poked me in the eye with her feather.

"Do you have to stay?" I asked her and when she didn't look up, I hooked a finger under her chin and nudged her to look up at me.

She was so soft under her chin. I couldn't stand it when she trembled at my touch and I felt a shiver run through me.

"Your eyes are pretty," I told her as she stared up at me and then she slowly pulled her hat off and let all her honey blonde hair cascade down out of the hat and over her shoulders. She only took off her hat but my face burned as if she had dropped all her clothes.

"Thank you," she said quietly and looked down again and let a sheet of shiny straight hair fall in front of her face.
Your eyes are pretty but your boobs are fantastic, I thought to myself and smiled like an asshole again.

**

"Don't drive like a dick," I told Jeff after I helped Faith climb into the backseat of the Skylark and before I climbed back there too. It wasn't work at all to get her to leave the game and go with me. She was sick of the crowd, the noise, the kids, the bleachers. She hated the bleachers and who could blame her.

"You getting in the back too?" Jeff asked.

"Yes. Take us to my place. Faith and I are going out."

I slammed the door and scooted closer to Faith. She looked scared in the corner of the backseat and she pulled the little red hoodie tight over her chest but it wouldn't reach to zip. She had no idea how she was built or what it did to me.

This was the night. I couldn't wait. She looked so good I wanted to devour all of her. I glanced up at Jeff as he grabbed the rearview mirror and slanted it down so he could stare at her.

"Eyes ahead. Get us there."

The closer we got to my apartment, the more frightened Faith looked and the more anxious I got. I imagined her hitting the ground running when we got there, when she got out of Jeff's car. I knew she lived too far away to run home, especially with a broken leg, but I had known girls to try to do crazy things, especially when scared, and this one looked like she was working herself into a fright. But she couldn't run. I wouldn't let her anyway. At this, I smiled. I wouldn't let anything scare her.

"Hey."

I reached over and took a hold of her hand. This was make or break time. I squeezed her hand that was small and cold in my warm one and felt her tense and then relax. I heard her sigh and then she smiled very small, but still a smile.

"Hi," I said to her and watched her turn pink.

"Hi," she said back.

"We here," I told her as Jeff pulled up in front of my apartment house.

I reached over her and opened her door.

"Do you need help getting out?"

"No, I can do it."

Her voice was so sweet it absolutely killed me. I wanted to crush her and make her whimper and cry, and take a bullet for her all at once. I tried not to stare at her ass as she got out.

She had on faded, worn jeans, that didn't have any pockets on the butt. She'd cut the right leg of them off for her cast. She got out very slow and it gave Jeff time to give me shit about being pussy-whipped.

I got out of the car to go around and help her and to also get away from Jeff and his mouth so I didn't have to pull him out of the car and kick the shit out of him.

"Here," I made it around the back of the car quickly without her even knowing I was going and I very carefully took a hold of her good arm and helped her.

"No crutches?" I asked her as she stepped up on the curb.

"I can't really do them good with one arm."

"When's all this come off?"

"Maybe Thanksgiving."

"Wow. No more bleachers for you."
I couldn't help but sound bossy.

"I know. I want to quit Marching Band but my parents won't let me."

"So don't tell them," I said and shrugged.

"They'll find out and be pissed at me."

"So? Let them. You're a good girl. It's not like you do anything else to piss 'em off."

Talk of her parents was making me angry. And I think it was making her angry as well. She shot me a blazing mad look. Her pale, heart shaped face had two cooking hot patches on each cheek. I found myself smiling like an asshole at her temper.

"What?" I asked and smiled once more as I led her over to my car, a 1978 Cutlass Supreme.

"That's what everyone says about me."

"What?" That you're a good girl?"

"Yeah."

"But it's true. You are a good girl."
I could not stop smiling to save my life.
Here her shoulders slumped and she let out a sigh.

"I know," she said and sighed again.

"That's ok. I like good girls."
And here she looked up at me and she too had a huge smile.
She had no idea.

Chapter Three

I had enough ideas for the two of us and I was glad she couldn't see any of them. I looked over at her body silhouetted against the window and gulped. I wiped the sweat off my palms and onto my jeans and started the car.

She wasn't high maintenance. She hadn't said a peep about my car or my worn-out jeans or even asked what we were doing. She was a good girl. She was a quiet girl. My God she had no idea what she was doing to me when she strapped her seatbelt over her tiny waist. I needed to calm down. I needed to take control of the night, of myself, of my heartrate. I was a good guy after all. I smiled at this. It was true though. I had manners. And they would be out in full force tonight. I looked over at her as she sat tense with her one good hand balled up tight in her lap as we rumbled down the road.

I asked her what she wanted at the gas station after I filled the tank.

"Grape pop please."

"Anything else?" I asked as I leaned in the window.

"Um a snack would be nice. Something small."

She bit her bottom lip after she said it and I wanted to howl at the night sky and scream and jump and yell it to the world that I was going to bang the Bleacher Girl in the back of my Cutlass. But I kept control of myself and only smiled at her and said, "Sure."

"Something small," I chanted to myself in the gas station as I grabbed a six pack and two bottles of grape soda. "Something small," I said again and snatched a bag of pretzels on my way to the counter.

Pretzels were a good girl snack. Weren't they? I had no idea and I picked up a small bottle of vodka at the counter. They never carded me here. I bought smokes and beer here all the time. No smokes for tonight though. Not enough money for everything and besides, my mouth was going to be occupied.

I smiled and winked at the cashier as she bagged it up and I watched her blush. The charm was working on everyone, even thirty-year-old cashiers. I gave her another wink when she told me to have a good night and I marveled at how red she turned. There was no stopping me tonight. Tonight, everything was popping along right on track. I was all lit up in all the right places. Faith did that to me. Bleacher Girl. Fucking Bleacher Girl going up the hill with me tonight.

I put the bags in the back. I didn't want Faith to see the booze. I didn't want questions. I didn't want her to back out on me before we even got out of town. I'd show her what I'd do to my grape pop with the vodka. And she could have a little sip and see if she liked it. Just a little. I wanted her a little loose. I didn't want her sick. I didn't want her drunk. I just wanted her to relax. I wanted me to relax. I popped my neck twice and rolled my shoulders when I saw her sitting with her hand still balled up on her thigh.

"Hi," I said and reached over and took her hand in mine as we took the steep curves up to Mint Falls.

Her hand relaxed in mine, her fingers cold and small in my hand. Maybe she was only cold and that's why she sat so tense. I pictured her guzzling all the booze and then puking and then I remembered it was Lori my old girlfriend with the Lita Ford Hair and the filthy mouth who was like that. She was not a good girl.

Faith was nothing like Lori. Lori didn't have any eyebrows. I always wanted to ask her where they went. What happened to them? But it never came up in the backseat of the Cutlass when she was taking her clothes off. It didn't seem important then. I laughed quietly and looked over at Faith and saw her looking out the window at the view as we crawled up the steep pass. Our hands bounced lightly on the top of her thigh. I wished she had that short skirt on again but she looked good in jeans too. Soft and faded and tight with a brass snap at the waist and four brass buttons where a zipper should have been. Damn.

Watch the road, I said to myself but my eyes went back to the brass buttons. Those wouldn't be easy. I glanced up over at her tits as they bounced with the bumps and then up at her face, her sweet face. I licked my lips and looked back at the road.

"You okay going for a little ride? You cold?" I asked her and glanced over at her again.

"A little," she said and used her good hand to try to pull the tiny red jacket across her chest again.

"Jacket's a little, little," I said and turned to face the road.

I couldn't stop smiling at how much I loved that tiny red jacket. My God what was under there that it couldn't strain to cover? I looked at her again as she jiggled next to me as we climbed up the twisty Mint River Drive.

"I didn't want to cut the sleeve off a good one. This one is from 8th grade."

"It's like wearing nothing. It's cute though," I added quickly and watched her throw all her long hair back over her shoulder and I thought my heart would stop.

"You're very pretty," I told her and let go of her hand and gripped the steering wheel and steered us around the tight curves.

Girls liked you to tell them they were hot or beautiful or whatever but it didn't feel right with this one. This one was hot and beautiful but she had no idea. She had no idea what she did to me. My knees were weak and I gulped again. I was ready for that vodka. I was more wound up than she was. I felt fourteen instead of seventeen.

"Thank you," she said and shivered.

I turned on the heater. We needed to get the car warm because I was not planning on leaving it running all night once we got up on Mint Falls. I took the risk of tearing up the Cutlass on the service road to get to the very top where no one else ever drove at night. If you took it slow and careful you wouldn't hit a rut or break an axel or bottom out. If you made it up there you could see the spray of the falls above the whole town and all its lights. If you made it up there, you could have some alone time with your girl.

"If you could get wet, we could go stand behind the waterfall," I told her and waited for her to laugh or get mad.

She didn't answer. She didn't get it. She didn't laugh or get mad or say something dirty back. She was that good of a girl. Lori would have told me she was already wet. Lori was good in a different way, except when she was mad and cussing. That was no good at all, that horrible temper she had.

Faith was good. Maybe she did get it and didn't like dirty talk.

"Maybe after my casts come off," was all she said.

She bit her lip and looked down at her knees. She looked nervous as we slowed down and pulled up to the edge of the falls in the dark. You could hear the water all around and you could see the spray above the horizon. I was happy as hell to have made it and ready to get started.

She was frightened though and a frightened good girl was new territory for me. I'd never been with a good girl before. They never had anything to do with me and now I wondered why.

"Faith?" I asked as I put the car in park and turned it off.

"Yes Mike?" she asked and her voice trembled.

I wanted to ask her why she went out with me but I lost my nerve. Smart girls, rich girls, cheerleaders, never had anything to do with me unless they needed their flat tire changed or their battery jumped and *then* they were all smiles. If I could help them out with something, then they were all smiles. But they never would go out with me no matter how hard I worked my magic. Now I wanted to ask her why a good girl like her would go out with a punk like me but I chickened out.

"Wanna get in the back with me?" I blurted instead.

"In the back? I don't know."

She glanced back at the white bench seat.

"It's scary up here," she said when she turned back around and looked out the window.

She gripped the dash with her good hand and scooted to the edge of the seat and peered out over the hood of the car at the falls and out over the whole town.

"It's beautiful but I feel like we're gonna roll over the edge," she said and turned and looked at me from where she gripped the dash.

She arched her back to balance on the very front of the seat and gave me a side view of her body and I swear I had chest pains as well as pains elsewhere. I adjusted my balls quickly while she looked out the window.

"Here."

I reached into the backseat and brought up the drinks. She watched me chug half of the bottle of grape pop and then I poured in the vodka. I drank a little of the mix and shivered and licked my lips. My eyes watered and everything looked clearer. I immediately looked at her. I could see every detail of her in sharp focus. She was small and soft and every inch of her was dangerous curves. I squeezed the bottle of grape pop hard thinking about getting on top of her in the backseat. I stared at the brass snaps at the waist of her jeans and clenched my jaw.

"Here's your pretzels and your pop. Do you want to try mine?" I asked her and took another sip of it.

She watched me drink it and her eyes followed my tongue as I licked my lips after I swallowed. I saw her gulp and lick her own lips.

She liked that, so I licked my lips again and the second time she turned pink and looked down at her lap.

"Try some?" I asked. No smile from me. All serious now. I was waiting. Her answer would tell me so much about my chances.

"Ok," she finally said and smiled just a tiny bit at me as if waiting for me to tell her what to do.

She started to take the bottle from me with her right hand,

the one in the cast. She made a frustrated sound and looked down.

"Here, let me," I said to her and held the bottle to her lips slowly.

Her eyes made contact with mine right before she touched her lips to the bottle and drank. I almost lost it. I pictured her looking at me like that with her lips on something else. But she was a good girl. I didn't know if we'd ever get to that. But my God, if we did. I shivered at the thought.

"Are you cold?" she asked me after she finished her drink.

She touched her lips with her fingers to wipe away any of the purple pop. Her fingernails were tiny and pink. Not filed sharp. Not chipped. Not red. Not dirty or broken.
Perfect. Not high maintenance, just perfect. Such a good girl.

"I good." My throat felt parched and I had a hard time speaking.

I cracked open a beer, rubbed my hand on my jeans several times and then drank nearly the whole can as I stared out the windshield.

"Wow!" she gasped.

I answered her with a smile, cracked open another one and offered it to her. She smiled back at me and held out both her hands to take it. It was going to be like that. Easy. So easy.

She was scared. But she was here. She was smiling. She was sipping a can of beer with her eyes on mine.

"Tilt it up," I told her and grinned and she did. And then she wrinkled her nose and stopped. "Oh my," she said and held the can out to me and shook her head no.

"Oh my," she said again and shook off the bad taste of the beer and I watched her jiggle.

"How old are you?" I asked her as I took her can and chugged it fast.

"Eighteen. You?"
She watched me chug the whole can with wide eyes.

"Seventeen. You want to get in the back? You look cold."

"Oh."

I wiped my mouth off with the back of my hand and then cupped it and breathed into it to check my breath.
She looked confused but she nodded all the same.

"Ok," she said.

I watched her as she pulled at one side of her red jacket and then the other. I'd have that thing off and balled up in the floor as soon as possible.
Fear rippled across her face as if she read my mind.

"Here," I said and slid through between the two front seats and on into the back. I was so skinny it wasn't a problem. Then I folded the driver's seat forward so she could come into the back and not have to squeeze through like I did. But the two casts were slowing her up.

"Here," I said again and scooped her up under her armpits. My fingers pressed in on the sides of her tits and I froze for a second. Then I pulled her from behind, up over the center console and into the back, right onto my lap.

A warm shot soaked the front of my shorts as her bottom smashed into my lap and as the side of her soft breast pressed into my chest. Welp. That was ok. There was a lot more fuel left in that tank.

"You are cold," I told her and wrapped my arms around her waist and pulled her close.

"You're really warm," she whispered and wiggled on my lap and made me think, oh no, here we go again.

She had to feel me pressing up against her ass. She was going to set me off again if she wiggled one more time. I shut my eyes and almost groaned. I opened them when I felt her fingers on my chin.

She rubbed my chin with the pad of her thumb and looked at it closely and I was scared to death she was eyeballing one of my pimples or maybe the scar where I went through the windshield when we were on vacation in Florida and Dad was driving drunk. I sat there silent as the blood pounded in my ears in slow throbs until she was done looking.

"Hi," she said and smiled and wiggled her bottom and put her hand on my chest.

Her face was glowing pink and she looked embarrassed.

"What were you looking at?" I asked her as I shifted under her to try to free myself a little and ease the pressure she was putting on me.

"Your, um," she faltered and reached up to my face and rubbed her thumb on my chin again.

"My beard?" I prompted and my voice cracked.

"Yeh."

"What about it?" I asked as she put her hand back on my chest and made me think that life was not fair that she could do that so easily to me, but I couldn't to her.

"It's so rough."

Her words were a spark in the dark car and I squeezed my eyes shut so I could slow myself down. She was winding me up and I was raring to go just from her saying that. I couldn't find words. I gulped a couple of times and wished I had the grape pop and vodka back with us. I tightened my hold on her waist. I was never letting her go. Ever. And this made her wiggle again.

"You should see it by tomorrow morning," I croaked out. "It's a lot thicker after a day and a night."

"I'm glad I don't have to deal with that."

My eyes popped open.

She pulled her long hair out from under her hoodie and carefully arranged it in front of her shoulder and down over her chest. I shut my eyes and couldn't watch it; it turned me on that much. Then she shifted around like she was uncomfortable sitting on my dick.

"You have other things to deal with," I rasped.

"I'm glad I don't have that, though."

"What?"

I thought she meant wood for a minute. I didn't know. My brain had stopped working in straight lines. I couldn't focus or speak anymore. I was heading into autopilot and pure male instinct.

"A beard."

"That makes two of us," I said and took a hold of her chin like she had done mine. But when I bent down to her, to act like I was looking closer, like she had done me, I kissed her open mouth and wasted no time sliding all my tongue in to greet hers.

Chapter Four

We were in Shane's white Malibu and I was nearly cashed out in the backseat as we drove to Sandy's to get shakes and fries from the car-hop. I'd worked ten hours after school and had already had three beers. I'd been out till 2AM with Faith working my magic on her in the backseat of my car. After that, I was nearly dead on my feet.

I hoped she didn't hate me for not calling her today. I worked all day and besides, I was never good on the phone. The phone was for wussies and girls.

I wondered if she was mad.

I wondered if she was upset.

I wondered if she was regretting our night.

My God she was incredible. But she hadn't let me go all the way.

Almost. But nope.

My God she'd taken all night to let me get her shirt off. We kissed for what felt like forever. She chased after my tongue when I pulled it out and she hungrily welcomed it back in when I slid it back in. We went on like that for a long time till finally she ventured her tongue into my mouth. Small and sweet, I never wanted it to leave. I ached when she pulled it away. I put my hand on her throat oh so gentle and stroked her neck with a finger slowly and then gradually moved my hand down lower, and lower.

She took a huge breath as if diving under water and didn't let it out as I touched the top of her breast with the back of my knuckles. I couldn't touch her with my palm yet. I was on that male autopilot almost. I was out of control nearly. I needed to watch it. If I touched her with my palm, I would lose all control of myself. I'd be a complete animal.

I moved my hand lower. I grazed her nipple with the back of

my knuckle and she sucked in another sharp breath and her tits rose up with it. I kept doing it. Down. Up. Gasp. Gasp. Down. Up. Gasp. Pause. Gasp. I lifted her off my lap and set her on the seat next to me and started to lay her back.

"Mike," she said against my lips.

Down. Up. Gasp. Then I used the pad of my thumb to nudge it. A little moan grew in the back of her throat as I nudged her nipple through her shirt and lay her on her back.

She had her eyes shut and I stared at her; at her hair splayed around her head in huge silky rivers, her eyelashes against her pink cheeks, and at her swollen red lips. I looked down at the rising and falling of her breasts, her nipples poking through the thin shirt in the moonlight in the backseat. I cupped one full tit and squeezed it and made her whimper as I lay on top of her and kissed her again.

I wanted under her shirt. I wanted her shirt off. I kept trying to get under there and I kept trying to pull it off and she kept pushing my hand away. Her fingers were tiny on the back of my hands.

Finally, all it took was for me to take mine off first. Who would have ever thought that was what slowed a girl down on taking her clothes off? I was sweating despite it being cold outside and I was getting so frustrated. I sat up and pulled my shirt off and sniffed. My deodorant had quit. It couldn't keep up with Bleacher Girl. It had given up.

She opened her eyes from where she lay panting under me as I straddled her and she watched me pull my shirt off and ball it up and wipe my armpits.

"Are you taking your shirt off?" she had asked all timid.

Her face glowed in the moonlight and her neck was bright red. It was either because she was hot and revved up or I was rubbing her soft skin raw from my stubble. Maybe both. Nothing rough had ever touched this girl and I felt bad for doing it. But yet I wanted to rub her raw everywhere. I wanted to send her home with marks to remind her of me.

"I want to take yours off."

She trembled at my voice. I was all serious. This was it. We'd go further or I'd take her home now. I couldn't take anymore. I felt like I was gonna die soon.

"Ok."

She stretched out with both arms above her head and shut her eyes. It took me several seconds to realize she was waiting for me to pull her shirt off for her.

When I grabbed the bottom of it and began to pull, her whole body trembled. She was like this 72 Dodge Dart I had had a year ago that trembled above 50. It'd still go faster but the tremble let you know you were pushing it. I always pushed it. But I eased it over 50 slow. I did this thing where I stuck my tongue out just a little and squinted my eyes down to slits when I'd ease that Dart up over 50 and on to 60. Then 65 we'd be shimmying, way past just trembling. I had a girlfriend then, Vanessa, who told me about the tongue thing back then. I liked Vanessa a lot back then. She had that huge, permed hair that would get stuck in the door of my Dart. She almost lit it on fire several times, she had such a cloud of hairspray above her head. I was always worried when she smoked, she would go up in a poof. She had tiny little tits and a space between her teeth. She loved to give me bjs but always wanted to do it while I drove and she always scraped the head of my dick with her teeth. I had to shove her head away a few times while driving. My hand would come away sticky with Aquanet. We broke up. She called me a fag. I liked her. She was smart and had sexy long legs but the teeth on my dick thing was too much and I didn't know how to tell her no. Or how to tell her about it at all. That wasn't the kind of thing you told a girl. Hey, by the way, can you not scrape your teeth on my dick?

Why was I thinking of Vanessa?

The tremble.

Faith.

I pulled her shirt slowly over her head to make sure I didn't pull any of that long hair. I gently tugged the sleeve over her cast on her arm. I laid her broken arm above her head where she still had her other arm. It was like she was giving herself to me. To do what I wanted. I wanted that bra off next. The little stretchy white triangles barely covered all she had and I wanted it off and I wasted no time unhooking it and flinging it over my shoulder. She covered her eyes with her free hand as she lay there topless below me as I stared at her body. I couldn't stop looking and there was so much to see.

"Hey asshole!"
It was Jeff yelling at me, bringing me back to now, back to where I was cashed out in the backseat of Shane's mom's Malibu.

"What?" I growled. I could hardly sit up right. My balls still hurt from the night before.

"You banged the Bleacher Girl."
Here, I smiled huge.

"Mike, you piece of shit," Shane looked at me in the rearview mirror.
They both wanted details.

They both had their Mommy and Daddy's money and their Mommy and Daddy's cars so I went to Sandy's with them, even though I knew they'd want details. I went with them even though I was dead on my feet and just wanted to crawl into bed. I was hungry and low on food, so I let them buy me a tray of food in return for a detail or two. Now I was stuffed and finishing a smoke.

"Where is Bleacher Girl tonight?" Shane asked.

"Home, I guess. I hope."
I tossed my smoke out the window.

"You better call her."

"It's after eleven."

"She's gonna be pissed."

"She be all right."

She was not all right. She didn't take my call Monday night. And she didn't take it Tuesday. Her mother said she couldn't come to the phone. I left my number but my phone never rang. I worked long hours at the donut shop. I went to my three classes at the New Directions High School for losers. By Wednesday I looked into a second job at the Thrifty Lube. I assured them I could work 7-9 AM every day they needed me and they said they'd call if they were short. I knew they were short because I had PE with their morning guy, Adam. I knew he drank hard and missed many mornings due to a hangover. That's why I dropped in there one morning when I saw a long line backed up for $12 Tuesday. Adam would be pissed at me for scooping his job out from under him, but too bad. I could use the money. I had rent to get. Gas to buy. Faith to take out.

By Thursday I was exhausted from chasing my tail working two jobs, going to school, and driving around with Jeff. Shane was taking Allison out and Jeff was trying to get Jennifer to go out with him, or as I joked, he was trying to get her to take him out. He didn't have a job or a car of his own. She had that Buick. It wasn't a turbo but it was a lot better than Jeff's mom's Skylark.

I had two jobs and a Cutlass and my own place and hopefully a new girlfriend.

Thursday evening, I finally talked to her.

Kahmir sent me home early because we got shut down by a surprise visit from the Health Department. When they came in and saw that the overhead lights were brimming with cockroaches, they closed us up. It always unnerved me to work below them, especially when they would cast a moving shadow over you as you got a refill on your Mountain Dew. That light was the one that they had always been in; over the pop machine. But just the other day they had multiplied and migrated to the light above the ovens where we baked the brownies and biscuits.

At least they hadn't moved into the light above me where I stood to fry all the donuts. But now it didn't matter. Now we were closed until we could pass inspection and until Kahmir paid the fine. I'd just come into the apartment, four hours earlier than expected, when the phone rang.

"Lo?"

"Hi, is this Mike?"

It was her. Bleacher Girl. My Bleacher Girl. Faith.

"Hi, how are you?"

I wasn't much of a phone talker but I loved hearing her small voice and couldn't stop smiling. She pushed all my right buttons and every inch of me lit up just for her.

"I'm good. I had to miss school two days because my ankle was swelling. But that's ok. My parents let me drop Marching Band."

"That's great news."

I kicked off my sneakers and began to pace the room, stretching the phone cord behind me as I went.

"Yeh, so I don't have to go to the games anymore and sit there on those cold bleachers."

"Or fall through them," I added and laughed and sat down on my bed.

"Yeh, that," she said barely above a whisper and I felt bad for making a joke of it.

She sounded as small as I remembered her in my arms under me and I had to suddenly stand up and readjust myself. I was glad she couldn't see me but I hated the phone all the same because now she was silent. I didn't know what was wrong or how to fix it.

"Are you ok, you know, after the other night?" I asked her.

I was never one to shy away from any topic. If I cared, I cared, and I asked. I'd talked to girls about their periods before, so asking her if she was ok after I had my hand down her pants didn't bother me. Nothing really put me off.

"You weren't too sore the next day, were you?" I asked her.

She cleared her throat a few times before answering me and I was reminded that she lived with her parents like a normal 18-year-old. I wasn't normal. I had moved out this past spring when being at home with Mom and her boyfriend Dennis and Dad and his girlfriend Linda had become unbearable. I lived on my own in a one room apartment with a tiny kitchen and a closet that had a toilet in it. There was a communal tub down the hall. Otherwise, I had my kitchen sink to wash up in or shave or brush my teeth.

The wood floor around the toilet was springy and rotten and about to fall through when I moved in. I had ripped out all the carpet in there and in my room the first day I lived here. I'd drained the toilet and fixed the leak with a new seal and repaired the floor. When the landlord Doris saw, she gave me half my rent off if I would do small repairs for her.

I was a busy guy and I forgot most teens lived with their P's and didn't share a tub with four other strangers in an apartment house.

"I'm fine," Faith said and I heard rustling on her end. "I wasn't sore. I'm good."

She was good. Very good. We hadn't had sex, not really. She had finally let me get my hand down the front of her pants and what a tight fit that was in more ways than one. Thinking about the pink triangle of wet cotton panties made my ears burn and I paced faster. Thinking about what was behind that cotton triangle almost made me stumble in my pacing. I was so whipped for a whole lot of not much.

She didn't let me keep my hand down there very long. She let me dip my fingers into her just enough to feel how slick she was and then when I slid one in all the way, I think she almost started to cry. That's how it was. I felt the cry coming before it arrived. I felt her freeze up and heard her hiccup and I stopped. I found her shirt and her jacket in the floor of the car. The bra was hanging off the headrest. But before I let her get dressed, I held her. I held her topless and soft under me and shut my eyes and listened to the falls and tried to memorize the moment because it was a good one. The best I'd ever had in a long time. I caught my breath with my face resting on her bare tits. And she caught hers too. It was all I could do to stop when she asked but I would never do anything to make her cry.

Shirley Johnson

But she started to get cold and I knew it was very late. You could see our breath in the car. I helped her get dressed and took her home. I walked her to her door. I wanted to carry her. I wanted to take her home to my bed and sleep next to her forever. It was so hard to drive away from that big, white colonial house and leave her behind. How would she get upstairs to her room without any help?

I had worried about her all the way home.

"When can I see you again?" I asked her now and felt like an eager fool.

"When do you want to?"

"Tonight. But..."

"But what?"

"How about tomorrow?" I asked.

I wanted to see her tonight but I was exhausted. But I didn't want her to know that. I could power through any exhaustion for her. But I'd rather see her tomorrow night.

"Sure ok."

"I'll pick you up at 7, ok?"

"Ok."

"Night."

"Bye."

"Stay safe," I told her and it was more like an order than a goodbye. I wasn't smiling.

"I will."

That night I used the shower at the end of the hall that the whole apartment shared and sudsed every inch of myself and shaved close and drank a beer in the steam and then wrapped a towel around my ass and strutted back to my unlocked apartment and collapsed into the old Ginny Lind bed naked as God made me.

Chapter Five

I was on the balls of my feet, my hair slicked back, toothbrush in my jaw, good Levi's stiff on the radiator, happy ass OMD on the radio making me happy though I would have never admitted it to anyone. Maybe Faith. I'd tell her anything. Anything she wanted to know. Maybe I was pussy-whipped. Maybe. I didn't care. It was like that. I smiled and nearly dropped the toothbrush out of my jaw and onto the linoleum floor.

We were going out. I was picking her up in an hour and could not wait.

"You have to meet my parents before I can go out with you."

"That's good. Whatever. I don't care," I had said to her; juiced about seeing her, her house, meeting her P's, which was something I had never had any interest in before. Me and parents didn't mix. I had too many parents back in the home I left behind. I didn't need more.

I could charm anyone. Everything would be fine. I put on a clean white T-shirt and my blue alligator collared shirt over it, my Levi's stiff and clean that had finished drying overnight on the radiator. Laced up my Nikes. Left my hair wet. It needed cut. It lay on my collar a little curly, a little too long. I ran my fingers through it to spike it up a little on top. It didn't matter if it was a little shaggy in the back. I was clean shaved and smiling and ready.

"Hey Mike!"

I crashed into Doris the landlady right outside my door.

"Hi Doris," the clitoris, I added to myself and smiled at her a real big one. I wanted that half off my rent.

"You going out, Mike?" She asked and pulled on her nose a few times like she had something stuck in there.

"Yup."

I locked the deadbolt on my door while she stood behind

me.

"I was just coming to see you."

"Oh yea?" I asked and smiled again and headed towards the stairs.

"Why's that?" I asked as I slid a stick of Juicy Fruit gum in my mouth.

"Sink is all backed up in Molly's unit."

"Oh." Not tonight, tonight was Bleacher Girl, I thought but didn't say it.

"Yeh."

"I'm sorry to hear that."

I stopped on the stairs with Doris breathing hard next to me. Her skin problem was like red lace throbbing over her nose and cheeks.

"Can it wait?" I asked and chomped my gum in a hurry to go.

"She really needs it fixed now."

"Ok. I'll need a plunger and a 2 liter of coke, some baking soda and vinegar, and the tool box."

I could do my best shot and keep myself in Doris' good book for half off the rent and then be on my way.

I made a show of taking off my jacket and my good shirt and laying them flat over a dining room chair in front of both Doris and Molly as they watched. Both of them had their mouths open above their double chins. I smiled at them as they watched me with wide, shiny eyes.

"Going out with the fellas?" Molly asked.
Big smile from me, big blush from her.

"Naw. Date," I told her and chewed my gum and winked.

"Oh my! A nice girl?" she asked and blushed harder.

Molly was just a couple years older than me, overweight, and with those giant boobs big girls had, in one of those pointy old lady bras. She always wore really bright sweatshirts and matching pants that were speckled with neon paint drips. I always wondered if she were doing aerobics or something in her place. She was nice but she was weird. She always wore her hair in a fat, short ponytail on the side of her head and it made her look off balance.

"A good girl," I told her and smiled again and watched her as she touched her face and flushed redder and grew fidgety.

"Oh. I hope you don't get any of this on you. It's very nasty," Doris stepped in front of Molly and warned me and pointed to the sink.

"In that case, I better," I said as I pulled my undershirt out of the waist of my jeans and over my head and hung it over my good shirt on the back of the chair.

A plunger, a vice grip, and a 2 liter of coke later and the sink was draining, slowly. And I was late.

"Can I use your phone?" I asked when I was done and shirtless in Molly's kitchen.

She gestured silently and looked like she was going to burp or something as I helped myself to the phone.

"Hi. Faith? Yeh. Something came up. No. I'm still coming. Running late. Mmmhm. But I'm on my way now. Yeh I remember how to get there. K. See you soon baby," I said into the phone while Doris and Molly watched me. Molly's eyes roamed over the little bit of dark hair I had on my pale chest that trickled down to below my belt.

"All right," I said and smiled and pulled the gum out of my mouth and put it in Molly's outstretched hand.

I needed a cigarette and a sixpack. I still hadn't decided what to do with Faith tonight either.
Funds were tight but maybe they just opened up with the sink clog fixed.

"Doris?"

"Yes Mike?"

"About next month's rent?" I asked as I straightened out non-existent wrinkles in my under shirt and undid my pants as the two women watched.

"It's taken care of Mike. The whole month."

"That's great," I said as I tucked the front of the T-shirt in as they watched.

Sometimes things were easy like that.

Just like meeting Faith's mom and dad. Except the dad wasn't her dad. Step-dad, Garrett. Shiny bald head, fluffy brown combover. I almost laughed thinking about him in the wind. But Faith's mom, Rebekkah. Va va va-voom! A looker. Big Farrah Fawcett hair. Dark eyes. Not stacked like Faith but leggy. I wondered who Faith inherited her figure from? She was certainly blessed. Double blessed. But her mom was thin, not stacked, but a looker all the same.

I gave her the big smile. The one with the eyes that said, yes yes and yes some more. I couldn't help it and she gave it right back. Faith's dad, I mean, step-dad, was a lucky guy. So was I.

Faith was shiny and clean and short between her P's. Hair blown straight and silky long and parted far on the side. She had on a ruffled dark blue shirt buttoned up the back. Who the hell helped her get that on? Who buttoned all those tiny buttons and who cut the slit up her sleeve and pinned it with a hundred safety pins? She had so many ruffles on her shirt she looked like that guy from the Flock of Seagulls video.

And then I saw the denim skirt. I had to look twice. Very short denim skirt. Merry Christmas to me. Acid washed and frayed. Big white cast on one leg and slouchy leather boot on the other one.

Holy Moly.

You could kids have fun.

Here's twenty dollars.

No questions at all.

No curfew given. Friday night.

"Sorry I was late," I said to her soon as we hit the porch. Arm around tiny waist all the way to the car. She smelled like cinnamon and apples. Baked apples. Soft and sticky. Mm. I could eat her. I could. I would. I should try at least.

I wanted to pick her up and carry her. When her arm snaked around my waist as far as she could reach, I wanted to howl at the moon right then and there.

I'd never been such a puss for a girl ever. Never. I'd never met any of their parents unless it was unplanned. Like carrying Kerri in with her wasted and puking, her crimped blonde hair swinging, that angry mouth cursing everything in sight. Her parents were nearly passed out on the broken sofa with a black bong between them, watching wrestling. It'd been a quick meeting and I wasn't even sure that was her dad. We never went out again. I don't like puke in my car. I don't like angry girls, and her house was too much like my parent's house.

Other than Kerri, I'd never met any parents. There was no mention of parents ever. I tried to stay far away from even the subject of parents, much less the actual ones. I didn't want to hear any bitching about them and I didn't want to meet them. I didn't want them telling me what to do or not do and God help if any of them threatened me. None ever did and they better not. Ever.

These parents were ok. Goofy. Too happy maybe. I didn't care. They didn't tell me what to do and they gave me a twenty to take their hot daughter out. It as a win win. It was like that. When it got too cold to park, maybe they'd let me bang her in the basement family room. Or even better, in my own bed in my own apartment with the radiator clinking next to us.

I was definitely whipped and acting tuff wasn't changing that.

"What are we doing?" she asked once she got the buckle across her lap.

I had her parent's twenty dollars in my front pocket and I suddenly realized I hadn't eaten really good in a long time. A lot of peanut butter sandwiches on cheap white Texas toast and a lot of milk. Apples. Cereal. Donuts from Kahmir. A Whopper or two from his sister's new Burger King. A lot of junk. But not enough.

"I'm hungry. You hungry?"

"Sure, I could eat."

She was game. She could eat. She had one cheeseburger and a vanilla shake and I had a sack of cheeseburgers, a coke, and a vanilla shake from Sandy's Drive-In. The car smelled heavenly of beef and cheese and pickles and her. The temps were dropping outside and it was lightly raining. There'd be no going up to Mint Falls. It could get icy quick up on that pass and the Cutlass would be a handful which didn't bother me but I knew that it made girls shriek. The wrong kind of shriek.

"Now where?" I asked her and she shrugged those little shoulders.

"A movie?" I asked and eyed her bare thighs in her short skirt.

"I don't know. I need to put my foot up on something because it's swelling."

I had something she could put her foot up on.

"Huh, uhuh," I laughed out loud thinking about it. My face burned as she looked at me, curious, as if she could almost see my thoughts but didn't get it.

"What?" she asked and then she looked down at her lap, then back up at me. When she returned my smile, my heart squeezed.

"I'm just foolin' with you," I told her and my ears burned.

Maybe she would taste like baked apples down there. Maybe someday I'd find out. But I couldn't ask her to put her broken leg up like that. That wouldn't be right. Not every girl liked to do that sort of stuff and anyway the ones who did were usually the ones you wished didn't.

Like Misti. Misti worked at the Y as a lifeguard and she did gymnastics there on Saturdays. Misti was the only lifeguard I ever knew who wore full makeup; dark eyeliner, the works, huge permed hair, while lifeguarding.

Misti was also the only lifeguard I'd ever seen who kept a

Marlboro behind her ear while she sat up there looking for drowning victims. She did the balance beam on the weekends. I wondered if she kept a cigarette tucked behind her ear then too.

She was the only girl I knew who shaved down there. Didn't help with the smell. One time we did the thing with her feet on my shoulders and that smell was enough that I was put off dating any girls a long time. Two whole weeks, no girls at all. And none of THAT; the ankles on the shoulders, my face deep in the apple pie, none of that since.

I sold that Galaxie after Misti. Couldn't get rid of the memories. That and the fuel pump kept going out.

"Mike?"

"Yes?"

"Where are we going?" Faith asked.

Poor Bleacher girl looked cold sitting there waiting on me to turn on the car.

"Where's your coat?"

"I didn't bring one."

"It's almost Halloween."

"What?" she asked, confused.

"It's nearly November! You need a coat. You're getting your coat."

I turned on the car and drove us back to her P's house. I left her sitting there looking astonished as I got out and ran up to the porch. I returned with a hot pink down ski jacket. Expensive stuff. She'd have to put one arm in it and pull the rest around her shoulders. I helped her shrug it on and pulled it around her best I could. Her eyelashes brushed against her pink cheeks as I came close.

This girl was so low maintenance she needed someone to watch out for her. This girl was so low maintenance that she didn't fend for herself. She definitely needed me. I'd look out for her. I could do it forever. I did it for myself. What was one more person to look out for?

"Jennifer and Allison are going to the bowling alley."
I had to look at her twice and think about what she said twice too.

"What?" I grinned because she was so cute sitting there.

"They're going to the Thunderbird, bowling."

"You want to go bowling?" I asked and glanced at her leg and her arm in their white casts. I couldn't stop smiling. She really needed someone to keep an eye on her. Keep her out of trouble.

"No, silly," she said and smiled back at me then looked down at her lap.

Everything she did, wound me right on up. She couldn't stop smiling at me and she turned away and blushed, and even that turned me on.

I waited for her to explain and as I sat patient, a sheet of hair slowly slid in front of her face. I couldn't help myself. I reached out and moved it back very gently.

"Then why do you want to go to the Thunderbird?"

"I can sit and put my foot up."

"Yeah? But you can do that anywhere."
I glanced back at the backseat.

"I know. But I thought it'd be fun. It's something we do sometimes. We sneak in booze and then we bowl."

I couldn't stop smiling at her. Thinking of her sneaking in booze to the bowling alley made me laugh. She wasn't such a good girl after all. Maybe that was how she fell through the bleachers. I would have to ask her sometime. Maybe not now though.

"Please Mike?"

She startled me by suddenly looking up at me and wrapping her good hand around the back of my neck. Goose bumps broke out all over my scalp and I had to pop my neck twice under her hand. She slowly ran her fingers through the back of my hair as she waited for me to answer.

Little minx knew how to get her way. Oh my God she was winding me up from touching my hair. If I could lay my face on those tits and have her run her fingers through my hair, I'd be happier than hell. And then she took her hand away and put it back on her lap and on top of that incredibly short skirt.

My God she was going to kill me. I was never going to get used to her. Ever. And that was fine. I'd die looking like an asshole with the biggest smile ever.

"Is that from 8th grade too?" I asked and bugged my eyes at her skirt.

"Yes," she said and blushed and we both laughed.

Maybe she wasn't such a minx after all. Maybe she was too low maintenance is all, if there was such a thing as that. She was throwing me so many signals, I couldn't figure her out at all.

"Ok. Bowling Alley. Let's do this," I said and threw the Cutlass into gear and began to back out of the drive.

"Really Mike?" she asked and I could have sworn she was trying to scoot closer to me but the middle console got in the way. Maybe I should trade the Cutlass off for a truck. A truck with a big bench seat. We could get cuddly and drive. That'd be nice. I looked over at her and winked as a car beeped its horn behind me. Tiny little Japanese thing. Everyone was buying them now and they all drove like assholes.

"Fuck off," I scowled and backed closer to the little car and then threw it into drive. I heard her gasp from next to me.

"Sorry honey," I said and reached over blindly and patted her bare knee as I took off toward the Thunderbird Bowling Alley.
**

I got Faith situated on the bench with her legs up. Oh those legs. God help any guy who stared at them. I'd bust loose some teeth, God's honest truth if that happened.

"You need anything from the counter?" I asked her a million and two times while her friends Jennifer and Allison with their huge hair and their caked up faces popped their gum and watched.

"Maybe a pop?" she answered but sounded like a question. So low maintenance. I couldn't help but smile. Maybe low maintenance was just as much work as high maintenance? It was all good to me. I wasn't scared of a little work.

"Grape?" I asked and winked at her and watched her blush.

"Sure," she said and smiled with her eyes shut.

She was so shy, I loved it so much. It lit me up in all my dark spots. She was so pretty with her long shiny hair and she was so hot with her short little self and those big titties packed in that blue ruffled shirt. My God. All those buttons up the back. How was I supposed to get under that?

I thought about it while I got my shoes and my ball. Then I ordered a pepperoni pizza, a pitcher of beer and a coke. They didn't have grape pop.

"Sorry baby. No grape pop. Is a coke ok?" I asked her as I handed her the cup with the straw.

"Thanks Mike," she said and held it and sipped it as I sat the pitcher and cups down on the table.

"You bought a pitcher?" Jennifer, the one with the Regal, the one with the wall of brown hair, asked me.

"You want a cup?" I asked her and poured one out the side of the pitcher to reduce the head.

"No. How old are you?" she asked with her face scrunched up so tight all I saw were plucked eyebrows and frosted lip gloss.

"17," I answered and sipped the little bit of foam off the top of the cup myself as my face hardened. This one did not light me up in all the right spots. Neither did the other one, the blonde, Allison, the one I had set my sights on the first time I saw her get out of the Buick. How wrong I'd been about that one. Skinny in acid wash jeans with a flat ass and a flat chest and hair fried, bleached, and huge.

"Beer?" I offered her the next cup I poured as I sipped steadily from the first one.

Cold beer from a keg is the best if you can't get a can. I didn't need bottles. I didn't need fancy. I needed it cold and flowing.

"What kind is it?" she asked. Her frosted lips sneered as she watched me drink. Her small eyes blinked under all that brown eyeliner. Her lips looked hard already from chain-smoking so many years. She'd look like my mom before long.

"Cold and free," I answered and smiled.

"No thanks," she replied and gave me the one-second smile before her face turned sour and she sat down and hunched over to put on her bowling shoes.

I chugged the rest of both cups and sat down across from Faith to slip on my own shoes.

"Pizza be out soon."

"We just had cheeseburgers," she said and laughed quietly. I shrugged and grinned.

"I'm still hungry," I admitted and made her giggle.

She looked so good sitting there with all her hair long and soft and her face pale and without make up. Her lips had a hint of pink gloss. I loved how unpainted and soft she was. I'd never dated a girl like her. The last time I kissed a girl without make-up had been in the sixth grade. Jennifer Denton. Wealthy. Bitchy for a 12-year-old. My God she had broken my heart. She taught me how to French. My one and only rich girl.

"You hungry, too, Bleacher Girl?" I asked her and winked at her and then leaned over and kissed those soft lips while her friends watched.

"Well, are you baby?" I asked her when I finished kissing her.

"Sure, Mike."
She looked confused.

"Huh, huh!" I laughed and grabbed my ball and marked my name on the card as first player.

"I'm up!" I called out and went up to the line. Slammed the pins down, a strike.

It was like that. Strikes and spares, goofing and showing off in the lane for Faith. I couldn't stop smiling at her. I drank my beer and ate pizza and fed her a slice, all while her two girlfriends watched. The place filled up with young and old. Kids from my old school and old men from the donut shop. Everyone came by to say hi and to meet Faith. Everyone was mesmerized by her.

I kept throwing the strikes while her friends threw gutters and bummed smokes off me all night and had me light them. I acted like it was nothing, even though money was tight, and there went all my smokes. I looked at Faith and couldn't help smiling. I oozed charm. I acted like I owned the world. And I did. I had everything a man needed and then some.

Then Shane and Jeff rolled in.

"Well, well, well. Look who's here with the three hottest hunnies in town."

Allison and Jennifer warmed right up to that. I looked at Faith. I couldn't remember if I'd told her she looked pretty or not tonight. I was buzzed. I couldn't think.

"What's the matter?" she asked and reached out for me and I took her hand and got on my knees in front of her.

"You need anything?" I asked her right by her little pink ear.

I didn't want to be here anymore. I wanted to get Faith out of there. Me and Bleacher Girl. I didn't need to show her off. I was sick of every man in the place, young and old, looking at her. Her legs. Her rack.

"I'm good, Mike. Are you having fun?"

"Sure. I'm here for you though. Are you having fun?" I took her face in my hands and it looked so small. She was all I wanted to see as noise bounced all around us.

"Sure, I'm good."

"Yes, you are good. But you been sitting there all night. You need the ladies?" I asked and tilted my head towards the girls room.

"Yeah, that'd be good," she said and started to get up.

"We'll walk her there." Allison and Jennifer both said at the same time.

"Well try to fuckin' stay with her," I said to their backs as they helped Faith hobble down past all the lanes and the counter to the girls room.

I watched as every male turned to stare.
That's how it was. That's why Jennifer and Allison wanted Faith around.

She didn't drink or smoke or wear makeup. She had nothing in common with them. But she was a looker. She was stacked like no other girl her age. She was famous. She was Bleacher Girl. She drew all the boys. That's exactly how it was.

I kept my head up and watching for their return. For the inevitable.

"Fuck her, Mike. Who cares?" Shane said to me when he saw me stand up and drop my cigarette butt on the floor and step on it.

"So not worth jail, bro," Jeff said to me and started to grab me.

"Don't have my back or nothing, you assholes," I said as I ducked out from under Jeff's grip. He had several inches over me and probably outweighed me by 50 lbs but I didn't care. I worked my ass off for my life and I'd beat his in a second if he got between me and Faith.

And now some guy was putting his arm around her and trying to help her walk against her will. She was batting at him with her tiny hand. Oh no. She looked terrified. He pulled her so hard her boobs jiggled against him. Nope.

I was on the balls of my feet, sprinting. My face hard. Jaw clenched. Body loose and hot. Running like a fucking wildebeest. Everything clicked into place nice and slow. Crystal clear. Fist back. Click. Dude looking up startled. Click. Dude letting go of Faith. Click. His eyes wide. Click. I leapt over a bench. Click. My teeth bared. Click. Faith stumbling. Click. Faith falling. Click. No. Click.

I shoved that asshole out of the way and grabbed her and pulled her into me. I crushed her against me as she tucked her head under my jaw.

"You ok, Bleacher Girl?" I asked her urgently, frantically,

my lips in her hair as I held on to her waist tight.

"Mike!" she cried out and wrapped her arm around my neck and smashed herself soft and bouncy against me.

"You ok?" I asked her 500 more times as she sniffled against my shirt.

I walked her back to our lane, grabbed her purse, and coat and helped her get situated.
No goodbyes. No paying for the lane, the shoes, the pizza, the beer, none of it. I kicked my shoes off and put them on the counter and slipped my Nikes on fast and got us out of there. Mine. She was mine. My Bleacher Girl.

I wanted to kill that guy. I had to get away. I would have crushed his face with a bowling ball. I was that mad and he had at least 60 lbs on me. Easily. I was skinny. But I was mean if I wanted to be. And I wanted to be but I didn't want Faith to ever see me like that. So, I got us out of there.

I was on her immediately in the car. I was halfway over the center console crushing her under me. I needed in her now. I needed her to be all mine. My hands roamed all over her; her knees, her thighs, her face, her hair, until they landed on what they really liked, a lot. My hands squeezed both of her tits again and again and that melted the anger. I couldn't get enough of their softness. They calmed me. I climbed on top of her in her seat right there in the parking lot of the Thunderbird. She was moaning and let me do what I wanted. She was soft and warm and she gave me run of all of it. I pushed that short skirt up all the way and she let me. Her forehead broke out in a sweat and her hair was wild. I was ready to unzip.

"Mike, slow down!"

"Baby, I can't! I can't stop!"

"Mike we're right by the door!"

I looked up. She was right. We were right there in the neon lights of the doorway with me on top of her and my hands squeezing her tits as people went in and out the door, laughing and lighting smokes.

I got off her and got back in my own seat. Lit a smoke and rolled down the window. Turned on the car and threw it in reverse.

"Where we going?" she asked as she pulled her seatbelt over her lap and pulled down her skirt so her panties weren't showing anymore.

I felt like I had on too many layers of clothes and was sweating all over. I was ready to take it all off.

"Tire plant," I answered her.

"Tire plant?" she asked and sounded frightened.

"Night guard owes me for several favors."

"What kind of favors?" she sounded so scared. So unsure.

"Oh, too many to name them all," I chuckled but that didn't satisfy her.

She was scooting away from me.

"Oh, nothing bad, honey. I changed his tire one night. Jumped his battery for him. I helped him change out his master cylinder one weekend. Things like that."

"How do you know him? Is he from your school?"

"Oh no, not from school. Sometimes I wax floors there at night when they're shut down over the holidays. And I was always the last one to leave and I'd have a cigarette with him sometimes. And then I helped him a few times. He has bad luck I guess. Or maybe it was good luck since I was there. Anyway, he owes me."

"But why are we going there?"

"Privacy."

Tucked between two semi-trailers in the back lot of the tire plant, I left the engine on and parked nose out. It felt safer nose out. I had to protect my Bleacher Girl. But who was protecting her from me?

I was on her quick in her seat, kissing her and pulling the lever on the seat all the way back. This was gonna be fast. No time for the backseat. No time for taking it slow.

She was into it. She was into me. But she was still scared. She was a little frozen, a little tense. I was all serious. I was all for me. I buried my face in all that hair. She was small and soft under me, I covered her with my body. My hands everywhere. She was warm and girly and oh so squeezable and she responded to my hands with cute little moans and gasps and her hand in my hair.

"You trust me?" I asked her.

"I don't know, Mike. I'm scared."

She knew where this was going. Her body trembled with fear but her face was pink with excitement.

"I won't hurt you."

I felt bad soon as I said it.

Her eyes opened wide in the dark car as if she knew I was lying.

"Don't be scared," I told her as I struggled with her shirt and its millions of buttons up the back of it. I gave up and yanked it apart really hard and popped most of them off. They flew through the car like little white candies as the sodium lights of the parking lot lit them up. I heard them clitter clatter all over the car.

"Oh my gosh!"

"Sorry sweetie, I'll buy you a hundred more I swear to God but let them not have any buttons."

"Mike!" she squealed and giggled as I pulled the shirt gently open up her back and off her uninjured arm and over the cast.

"Oh my God."

"What?"

"Is this bra from 8th grade too?"

"No, silly, why?"

"It has a tiny flower right in the middle of your tits."

She giggled.

"It looks like it would have fit you in 8th grade. Jesus. You're gonna kill me."

Her tits were popping out of and overflowing the tiny triangle cups. The stretchy thin cloth covered the sides of her tits but barely contained her nipples as the rest of her was pushing out and hanging on for dear life.

"No, I was this big then too."

"My God."

I couldn't even imagine a stacked Faith in 8th grade. Why didn't we go to the same school? I would have made such a fool of myself over her then. I would have panted at her heels like a dog. Thank God she was 18 now. Thank God she was mine now.

I kissed her and she wrapped her leg around my waist and that was the end of all restraint for me. I ground against her and she rubbed against me in response. Yes. It was go time.

"Tell me about the bleachers," I whispered to her as I reached under her skirt and touched her damp panties and made her arch against my fingers.

"Mike no, I don't like you touching me there."

"Why not?" I asked with my lips against her neck.

"It scares me."

"I won't hurt you."

"It's not right."

"Why not?"

"I'm not nice down there."

"What does that mean?" I asked and sat up, very curious. I cocked my head at an angle and waited for her to explain.
She had her eyes closed but her face looked soft and relaxed even though I knew she was scared.

"What does that mean?" I asked her again, "Not nice?"

"It's not nice down there. It's really wet."
I gulped. Did she not know she was supposed to be like this?

"How old are you again?" I choked out and could barely talk. I buried my face in her hair that spilled all around her head on the back of the seat.

"I'm 18, you know that. Why?"

"Don't you know you're supposed to get wet?"
She didn't answer. She froze up rigid. This wasn't good.

"It means you like me," I whispered in her ear and gently

stroked her cheek.

I could wait. I bit my lip and stroked her face and her hair very gently till finally she opened her eyes and looked at me and then she smiled.

"Is it dirty? Is it bad?" she asked with her face close to mine, and then she squeezed her eyes shut tight as she waited for an answer.

"Naw, it's good," I said with my mouth grazing her sweet pink lips and I watched as she opened her eyes again and smiled even bigger.

She relaxed and spread her knees apart and I wasted no time getting back down there. I pulled her panties down on one side. They were so flimsy I was afraid I'd break them.

"Tell me," I panted as I reached down her leg and slid her slouchy leather boot off. She had a tiny white lacy sock on and my stomach muscles clenched hard when I saw it. "Tell me about falling on the bleachers, Faith," I said to her as I pulled her cotton panties all the way off; over her socked foot and over the cast on her leg.

I held her panties in my hand a moment. They were so tiny and so thin, I crushed them in my fist. I wanted to hold them the rest of my life. I loved those panties. They were damp and sticky against my palm.

"Tell me all of it Faith. How you fell. How you survived. I want all of it. I need all of it from you now," I prompted her as I nudged her knees further apart.

My mind and fingers were a million miles away from the bleachers.

My heart was going to kill me as it pounded harder and harder. I took a deep breath and pulled my shirt off and wiped the sweat from around my neck and under both arms. The windows of the car were steamed up in the cold night.

"Tell me how it happened," I urged her as I reached down and touched between her legs and lay my face on top of those wonderful soft tits.

I could touch her forever the rest of my days and never get enough. Her breasts rose and fell faster and faster and I watched mesmerized as one swollen pink nipple pushed free of the stretchy white cotton bra. I held my breath as I watched it rise and fall with her breathing. I watched it harden in the chilly air. I sucked it into my mouth and lapped at it to warm it up and then I asked again, "Tell me how you fell."

I slid my hand between her thighs as I waited for her to answer.

"I couldn't see," she said and began to pant as I touched her slow with just one fingertip on the very edge of her wet little folds.

Her breasts heaved under my face as I slowly slid two fingers between her slick lips as she remembered her accident. I kissed the freed nipple and sucked it just a little and she sucked in a sharp breath and then got very quiet.

"Was it too dark?" I asked her as I scooted down between her creamy thighs. She dripped steadily on to my fingers as I slid them slowly up and down her slippery valleys. She shuddered like a bad roller skate with every stroke. "Was it too dark to see?" I asked her again.

It was dark for me right now. I couldn't see a thing. But I could feel her. I could feel her light little curls on my chin. I could smell her. Not baked apples.

Pancakes. Butter. Chicken in a skillet. Something rich and alive. Dark dirt in the countryside. I didn't know. Nothing had meaning. I remembered nothing from my life at that moment. My mouth watered. I eased her ankle onto my shoulder. I took it slow. Not all girls liked to open their legs that wide for you. I paused here a moment to see how she reacted.

"Keep talking," I told her and then I said, "You couldn't see. Tell me how you fell."

"It was dark."

I heard her say that and then I wrapped her leg around the back of my neck and I went into the dark myself. She whimpered and whined like a pup stuck in a fence. She bumped herself lightly against my face and I growled hungrily at how bold she was letting herself be. I searched for her little bean with my tongue. I took my time tasting her every fold and every sweet crevice. I lapped and sucked all of it.

"I, I," she bucked and stuttered when I found her hard little nub. I reached up and found her hand and squeezed it for reassurance as I stuck my whole face into her and lapped it all up.

"What are you doing? Mike? No, Mike, no!"

She tried to pull her hand away from mine. I squeezed it gently and placed it on the back of my head. She wove her fingers into my hair and drove me wild.

"Keep going," I told her.

"Your hair is so soft," she said dreamily and sighed and opened wider.

"Now, tell me what happened, the bleachers."

"I couldn't see and I," she trailed off as I went deeper with my tongue.

She was soft and wet and tiny and hot and so full of life throbbing against my mouth. I buried my face deep when she pushed gently on the back of my head. I wished she had the use of both her hands to shove me deeper between her legs.

"I tripped!"

It came out as an exclamation as she arched under me.

"I tripped! I didn't fall!"

Her hand now limp in my hair. She was panting and whimpering.

"Mike? What are you doing to me? I can feel your beard," she cried out in between deep breaths.

"Do you like it?"

"Yes. But what are you doing to me?"

"Getting you ready for me. Keep talking Faith. Tell me all of it."

I went back in. She was silent except for her breathing. And then she startled me. She bucked and ground all her wetness all over my face. I had to pause. I shuddered like a wet dog with ecstasy rippling up and down my back. I had never tasted a girl like this. I'd never had a girl this wet before and she just got slicker with each lick.

"Don't stop," she whispered and so I dove back in and felt her shimmy a bit before she bucked hard three times against my face with all that wet pie and she cried out, "Someone pushed me!" My head popped up.

"Someone pushed you?"
This was news to me. I sat halfway up. The air was cold on my slick cheeks.

"Yes. Someone shoved me." She sounded impatient.

She wiggled and arched under me. She wanted more. She squirmed around. Her hand nudged me down but I wanted to hear this.
I hoped the callouses on my fingers weren't too rough for her compared to my tongue. Now she squirmed harder. Did she like that better? I went slow and easy. I had to remind myself to go slow with my fingers. Good girls were probably fragile, but what did I know?

"Who pushed you?" I asked her with her ankle with the lace sock back up on my shoulder again.
My God she was flexible.

"I don't know. I heard laughing and then screaming."
"Screaming?"

I went in a little too fast and she cried out. I eased out and went in a little more deeper. My God she was slick and tight and ready for me but I needed to hear all of this. But I also needed what I needed and, in the end, my need to be inside of her, pumping hard, was driving me on. I was rock hard.
I unzipped and pressed myself against her wetness to let her know what I wanted to do; to let her know what was going to happen. She shifted around under me, her ankle still on my shoulder. She was so

open for me. She rolled her hips and I felt how slippery she was with the head of my cock and I went in just a little. She whimpered and wiggled and then stopped moving.

"I'll be careful, I'll try to be gentle," I whispered in her hair.

I went in all the way with her foot up on my shoulder and she sucked in a deep breath.

"It'll be over soon!" I assured her. That was not a lie. I couldn't hold on long at all. Male instinct was driving me now, driving me hard.

Her face twisted in pain and she bared her teeth at me. They were straight and white and her canines looked sharp. She looked like an animal. It turned me on. She was scorching hot and squeezing me tight as I sank into her. That turned me on more.

"Faith!" I called to her.

Her eyes popped open. They were wide and scared.

"I love you."

It just came out. I don't know why I said it. I'd never said it to anyone. I couldn't even remember any girls I'd ever had sex with at all at that moment, much less any that I had told I loved, because I hadn't loved any of them.

"Mike," she gasped as I drove deep in her and pulled out halfway.

"Are you ok?" I asked her and held her face tight.

I cared about her. I didn't want to hurt her. But I sunk back into her as far as I could and just as quick pulled back to the tip and dove back in. I couldn't stop. I was pumping her too hard. I had no control. None.

"Mike, please," she begged. She panted. She hiccupped.

She held onto my shoulder with her good hand; her nails raked my skin and drove me wild.

"Who was screaming, Faith?"

I slammed into her again and again with one of my hands gripping the center console; the other gripping the headrest.

"It was me!"

"Why?"

"I was falling! I was dying!"

"Who shoved you?" I demanded to know. I had to know. NOW.

I only had a couple seconds left that I could hold on.

"It was Allison!" she yelled as I came.

I hoped I didn't hurt her. I couldn't stop. I couldn't hold back. I was in it on pure male desire, pure gluttonous pleasure and I was nailing her hard in the seat of the Cutlass.

"Allison! That bitch!"

I growled it out too loud. Too frightening.

I sounded exactly like my dad when he back-handed my mom last Easter and I shivered on top of Faith, on top of Bleacher Girl, and I thrust deep inside her, in all her tight wetness, and I came again and kicked the dashboard with the heel of my foot. I kicked the thought of my dad right out of my head.

Chapter Six

Clear eyes full tank can't lose.

I chanted that to myself as I gently fingered my fat bottom lip.

It took Adam a week to realize it was me who took his job at the Thrifty Lube. He was not happy about it at all and now I had a fat lip and busted-open knuckles on my right hand. I also had two days suspension from school which was fine by me. It gave me time to work more hours.

I needed to put the fight behind me. I'd still be his friend if he wanted. But I'd be watching that guy.

I checked in at Thrifty Lube that Monday afternoon with a huge smile on my face to see when they wanted me next. I informed them that I was free to work all day Tuesday for $12 Tuesday and not just the early morning since I was suspended from school. Adam was free to look for new work since he was the fucker who sucker punched me when I rolled into PE that morning wearing a Thrifty Lube t-shirt after my first early shift in the bays. I didn't think he would ever try that with me again as I didn't react well to being sucker punched. If he got his job back at the Thrifty Lube, he'd be doing it with one eye swollen shut and a busted nose and he'd be doing it next to me. And he'd better watch his step.

"Down below or on the counter?" My new manager asked the assistant manager.

Everything they said to each other sounded dirty.

"He's got a way with the ladies when he's up top but he also knows what he's doing underneath."

"I bet he does."

Those two assholes talked to each other like they were boyfriends but I didn't care. I just smiled at them and waited.

"We'll put him in the bay," the manager Fred with the handlebar mustache said to the assistant, Skip.
He looked like a Skip.

"In the bay. Nice. He can still interact with the ladies and do all the things on top."

"Nice."

"Nice."

"You'll be in the bays tomorrow for $12 Tuesday. Help pull the cars in straight, clean them out. New wipers, inspect the filters and all the lights and signals. Charm the ladies. But charm them fast."

"Sounds nice." I shot him a fast smile.

"Any questions?"

"Yeah, can I get a couple more shirts?"

"Sure. Help yourself. Anything else?"

"When's payday?"

"Next Friday but Skip can front you $40 if you need it."

"I'm good."
I didn't want to owe Skip anything.

"By the way, what's the other guy look like?"

"Oh, you mean this?" I asked and pulled on my fat bottom lip. "He looks like a guy who used to work here."

"Adam," they both said at the same time.

"He didn't take it well that you took his job," Fred said.

"Naw, but he'll be fine."

I wore a Thrifty Lube t-shirt Thursday and Friday when I went back to school and greeted Adam with a shit-eating grin on my face but he didn't say a peep.

The two days back at school crawled by and I hated being stuck at a desk all morning when my suspension was done. I missed my little Bleacher Girl but could not get up my nerve to call her after we had done it behind the tire plant. She had cried and cried after we did it and I hadn't been able to get her to calm down and couldn't get out of her what was wrong. But I knew what was wrong. I popped her cherry, me, a third-rate punk from the east side of town. Me, white trash from the Bird's Nest, a neighborhood of dead-end streets named after birds. Not even fancy birds.

I grew up in a split-level house on Robin Court. Piece of shit house. Mom and her boyfriend Dennis upstairs and Dad and his girlfriend Linda downstairs. Me on the couch trying to avoid them all. The drinking, the chain-smoking, the cards, the hamburger helper dinners, and the fights and the never-ending beer and cigarettes. That's all they were good for to me; beer and smokes. Dad beat Mom, and Mom slapped me around, and Dennis was like a ticking time bomb likely to go off yelling at anyone in the house and randomly beating the hell out of me. But Dennis throwing me off the deck was too much. Throwing me off the deck, breaking my arm, crossed a line. If I would have stayed, I would have killed him with my one good arm.

As it was, he called the cops on me after he threw me off the deck. And for what? For taking a pack of his smokes. For using his tools to drain my brake lines on the Cutlass without asking and for leaving them on the garage floor when I was done. He was never sober enough to talk to, so how could I ask him if I could use them? The cops didn't even arrest him or ask questions, they just asked if I needed an ambulance.

I couldn't blame Faith for crying. Why would she want some skinny punk like me busting her cherry? Why would she let some grease monkey from a retread high school touch her beautiful body? She probably regretted all of it. Why would she love me? I just needed her to love me. She didn't have to let me touch her ever again. Just let me love her. I'd do anything for her. I'd do anything to make her smile at me. My God I was so whipped.

I knew one thing for sure. She regretted telling me that Allison shoved her on the bleachers. She swore me to secrecy that night after she got done hiccupping and crying. I promised her I would never say a word to anyone about it. But that word, that promise was dead in the water if she broke up with me. I felt it coming. And I would take my anger out on Allison for pushing her. For hurting her. The secret would be out.

I didn't hear from Faith all week. She didn't call me. I didn't call her. I wasn't chicken. I was busy. I was giving her, her space. I was waiting for her to call me. I pulled as many hours as I could at the Thrifty Lube which is why I was exhausted and sitting on the kitchen table next to the windows with one of them cracked open while I ate a peanut butter and jelly sandwich on Texas Toast that Friday night.

I had my feet propped up on a kitchen chair, watching a freezing drizzle come down when the Regal rolled up and bumped the curb.

The passenger door opened and a white cast came out followed by Faith. Shiny haired and wearing that brown mini skirt that buttoned up the middle and her pink puffer jacket pulled around her. A lime green knee-sock and a hiking boot on her good leg.
My God she was going to kill me.

I rocketed off the kitchen table so hard a leg broke right off it. I had to get downstairs before she got back in that car and disappeared. I had to see her up close. I couldn't believe my eyes that she was there. At my place. All doubt was gone about her as soon as I saw her but she looked uncertain. She looked scared. She looked incredible. I never felt better in my life.

I had too many emotions at once. I'd never felt so confused in all my life.

"Bleacher Girl," I said under my breath.
I hoped she wasn't there to dump me. I started to touch her arm. I started to pull her into me. But what if she came by to dump me? So, I hesitated.

"Hi Mike."
She glanced up at me uncertain. Her cheeks blazed pink.

"Hi Faith."
I stood back from her, waiting. She was lighting me all up

inside. I couldn't help but smile huge. If she dumped me, if she crushed me, then she crushed me. I'd take it smiling, I'd take it grinning, I'd take anything she wanted to do to me.

"Are you mad at me Mike?"

"No, of course not, why? I could never be mad at you."

"Because you haven't called."

"I been busy."

I sounded defensive. I sounded like an asshole.

"With who?" she demanded in her small voice.

"With who?" I repeated like it made no sense to me.

"Yes. Who?" she asked and started to cry.

"With no one. With work. With school. With looking for a better job!"

Now I really sounded like an asshole and she began to cry more.

She wiped at the tears with the back of her hand. Freezing rain fell on us and Jennifer rolled down the window on the Regal with the push of a slick button.

"You coming?"

"Don't go. I'm sorry Faith! I should have called. I'm not good on the phone. I don't know how to talk on the phone. Come upstairs. Let's talk!" I pleaded with her.

"I don't know, Mike."

She looked back at her friend who sat impatient behind the wheel.

"She push you too?" I asked Faith.

"Mike! You promised!"

"Sorry. Come upstairs. Please. I'll make us dinner."

"I can't. But you didn't answer the phone. I've called twice!"

"I been out. Working tons. I'm sorry, honey, please, come up."

I wanted her so bad. I wanted her to see where I lived. I was proud of my little apartment. I wanted her to come upstairs and light it up with her magic like she did me. I wanted her to see how nice it was. But she wouldn't.

"I need to go. My casts are getting wet."
She started to go back to the car.

"Please. Faith."

I reached out and wrapped my arms around her tiny waist. She pressed her face into my chest and I kissed the top of her hair. She smelled so good. She felt so warm against me. It thundered once and began to rain harder.

"Faith come up. I'll take you home soon. Just come up for a little."

I squeezed her tight to me. She looked up at me as the rain turned to hail and she winced and tucked her face into the front of my shirt and shivered. She glanced up at me at the same time as I bent down to kiss the top of her head.

"Ouch," she said and rubbed her forehead where my whiskers burnt her soft skin when we bumped. I kissed it and touched it with a finger.

"I need to shave again. Come up and I'll show you where I do that," I said down to her as I stroked my face with the back of my fingers and I smiled at her and tried to work my magic on her. And it worked because she blushed and smiled back and said, "Ok."
It was like that. It was easy magic. It was soft magic.

Shirley Johnson

Chapter Seven

I carried her in my arms up the stairs, past Molly with her door open, licking a spoon of yellow batter from a large plastic bowl.

"Hi Mike."

"Hello," I answered all polite as Faith clung to me, her good arm around my neck, her fingers entwining in my hair that curled under the collar of my shirt. I needed a trim bad. But no money and no time.

I wanted to roar in pleasure as her fingers touched me softly. I popped my neck twice and continued up to my floor. She was impressed with my tiny apartment as soon as she saw it. I didn't want to ever put her down. I carried her into my one big room that had a twin bed, a recliner, a dresser, and a weight bench. It had a tv tray and a small color tv with rabbit ears. I hoped the two posters of Samantha Fox's naked tits on the wall didn't upset her. My ears burned hot and I told myself I needed to get rid of those as soon as possible.

I carried her sideways out of my room into my little entry hall and over to my tiny kitchen with the sink, stove, the hutch, and the now broken table. There was also the small white fridge that sounded like a model T car chugging along.

"This is it. You like?" I asked and felt my smile blast its way across my happy face.
She liked. She liked it all. She said it needed a woman's touch. It was that easy. She walked right into that one. I could not stop grinning.

"I would like a woman's touch," I said to her and kissed her soft cheek.

"Why do you like me?" she asked as I took her back into the

bedroom and set her gently on my bed and propped her leg up with a corduroy pillow that was worn threadbare on the corners.

There were so many reasons all dancing around each other in my head about why I liked her. That short skirt was number one. I slid her puffy pink coat off and folded it carefully over the headboard of the bed and used the time to calm myself down and then I sat next to her. I hoped she didn't notice what she did to me. I hoped she didn't notice how much I liked her and where it was showing.

"I like you because," I said playfully and began to laugh. "I like the crazy way you dress."

I eyeballed that incredibly short brown skirt and the brass buttons going up the middle. I eyed the hot pink tight wool cardigan sweater she had pulled up over her broken arm.

"I like this sweater, and how you always wear one sock and one shoe."

"Mike," she laughed.
I kicked off one of my shoes and started to pull off one of my socks.

"Mike! No!" she squealed and tried to stop me as if I were taking off my pants or something unacceptable. I wanted to. I wanted to unbuckle them right then.

"Really Mike, why?" she asked as I came close to her face.

I stopped smiling. She smelled so good. Not like cigarettes. Not like hairspray or bad breath from bad cooking. She smelled like honey and something sweet like a cookie right out of the oven. I'd had them once when I was eight and school took us to meet the "real" Santa and his wife gave us cookies right out of the oven, sugary and warm.

"You're like Mrs. Claus," I said with my eyes shut.

"What does that mean?" she shrieked and shoved me away just as my lips brushed against her soft ones.
But I held her by her tiny shoulders and pushed her back onto my bed.

"Because you're like a Christmas cookie," I said and kissed

her slow and gentle despite the fact my whole body throbbed to be inside her.

Then I kissed her deeper and harder. She was much more than just a lay. So much more and for that I could wait. I could wait and savor the so much more even if I didn't understand what it was, I told myself as the kiss grew hotter. There was much more going on than just sex between us. It was good in a different way. Oher girls were just lays. Noise and money spent on smokes and gas and a lot of fighting and drama in between a few screws in the backseat. I saw that now, here in the quiet of my apartment, kissing Faith with all the time in the world to get it right.

"Why do you like me?" I asked her with my eyes close to her own.

Her eyes were deepest dark blue and beautiful, nothing like my plain brown ones. She looked away so I couldn't see them. I could feel the heat blaze off her face though. She tried to push back from under me but I wouldn't let her. The smallest smile curled on the corners of her pink lips. But she would not look up. She hid under those dark lashes.

"Come on Faith, there has to be at least one reason you like me," I said to her and tilted her chin to make her look up at me. She finally looked up and stared deep into my eyes for a long time before she blushed pink.

"I don't know," she admitted coyly and smiled and let her hair fall in front of her face. "I like you because you like me. And I like you because you're happy," she said as she peeked out from behind all that hair.

"Yeah?" I asked and let the huge smile I was holding back rip across my face.
I WAS happy. She did it to me.

"Yes, and you're, I don't know, you're so polite, you're like a grown man and you're a gentleman too."

I was a gentleman. I let it echo around in my head a while as I tried to take it in and understand it. No one had ever described me like that. I had never thought of myself like that; a gentleman.

She blinked and blushed and looked away.

She thought I was polite. She thought I was happy. She thought I was a gentleman. When all I thought about all the time was getting her naked and pounding into her 'til she shrieked.

"You think so?" I asked and felt like a wolf. A wolf in boy's clothing. A wolf with a giant boner I was trying not to press into her.

"I don't know, Mike. I feel good when I'm with you. You're so handsome," her face blazed redder on those words and she tucked her chin into that amazing chest and shut her eyes.

"I feel good with you too, baby."

I feel good when I look at that skirt, I said to myself, I feel good when I see those beautiful huge tits in that sweater, I thought and lay down on top of her as the hail pounded the windowpanes and the radiators began their nightly clinking as they sent steam gushing through the pipes of the apartment.

I wanted to run my hands all over her, but she wasn't having it. She pushed my hands away from her boobs. She smacked at the backs of them when I squeezed her with both of them. I eased up but she wasn't having it.

It was like that.

She shoved me away. My smile froze on my face and I felt like the world's biggest dickwad. I was acting like a kid who'd never been with a girl. And it was sort of true, I'd never been with a girl like Faith. She drove me wild.

"What?" I asked and reached for her tiny waist.
Her chest rose and fell as she pried my hands off her. I couldn't take my eyes away. I licked my lips and nearly panted. She was killing me.

"I need to get home."

"But Faith, you only just got here. Stay. Stay the night. You and me cuddling here all night while it storms. You can keep your bra and panties on."

I was unbuckling my pants, ready to go. I was a man possessed. I was running ahead and making all the wrong choices and I knew it and couldn't stop myself meanwhile she was pulling the rug out of from under me. She was hot and then she was cold.

"Mike!" she shrieked, "Why are you taking your pants off?"

"You can keep everything on! Honest! Truth!" I held up my hand as my pledge, my honor. "I'm a gentleman, remember!"

"I'm not that kind of girl!" Her eyes grew rounder with every word as she stared at my dangling belt.

Her heart shaped face hardened. Her swollen lips disappeared in a point as she struggled to get up, get out from under me.

"What kind a girl?" I asked, my voice sounded weak. I was whipped. I looked down at my unbuckled pants and back at her face which was turning red with exertion to get out from under me. Oh, why did I let this girl whip me? Why did I let her do this to me?

"A fast girl! A slutty girl!" she cried out from under me. "A girl you just undo your pants in broad daylight with and just want around for sex!" she ticked off on her fingers as her eyes widened bigger and bigger.

"I don't think that about you. Not at all," I said and rolled off her and let her get up.

I followed her as she hobbled to my entry-way, her cast sliding on my waxed hardwood floor. She glared up at Samantha Fox as she went.

"I can take you home whenever you want. Just stay a little."

"You just want to get up my top! You just want to feel me up!" she snapped.

Yes. That was true. I wanted up under that sweater. But I also wanted up under that short skirt. My God, I knew her little panties were right up there. Why was she doing this? I'd already been up there before.

"I'm going now."

"What'd I do wrong? I thought I was a gentleman?" I

pleaded with her.

I got a growl from her in return but my God she was hot when she lost her temper. She was so cute. She was so irresistible. She was going to kill me. I was trying to so hard to live up to her view of me as a gentleman. But I'd already messed it all up. Her growls turned to snarls and it was over.

I knew then I'd lost her and I'd never get her back. My voice sounded so wimpy. She'd never want to be with me again. She was closing up shop. She was leaving. She only came here to rub it in my face one last time how beautiful she was and how she would never let me near her again. She only came here to show me what I'd never get to touch or even see ever again.

We went to two different high schools; there'd be no chance I'd ever even run into her again if she broke up with me. How had it gone wrong so fast? I was going to lose her forever if I didn't do something quick. This was what all girls were like. Everything could be fine one moment and a complete mess the next. There was no sense trying to figure it out because you never would understand it. But I couldn't let go of her.

"Faith. Let me help you get down the stairs at least," I begged her as she pulled on her puffy coat and opened the door to the hall.

"Because you're real strong?" Her voice was high and so was the color in her face.

"Yes Faith. You're so light, I could carry you the rest of my life."

I sounded like such a loser and there were Molly and Doris opening their doors and watching me. I couldn't let them see me like this; this weak boy.

"Why are you being such a bitch?" I snapped and watched Faith recoil as if I'd smacked her in the face.

That was when her face turned blotchy and it crumpled soft and destroyed right in front of my eyes and she began to shake and sob and her puffy coat slithered off her shoulders and onto the floor.

"Jennifer was right, she told me you only wanted me for my body!" she wailed and began to cry harder; her little shoulders shook on every word and pierced my heart. "Jennifer told me I meant nothing to you and that's why you didn't call or answer the phone!"

Jennifer was also one of the ones who nearly killed her but I didn't mention that. Even I was smart enough to know not to mention that right now if I ever wanted to touch her again.

I kept quiet and she let me hold her hand all the way down the stairs. I went down them backwards, one step at a time, making sure she didn't fall. I wondered how she managed high school and all the steps, the crowds, her books. Were random boys helping her? Were they copping feels every chance they could? I wanted to ask all these things but couldn't. Her face was pinched and hardened to me.

"I'll take you home but why are you mad?"

"You don't listen to me! You know why! I told you why!"

"I don't, Faith, I swear. I don't. I'm sorry I didn't call. I'm bad on the phone!"

I was back to being weak again and wasn't able to stop her from going.

Chapter Eight

"Mike, you are so pussy whipped."

"I'm not."

But I was. I couldn't follow any of the conversation in the car riding out to the party in the country. I kept spacing out, staring out the back window into the dark night. I could not stop thinking of the last time I'd seen her. Five days ago. It felt like five years. My chest hurt. I'd stopped smoking, I was certain I had cancer or heart failure. And I found myself staring into space at anything and nothing.

She wouldn't let me give her a ride and she wouldn't tell me why she was mad. She simply left. Jennifer had been there in the Regal, waiting to take her home, take her away from me. Jennifer knew she wouldn't be staying long. It was planned. I had stood there in the frozen rain long after they'd left and thought I'd imagined the whole thing; the Buick pulling up, Bleacher Girl in my apartment, in my arms. How would I see her again? I needed her in my arms now. I thought about calling her but didn't.

"Look at him," Shane said to Jeff and I saw his face in the review mirror as he glanced back at me and smirked.

Jeff turned all away around in the seat and looked at me around the headrest of Shane's mom's Malibu.

"Fucking whipped," Jeff said and shook his head back and forth at me.

"He won't even smoke," Shane quietly told Jeff and at his words I pushed on my ribs above my heart with my fingertips as if I could push something back into place and make it stop hurting. When would it stop hurting? I had never had anything like this before with any girl. My throat hurt. I couldn't swallow. I couldn't talk.

"Dude, have a fucking smoke already, you're scarin' me,"

Jeff begged me and handed back his pack of cigarettes.
I took one out and put it behind my ear for later and handed the
pack back to him half-heartedly. I was looking forward to slamming
beers, as many as possible, as soon as we got there. I didn't care
about other girls, I just wanted to drink myself into nothingness.
But the place was packed with kids, all dressed up for Halloween.

"Oh my God, there's a chick here dressed like Elvira!" Jeff
exclaimed as we stepped inside and scanned the room.

"Where" Where?" I asked and punched him in the bicep
with the back of my fist.

"There, dickhead. Sitting by the fireplace."

"My God."

"Fucking right. She'll take your mind off things."

"Jesus, ten dollars say she loses a titty before ten o'clock," I
muttered out of the side of my mouth to him but it didn't matter. It
was noisy and no one could hear us and even if they did, no one
would have cared.

The girl in question was laughing loudly and leaning
forward and taking deep breaths and fanning herself. Every time
we thought she was done laughing, her friend would say something
to her and get her going all over again. The laughs were as fake as
her hair; a black wig that sat crooked and wobbled on her stupid
head.

"It's 9:45. Those tits won't be out by 10," Jeff declared to me
as he stared at the girl and licked his lips.

"Is it a bet?" I asked him with a grin.

"I see that grin. And yes. I'm in for ten. But no interference!"
He smiled devilishly as he pointed his finger at me. "No
interference," he repeated and shook his head at me and I couldn't
help but start laughing.

"Or what?" I asked and my voice broke apart with laughter
and I felt the shell of hurt around my heart crack a little.

"Or it doesn't count."

"What doesn't count?" Shane asked as he pushed his way

thought the crowd carrying three cans of beer. He didn't wait for an answer as he passed us the cans.

"Here's to getting' laid," Jeff nodded at us and we all clunked cans and chugged.

"What were you guys talking about? What doesn't count?"

"Elvira over there," I tipped my beer can in her direction where she sat on the brick ledge in front of the empty fireplace.

"You gonna bang her, Mike?"

"Naw, we bet she gonna lose a tit. And Jeff says I can't help it come out or it's interference and doesn't count."
Jeff snorted and we all started laughing.

"Well obviously. There's her nipple now," Shane announced and chugged the rest of his can and belched.

"Fuck!" Jeff and I both yelled at once over the noise of the party and caused Elvira to look up at us under her heavy lined eyes. Her nipple and bare breast completely fell out of the low open neck of her dress as she stared at us.

"Jesus fuck, pay up," I said and slapped Jeff's arm with the back of my hand, never taking my eyes off that hard little nipple. Every boy around her drank their drinks and stared until her girlfriend sitting next to her elbowed her, causing her to jiggle, and then yelled at her to cover up. Elvira-girl faked surprise and embarrassment and pulled her dress over her beautiful free tit and stood up and walked away on stilettos, giggling as it popped out again.

"Jesus wept!" Shane whispered. He looked like he was going to follow her as his eyes were glued to her swaying ass as she went.

"Gimme my ten," I told Jeff who pulled out a crumpled ten and slapped it in my palm.

"She here alone, you think?" Shane asked me.

"Fuck yes. She has to be. If she was my girl, I'd have her covered up and out in the car!"

"Speaking of your girl, look who's here," Shane's eyes popped once more and he blinked as if to clear them.

Shirley Johnson

"Little Red Riding Hood, how appropriate with those wolves all around her," Jeff snickered.

"My God, a stacked Red," Shane whistled and shook his head.

Faith had a swarm of boys around her all eyeballing that body of hers in her white, low-cut blouse with a red cape tied over her pale cleavage. Her cheeks were rosy and she looked very uncomfortable. She was the perfect Red Riding Hood in a room full of leering wolves. She was pure white girliness popping out of that top, not to mention the red little skirt riding high on her thighs. With her white cast on her arm and her leg, she looked absolutely helpless. That was ok, I was here now.

I stood by myself and watched her from across the room as she batted her lashes and smiled down into her cup. I sipped my can of beer and licked my lips and smiled and wondered if she was still mad and hoped like hell she wasn't.

Her poor arm was huge and awkward in that cast and I could see that she was using it to bump guys away from her and make it look like an accident. Her eyes flicked around the room, looking, looking for someone. Was it me she was looking for?

Where were her friends? Where were Allison and Jennifer, the ones who knocked her off the bleachers? Who was she here with? It couldn't have been a guy. No guy would let that many dudes near his woman. Not a woman like Faith. A guy would have her off in the corner on her own or at least have his arm around her, drawing all of her attention on himself. A guy, I started to say to myself and she looked up from her cup and right at me. The small smile froze on her face and my heart skidded painfully to a stop in my chest and didn't revv back up again until I saw her face turn pinker than it was. Then her eyes sparkled and she smiled wide and batted those thick lashes at me.

She was mine still.

She wasn't mad. That smile was all for me.

I drained my beer can and set it down and crossed the room

in two huge strides and watched the bevy of assholes part for me.

"Hi baby," I said to her with a huge grin spreading across my face, the kind of grin that could light up even my plain brown eyes.

"Hi Mike."
She looked up at me and smiled right back before biting her lips and ducking her head down below all that shiny long hair.

"I'm still mad at you," she said and peeked up at me and pulled a pout.

She put her hand on my chest as I went to close the distance between us. The guys around her closed in and tried to edge me out but I wasn't moving till she told me to go and if she did, I was taking all them guys with me, the hard way.

"Tell me how to fix it. How do I make it better?" I asked and smiled down at her, my eyes lingering on the beautiful swells of her pale breasts as they rose and fell with her quick breaths.

"I don't think you can," she glanced up at me and started to smile and quickly looked away.
The douchebags all around us still hadn't backed off and they too were waiting to see which way she landed on this. As a matter of fact, it felt like they were edging closer to us.

I looked down at little Bleacher Girl as she used her good hand to pull her broken arm across the front of her body. She was so uncomfortable here. It wasn't her scene.

"Little Red," I whispered down to her and when she looked up at me her eyes were round with worry and I tugged on her hand and spoke in her ear, "Let's bail."

She looked uncertain. She looked like a 'no'. I knew if she got out that first 'no' it'd be no all night long. This was either gonna end happy or I was gonna kick the shit of a bunch of these Sand Creek assholes. Rich kids. I used to wrestle those douchebags before I got kicked out of Carroll County High and sent over to delinquent school. I used to love roughing those soft bastards up. I wondered if any of their wrestlers were here tonight. Maybe I'd pick one out in advance. I glanced around the crowded room as a wave of yelling and cheering burst through all the small talk.

"What happened?" she asked and suddenly pressed herself against me tightly.

I felt her little hand crawl its way up my stomach to my chest as she quickly shot glances around the crowded room. I lost no time snaking my own arm around her tiny waist as I peered around the room and saw most of the kids begin to press their way towards the kitchen where most of the cheering came from. Too happy and too early for a fist fight.

"Must be the keg. They musta got it tapped finally." I smiled at this. Beer. Yes. And Bleacher Girl pressed up tight against me.

No sooner than I said it, loud pulsating music began to throb from speakers by the front door. Bass thumped as Billy Idol shrieked and Faith pulled me closer and tucked her forehead into my chest and hid from all the commotion.

"I don't like the crowd," she whispered up at me. "I don't like this song and I don't like all the pushing."

Of course she didn't. The last time she was in a crowd with loud music and pushing, she nearly died. Poor girl. Poor little Bleacher Girl. I kissed the top of her forehead as gentle as I could and felt her relax into me.

It was that easy. I grinned at the douchebags all around us and they all split; some of them groaning and cursing as they went.

Chapter Nine

"How'd you get a pitcher?" Shane asked me.

I had Faith set up on top of a freezer chest out in the back yard and I was standing by her bare knees that were clamped together. I'd asked her a hundred times already if it hurt her leg for that heavy cast to dangle there, hanging. But she said she was ok. I topped her beer off in her red cup and poured me another one.

"Come on, Mike, where'd you find a pitcher?"

"I found it in the cabinet by the card table," I answered, distracted.

My eyes could not stop dropping down to the tops of Faith's thighs where the red wool skirt ended and her creamy skin glowed in the cold night. I licked my lips and started to ask her if she was cold and then remembered I had no jacket to give her this time.

"You found it in the cabinet by the card table?" Shane asked and looked at Jeff like I'd said the most ridiculous thing he'd ever heard ever.

I didn't bother commenting. I sucked the foam off the top of my beer and encouraged Faith to do the same. People were all the same. Wealthy, or poor, or country bumpkins. If they had a card table set up in some way in their house, no matter if it were set up in a dilapidated washroom with linoleum on the slanted floor in front of a cabinet with red plastic doors, there was always a beer pitcher inside it. Whether it was glass or plastic was anyone's guess. This house might have had a plastic folding table for cards and not a felted one like I'd seen at the parties in town, and the pitcher might have been scratched nearly white with wear, but it worked. It looked like it'd been used for decades, so it'd definitely work for me; poor white trash Mike from the Bird's Nest, the shitty side of town.

Poor Mike, the only one not wearing a cool costume. I had

on blue mechanic's overalls over my jeans. I'd borrowed them from the Thrifty Lube. No shirt under it. Didn't think I'd need it but now I was cold in just the coveralls.

Beer would fix it. And Bleacher Girl. If I could get her to loosen up. She didn't like crowds and noise and there were kids from at least three high schools and four counties here. Which reminded me. Adam was probably here. I looked around to see if anyone from my high school for losers was here. Nope. Not close by at least. But about two hundred kids had to be here. The yard was packed and so was the house. Which was why I'd gotten the pitcher. That keg wasn't gonna last.

But no sooner did I think that than a wood panel station wagon rolled up and seven guys got out shouting and laughing and rolled a keg out of the back of it.

"Well I'll be," I said and chuckled and Bleacher Girl followed my gaze to see what I was looking at.

"Mike," she said and giggled.

"What?" I asked her and felt the smile light me up. She lit me up.

She'd drank one cup of beer to my four and she was getting giggly and then she opened her legs a little and I wasted no time getting in there, scooting closer to her, getting where I wanted to be.

"What, my little Bleacher Girl?" I asked her and was aware out of the corner of my eye that both Jeff and Shane were staring at her hungrily. I couldn't look at them and watch their eyes devour her bouncing in that low cut peasant blouse. Nor could I watch their feely eyes crawl up her bare thighs where that short red skirt rippled in the cold night.

If I looked at them, I'd beat the hell out of one with the other. They always checked out my girls and sometimes I threw my leftovers their way when I was done. But Faith was different. Faith, I was never letting go.

"Mike, I can't sit like this."

"Why not?" I asked her in my most innocent voice as she

pushed at me gently to move.

"It's not very nice," she said and blushed.

"Oh I think it's very nice, Faith," I said close to her face so only she could hear me and then I looked back to watch the guys rolling the keg up to the house.

"You have a whole pitcher!" she said to me and giggled and swatted my arm playfully to get me to look back at her.
I glanced down at the pitcher that sat on the freezer chest next to where she was perched.

"Half a pitcher," I said. "Even me who failed math knows that," I laughed.

"Mike, why did you fail math?"

"Because I'm stupid."
I shrugged.

"You are not. I think you're smart. You live on your own. You can't be stupid."

I rolled my shoulders and popped my neck a couple of times and grinned. I could feel Jeff and Shane rolling their eyes next to me without even looking over at them.

She thought I was smart.

I felt like the tallest man on the planet. I bounced on the balls of my feet. I stood up straight and ran my hand through my hair and moved closer to her.

"Mike," she said and smiled and wrapped her legs around me. The large white cast bumped the back of my thigh as she kicked her feet slow like the happy little girl she was.

"Mike," she said and reached out and popped the collar to my mechanics overalls, "I can help you with your math if you need it," she assured me and ran her small hands over my chest and drove me wild.

She bit her bottom lip and stared at me while she waited for me to answer but I couldn't speak because she was fiddling absent-mindedly with the snap of my coveralls at the middle of my chest and when she popped it open, I nearly threw her over my shoulder and ran off with her.

"Jesus, you two get a room," Jeff grouched next to us.

"Where's Jennifer? Where's Allison?" I asked them, looking first to Jeff and then to Shane.

"Inside. Too many bugs they said."

"Bugs?" I asked and laughed and looked all around at all the kids huddled together against the chill. It was almost November and you could feel the cold moisture in the air as if snow were only weeks away.

"Too cold for bugs," I mused and looked at Faith. She would not meet my gaze. She looked like she'd swallowed wrong.

"Faith knows where they are," I blurted without thinking, a laugh on the edge of my words.

"Faith knows what?" Jeff asked, his voice sharp and it caused Faith to flinch and pull me closer to her.

"Chill out man, back up," I warned him.

"Knows what? What does she know?" Shane asked and he too pressed close to us, impatient.

"Faith," I said to her quietly, I wanted her to give it up quick before these guys crossed a line with me. "Tell us what you know."

"Yeah bitch, what the," but that was all Jeff got out before I turned and socked him in the jaw and spun him around.
The hit made a hard, wet sound in the dark and I felt Faith flinch behind me.

"Jesus Mike!" Shane yelled from where he'd jumped away from us.

I was still standing between Faith's legs but Jeff was no longer close to us. My punch spun him around and almost laid him flat in the gravel of the drive. He crouched there on his haunches, rubbing his jaw.

I patted Faith's bare knees to let her know everything was ok. I was pretty certain Jeff would not be wanting more but I was ready to step away from Faith if he did. I didn't trust him to not try to hit me while I stood close to her, close to my little Bleacher Girl.

But he got up and turned around, rubbed his jaw and smiled. He knew he fucked up.

Girls were sacred. You didn't cuss them. Not in front of me. Not my girl. Ever. Even if she had a filthy mouth herself, and most of my girlfriends did, I admit it. But still, you didn't cuss someone's girl.

I smiled back at Jeff and we both started laughing. He was coming close, his arms out. I didn't want him that close to Faith but I didn't want to move away from her either.

"Sorry, bro," he said to me and clapped me on the back in a half hug.

"Yeah, well," was all I said and pushed him away and then I smiled and winked at Faith to let her know everything was under control.

"Tell him what you know, honey," I said to her and squeezed her hand gently.
I could feel my eyes working their magic on her. The blush heated her cheeks and spread down her neck and disappeared into her deep cleavage. She looked delicious but her eyes widened with worry.

"They're inside smoking pot, with some boys from St. Thomas," she said to me barely above a whisper, her words trembling on the ends.

"They're what?" Jeff yelled.

"Stand back. Step off."

"What'd this bitch say?" he demanded and came even closer to us.

I touched his chest and pushed him back. His face was too close to Faith and I did not like how his veins and tendons stood out in his neck.

Some people when they drink, get mean and aggressive. I knew that first-hand. It's a wonder I drank beer because just smelling the bitter stickiness of it sometimes made me think of getting popped in the face by Mom or Dad or both because both of

them were mean drunks. Mom's boyfriend Dennis turned out to be the meanest of them all. But mean ain't the same as tough.
Jeff looked like he was turning out to be a mean drunk. I'd seen it a hundred times. Red face. Red nose. Shiny blue beady eyes. Mean stares. Big mean fists balled up. But mean ain't tuff. That's for sure. I wanted to kick the shit out of him for acting a fraction of mean toward Faith. I felt the change in my own face.

I was a happy drunk but now I was sober quick and ready to teach him a hard lesson. I began to roll up the sleeves of my coveralls without taking my eyes off him and I watched his face contort in confusion as he watched me.

He was a couple inches taller and more than a couple of weight classes heavier but he was stupid and fat and slow and home-fed and soft. He'd never had to sleep in his car. He didn't even have a car. He had his mom's car. And he had a mom who never walloped him upside the head. He had a spoiled greedy look on his face. A hungry look. Hungry for someone else's spoils. His eyes were always bugged and searching. Now he had his fists balled as if he were going to hit someone. And he was glaring over my shoulder at Faith as I began to roll my second sleeve.

His mouth dropped open. He saw me finish rolling my second sleeve up as I stepped away from Faith.

"Fuck," I heard Shane whisper. He knew what was coming.

"What do you think you're doin, Mike?" Jeff asked me and glanced down at my fists that I held for now, loose and down by my waist.

I didn't have words. I was pulling air in and out through my nose hard and slow as I took a step towards him and made him back away.

"I'm sorry Mike," he said and put both hands up, palms out.

"But bros before hos!" he said and grinned and then he dropped.

I popped him so hard he went down in the dirt and the gravel as if his strings were cut.

**

"Mike! You dick!" Jennifer screamed from where she knelt in the dirt near Jeff's head.

He was out cold and I was disappointed.
I wanted him to fight back but the fat fuck dropped like a rock with one hit to the kisser and didn't look like he'd be waking up soon. I glanced back at Faith and saw that she was holding her hand over her gaping mouth in shock. I couldn't help but smile at her, a huge one. I felt great. I felt like kicking the tar out of a few more guys. Maybe somebody with some real skill. Where was Adam when I needed him? He had a pretty good sucker punch. Maybe he'd take a swing if I called him a pussy. It was more fun when they fought back.

I bounced on the balls of my feet and looked out over the crowd that was moving away from Jeff who as still knocked out with Jennifer kneeling down next to him, stroking his hair.

"Jesus," was all Shane could say and shake his head while Allison rigidly remained next to him, seething at me.

"Y'all done smoking your pot?" I asked Jennifer and Allison who'd come outside to see who was fighting. They were shocked to see Jeff on the ground, knocked out.

"There isn't any pot," Allison snarled at me and gave me her bitchiest look.

"What are you supposed to be anyway?" I asked her and eyed her outfit. Her bleached hair was teased and frizzed and sprayed into a huge wall around her caked up face.

"I'm a vampire, can't you tell?"

"No," I said grinning as the adrenaline still pumped through me and lit me up all over.

"I thought you were a whore with a bunch of hickeys," I cackled at her and stepped back between Faith's legs again.
I glanced at Shane to see if he was gonna stand up for his woman but he hung his head and refused to look at me.

Faith put her little hand on my shoulder and squeezed it and

I felt emboldened and tucked my chin down and smiled at Allison and winked and watched her face turn red with fury.

"A whore?" she screeched and caused Shane to jump away from her.
I felt Faith squeeze my shoulder harder.

"Yeh, a whore! What's with all those hickeys on your heck? My God!" I hooted.
I was feeling all good from the beer and the punch I had landed on Jeff and from Faith's legs wrapped around me tight from behind.

"I'm a vampire!" Allison yelled.

I felt Faith's legs squeeze me on every word. Girl was holding on to me like she was riding a horse. That gave me ideas. And that gave me a hard-on. I smiled again and watched the rage burn on Allison's ugly, made-up face.

"You dick!" she yelled and lunged at me.

Without thinking, I ducked from her punch forgetting Faith was right behind me.

But she didn't throw a punch. She didn't even throw claws with those long black fingernails she had on. Oh no, she lunged and grabbed my pitcher of beer, the one that was half full or half empty or whatever Faith had said. The one that still had a lot of foamy, cold beer in it. She flung it while I was ducked out of the way.

"Oh my gosh!" Faith gasped from behind me. "Oh my gosh!" she cried again as I turned around to see her with both hands in front of her face; the one in the cast and the uninjured one wiping at her face and pulling her long, wet hair back.

She was dripping. Her mouth was bleeding.

"Oh Faith, oh no," I uttered and pulled her face towards me. "What's bleeding? Are you hurt? How bad are you hurt?"
I held her face in my hands and examined her closely and saw that her top lip was busted open.

"Did you get hit with the pitcher?"

Thank God it wasn't glass I thought and then I was upset that I let this happen. How did I let this happen? I was supposed to protect her and here I was, ducking out of the way.

"No, I did it myself," she said and held up her cast. The plaster near her thumb was bright red with blood.

"Oh, my poor girl," I said to her as she hung her head. "Did your cape save you?" I asked as I watched her bottom lip begin to quiver.

I looked down at her hiccupping chest to see that most of the white peasant blouse was soaked in an ugly wet pattern.

"But your cast is dry?" I asked her as my hands ran all over her, checking every part of her.

"I think it's dry. I think it's ok," she said and held it up for a second before letting it drop heavily.

"Why'd they put such a heavy cast on you? This is way too big for you!" I was furious about everything but she knocked the wind right out of my sails when she started to peel that wet cape off.

"Oh Mike," she said and shivered and began to cry and tried to hide her chest with her good hand. I know it wasn't right to stare, but she was soaked in beer and nearly topless and it was really cold out. I had to pry my eyes away.

I turned around to see Shane pulling Allison backwards away from us. Allison had her hands over her face and a look of pure joy that exploded into throaty laughter when she saw my face. Then she looked at Faith, snorted back a laugh and yelled, "Sorry!" as they both stepped around Jeff who was still out cold on the ground. This sent Faith to crying even harder.

"Honey, no, come here," I said to her and held my arms out to her and rocked back on my heels as she crashed into me with her arms around my neck, her face wet against me. I pulled her to me and was shocked when she wrapped her legs around my waist and her bottom slid completely off the ice chest and into my cupped hands.

"Oh, poor Bleacher Girl," I whispered in her hair and held

her easily off the ground. "You're soaked, poor baby."
The front of her thin blouse was soaked in beer and she pressed it against me.

"Oh Mike, I want to go home. I smell like beer," she wailed as I carried her away from the staring crowd like a backpack worn on the front of my chest.

"I know, honey, I know, baby," I cooed to her and smoothed her wet hair down as I carried her away from the noise and down the gravel lane towards the way-back of the house where all the cars were parked.

"Hey buddy."

A huge, shiny black jacked up Ford truck rolled up next to us, growling and trembling on its fat mud tires. It was sweet. I would have killed for a fun new ride like that. I looked up to see the cab was full of wealthy Sand Creek jocks sitting three across.
Fuck.

"Hey buddy, she ok? Is that Bleacher Girl?" the guy asked as he leaned out of the window towards us.
I didn't want any trouble with him. Not now. Now I just wanted to take care of Faith.

"Where you taking her?" he asked as he idled in step with me walking, carrying Faith down the lane towards an out-building where I thought I might be able to clean her up or give her my coveralls at least to change into.

"What do you want?" I asked him and stopped in my tracks. I heard Faith sniffle and felt her grip me tighter as if she were afraid I was gonna drop her.

"I want to help. That's all," the guy in the letterman jacket said and he looked genuinely concerned but I didn't trust him nor his two buddies. Not where Faith was concerned. Nope. Not at all.

"I don't need your help."

"But that's Faith."

Him saying her name stopped me in my tracks and sent my temper boiling to the top of my eyes.

"She's in our marching band. I gave her first-aid when she fell. She looks hurt now and I don't trust you with her."
Faith's head popped up and swiveled around to look at the guy.

"You know this guy?" I asked her out of the side of my mouth while never taking my eyes off him.

"Yes, that's Derek Charles."

"Derek Charles?" Only a rich asshole in a new Ford truck would have two first names like that.

"He was there when I fell."

"He push you?"

"No, he was playing football. He was the first one to get to me. He kept them from moving me until help came."

"Faith, are you ok?" he asked. His voice was high and felt like soft chalk dust in my hand.

"I'm ok. I'm not hurt. Someone threw beer on me. Mike's my boyfriend."

It echoed in my head. Mike's my boyfriend. I heard it a hundred times as if she shouted it in a silo. She felt light in my arms. I wanted to crush her into me and kiss her hard. I wanted these guys out of here.

"Here," Derek Charles said and stopped his truck and got out. "Use my truck and take her back to your car or wherever you're taking her. Leave the keys in it."

The whole thing felt fishy and I trusted none of it. I watched as the other two dudes slid out of the truck and walked around to where I was standing with Faith. I held her to me tighter. I would never let go of her. There was no way I was putting her in that cab with them around. Panic squeezed my heart just thinking about them driving off with Faith between them, helpless on that bench seat.

"Maybe we'll see you later, back at the party," Derek Charles said as he forced a smile full of huge square teeth as his friends walked away with scowls on their faces but without a word or a glance back at me. They were his lackeys. He had the Ford. He called the shots.

"Faith?" I asked her quietly because she was resting her cheek on my shoulder again.

But she didn't answer. She was still crying softly.

"Are you hurt?"

"No."

"You want to change your clothes?"

"I don't have anything to put on," she said and hiccupped.

"You can put on my coveralls."

"And I feel drunk."

I laughed at this. She had had one beer and she felt drunk. Oh, how she made me happy.

"Let's ride in this guy's truck back behind that barn way back there and change. It'll be fun."

"Okay."

She sat up. She was interested in the truck. A pang of jealousy clinched my stomach low and sharp.

"I always wanted to go for a ride in the back of a truck. Can we get in the back?" she asked.

She was crazy or she was drunker than I thought. She had to be. I peeled her off me and set her down on the ground and watched as she flung the red cape into the bed of the jacked-up Ford. She backed up to the tailgate and pressed her back against it and waited for me to answer or waited for me to lift her up into it, or waited for me to peel my popping eyes away from the soaked front of her white blouse.

"Mike," she said when she was tired of waiting, and tilted her head a little and smiled.

I went to her instantly, my arms around her waist. She had her good hand in the back of my hair, at the nape of my neck, where it was grown out and starting to go curly. She wove her little fingers in there and made me shiver all over. I rolled my neck and shivered like a wet dog and stared up at the starry sky and felt the world spinning beneath my feet. This was all too good to be true.

"Mike," she breathed and I could smell a sweet sugary fruity smell on her breath as she came closer.

I started to say, "Yes?" but she kissed me.

She. Kissed. Me. I froze in shock for a moment. Her lips soft and sticky barely brushed over my own. I let her do what she wanted. I let her figure it out and I went with whatever she wanted. I followed her lead, I let her be in control. She made me smile, her tongue was so timid. She touched my lips with it, a tiny small touch and I replied back the same way. She grew bolder and I did too. I went with her rhythm. My head swam in the dark, drunk on her sweetness.

Then I lifted her, oh so gently, my hands on her ass under that skirt, cotton panties against my palms, up on the back-end of that lifted Ford. She wrapped her legs tight around my waist as I set her down and I heard the shocks of that 4x4 sigh in the dark night over the noise of the party behind us. That was the only thing that made me stop kissing her. That was the only thing that snapped my eyes open. She kept hers closed after I pushed away from her.

"We shouldn't do it here, babe," I said to her and still she kept her eyes shut. I could see them flutter in the moonlight and wondered what she was thinking about.

"No? How come?" she asked, her voice clear like a tiny silver bell in the dark.

"The party is right there, sweetheart."

Her eyes opened at that and she strained to see far off back towards the house.

All you could really see of the party were the glowing lights thrown off from the house and the flickering of a bonfire they had started out in front on the driveway; it's tail of smoke went straight up into the black night.

"Not here, but I want to do it in the back of the truck," she said and then coughed several times.

"Did you say, you want to do it in the back of the truck?" I asked her.

I couldn't help but smile. She couldn't answer for coughing. But she nodded yes. I patted those bare knees and looked to see if she was going to be ok. She was smiling too, with her eyes watering.

"Quick Mike, the bonfire is making me cough and this shirt stinks and is cold and I want to take it off."
That's all I needed to hear.

"Drive slow, don't bounce me off," she called to me as I walked to the driver's door. I nodded yes, but she was facing the other way and didn't see.

That truck was the sweetest ride I'd ever been in. Brand new. Gear shift shiny and black and the transmission made that smooth, clear, yawning sound as the clutch went in easy. But all I cared about was not dumping little Bleacher Girl off the back end. My God, I wheezed to myself, don't goose it and dump her off the back because my God, she said she wanted to do it in the back of the truck.

Chapter Ten

"Mike, are you talking to us?" Shane asked me from where he and Jeff sat on top of the picnic table in the grass behind the Thrifty Lube.

I wiped my hands on a rag and shoved it in the back pocket of my coveralls, the coveralls I'd worn to the Halloween party the night before; the ones that Faith had eventually changed into. The ones that smelled like her most intimate places.

"I don't know, are you guys still being dicks?" I asked and braced my feet apart, ready to take on both of them at once.
But they both continued to sit there.

"We're here as your friend," Shane said and then he looked over at Jeff.

"What about you?" I asked Jeff.

"Fuck, Mike, you nearly concussed me with that punch. But of course I'm your friend. I sort a deserved it," he said and rubbed his jaw where it was still swollen and purple.

"What do you want? I have to get back to work."

I turned around and saw Skip watching me from where he stood in the empty bay. It wouldn't be empty long. We'd had the first frost of winter last night and people were coming in all day to winterize their cars and change their oil. I wondered how long Shane and Jeff had been sitting there before I noticed them. My head wasn't exactly on a swivel at the Thrifty Lube this morning.

My brain was still reeling from the night before. Every time I moved, Faith's aroma came flooding up to me from the coveralls. So many scents. Every time I got focused on work, every time the smell of exhaust and oil and tires and cigarettes overrode her scent and I'd get my mind off her, the bay doors would go up to let a car out and another in. Then the fresh air would whoosh away the exhaust and I'd be left with the perfume and the thick earthy aroma she left behind from wearing the coveralls without her panties.

My God, I ached. I needed to trade the Cutlass for a truck. I'd never be able to get a new one like we used last night but hey they all had cabs and they all had beds.

This was the way my mind was running today. It was all Faith. Her body. Her little white ass sticking up helpless in the moonlight as I lifted her up and bent her over the roof of the cab of that guy's truck. Oh, she had been scared but she had also trusted me after an eternity of necking and other things on the back end of that truck bed to make sure she was as revved up as me and make certain she was ready for me. She trusted me to put her up there in only her bra and her skirt, which I wasted no time lifting up over her round little rump. Those white bikini panties were blinding bright in the glow of the moon even way down the dirt lane, way out in the middle of the prairie far away from the house party.

She wiggled and tried to help me get them down faster but I wasn't in any hurry. I savored every bit. I wanted to remember her laying on her belly on top of that cab with her cheeks exposed forever and I did a good job burning it into my mind because the memory of it had distracted me all day.

"Mike!" Shane and Jeff brought me back from the memory movie playing on repeat in my head.

"What?" I shook my head and pulled a cigarette out of my breast pocket.

"We are here to warn you."

"About what?" I asked and watched an old Plymouth Volaire roll by on bald tires and slow down near the drive of the Thrifty Lube. If they pulled in, I'd have to go. I turned around and saw Skip watching them too. But then they rolled on. Maybe they didn't want to face what all was wrong with their car. Some people were like that. They think if they don't look at it, or listen to it, it'll be fine.

"Mike! Pay attention! Jesus!" Shane snapped at me.

"What? What do you want?"

"We came to warn you. Dude that owns that truck, is looking for you."

"What for?"

"You tore up his truck."

Jeff and Shane leaned towards me as one and waited for me to understand.

"What?" I asked, and took off my cap and scratched my head.

"They're driving all over town, past your school, and your parents' place, and even Kahmir's, looking for you."

"No shit?" I asked.

"No shit."

"Kahmir's back open? And he didn't even call me. What the hell?"

"Dude. You don't get it. That guy, that Sand Creek football guy and a shit-load of his friends are driving around looking for you. They're shaking down everyone."

"What for again?"

I wanted Jeff and Shane gone. I was tired and they were interrupting my daydream time and also my time at work with their bullshit high school drama and I liked this job and I needed to keep it.

"You tore up that asshole's truck!" Jeff yelled and stood up and flicked his cigarette away.

"I did not," I answered and stepped on my own and ground it out and eyeballed him and his aggressive stance until he stood down.

"You did. We just saw him at McDonald's and the back glass is kicked in," Shane said matter of factly and smirked at me like it was the funniest thing he had ever seen but he was trying not to laugh.

"What? How? He's blaming that on me?" I asked Shane.

"There's a huge dent in the back glass."

Shane held up his hands and made a circle the size of a waffle.

"Like this big," he said, "all splintered in on the back glass."

"I didn't do that. That wasn't me," I countered with certainty and then remembered last night and let the huge smile spread across my face.

Technically, I was telling the truth. I hadn't done it. Faith had. With every stroke I pumped her from behind she had kicked the back glass with her cast as her feet hung, legs spread apart, me behind her, holding her waist tight and slamming into her as she cried out my name in the night.

That had been a good time. That was one for the bank. Just thinking back on it now was getting me going. But that wasn't nearly the best part of last night oh no. But I couldn't think about that now. Now, I had a lot of other pots in the fire.

"I didn't do anything to his truck. Who the hell knows how many assholes that guy lets drive his truck? Who does that? He's probably queer. And he can't prove Jack."
Shane and Jeff both recoiled at my words and I let them. I mean seriously, what kind of guy gives his keys to his new truck to another dude, one he doesn't even know, to take a girl out in the country and bang? Something was wrong with that guy.

"Well, he's looking for you. And he'll be coming in hot when he finds you."

"That's what he thinks," I said and turned away to head back to work.

"You want us to help?" Shane called to me.

"We got your back, bro," Jeff added and it reminded me of him saying, 'bros before ho's' the night before and I felt my anger bubble up again.

"Whatever," I called over my shoulder and pulled the rag out of my pocket and went back to work.

Smashing the back glass of the rich kid's truck was the least of my worries. I still had the two-stroke bike I'd taken from the barn at the party to get Faith and I home. I needed to get rid of that thing quick, even if having her on it behind me, her arms and legs wrapped around me tight, was the best feeling in the world. Jail would not be such a good feeling. There would be no beautiful Faith in jail and that bike was hot!

That party must have been really hot as well as it was on the news later that night as I ate a late supper of triple decker peanut butter jelly toast in front of the TV and chugged a glass of whole milk.

The party house was trashed. Half the woods nearly burnt down from the bonfire. A couple of car wrecks. Several fist-fights. The police were called. And the motorbike reported stolen by the kid who lived there.

"He was about five and half feet tall and really white," the buck-tooth kid who lived in the house and owned the bike told the news reporter.

"Five and a half feet tall!" I was mortified that I looked so short on the motorbike. I was taller than that. I was at least five-nine. Maybe five-seven.

"Really white? How so?" the reportet interrupted my indignation.

"He didn't have a shirt on or pants! He was only wearing his jeans and he almost glowed like a ghost! And he had a gorgeous blonde girl on the back of the bike. MY bike!"

"Any other details that might help catch him?"

"He had one of them angry noses."
The kid looked like a well-fed squirrel with his buck teeth and his wavy blonde hair and his chubby cheeks.

"A what?"

"You know. One of them noses that's been busted a few times, the sign of a guy who fights a lot, and loses. I saw his face good when he smiled and waved at me, the happy son of a ...." The kid trailed off.

I fingered my nose at this. My nose wasn't too messed up. I mean sure, it had been punched a time or two. The last time was

Velvet Lucille's brother who shattered it after finding us necking in the front seat of his '59 Bel Aire parked in the alley behind their house. Velvet Lucille. She was a dish. But a dish many had had their hands in, not counting mine because mine never got in there. She was all perfume and hairspray and shoulder pads. She looked thirty at sixteen. She looked like a bank teller in that black velvet jacket she always wore and those stirrup pants. Velvet Lucille. Yep, my nose was shattered from her brother Lonnie's super punch. Crossed my eyes. Blacked them too. But I didn't think it had healed up too bad.

Of course that wasn't counting all the times Mom and Dad had popped me in the nose with the back of their hands or a book or Dad's fist. I didn't think they'd ever busted it. Not really. I mean it'd bled a lot every time but I don't think it was ever broken. Not on purpose at least.

"Anything else you can tell us about the person who rode off on your motorbike?" the news reporter asked the kid as he stared blankly into the camera.

"Yeh," he said with a far-off look in his eyes, "The blonde on the bike with him? She had big you knows," he said with a smile.

"Big what?" the reporter cawed in horror.

"Big, you knows" the kid said and made a squeezing motion with both hands and the newswoman cut away immediately.

I almost choked on my peanut butter and jelly, it took me by surprise so hard!

Big, you knows. Squeeze squeeze. Honk honk.

I knew.

I *really* knew.

**

The motorcycle was just part of the trouble I was in. But it was worth it. Same went for the smashed in back glass. I'd had trouble with smashed glass before and it wasn't nothing I couldn't walk off. Mom and her boyfriend Dennis both had belted me over smashing windows with baseballs in our weed-grown backyard and for throwing rocks at the empty old grade school outside our neighborhood when I was six. Throwing rocks at those school windows wasn't hurting no one. And busting the kitchen window twice was an accident both times. But I got belted raw all the same. Didn't matter I was only eight the first time and fifteen the second time. They didn't think nothing of belting my bare back and ass at fifteen. And I took it.

But at sixteen I was done taking it. I was giving it back. Smashing Dennis' windshield on his black Toronado was on purpose, but he never did put that on me. He was on a three-day bender after getting fired from the casting plant. He didn't even remember how he got home from the plant after they fired him and had security throw his ass out, which shows he was already drunk on the job.

When he came home that afternoon, red-faced and drunk and pissed as hell, he back-handed me as soon as he came in the door for no reason. As I wiped the blood from my nose and my split lip, I plotted revenge. I lay in wait the next two days till I knew he was blacked out. Then I went to the front yard where he had parked his huge car on our lawn and I smacked the windshield with my Louisville slugger till the glass webbed like rock candy in the sun.

I waited for him to accuse me. I waited with the bat nearby and ready to tool the side of his head with it. Just like now I'd be waiting for Derek Charles to roll in hot, like Shane and Jeff said he was, to kick my ass. Go ahead, rich boy, I thought to myself as I pushed the two-stroke motorcycle down the alley behind my apartment and jumped on her and rode her south to the wealthy side of town on her final ride. It was worth taking but not worth jail time.

I'd leave her as a little gift for Derek Charles to make up for smashing his rear window with my girlfriend's cast. I wasn't mean. But I was tuff. And I was smart.
Explaining how the stolen bike ended up in his front yard ought to

keep him busy enough to leave me be. He still lived with his parents. They'd be hot on him for the truck getting banged up and now for this stolen motorbike. Let the shit rain hard on Captain Squarejaw, varsity dick-head, for a change, I chuckled. Doubt his parents would belt him, I thought while I ran home with a huge smile on my face.

I was still in shape from years of wrestling; even though I hadn't worked out since last March. Running in the cold dark felt good. I needed to take better care of myself. Maybe quit smoking. Maybe not. I felt like I could run a hundred miles right now, smoking or not. I'd do it with a cigarette in my mouth if I wanted to, I was my own man.

Chapter Eleven

I had so much energy, I could have run a hundred miles but instead I was moving a hundred tires. Or more.

I ran into my friend Carter from the guard shack at the tire plant on my way home and he clued me into a job lead as he gave me a lift the rest of the way home. He let me know they needed temporary help weeding out and moving bad tires by hand. He said to show up right after class Monday at noon, bring gloves, and I could work till they were all moved onto the truck.

"Why not use a fork lift?" I asked that evening when I saw the huge pile of odd shaped tires and then regretted it.

"Because the fork lift guys aren't in the union and they don't want to use their time fixin' some mistake the union guys made," one of the line workers told me.

It was a headscratcher for sure and I didn't really care enough to try to figure it out. It paid $10.50 an hour instead of the $2.44 an hour I made at the Thrifty Lube. I'd do whatever they wanted, union work or not. I didn't play sides. I just needed the money.

I moved tires from noon to three and took a required break when the line foreman told me to. He bought me an iced tea and a bag of popcorn which I gladly ate and then used the empty cup to refill from the fountain the rest of the shift as I stuck around and made myself useful.

"Fucking toilet's clogged!" The foreman could be heard bitching clear down the line.

I stopped what I was doing, which was sweeping up thousands of tiny hair-like rubber shavings off the concrete floor and looked around to see the whole line had stopped working one by one when they heard him bitching about the toilet.

"McEllroy dropped a double deuce again after chili night at

the VFW!" I heard someone bellow down the line and then laughter broke out.

I leaned my push-broom against the wall near the time clock and made my way down to the toilets.

"Fuckin' hell boy, don't go in there! The toilet's jammed full and over flowing!" the foreman warned me, his face red as a boil.

"I'll take care of it," I told him and pulled a handful of rubber bands off the shop desk and fixed the cuffs of my jeans and went in to the toilets and didn't come out til it was unplugged. And then I only came out to get a mop and a bucket and a screwdriver. I had the grate off the floor drain and cleaned it out before mopping twice.

"You're right handy son," the foreman clapped me on the back.
I smiled at him and looked hopeful.

"But we can't hire you fulltime till you're eighteen. Come back and we'll have a spot for you making tires."
I let him know I'd be back to do odds and ends work every Monday at noon until I turned eighteen. Every little bit helped and I didn't want him to forget me. I liked that $10.50 an hour.

I couldn't wait to turn eighteen. Though it didn't really mean much. I'd been on my own since last March, right after turning seventeen. In my eyes, I was a grown man. I lived on my own. I answered to me. Except when Faith called. Then I answered to her.

"Mike, why don't you ever call me?" she asked when I answered the phone that night.
I was heating up a can of Dinty More beef stew on the stove and buttering a stack of Texas Toast.

"Because I'm working so much, honey."

"What are you doing now?" she asked.

"Making dinner. I'm starved."

"Oh, poor Mike," she sighed and meant it.
She worried about me.

"Poor Mike, indeed," I agreed as I shoved a folded-up slice of Texas Toast in my mouth and got butter all over my upper lip.

"You need somebody to feed you."

I glanced around the kitchen as I dragged the phone across the floor on its long cord. The blue gas of the stove danced low under the pot of canned stew. It smelled amazing. Maybe I would dump a can of green beans in it. I was that hungry.

"Aw, I think I'm doin' all right, unless you meant you. I'd let you feed me. Hell, I'd eat you right now if you were here," I said and licked butter off the edge of my hand as I wedged the phone between my shoulder and cheek and stirred the pot.

"What?" she hollered. "You'd eat me!"

"Lord! I hope your parents aren't near!" I laughed into the phone.

"Oh my gosh! Mike!"

"That's funny."

"Be good."

"I am good."

And good at it, I thought to myself but didn't say it out loud.

"Can you come to dinner Friday night?"

"Friday night? This Friday?"

"Yes. Unless you're busy."

Now she sounded sad.

"I'm not busy," I assured her around a mouthful of buttered bread.

**

She couldn't wait for me to come over for dinner with her parents. Me, I could have waited forever for that to happen. I never met the parents of any girls. Never ever. Not before I moved out on my own and definitely not after I moved to my own place. Never. It was a dealbreaker.

I didn't even try to explain it to Faith. I didn't say no. I didn't say, maybe. I didn't say I'd think about it. I said, "Sure Honey, what time?" And then I said, "I love you, sweetheart." To which she answered, "I do too," and then she giggled at what she said.

I pictured her blushing. I pictured her smiling. I pictured that glorious long blond hair falling over her shoulder. I pictured myself telling her I loved her again as I made it with her on the couch in her parent's house.

The thought of her parents being there, of having to spend an evening with them, didn't even faze me. Her mom was a looker. That'd be interesting. I'd never known a girlfriend to have such a looker for a mom. She wasn't a beer guzzling, cigarette sucking mom. I'd seen several moms. From a distance. And stepdads too for that matter. Dads maybe. Boyfriends of moms, definitely. Uncles. Whatever. None of the moms looked good, not even from far away. They looked like house slippers worn too long. Sure, you could see they had once been pink and fluffy, but that was a long time ago. Now they were scuffed and matted and worn hard. But Faith's mom didn't look like that and I was curious what her family was like.

More than anything, I simply wanted to see Faith. I'd go wherever she asked me to go. Boy, was I glad I went when I got there.

Faith was a blur; a shrieking blur. When I knocked on the door it was answered by a shrieking blur who wrapped two arms around me. TWO arms around my neck. And her two, big, soft, tits pressed up against me that took my breath away. I would never get used to her. Never. I was instantly hard as a rock.

"Heyyy," I said as I looked at the two arms reaching up for me as she bounced up against me.

One newly bare arm had a long scar up from the wrist to the elbow with little dented holes all the way up.

"You're healed there, Frankenstein!"

I held her back from me and looked down at her legs and let out a low whistle. She had on a short, tight dress the color of a suntan. Her leg was free from its cast as well. It was pale and skinny and looked vulnerable and bare.

"Why are you wearing those shoes?" I asked, my voice high and echoey in the tall entryway of her house.

"You like them?" she asked and held her leg out for me to admire her leather sandals with the stacked wood heels.
I gulped. I blinked several times. I started to talk but my throat had dried shut.

"What's wrong?" she asked me and took a hold of my arm.

"What's that?" I choked out and my voice cracked like I was fourteen.

She rotated her thin ankle as she held on to my shoulder for balance.

"What?" she asked.
A tiny delicate gold chain circled her ankle and glinted in the low light that shone down from the ceiling lamp.

"Mom let me pick out heels after I got my cast off. I only got them because I didn't complain this time about my casts being itchy. And Garrett got me the anklet."
Step-dad got her the anklet??? I didn't like that at all.

"It's dainty," she said and squeezed my bicep with both her hands and I realized I was tense and angry and I took a deep breath and I tried to relax.

"He said it would be a reminder for me to be careful and that I'm fragile and need to act like it."

She WAS fragile. But if anyone was going to remind her, it was me. Not step-dad. Not Garrett. Where was he? I rolled my shoulders and popped my neck two times. My hair was still wet on my collar and it made me shiver. Everything looked too clear, too sharp. I tried to calm down. I couldn't stop looking at that gold chain around her ankle. I had visions of where I'd like that ankle to go, chain and all up on my shoulder. I shook my head to clear it.

"Mike," Faith said to me and adjusted the collar of my good alligator shirt and then she ran both of her hands up through the back of my hair.

It was like that and it was that easy to calm me down. Then she pressed up against me, soft and bouncy, and I let out a small growl and pulled her close and kissed those lips. And I would have been happy to kiss them all night but her mom called us to dinner.

"I'm so glad Faith got her casts off. Now maybe she can be a help around the house again," her mom said as she passed me the platter of meat.

I had a hard time following what she was saying. My eyes were on her huge feathered waves of hair. That was not mom-hair. That was TJ Hooker hair. Or Farrah hair. It was not mom hair.

"Mike, tell me when to stop," she said to me and brought me back to earth.

"What is this? It smells amazing!" I said, blinking my eyes fast and watching her serve me two slices.

I sniffed the gravy covered meat and motioned for her to slide me a third slice off the platter. I'd never seen or smelled meat like it before.

"It's Salisbury Steak and I helped make it!" Faith chimed in and smiled and took the platter from me.

"Yes, when you're not injured, you're a good help to your mother," her step-dad said and I watched him look from Faith back to her mom and back to Faith.

Faith slid off one slice of meat and sat down. Her plump pink lips twisted in a pout as she stared down at her plate. Something was going on here but I wasn't quite sure what. I started to ask but was distracted by her mom scooping mashed potatoes on my plate and asking me to say when again.

"Now, now, when, when, that's fine," I waved my hand over my plate to get her to stop as I watched Faith fume silently in her seat. She stared down at her plate and would not look up.

I started to say something to defend her but her mother crossed her arms over her chest and said, "And since you're not in band anymore either, you'll have more time to get your grades up."

Red blotches spread across Faith's face and down her neck.

I didn't understand what was happening but I didn't want to be here anymore. I wanted both Faith and myself gone. I started to fold my napkin. I had zero tolerance for family turbulence.

My family had not had dinner at the table since I was small enough to watch Sesame Street on the portable tv next to the table. I remembered that we ate at the table at Grandma's last year for her birthday and also last Christmas, but we hadn't sat at the table at my house in a long time. I had eaten every meal either standing at the stove or at a metal tv tray in front of the tv since I was about 8.

I didn't know what was expected for dinner conversation at regular families' homes. Someone always threw something at our dinner and I wasn't waiting around for that to happen here. I folded my napkin and placed it next to my untouched silverware.

"I just hope this is the end of the injuries, honey," her mom said and I looked up to see her patting Faith's head as a tear rolled down both their cheeks.

"That's it," I said and pushed back from the table and stood up.

Everyone froze and stared up at me. Faith's mom took a hold of her hand and her step-dad clasped the other one and they all turned to stare at me. They looked confused. And scared.

"Mike," Faith whispered, "Sit down," she urged me. She let go of her mom and step-dad's hands and stood up and came to me as I stepped out of the dining room.

"Mike, what's the matter?"
I leaned down and pressed my forehead against hers.

"I want to go." I was serious. I meant it.

"Why?"
Her eyes pleaded with me.

"I'm not good with family stuff."
I shrugged.

"But you haven't eaten."
I pulled her into the kitchen and out of earshot of her parents.

"I don't do families. I don't do all this emotional stuff."

"What does that mean?" her voice climbed higher.

In her high heels she was much closer to my face and she intimidated me a little with how fierce she looked as she backed me against the sink.

"Why are they raggin' on you?" I asked her urgently.
I wanted to understand.

"They're not raggin' on me."
She sounded confused and I didn't like my bad language coming out of her sweet mouth.

"They sounded like they were."
And then they were there, at the door.

"Kids," Faith's mom said to us with her step-dad right behind her. Her voice was quiet and her eyes were kind.

"Come back to the table, let's enjoy dinner," her step-dad said.

Faith looked up at me with those big eyes and wove her little fingers in between in my own and pulled me back to the table.

"It'll be fine," she whispered as I pulled her chair out for her.

She surprised me when she kissed my cheek and I held my fingers over it and stared off stunned like a dumbass as her mom began to scoop peas onto my plate.

Chapter Twelve

"Homecoming? You're going to homecoming?" Shane was nearly freaking out at me as we sat on top of the picnic table behind the Thrifty Lube having a smoke in the wet cold on Tuesday afternoon.

"Yep."

"At Sand Creek High," Shane said and shook his head in disbelief.

"At her school, yes," I told him as I zipped up my gray winter coveralls.

Neither one of us looked at each other. We stared ahead in silence and smoked.

"When is it?" he finally asked.

"Next Saturday."

"Fuck."

I didn't answer.

"How'd that happen?" he asked me and I shrugged as if I didn't know.

I knew all right. We had dinner at her place where I ate my fill of Salisbury steak and mashed potatoes. I figured Faith would help do the dishes and I'd get stuck with her step-dad while he smoked a pipe and talked sports but it wasn't like that. Not at all. He and Faith's mom left. They had plans to go dancing with another couple at the Holiday Inn two towns over. Said to not wait up. Said they might be very late. All of which had me revved up and ready to run all night.

"I can't believe them!"

Faith was upset.

"Believe what?" I asked.

I couldn't believe them either but wanted to make sure her disbelief and my disbelief lined up because I was sure they did not.

"I can't believe that she'd wear that out dancing."
Faith rolled her eyes as we carried the plates to the kitchen sink and I helped scrape and rinse them.

"What'd she have on?" I honestly couldn't remember. All I could think of was what Faith had on. Tight little dress the color of summer-time skin and that sexy gold chain around her ankle that kept catching my eye.

Faith's mom was a looker but my eyes had been all on Faith all dinner. Faith and her arm free of the cast and the bare leg with the little anklet and the high heels.

"She had on a sweater and slacks. Who goes dancing in that?" she had demanded to know, her voice shrill.

"I dunno." I shrugged.

I was hoping we'd go to Faith's room soon. I was hoping we'd be kissing soon. But we went to her parents' room instead where I sat on the huge bed while she flipped through her mom's closet.

"Be right back. Don't move," she told me as she tossed a stack of dresses over her shoulder and grabbed a pair of strappy heels and disappeared into her parents' bathroom.

I waited for what felt like forever but it was worth it. The door opened and Faith emerged and stood there with the bathroom lights glowing behind her. I sat up slow from the bed and took her all in as the breath caught in my chest and squeezed my heart a hard one.

"If we were going dancing, this is what I'd wear," she said and smiled and twirled and everything twirled with her.

The dark red shiny dress clung to her in all the right places as she twirled and swung her hips. It was low-cut with straps that crossed her bare back and tied over her shoulder blades. My God, I couldn't breathe seeing that little bow tied back there. I had to look away. I looked down. No better. The bottom of the dress was uneven and jagged and looked like she'd fought a wild tiger or something.

I swung my legs off the bed but couldn't stand. Not yet. I had to get a hold of myself. I was shaking inside and out.

"What do you think?" she asked and smiled.
Her dimples popped up when her little lips curled up into a smile; they stabbed me in the heart, I swear.

"I've never felt more like going dancing in my entire life," I said under my breath.

I was struck dumb and smiling like an ass but I'd never seen a more delicious looking girl in my life. I couldn't tear my eyes away from every inch of that dress. It had to have been designed by a man. My God, the plunging neckline that criss-crossed in the front was ridiculous. Any moment it was going to come all the way open and all those glorious jugs of hers were going to be bouncing everywhere, naked and free.

It was the sexiest thing I'd ever seen in person in my life. It was a dress with so much going on I couldn't look away. It was a dress with a lot of promise, was what it felt like. It was a dress that said, don't look away because it's all going to happen any moment. At least that's what it felt like in my shorts.
Any moment.

"What about the shoes? Are they ugly? Because I kinda like them."

She had on black heels with skinny leather straps that criss crossed her feet and ran on up her calves and tied on the backs of her legs. The gold chain twinkled in the low lights. I immediately pictured her naked and wearing them and I groaned.

"They're great."
My voice sounded weak like a croak.

"This is what you wear dancing," she smiled and took my hand.

I looked down at her as she swayed and dipped and shook her bottom and I saw nearly everything she had on top as she bounced and jiggled in every direction.

"What do you say?" she asked and smiled up at me.

"I've never needed to go dancing so bad in my life as I do right now," I said again, this time louder and then gulped.

Which was how I'd gotten myself into this predicament.

"Fuck. I should ask Allison," Shane snapped his fingers and tossed his cigarette butt onto the wet drive of the Thrifty Lube.

"You should."

My mind was still on Faith and that dress. That dress danced in front of my eyes every time I tried to sleep. That dress kept me awake tossing and turning and kept me so turned on I almost felt ashamed.

"We could double date," he said and turned and smiled at me.

"Nope," I answered and hopped off the table and tossed my butt.

"Why not?"

"I don't need an audience."

"Come on, it's a dance. You won't be fucking her at the dance."

I didn't plan to stay at the dance very long. I wanted to leave when I wanted to leave.

"Come on its Sand Creek. We gotta stick together. Those guys are dicks. We could get jumped."

He sounded scared. I couldn't let him down.

"Ok. Ask her. If she says yes, we'll meet you there."

I didn't like Allison. I didn't like formal dances. And I didn't like double dates either. I liked to act solo. For everything. But I agreed to do it against all better judgement.

"It's not that big of a deal."

My famous last words.

**

Saturday night found me outside Faith's house standing in the grass, smoking a cigarette, smiling my butt off in black dress pants, white dress shirt, and pink suspenders and a black leather tie, waiting for her to come out. I was too nervous to wait for her inside.

ZZ-Top played on a loop in my brain.

I could feel her step-dad watching me from the porch as I smoked. I didn't care. My own mom had taught me to smoke at fourteen. It wasn't nothing to be upset over.

"Here she is!" her mom called to us and I turned around and tossed the butt on the wet sidewalk.

She wasn't wearing her mom's satin strappy dress like I had pictured a thousand times when I fantasized about this night. Nope. She was wearing a hazy cloud of lightest pink. I was scared to touch her. She looked as if her dress would melt if I laid a hand on it. Pale pink mist. I rubbed my hands together and wiped them on my pants twice before approaching her. I double checked that they weren't dirty from changing oil and lifting tires all week before I touched her bare shoulders.

She matched my pink suspenders perfectly and now I understood why Faith gave them to me and asked me to please wear them.

"Mike," she gasped, her eyes wide in wonder.

"What?" I asked with the hugest smile on my face. I couldn't stop blinking. Something was in my eyes.

"Your hair!"

"What?" I asked and ran my fingers through my newly cut hair. It was very short and spiky with just a little mousse in it. My neck felt naked and white.

"You like it?" I asked and cracked another smile at her.

"Yes!" was all she said in a gush.

"I like yours," I tried to say but couldn't get any wind and it came out broken.

She looked down at her pink pointy heels where the gold chain twinkled around her little ankle. She turned this way and that so I could admire her dress and then she smiled in the light of the porch while her parents watched. The smile lit up her face and she gazed up at me all dimples and gorgeous huge eyes.

We posed for a million pictures but I couldn't stop looking

at her. Her bare shoulders. The tops of her breasts rising and falling in excitement. That dress made out of pink mist. Her hair piled up loosely on top of her head with the long strands falling down her neck. She looked so sexy with her neck exposed.

I wanted us to leave. Her parents wanted more photos. And there were things we had to do such as flowers had to be pinned and strapped here and there. Her hair had to be sprayed one more time. She came down the porch steps one more time in a shimmering pink cloud of perfume that made me drunk. I sniffed my armpits and smiled and rolled my shoulders and popped my neck and pulled her in for a kiss all while her parents hustled around us, snapping photos.

"Let's get this over with," I whispered with my lips against her ear.

She giggled and bounced against me and we left with the promise of no drinking and driving, and to not be out ALL night. Her mom cried.

But Faith didn't notice nor look back even once as I slid her into the car.

Chapter Thirteen

"Mike, oh my God, you're here," was the first thing Shane said to me when Faith and I walked up to the doors of the gym.

He looked like a dork. He'd gotten his hair cut too but only the front. The back was long and straight and looked stupid. I frowned when I noticed he had on suspenders too. Red ones, and they matched Allison's red dress too. Her and Faith must have planned that together. Allison scowled at me when she noticed me looking at her.

"What's up?" I asked Shane as I put my arm around Faith's waist and pulled her close.

"Bunch of guys are looking for you!" Shane said with his eyes glassy and wild.

They'd been drinking already where Faith and I had shared a vanilla shake and fries at Sandy's drive up like it was 1953. I hadn't had a beer in ages. Working too much. Or out with Faith. Hadn't crossed my mind to sneak alcohol into the dance. I looked down at Faith to see if she noticed Shane and Allison were drunk. Maybe she'd think I was uncool for not bringing booze. She looked worried.

"Whatsamatter babe?" I asked her.

"Buncha guys looking for you," she said and bit her lip.

"Eh, I'm right here if they want me. Who cares? Let's go dance."

I took her hand in mine and we made our way into the dance.

She was the beautiful angel of the dance. Oh sure some girl with a broom handle up her rear with huge hair won homecoming queen with her squarejaw preppie boyfriend for king, but Faith was the star of the night.

Everyone seemed to know her. Everyone had to say hi. I was

all smiles and polite nods. It was a blur to meet so many people. I had never been popular and it was making my head spin. But I put on the charm for all of them. For her. It came easy. I had the most beautiful girl in the world on my arm. She was dressed like a soft pink cloud; like a ballerina.

The charm was real. I nodded and smiled and said hello to every single person and couple who came by to say hi to Faith as the gym filled up. Finally, I decided to get her on the dancefloor just to get her alone.

She was a little shy about dancing to the fast songs. Nothing could make me shy or insecure. I was that happy with her. We fast danced to goofy new wave music by The Cure, and The Psychedelic Furs. We slow danced to my favorite, The Scorpions and Journey! We jammed to Bad Company and 38 Special. We did the Time Warp with Shane and Allison and the rest of the school. We got our picture taken under a plastic gazebo. I forgot that I didn't want to stay long. I forgot a buncha guys were looking for me. I forgot to watch my back and I forgot to watch my front as well and that was the direction they came from.

They did it all wrong. But I was good with that.

They came at me just as I walked out of the men's room; grabbed me from both sides and one punched me in the gut when I wasn't expecting it. I sucked in air and sucked in pain and swung my leg hard and kicked the balls of the guy who punched me and watched him drop to his knees, spit dripping from his mouth as he heaved. Behind him, I saw two more guys grab Faith and pull her backwards across the dance floor and towards the doors.

Nope. I tore my left arm free and I climbed right on top of the guy still holding me. Climbed right up him and wrapped my left arm around his head. Put all my weight on him and forced him onto the floor, fast. His head banged on it, hard. As soon as I saw his head bounce, I yanked myself free and I ran after Faith.

I felt sick when I saw Faith in her beautiful dress being lifted right out of her shoes as she struggled against the boys who were carrying her off. Half her hair had fallen out of the clips that held it piled up on her head. The top of her dress was slipping down as they yanked on her newly healed arm.

Nope. I was not having it. I ignored the pain in my guts and I ran fast, fists drawn back as I went. I yelled at the backs of the jerks dragging her away and I landed a good one in the middle of Derek Charles' ugly face as he turned to sneer at me. I snapped his head back a good one. He let go of Faith and came at me hard. He was red-faced and ready to pummel me but I was concerned about the creep who was still pulling Faith across the parking lot while she smacked at his hands as he squeezed her newly healed arm. She was barely strong enough to do anything.

So that's how it was. That's how it would be at Sand Creek High.

One would drag off my girl while the others jumped me. Derek spat blood and ran at me with all his football training and knocked into me so hard I would have slid backwards across the parking lot blacktop if I had of been wearing slick dress shoes. But I wasn't. I had on cheap Kinney topsiders. That was as fancy as I owned. And the bottoms were rubbery and gripped the pavement. I took his full hit from his thick body and everything rattled inside me and hurt. As I scrambled to keep on my feet, Derek caved in my nose with a pounding jab from his fist.

I had two seconds to think; not broken. Yet. But soon. If I didn't stop him it'd be crushed. For now, it only hurt like hell. Dad used to like to backhand me in the nose because it smarted so much it'd instantly bring tears and then he liked to swat me another one for crying like a baby. By the time I was ten I didn't have any more tears. But a hit to the nose was still painful. But I was fast and before Derek Charles, preppie jock of the football team could step back, I tagged him a hard one in the side of the eye. It crunched under my knuckles. I quickly pulled back my fist and pumped another one in the exact same spot and felt his eye socket cave in under my fist. That shook his marbles up a bit. I saw the dazed look in his eyes. He reeled and swayed on his feet with his eyes glazing over.

I hesitated and he caught me one under the chin; a big wide arching pop I should have been able to block but wasn't on guard. I wasn't expecting him to be able to move after crushing his eye like I did. He didn't feel pain like I did. He shouldn't have been able to swing on me with that much power after I shook his brains up for him. Maybe he didn't have any brains to shake.

I spat blood all over the front of my new white shirt.

"You asshole!" I screamed, my throat raw and salty with blood.

I launched myself in the air at him with everything I had, with every fear I had for Faith being hurt at that moment, and I jacked him in his big square teeth and gashed open all my knuckles. The split skin burnt but not enough to keep me from jabbing him there again and again as I squeezed his throat with my other hand.

"Mike!" Allison screamed from behind me.

I whirled around to look at her and the whole dark night whirled and spun with it. I was never so glad in all my life to be sober than I was at that moment. I needed every ounce of everything I had to give to protect Faith.

"What?" I asked her and spit great globs of blood out my throbbing mouth.

She screamed and pointed across the parking lot.

Faith! NO!

I saw Shane running across the blacktop, his shoes slapping loud in the night and then I heard Faith screaming! Shrieking! No! No! No! No! she shrieked on and on.

"You bastards!" I yelled and punched Derek one last time low in his gut as hard as I could. He was soft there and he made a deep hollow sound in his throat and then spewed foamy puke all over the ground.

Kids were now pouring out the doors of the gym and adults were yelling at everyone. I let go of Derek and ran, almost tripped over something, and was righted by Allison, and then ran hell-bent for election towards the terrified shrieks of Faith.

But it was Shane who was yelling when I got to the purple Buick Century where two guys were cramming Faith into the backseat against her will.

"What do you think you're doing to Bleacher Girl?" Shane screeched and then I heard him scream, "Ya dick!" and the sounds of smacks and knuckles on skulls came in a fury as he scuffled with the two football teammates of Derek's.

"Someone's gotta pay for Derek's truck!" one of them yelled but was cut off by Shane ramming the guy's forehead into the doorframe of the car.

"Mike! Help!" Faith pleaded in panic from the backseat of the car where she had a front-row view to Shane fighting the two guys at once.

"Right here babe!" I shouted as I skidded into the front fender of the car and shoved a big blonde dude head first over the hood of the car!

It was the Homecoming King! He went over the hood with a squeak and a squeal of clothes and belt buckle on the finish of the car and left behind a smear of blood that looked black in the night.

"Woo hoo!" Shane hooted and jacked the other football player in the chin but it didn't even snap his head back. It only seemed to make him angrier and he took it out on Shane's face.

Since the fist wasn't working, Shane decided to hit the guy between the eyes with the open car door. That turned his lights off for him. I laughed even as the guy I was fighting was joined by four more.

Chapter Fourteen

A bunch of us got arrested. That's all that saved Shane and me. We were in over our heads. Shane and I both were thrown in to the paddy wagon with a bunch of Sand Creek jocks. I felt as bad as he looked, as much of him as I could see, that is. Both my eyes were nearly swollen shut. My nose was swollen, which was fine, that stopped it from bleeding at least. My lips hurt and were split and cracked and puffy. Shane looked a mess. But we were still smiling. We still had a lot of gas in the tank but the cops had shut us all down.

Lucky for the Sand Creek boys we were all handcuffed with our hands behind our backs or I'm sure Shane and I would have continued to bust heads in the back of that truck. As it were, I kicked one with both my feet in the side of his knee-cap because he wouldn't stop glaring at me in the paddy wagon. I made that kick count too. He yowled like a baby. I hoped I kicked his knee cap around to the other side of his leg for him.

"Get that smirk off your face!" the guy sitting next to him spat at me.

"Make me!" I came back at him with an even more sinister smile on my busted-up face.

The wagon got quiet after that. Except for the guy with the busted knee. He couldn't stop yowling. I didn't feel bad for him either. He wasn't glaring at me now or anyone else and wouldn't be the rest of the night.

Shane and I looked worse than any of them. Besides our faces being busted up, I had blood all down the front of my white shirt and Shane did too. My suspenders were gone. The cops had ripped them right off me when they pulled me off the dude on the hood of the car. I wasn't sure where Shane's were. Probably gone the same way mine did.

When we got to jail, they tested all of us for alcohol. I was the only one who tested clean so they tested me twice. But I was the only sober one. And out of all the football players brought in and booked, I was the only small one. So, I got told I was gonna get kicked loose if a parent would come get me.

I didn't know who to call to bail me out of jail so I called the foreman from the tire factory. Luckily, I knew his full name and he came and got me. No, he wasn't my parent, I explained to the cop at the desk and the cop seemed to like that I lived on my own. And Mr. Herman the foreman, vouched for me. He told the cop I was a solid kid and a good employee. And he paid my $50 fine.

"Don't worry kid, you'll work that off for me in one day. If I were you, I'd be worried about those Sand Creek boys coming after you again."

He was right. But I wasn't scared about the Sand Creek boys coming after me. I had a thing or two to settle up with them for touching Faith. That wasn't getting dropped. For now, I needed to find her. I was worried to death. I would be going after them eventually and settling that score and if they came looking for me, that was fine too.

"Please," I pleaded with Faith's stepdad Garret. "Please. Can I see her just a second?"

He stood in the doorway and wouldn't budge. It wasn't even that late after I got out of jail, got my car from school, and drove over there. Mr. Herman from the tire plant told me to go straight home. I couldn't lie to him. I told him I had to make sure my girl got home safely. He understood, but he grabbed me by the shoulders before he let me get in my car.

"Mike. You look like absolute shit. Are you sure you want to go now? Will she be able to handle seeing you like this?"

"She'll be fine. I'll stay on the porch in the dark."

"Ok, but the dark isn't going to be able to hide that face. You are jacked up. I think maybe you might even need the hospital."

"I'm fine."

I shrugged his hands off me. I didn't like adults touching me and the whole time his hands were on me I was jumpy and ready to spring.

But I promised him all the same that I'd stay in the dark and not let her get a good look at me. But I didn't. The more I pleaded with her stepdad, the closer to the lighted doorway I stepped. He gasped when he saw me.

"Please, please just so I can see she's ok. Please, sir," I begged and was shocked to feel the tears dripping off the tip of my busted nose as I hung my head.

I felt very nauseous, which didn't make sense to me. I was beat up, but I wasn't drunk. My eyes were swollen and puffy purple, my lips busted and crusted with blood, my nose broken and nearly black. I was a mess and it all hurt a hell of a lot.

"Please?" I said one more time.

But he wasn't having it and I felt so sleepy and dizzy, I couldn't stand on the porch anymore. I thought about curling up right there on the porch and sleeping on their flowered welcome mat till morning. It was freezing out and I'd probably die but what else could I do?

I couldn't believe I was bawling like a baby. I couldn't believe I was being kept away from Faith by the likes of this guy, Garrett and his bad combed over hair.

If my head didn't hurt so much, if I could have stopped crying, if I hadn't just gotten out of jail ten minutes ago, I would have pushed on past him and gone and found Faith and passed out next to her in her soft bed. I bet she had on a short nightie. Maybe one with pink hearts on it or kittens.

My mind was off the rails while I staggered back to the car. I was in no state to drive home and I sat there so long with my head on the wheel I almost fell asleep.

"Leave."

Faith's stepdad woke me up.

"Leave or I'm calling the cops," he said to me as he stood there in the dead rosebushes with his arms crossed over his bathrobe.

I left and went home and I slept fourteen hours. Lucky for me, no work at the Thrifty Lube nor at the tire plant on Sunday. No school either. But I rolled out of bed fast when my eyes finally peeled open a crack, to go see Faith. Then I nearly fell headfirst into the tv set.

The whole room spun and I didn't understand why. I didn't drink the night before. Maybe I hadn't eaten enough. I held the wall as I walked to the toilet. I swayed as I pissed on and on and then the toilet flusher snapped off in my hand when I tried to flush. Great. And then it slipped between my fingers and I dropped it into the toilet. And then I puked on it. Double great.

After that I wobbled my way back to bed and slept another four hours. By the time I woke up and made a pitcher of cherry kool-aid and chugged down two glasses and kept it down, it was almost 6pm. I called Faith and her stepdad told me it was dinnertime and no, Faith could not come to the phone.

I was starting to hate that guy. I remembered the gold ankle bracelet he had bought her to remind her she was delicate, and my anger clicked up even higher till my head pounded.

I'd see her soon. Whether he liked it or not. And I'd get that anklet off her and toss it out of the open car window at a high speed, no matter how sexy it was.

I slept almost all day Monday. I missed my early shift at the Thrifty Lube and I missed all of school. But I woke up at noon, ate three bread and butter sandwiches, flushed the toilet manually, showered, and went to the tire factory.

"Jesus, what's the other guy look like?"
Everyone I worked with asked me that again and again when they saw my busted-up face.

"They looked like a football team," Mr. Herman yelled at

everyone and pulled me over to the time clock.

"We got ya a real time card, so punch in and punch out, Mike."

"All right."

"You feel ok?"

"I'm all right," I answered and refused to look him in the eye. I wasn't too happy about not looking the boss in the eye but I wasn't happy about lying to him either.

I felt like hell. But I put in ear plugs and I worked from 1 till 6 when I left for home in the blissfully silent car. I stopped to call Faith from the payphone across the street at the Thunderbird Bowling Alley. The phone rang forever. Finally, Garrett the stepdad answered. It was like he knew it was me before he picked up. He sounded ticked off. He told me they were having dinner and no, Faith could not come to the phone.

If my head wasn't pounding so hard, I would have driven over there and made sure I saw her. But my head and face hurt like hell. My ribs didn't feel so good either. I rolled into the gas station and picked up a bag of ice and a six-pack of beer, and two packs of cigs to get me through the night.

I slept till noon again the next day; missed the early shift, missed school, rolled into the tire factory looking worse than the day before.

Bruises always look worse the second day, I assured everyone as I picked up the nearest push broom and began to sweep the mold-making assembly line. The guys stopped working when I got near and they stared at my face.

"You don't look too good, kid," they kept saying as I shuffled along. I forced a smile, a big one, so they would stop saying things like that. It was making me feel worse than I did. But the smile seemed to spook them even more.

"Kid, you look goddamned scary," Mr. Herman said to me as he pulled me aside. "Kid," he said and shook me by the shoulder. I didn't usually let adults touch me, much less in such an aggressive way, but I was unable to shrug him off. As a matter of fact, when I tried to slip out from under his meaty fist gripping my arm, I fell on the ground.

"Listen kid, either have someone pick you up and take you home, or I'm taking you to the hospital."

"Nah, I'm fine," I said to him from where I was splayed out on the shop floor and I laughed it off to show him I was ok. But he wouldn't move and let me up.

"Give me a number to call to have someone come get you. Someone who'll stay with you. You got a concussion kid. A bad one."

"Nah, I'm ok. I don't need anyone. I don't have anyone to call anyway."

I slithered out from under him but swayed on my feet when I tried to stand up. He started to catch me but he didn't put his hands on me at the last second, and at that, I really did smile at him, an honest to goodness big one; one that could light up even my eyes, even if they were purple and bloody.

"I'm not gonna hurt you kid!"

"I know, Mr. Herman. Sorry."

"No need to say sorry to me kid," he said down to me and gave me a hand up, which I accepted.

"You're all right, kid. You're tuff too. But I gotta send you home with someone else at the wheel. I'll have Carter drive your car home to you tonight when he gets here for the late shift. He owes ya one!"

"I need the hours," I said and felt ashamed.

"Here," he mumbled and pulled a worn, fat leather wallet out of his back pocket.
It was stuffed full of tissue thin white and yellow receipts.

"The wife makes me keep them," he shrugged and with his fat fingers he pulled out two crumpled and soiled bills and pressed them into my fist.

I didn't want to take them. I already owed him $50 for the

fine at jail.

"Just take it, kid."

I straightened out the two bills, a $10 and a $20 and carefully folded them and put them in my own much thinner, much shinier wallet and followed him slowly out to the parking lot so he could take me home. I agreed he was right. I should go home and maybe even go to the hospital but I didn't have the money for that either.

Chapter Fifteen

"Mom! Why are you here?" I cried in shock.
It was my worst nightmare come true.

"Got a court summons, Mikey. Child protective services for neglect," she said and when I didn't respond, she continued. "I said to them, how can I be neglecting him when he doesn't even live here?"

She snorted and waited for me to laugh and when I didn't, she scowled at me.
My mind was still trying to understand why my mom was in my apartment, pacing around, touching all my things, which were few.

"So that's where the good rabbit ears for the portable tv went," she said and gave my tv antenna a good twist with her thick fingers.

I shut my eyes as she went out in the hall and on into my kitchen. My mom, in my apartment. I must have left the door unlocked the night before. I couldn't remember getting home. I remembered the ride home in Mr. Herman's car but it was hazy. I remembered Molly's big arm around my waist, helping me get up the stairs.

"What time is it?" I called out to Mom.

Had I missed my shift at the Thrifty Lube and school again? I rolled over and looked at my Timex on the windowsill. 8 AM. That was perfect. I could make it to work and then school. I shut my eyes a minute. Sleep beckoned me to drop off deeper. Maybe Mom being there was all a bad dream.

"Well?"

Mom was back in the doorway. She wasn't a bad dream. She was a living nightmare come back to haunt me after seven months of freedom.

"Why are you here, Mom? How did you find out where I live?"

"I told you. I got a summons to court this morning from child protective services. We have to be before the judge at 10. Get dressed in something nice. And my God, do something about your face!"

I ignored her and made my way past her as soon as she moved out of the doorway and back into my entrance hall. It made me sick to my stomach to see her in my apartment. I shuffled to the kitchen where I mixed up a pitcher of cherry kool-aid and filled a glass and chugged it down. I waited by the garbage can in silence for it to come back up but it stayed put. My stomach grumbled but it was a hungry grumble. Cereal. I needed cereal.

"Mike! Hurry up!" she snapped at me and I nearly dropped the milk as I looked for its date.

"Mom, you need to go," I told her as I dumped the milk down the drain and sniffed its soured stink as it went. "I don't need you here," I said over my shoulder.

"You never did listen," she said and took three fast steps in her cheap sneakers over to me and slapped an envelope down and made me wince.

"This one's for you."

"Is this from jail?" I asked when I saw the courthouse return address on the front.

"It's a summons for court," she brayed like a donkey at me and I felt sorry for her that she never had the money to take care of her teeth because her and Dad drank it all away.

I pulled the envelope open, my heart racing, expecting it to be about the massive fight at school. Maybe they didn't mean to turn me loose from jail, maybe they wanted me back. Or maybe they knew it was me who stole the motorbike. Maybe they were coming for me. I opened it with shaking hands.

Child neglect.

I read it two more times and it all equaled child neglect.

"I don't have any kids."

I wadded it up and tossed it onto the table and kept looking for something to eat for breakfast besides peanut butter and toast and wasn't prepared for the hard wallop she hit me with on the back of the head.

I don't know if it was the beating my head had already taken or the fact that I was in my own home and not expecting to get hit, but it shook my marbles up hard.
I glared at her and she froze where she stood.

"You idiot! You're the child who's been neglected! Get dressed! Dennis and your dad are downstairs waiting to take us to court! You need to get cleaned up!"

"Out. Get out."
I rolled my shoulders and popped my neck twice and pointed to the door.

"Court's in an hour, if we get there early we can get this whole thing dropped, Mike!" her bitter voice and its panicked edges bounced off my bare walls and set my teeth on edge.

"Get out."

"Mike!" she yelled and then winced and I realized I had raised my fist to her.

She ducked and I realized she was shorter than me now.

"Mikey," she said softer. "We have to go."
She looked like she was going to cry. I could see the tears welling up in her eyes. But she wasn't crying for me. She was crying for herself. For the interruption in her life. For someone on the outside peeking in to their mess of their life over there on Robin Court.

"I'll take myself."

I hoped Carter from the tire factory had brought my car home like Mr. Herman had said he would. I looked out the kitchen window and there it was, my beautiful yellow car snugged up to the curb with rain falling on it in the cold morning.

"Yes. Court. Child neglect. What else can go wrong?" I asked myself.

**

"Emancipation," Jeff said the word slowly and then looked up at me. "That sounds gay," he scoffed and handed me his pack of cigarettes.

I took one and passed the pack to Shane. Shane reached out with a shaky hand and pulled one from the pack. He was banged up just as bad as me. Both eyes purple and swollen. Busted lips, puffy black nose with blood crusting the nostrils still a week later. He noticed me checking out his face and smiled. He still had all his teeth and I did too and when he realized I was counting his, he smiled even bigger which sent me into laughter that made my ribs ache.

"More gay," Jeff said and shook his head from where he sat below us on the front steps of the apartment house.

"What's all this mean? Is this good?" Shane asked.

"Yeah man. It's real good."

I was declared to be emancipated, but not just emancipated, I was declared by the judge as being *forced* emancipated. Forced to move out to escape physical abuse, mental abuse, and general neglect.

Mom was silent for the first time ever when confronted by authority. Dad was threatened with jail time because he wouldn't stop interrupting the judge. When Dad yelled, "What the hell?" at the judge in the first five minutes of court, the judge had him removed until he could control himself. Once he promised to get himself under control, or be jailed, the judge began to question me, and our secret lifestyle that had always been hidden, and that I never wanted to unearth, was forced to bring out in the public eye.

"Do your parents hit you, son?" the judge asked me as I stood there in my good Levis and best blue alligator shirt with the collar respectfully down.

The judge was a looker. I'd seen a couple of judges in my short life, but none of them had ever been women, much less one that was such a looker. Her shiny dark hair lay in thick waves and framed her face. She had deep dimples on either side of her mouth and if she would smile, I'd bet she'd be adorable. My busted and swollen face burned hot as I smiled at her. When she smiled back, I forgot where I was for a moment.

"Mike?" she prodded.

"Yes?"

"Do they ever hit you?"

"Not anymore, no," I told her and tried not to fidget. I felt ashamed to be telling such a good-looking woman that my parents slapped me around. I stared hard at the tops of my shoes.

"Not anymore?" she asked and I raised my head up and looked at her.

"No, ma'am, I mean, Miss, uhhh."

My heart thudded fast and light. I hated everything about this; the cops on the edges of the room, the lime green and grey linoleum, the smell of jail, the having to tell a pretty judge my parents hit me, my parents and mom's boyfriend Dennis sitting across from me. I hated all of it.

"Your honor will suffice."

I glanced up at her to see if I was in trouble. Nope. I didn't think I was.

She had a small smile and I swear she had a twinkle in her eye. I was going to be okay.

"Your honor," I echoed and felt my own smile rip across my face. She was cute.

"When's the last time they hit you?" Now she was all serious.

I glanced at Mom over at the next table. She had red patches not only on her face and neck but also flowering up the pale skin of her thick arms. She scratched at them with her yellow nails as she glared at me.

"Just a little bit ago."

"Just a little bit ago?"

"Yes, your honor, ma'am."

I flexed my hands and fingers down at my side. I wanted to pop my neck but I was scared to fidget too much in front of this judge. Something important was about to happen and I wasn't sure exactly what, yet. All I knew was, it was going to affect me, and it was going to involve my parents, and I didn't like it one bit.

"Define for the court when exactly that was."

"Um, this uh morning about 8."

I glanced over at Mom as if to see if she agreed. She glared back and so did Dad. Dennis looked asleep or high or both.

"This morning around 8? Who struck you?"

"My mom."

"Your mom," the judge repeated.

"Yes, your honor."

"Please describe for the court how you were hit," she instructed me and I did.

The judge was not happy to hear that Mom had walloped me in the back of the head when I wasn't looking, in my own apartment.

"She hit you this morning in the back of the head with her hand, in your own apartment?"

"Yes ma'am, your honor."

"What were you doing when she hit you?"

"I was looking for something to eat besides peanut butter and toast."

Dad laughed at this and that got him yelled at by the judge again and we had to wait for him to promise he would respect the court. After that, the details flowed out of me.

"So what you're telling me Mike, is you were looking for something other than peanut butter and bread to eat and while you were looking, your mother hit you in the back of the head?"

"Yes."

I licked my lips and gulped and yet the Judge continued to ask questions.

"Is this true, Ms. Kilo?"

"Well, see Mike was making me really frustrated because he wouldn't listen to me that we needed to go. He was ignoring me and I just wanted to get his attention."

"What did you do to get his attention?"

"I just you know," Mom said and made the motion of walloping me in the back of the head.
I winced when she did it and the Judge noticed.

"Tell me everything, Mike," the Judge instructed me.

"Everything what?"

"Tell me why you moved out."

I told her everything. The drinking. The smoking. The fighting. The all-night partying. The throwing things at me. Breaking my arm. Never having anything to eat. Sleeping on the couch. Everyone hitting me whenever they wanted. All of it.

"So what you're telling me, Mike, is you moved out March the 3rd, the day you turned seventeen, to get away from your parents because they hit you, they drink in excess, they have their live-in lovers there who also hit you, is that correct?"

"Yes, I remember it was March the 3rd because it was my birthday present to me."

I smiled at the memory but the judge didn't return it. She seemed to be studying my face and it reminded me I was all bruised up bad still, and I quit smiling and looked down and waited quietly for her to say something. But she didn't.

I peeked up to see what was happening and found her glaring at Mom and Dad and Dennis. I wondered where Linda was but did not care enough to ask. She was probably hung over and sleeping it off at home.

"You work several jobs, go to high school, and do maintenance for your landlord," the Judge said and here she tilted her head up to acknowledge someone behind me.

I turned and saw Doris and also Mr. Herman sitting behind me. Doris had tears in her eyes.

"Yes, your honor," I said as I turned back around to face the Judge.

"And your mother came over this morning and she?" she trailed off.

"She let herself into my apartment to tell me about court and then she smacked me a good one in the back of the head," I said and rubbed the back of my head where it was still tender.
I'd be ok. I'd been hit harder by Dad and Dennis.

"Do you feel secure in your apartment?"

"Yes."

"Do you worry about having enough to eat? Rent?" the Judge asked me.

I took a long time before I lied and said, "I'm okay."

"Mr. Kilo," she started to say and Dad and I both answered.

"Yes?"

"The senior Mr. Kilo."

Dad stood up.

"Are you employed?"

"Yes."

"You'll address me as Your Honor."

I looked at Dad and when I saw his face turn red and his temper begin to boil immediately from being dressed down by the Judge, I grinned just a little.

"Yes, Your Honor," he choked out.

"Where are you employed, sir?"

"Morgan Dooley, Your Honor."

"How long have you been there?"

"Since June, Your Honor."

This was new.

"Ms. Kilo are you employed?"

"No, your honor."

"Ms. Kilo, what does a mom do for her children?"

Here, Mom shrugged and then she held up her finger and said, "Mike's not really a child anymore, your honor, so I don't really need to do anything for him."

Here, I nodded my head in agreement. She didn't ever do much for me as a kid and she didn't need to now. She smacked me. She baked tv dinners. She smoked and she drank coffee all day and smoked and drank beer all night. I didn't miss her. Maybe I missed what she could have been, but I was fine. And when I told the judge all of this, it just poured out of me, all the years of being knocked around, flying through the windshield of the car, dad running over my foot, the cigarette burns, them ganging up on me when they were drunk or hungover.

"You two are in fact still married, correct?" The judge asked as she flipped through papers on her desk.

"Yes, Your Honor," they both answered and stood up together.

Mom looked hopeful like that was gonna go her way.

"The court orders you both to begin paying your son financial support of $250 a month starting today, right now and you will meet next week with Judge Blumenthal of Family Court and discuss past payments. Even though Mike is emancipated, he has done this to escape years of abuse and neglect which you seem still intent on afflicting on him. Pay him now with your check or you will both be handed over to the bailiff. And if that check is cancelled or bounces you will both do jail time."

I almost ripped the check up when Mom gave it to me. But I felt the eyes of the judge on me and I didn't want to make her mad. Besides, I needed the money. I need to take out my little Bleacher Girl.

Chapter Sixteen

But it wasn't going to be that easy. The truant officer was waiting for me outside my apartment when I got up the next morning to head into my early shift at the Thrifty Lube. I recognized him from all the trouble I was always in at my old school.

"Hey it's you, how are you, Officer Carr?"

"Mike. You're missing school again."

He was all serious, his eyes like green little marbles in his pockmarked face, put a bead on me, on my bruised face, my Thrifty Lube coveralls.

"I got banged up in a bad fight and then I was at court yesterday for child neglect," I told him.

"Child neglect?" he asked and pulled a pack of cigarettes out of his winter coat pocket and offered me one and I gladly took it because I was out.

He looked around the big room of my apartment as he lit our smokes as if he were looking for a child but all he saw were the Samantha Fox posters and her beautiful jugs. Those posters were nothing but trouble for me and I needed to get rid of them soon.

"I'm gonna need to look around, Mike."

He was still gazing around as if he'd find a baby or something left alone here behind my weight bench or under my bed.

"The child neglect was for me, Mr. Carr. I'm the child being neglected."

"You?"

"Yeh, me, funny ain't it?" I asked and laughed and waved him in the rest of the way. "See?" I said to him, "No kids, now can I go? I'm late for work."

"I gotta look around for drugs or guns or booze or girls," eyes back on Samantha and her tits, "and make sure you're keeping clean."

"I'm very clean, Mr. Carr, you know me."

"That, I do, which is why I gotta look. I'll be fast."

And he was. There wasn't much to look at it. Everything was squared away.

"Table's busted," he said to me.

"I know," I answered and passed him the ashtray and we both put our smokes out.

"Where's your parents?" he asked as he glanced at my banged-up face.

"At their place, I guess." I shrugged.

"You live here alone? No roomies, no girls?"

"Well, I have a girlfriend. But she lives with her p's like a normal kid. I live here alone. Which is why I was at court for child neglect. I'm the child."

"You look like a man to me."

"Thanks."

"Ok get to school, don't miss."

I got rid of him with a promise that I would do just that and he started to go but then his mood changed.

"Cuz if you keep missing school, you won't graduate. If you don't get your grades up, you won't either and now the court is involved! They could order you to go back home and you don't want that."

"No sir!"

After that, he wanted to hear all about the big fight but I was already late to work and needed to get there as soon as possible which proved not soon enough.

"You're late. We don't need you today. Or tomorrow for that matter," Fred told me, his face angry behind that ridiculous mustache.

Skip peeked out from behind a Dodge van. I stared at him as

he twisted a rag in his hands. He had on a stocking hat with a big stupid pompom on top and a scarf wrapped around his neck. If he was changing oil, that stuff would be filthy fast.

"What about $12 Tuesday? It's snowing too and you know that brings them in like mad." I flashed them a smile, hoping they would forgive me.

"You're not needed."

It was Adam. He had a stinky smirk on his face and if I wasn't already barely skating by in life as it were, I would have had a go at him right there. But I said nothing. I did nothing. I turned around and got in my car and was planning to go home but not before stopping off and picking up a case of beer and a couple of cartons of smokes to have later that night and the rest of the week. It was going to be a long night.

Fired from one job. Maybe no graduation if my grades didn't get up. Then no living on my own. No girlfriend if her parents never let me see her again. It all looked bleak as hell. I was planning on throwing myself a pity party. But it wasn't like me. I wasn't a complainer. I was a do-er. Wallowing in all this mess didn't help me.

Tomorrow would be a new day. I'd pull it all together tomorrow I told myself as I flicked on the windshield wipers to brush away the flakes that were beginning to pile up fast. I'd get another job. For now, I'd go to school today and do my homework tonight and throw myself a little pity party but just for one night. Then I'd go see Faith soon. Things just felt bad today because it was all happening now. But tonight, there'd be beer and smokes and tv in my own place alone while it continued to snow outside, nice and cozy, no Mom or Dad or Dennis knocking me in the head. Which reminded me; I had $250 a month coming to me from Mom and Dad and they'd have to pay or get thrown in jail. That made me smile as I headed to school.

School sucked and I had to stay after and make up missed work and missed lessons that I'd gotten zeros on when I missed from having a concussion. Geology lessons alone with that creepy Mr. Cargill were worse than lessons in the class with him staring at all the girls. He talked on and on about rocks and I nodded my head. I'm sure it was interesting but his delivery sucked.

Then it was typing by myself with the teacher up at the corner desk eyeballing me over her magazine as I slowly pecked out the lessons on the vibrating electric typewriter. Without anyone else in the class you could really hear how slow I went.

Then on to the gym. PE wasn't so bad. I liked to run and do push-ups and pull-ups while the teacher counted them off and marked things in his book. He was the only one happy with me. When I was finally allowed to leave, my car was a soft lump under a foot of snow. I warmed it up and cleaned it off and headed to the gas station on the way home with every intention of getting drunk while dinner cooked.

I threw the beer and smokes into the passenger seat and started the car. I wished Faith was there in the seat instead. I glanced over and remembered how she looked sitting there in her puffer jacket and her short skirt. I ripped open a carton and took a pack out and lit one with a match that burnt too fast and singed my finger.

"Dammit!" I hollered and flung it onto the floorboard on the passenger side where it hissed in the puddle on the rubber mat.

Shit. Something must have been leaking or rusted through. I didn't remember tracking snow into that side. Maybe Shane had when he rode with me the other day. Whatever it was from, there was an inch of water sitting on top of the rubber mat. I'd have to clean that up before letting my little Bleacher Girl sit there.

And that'd be soon. I'd get her back. Maybe my face would look better this weekend and I could take her out. Her parents couldn't keep me away forever; not once my face was healed. There'd be no reason to, I thought as the carton of cigarettes began to slide off the seat.

I reached over to grab it and when I did, several slippery

soft packs of smokes slid out of the carton and into the floorboard and plopped into all that water.
Shit.

I grabbed for them with one arm while still holding onto the wheel but as my fingertips grazed the slick wrapping on a pack, my vision exploded in sound and light. All I could think of was, WHAT EXPLODED?

The car was sliding, spinning, gliding fast, like a giant ice-skate. I had a second to think, damn! I'm doing the coolest 360 ever and can't even see what's going on. The force of the car spinning kept me pinned down sideways in the passenger seat until the passenger door slammed into something with another explosion of sound and light.

I flew off my seat and clear over into the passenger door like a missile, headfirst. I reached out to protect my head and the last thing I remember thinking was, "At least I'm not going through the windshield this time, I'm going through the door, ouch!"

Chapter Seventeen

"Hey kid, lay back down."

"Where am I? What happened?"

"You were in a bad accident. Help is on the way."

"Bad accident? With what? How?"

I blinked my eyes as fat cold snowflakes fell into them one after another and I tried to focus on the stars above me in the dark sky.

"You ran a red light and got hit by the dry-cleaning truck and then you spun out of control and hit the light pole."

"Shit."

"Don't worry. Help is on the way."

"I'm fine." I tried to get up but strong hands held me down.

"Ger off me!" I yelled. I struggled against the guy holding me down.

"Stay down little fella."

"Little fella? Fuck off and get off! You're hurting my arm!"

"Your arm's busted, man, and your face is all jacked up too, lay down."

The guy sounded tuff. I opened my eyes again and saw that he wasn't that much older than myself but he was twice as big.

"My face was already jacked."

"Oh. Hey. I think I know you."

I squinted at him but his face was a bright halo of light with the street light behind his head.

"From where?"

"Sand Creek High," he said and smiled.

"Naw man. I don't go there," I answered and collapsed back on the ground and shut my eyes.

"No, from the fight! I watched you kick a lot of the football team's ass! You're Bleacher Girl's boyfriend!"

My head popped right back up. I didn't recognize the guy at

all. He was so huge he was probably a football player.

"I don't go there either," he said, "but I was at that dance with my girlfriend and I watched the whole thing. I was cheering you on, man!" he said and smiled and smacked my arm which sent me yowling in pain.

"Sorry," he apologized and scrutinized my face. "Wow, sorry man."

"Don't worry," I croaked out, "It's all right. I'm fine. Let me up."

I could hear all sorts of sirens and horns blaring, getting louder every second. It sounded like they had an important place to get to, quick.

"Let me get up so I can get out of the way. Gotta move my car."

"Just relax. Let the medics look at you. Let them decide if you can go."

"All right. But stop touching me. I don't like people touching me."

He backed off but only because the medics shoved him out of the way. I was lifted from hard concrete and onto a hard gurney, and given a rough ride to the noisy ER.

"Someone's coming to pick you up and when they get here, we'll send you home, soon as we get a cast on that arm."

That was the answer I finally got after asking when could I leave. I needed to leave. I had so much to do. I had work. I had homework. I had to find more hours to work, I needed to see Faith. Faith, Faith, Faith, I said it a hundred times in my head till one of the nurses patted my shoulder and whispered, "Yes, keep the faith, you'll be fine. We're going to fix your arm."

"What about my car?" I called after her as she left through the curtain.

"Dunno about any car, but your arm we can fix!" she shot back over her shoulder.

She was a sassy one. I hated to see her go.

Jeff and Shane picked me up two hours later and took me to the impound lot and helped me get the tires off my destroyed car. I wanted to cry, but I didn't. I wanted to strip it of every part but Shane and Jeff wouldn't help me do that, and with my busted-up arm, I couldn't do it either. But we got the tires off, or they did, for me. I got three of the beers out. The others had exploded all over the door and the dash. I got five packs of cigarettes out too. They were the only ones that weren't soaked in beer and water.

I stared a long time in silence at that front passenger seat and the backseat. That was where I had first touched my little Bleacher Girl and I'd never touch her there again. It was the end of my car but hopefully it wasn't the end for me and Faith.
The guys helped me carry the beer and the smokes and even the tires up to my apartment because I was useless at the moment with my busted right arm. And then they left me because it was so late. Alone.

I drank the three beers fast and smoked five cigarettes right in a row as I sat on the back of a kitchen chair watching fat snowflakes falling softly outside. I needed a car. Soon. No car, no work, no school. If I didn't have those things, it'd be no apartment, no freedom, no me.

I had some money saved but I wanted to keep it. I was going to have money coming in from Mom and Dad but I didn't want to have to use it. I didn't want their help. The only reason I didn't tell them to stick it was because I was scared to see that judge again, even if she was a looker!

I'd have to dip into savings to buy a car; something small, reliable, something that sipped gas, just to get me around. Something just like the little red hatchback pulling up to the curb. It was a girl car and oh what a girl who got out of it, the most beautiful girl ever.

I flew down the three flights of stairs, broken arm held high in the air, huge smile on my face, eyes shining in the night, hard-on in my sweatpants, to Bleacher Girl pulling up to my place at 11 at night on a school night. This was a fantasy come true.

"Mike! Mike! Mike!"

It was like that. It was that easy.

"Your face! Oh my God!"

I tried to tell her I was fine but she kept going.

"Oh my gosh! Your arm! I heard about your car! I heard about you going to jail! Then you went to court! Then you crashed your car!"

Girls were like that. They had to say everything at once. Her hands fluttered all over my face, they danced through my hair and sent electrical zaps all over my body. She was, "Mike Mike!" this and "Mike! Mike!" that as she worried over and inspected every inch of me. I let her until she kissed my fingers poking out of my cast.

When she, "Mike! Mike! Oh Mike!" kissed my fingertips I sprung on her. Wrapped her in my arms and kissed her hard on the lips. The only other "Mike Mike!" I wanted coming out of her was from her flat on her back, naked in my bed.

I scooped her up in my arms and ran her up the three flights to my apartment. I made sure to lock the bolt behind us. Thoughts of my mom letting herself in again made me shudder. But thoughts of my mom were blown away by Faith who filled up every corner of my apartment with her presence.

"Oh my gosh! Your face! Is that from the fight?"

"Yes."

"Oh my, your arm, Mike, they broke your arm!"

She held my cast gently with her little hands and I swear I could feel it through the plaster.

"Naw, it got broke in the car wreck."

"I'm so sorry."

"Don't be. It's just life," I said and shrugged and then I remembered how Derek Charles and his friends had dragged her out of the dance and I grabbed her arm and looked her up and down.

"But what about you? Did those guys hurt you, hurt you in any way?" I asked her, close to her face.

She assured me they had not but then I had to ask, "Did they touch you or look at anything they shouldn't have?"
She shook her head no. She promised me that no they had not. And she smiled, an honest to goodness happy smile so I knew she was telling the truth.

What had felt like too much to handle before, seemed as easy as pie to solve now. I'd get a new car. Soon. Tomorrow maybe. Then off I'd go to work and school and wherever I wanted. Nothing could stop me. I was the happiest asshole in the world. I couldn't stop smiling, at Faith, at my girl, my Bleacher Girl.

She pulled off her pink puffy ski jacket and went and sat on my bed. She grew quiet. She was all pink; her cheeks, her lips, her wool sweater buttoned up all the way, even her corduroys; all pink. I got even harder and adjusted my sweatpants to try to keep her from seeing. But she noticed and she turned even pinker.

I didn't say a thing. I kept smiling. Good things were about to happen. I knew it. I didn't ask what brought her by so late. I didn't ask if she'd snuck out. I didn't ask a thing. She was here and that told me everything. She wanted to see me. And I wanted her.

I just watched her. I wanted to kiss her. Devour her. Hold her. But I paused. I'd forgotten how to approach her. And when I paused, the most wonderful thing happened. She stood up. She smiled. And then she started unbuttoning her pink cardigan.

Please don't stop, I begged silently in my brain when she got down to the fourth button. When she undid it, she did stop, and she let go of the sweater, and it sprung open to reveal the sexiest cleavage I'd ever seen in my life. No girl had when she had.

I started to pounce but she held up one finger. I wanted to suck that precious finger but she smiled at me a hot little twist of her lips and then she unbuttoned the next one. I held my breath. Now the tops of her breasts were exposed and I watched them rise and fall with her quick breathing. I could hardly resist. But she held that little pointer finger up again and flashed me that tiny smile and then she unbuttoned the button under her tits. Now the cardigan pulled open to reveal the middle of her bra; the tiny pink flower.

I started to walk towards her but she pointed at me to stop and I did. I even took a step backwards and waited eagerly with a pounding erection poking my sweatpants out, for her to finish unbuttoning to grab her. But she stopped unbuttoning.

Her face turned serious and her eyes blazed fierce as they locked on to mine. I forgot all about my banged up face, my totaled car, and my broken arm. That look on her face wiped all those thoughts out of my head.

The sweater still had three buttons to go but she didn't undo them. She pulled it open all the way as she watched me, as I took in all her curves with my wide opened eyes. I watched her hungrily as she giggled a little and bounced a little too. I needed to get a hold of her now. I smiled at her little teasing smile and her batting eyelashes. She was so cute trying to be sexy for me and by God it was working. She was sexy as hell and had no idea. My tongue nearly fell out as she finished unbuttoning and slid her arms out of the sleeves and dropped it all on the floor.

Then she turned around and showed me all that long glorious golden hair. She pulled it over her shoulder and I held my breath and watched as she reached both hands behind her back and undid her bra. Her tiny pink fingernails flashed in the dim light of the lamp on my dresser.

I took a deep breath as she dropped the bra on the floor. I waited for what she would do next but she seemed unsure, frozen for a second. She held her arms out to her sides a little as if she were a ballerina and then she slowly turned around to face me. She hooked her thumbs into the belt-loops of those pink corduroys and tilted one hip up and I couldn't hold back anymore.

I grabbed her by her arms and had her on her back on my bed as fast as I could and still be gentle with her, as fat snowflakes drifted past the windows next to my bed and the radiators clanked and whistled.

Chapter Eighteen

"Is that a girl car?" Jeff asked and cackled as he punched Shane in the arm.

Faith had insisted I keep her car for a couple of days right after she insisted that I take her home because she could not spend the night.

"Take me home and drop me off and keep my car a couple of days till you get a new one," she had told me when we were finally tired out.

I felt horrible borrowing it. I felt less than a man. But I had a million things I had to do that required me having wheels: school, work, even finding another car required having a car.

"Will you be able to drive it? It's a 5-speed," she had said to me as we kissed the whole way down the stairs.

I could not stop kissing her. But that comment stopped me.

"Of course I can drive a stick. I'm a man." I threw out my chest for emphasis.

"No, silly, I meant with your cast."

"Oh that," I shrugged. That was nothing.

I'd jumped motorbikes while wearing a cast. I'd spent a good portion of my life in a cast. Driving stick shift would be nothing.

"I'm a man, like I said. No big deal."

"Mike," she had giggled.

"Get over here," I growled at her and grabbed her as we continued down the stairs and out into the cold, snowy night.

"I love you, Mike," she said and smiled up at me as snowflakes melted in her eyelashes.

"I love you too, babe."

It came so easy and I meant every word. I kissed her hair where it parted on the side so she couldn't see I had dirt in my eyes, even though it was snowing.

"Mike? You there?" Shane blurted at me now.

"Sorry, yeh, what?"

I wiped the stupid grin off my face.

"IS this a girl car?" Shane asked me again and shoved a handful of fries in his mouth.

We were behind McDonald's eating a free dinner out in the cold, in Faith's car with the engine off. It had snowed all day but it wasn't very deep. I had taken Faith home late, after 2am, after making love to her every way I knew how. After she had even got brave and got on top of me the last time we did it. She was beautiful. Gorgeous. I loved being able to look up at her and watch her face go from afraid and unsure to sweaty and rippling with pleasure. I loved looking up at the undersides of her beautiful tits.

"Mike! The fuck?" Shane yelled and pelted me in the face with fries.

"Dude. Fuck. This is Faith's car! I'm just borrowing it till I have a new car! Stop throwin' shit!"

"Dude? How do you afford all these cars? You've had like five I swear in the two years you've been driving." Jeff said from the middle of the backseat where he sat hunched, drinking his coke, and shoving the last bite of his Big Mac in his mouth.

"What? I had a couple before I got my license too," I mused and laughed.

"Exactly. How does a fourteen-year-old buy a car?"

"I fucking work, you asshole! I've always had a job, all my life!"

"Fuck you, John Denver," he yelled back at me and punched me in the arm.

"Fuck off, what's that supposed to mean, John Denver?"

"Your coat, man! What's with the coat?" Jeff asked and laughed and I could see sauce all over his lips and teeth and I turned away from him and watched the snow fall onto the windshield, light and fluffy.

"Man, you look like you wrestle cows or something," Shane said over the top of his giggles from where he sat next to me in the passenger seat of Faith's car.

"It's my winter coat. It's snowing. Can't you see? Maybe you need to walk home in it."

"Come on. Where'd you get that?"

"What's it matter? I got it at work."

"You got a job at a ranch now?"

"No. At the tire plant."

Jim Mooney, the quality inspector had given it to me after he saw me roll in wearing my Members Only jacket, covered in snow, and pulled up over my cast. He'd insisted on giving it to me.

"Hey, it's just hanging here for an emergency like this," he had told me.

He never wore it, he'd assured me. Still, I didn't feel right taking it, till he showed me how he'd gotten too fat for it. That was when I agreed to try it on. It was pretty big on me but it was very warm. It felt good. It smelled good like worn-in cowhide. It reminded me of my old baseball glove Dennis had taken from me after I broke the second window on the back of the house.
I wasn't about to tell these guys all that.

"Dude. Everyone is giving you free stuff all the time."

"Fuck you. I'm giving this car back to Faith tomorrow."

"It smells good in here," Shane sniffed.

"It does," Jeff agreed from the backseat and he too was sniffing around.

He even bent over and started sniffing the seat back and I felt my temper begin to simmer. I took a deep breath and said, "Dude quit sniffing back there. What's wrong with you?"

"I smell something good back here. Girl smell."

"I wonder how many guys she shagged back there?" Shane asked and looked like he was seriously thinking about it and not just taking the Mickey out of me.

"Short guys, it had to have been short guys like Mike. It's

cramped back here," Jeff said while bent over with his face close to the seat.

"Knock it off."

"Why?" Jeff asked and stopped his disgusting sniffing and sat up.

"Stop sniffing while you still have a nose."

"Where is Bleacher Girl?" Shane asked and tried to change the subject before I lost my temper.

"Girl's night," was all I said as I gripped the steering wheel and stared straight ahead.

Bringing these guys in Faith's car was a bad idea. I should have stayed home and tried to do homework even if I had no idea how to write a paper on erosion or soil failure or whatever I was supposed to be researching. If I didn't do it, I wouldn't graduate.

"Girl's night?" Jeff asked and brayed out a laugh.

"Didn't you know that?" I turned around and looked at him. His face froze mid donkey laugh when he saw my patience with him was getting sparse.

"No. She's not talking to me," he owned up.

"How come?" Shane asked which was good, because I didn't really care.

Allison and Jennifer were the ones who nearly killed Faith and though I had promised to never bring it up again with her, I would never forget it or forgive them either. I didn't want her going out with them. I was worried they would get her hurt again.

"I don't know why Jen isn't talking to me," Jeff admitted as he wiped Big Mac sauce onto the sides of his jeans.
Shane looked as disgusted as I felt watching him.

"Maybe because you're a nasty goddamn pig!" Shane yelled at him and pointed as his jeans and threw a handful of napkins back at him.

"You're a mess! Maybe that's why she won't let you bang her! MAN! Keep that shit off the seats, bonehead!" I added.

"Shut up. I'm not like this around Jen!"

"When was the last time you were around her?" I asked.

"Last time we did it?"

"Sure, yeh, that."

Shane and I watched with curiosity as Jeff shut his eyes and ticked things off that only he could see on his fingers.

"A long time man. Been a long time, a very long time," he admitted and sighed.

"The heck with them," Shane muttered as he crossed his arms over his chest and sat back in his seat.

He had given up and was ready to join Jeff in his misery. But as for me, the wheels were turning every direction in my brain. It was hard to keep with all my thoughts as they chased each other around. Some of them crashed into brick walls where they fell apart and some dusted themselves off and got up and ran faster till it all clicked.

"That smile," Jeff pointed at me and Shane's head whipped around to look over at me.

"I know that smile," Shane said and now he too was starting to grin even though he had no idea what I was thinking.

"I know it too, but I don't know what it means. It usually means girls, I hope it means girls," Jeff said quickly and he looked from me to Shane and back to me as if the answer were zinging between us.

"What if boys' night out, ran into girls' night out?" I asked them and let the smile rip across my face.

But boy's night out couldn't collide with girl's night out if we couldn't find the girls.

We found *some girls* but they weren't our girls. Shane and Jeff didn't care. Not when they saw the group of girls standing around the bonfire behind the abandoned Lakeside Motors.

"They're babes, all of them," Shane insisted as he hung his head out the window as I drove around the edge of all the kids, mostly girls, girls in rabbit fur coats, girls in Sand Creek jackets, girls in puffer coats everywhere.

"They aren't our babes," I said as soon as I slowed the car down a little and got a good look.

None of them were anything like Faith. I didn't want to stop and was still rolling but Shane had his door open and way getting out whether I stopped or not. So I stopped. I wanted a cigarette. We all did and I wouldn't let them smoke in Faith's car. I didn't want to cover the scent of her. Shane and Jeff weren't the only ones who had picked up on that intoxicating scent. That was the first thing I noticed when I was alone in the little car. It was a little cloud of heavenly Faith.

"Come on let's go," I called to the backs of Jeff and Shane as I flicked my cigarette butt on the cold wind when I was done.

"Mike, why would you want to leave?" Jeff turned around and asked me with his hands out. "You always get swarmed by chicks, so let's stay."

He was right. But I didn't want to be swarmed by these chicks. Even though some of them were pretty hot. There was a lot of beautiful, thick hair going on here and a lot of flashing smiles and pretty eyes looking my way as soon as I got close to the bonfire. Soon they were all over me. I wanted to tell them to get off but I didn't want to be rude to them. I didn't want to hurt anyone's feelings.

"Ladies," I said to them, "I'm taken," I told them gently but that only made them press closer and one even pressed her sticky lips against my cheek in a warm kiss that sent shivers all over me. I couldn't help but smile from ear to ear. Being surrounded by girls felt good. Felt very good. Their hands squeezing my arm and my shoulders, asking me about my cast, my broken arm, my face that was still slightly bruised. Their fingers zinged through my hair; they were all over me. They weren't nearly as beautiful or sexy as Faith. None of them were sweet like Faith. None of them were as good as Faith. None of them were her.

But girls were girls and I was weak, I admit it. These girls were pretty and smiling and made up gorgeous and eager to please.

I may have been taken but I wasn't dead or numb to them rubbing against me all at once. I'd never been with more than one girl at a time. I mean, that was just something you read about in Hustler when you were tired of looking at the pictures. But here were all these girls trying to get a hold of me at once. It threw me off. It gave me ideas. Bad ideas.

"Who are you girls?" I asked and laughed and they told me their names but I didn't know them, but they all knew who I was.

"How do you know me?" I asked and could not stop smiling.

I felt stupid but they all looked very serious and intent on making me.

"You're Mike, Mike Kilo," they said as they petted my cowhide rancher coat.

"How do you know that?"

"You're the guy who got in that huge fight at Homecoming with the whole football team at Sand Creek. You're Bleacher Girl's boyfriend."

"I am. I am! See? I'm taken," I said to them and tried to snake my arms away from their hands and their grasp.

"Mike! You asshole! Look!" Jeff interrupted my struggles with the girls.

I pulled away from the ladies abruptly and saw Jeff point at a maroon Buick Regal cruising slowly by, crunching across the snowy blacktop. I could make out Allison's face in the front passenger window but didn't see Faith, my Bleacher Girl. She was probably in the back, I told myself as I started to jog after the car, my heart thrumming fast in my chest.

"Sorry ladies," I called back to them and looked to see them pouting.

But when I turned to keep jogging after the Buick, I ran right into another girl and nearly knocked her down.

"Oh man, sorry," I said as I grabbed her by her fake fur coat and kept her from falling. Then I looked down at her face.

"Hi Mike," she smiled and flashed that gap in her front teeth and made me wince.

"Hi, Vanessa."

Vanessa, the giver of the toothy blowjobs.

Chapter Nineteen

"Hi Mike, lookin' good even though you look kinda bad," she said as she righted herself back up on her two feet in the slippery slush the snow had become on top of the shiny blacktop.

The snow pelted down harder now and the temperatures were dropping steadily. The flakes were beginning to pile up on the blacktop and from the looks of the white night sky, it wasn't going to quit any time soon. The flakes gusted in the wind that blasted us randomly in the backs of our legs. Everyone had steam coming out of their mouths as they laughed and talked all around the bonfire.

Vanessa took her time looking at my face. She tried to bring the smoke show with her dark eyes lined in thick black and her huge moussed bangs and dark mane of teased hair. But it had absolutely no power over me. I smiled at her when I realized I didn't miss her at all anymore; especially her teeth scraping the head of my dick. I'd have to see if I could to get Faith down there and see how she did but anything Faith did would be better than Vanessa and her horrible gapped teeth. There was no hurry. But there was a hurry to get away from this bad blast from the past.

"Hi Nessa," I said to her and tried to get around her now that she was standing on her own feet.

The Buick was parking! The Buick was parking, I repeated to myself and stepped around Vanessa once more. She knew what she was doing and grinned at me. I didn't care, my Bleacher Girl was here! Boys' Night was about to collide with Girl's Night and I was bouncing on my feet as I watched Jennifer get out of the driver side door, and then Allison and her huge blonde hair got out of the passenger side.

"Who you looking for Mike?" Vanessa said from next to me.

I was vaguely aware of her pulling a green pack of cigarettes out of her coat pocket and heard her snap her zippo and light it.

"My girlfriend," I said without looking over at her.

"That him?" she asked smartly and nodded her head towards the Buick.

I turned and saw Allison pull up the passenger seat and I watched as a guy in a bright multi-colored ski jacket got out the back of the car. He had gold highlights in his sprayed hair and his jeans were frosty blue.

"What a fag," Vanessa said as she blew out a long stream of smoke from next to me.

"There she is," I breathed as I saw Faith's tiny hand grip the side of the car and start to pull herself up and out.

"Who's she?"

"My girl. What the heck?"

I watched for two seconds as the guy with the frosted hair reached down and took Faith's hand and pulled her up and out of the car. He ran his hand down the back of her pink puffer coat and pulled her into him as he shut the door to the car.

"Nope."

I took off running across the slick parking lot, past all the kids with their backs to the lot, unaware of what was going on behind them as they squeezed as close to the bonfire as they could, and towards the dude putting his hands on my girl.

"Nope!" I chuffed as I breathed hard and almost closed the space when Jeff grabbed me from one side and Shane from the other.

"Nope is right bro!" Jeff said and laughed loud as he pulled me backwards.

"Dude!" Shane breathed hard from next to him. "So. Not. Worth. It."

He was out of breath but not grabbing me. But Jeff gripped me hard and pulled me into a half nelson and wasn't letting go.

"Let me go!" I snarled at him and he loosened up a little bit.

I tried to shake him off me but he outweighed me and I couldn't get him off me. When Faith and the frosty headed dude turned around and saw me, I yanked my arm, the one in the cast, away from Jeff and ran. I drew it back as I went.

"NO! MIKE! NO!" Faith shrieked and pushed in between me and my fist before it connected with that asshole's tan face.

I slammed on the brakes fast when I saw Faith's beautiful eyes wide open in fear looking up at me.

I kept from socking her but I reached over her shoulder and jabbed the guy in the shoulder hard with my plaster casted fist and rattled him a good one. He was more than a head taller than me but I didn't care. Being small wasn't nothing new to me.

"What you think you're doin', buddy?" I hollered at him over Faith's shoulder.

"Faith? Who is this guy?" he asked her. His voice shook.

"Pussy! Puttin' your hands on my woman! What the fuck you think you're doing? I'm gonna fuckin' kill you right now!" I spit at him.

"Mike! NO! This is my cousin Tad!"

"What?" I asked her and laughed at the guy's name.

"This is my cousin! Don't hit him!"

"Your cousin?" I asked as I pulled her away from the guy and wrapped my arms around her tight.

He smelled like some fruity cologne. He was nasty. Tan. Frosted hair sprayed stiff. White leather high-tops. Bright geometric shapes covered his puffy jacket. I wanted to kill him.

"Who is this guy, Faith?" her cousin asked in a dramatic voice.

"This is my boyfriend, Mike and Mike, this is my cousin Tad." Faith snapped and pulled away from me as she shot me a hot glare that made me want to play nice for now.

I stared at the guy and held out my left hand, the one that wasn't in a cast, and dared him to take it. When he did, I crunched it in my much bigger hand and shook it hard as I glared up at him.

"Hey Mike, who are your friends?"

Vanessa draped her arm around me and rested her chin on my shoulder as she exhaled smoke towards a visibly disgusted Faith. I hated to see Faith's face pinched up like that but I admired her lack of fear of Vanessa. Faith waved the smoke away and then looked away as she tried to comb the snowflakes out of her hair. I wanted to do it for her. I wanted to kiss every single one of them away but I wasn't brave enough to touch her while she was glaring at me like that. But all the same, her temper turned me on and made me smile and smile I did. I'd get her back. Angry or not she'd be in my arms before the night was over. I was certain of it and I licked my lips at the thought of it.

"Nessa, this is my girlfriend Faith, and her cousin," I said, while removing Vanessa's arm from around me, without taking my eyes off Faith.

I slipped out from under Vanessa but was too scared to touch Faith and have her reject me in front of everyone. She had a hot temper and I didn't want to send her running. But I wanted to stake my claim on her. She was mine and I was eager to get my hands on her but I knew that right now, she wasn't having it.

"Who's that?" Faith countered back to me and I felt horrible in my heart to hear the quiver in her words.

"No one, just and old girlfriend."

"Mike, you're still a dick!" Vanessa screeched and punched me hard in the arm but I didn't care.

As long as she wasn't scratching my face, like some girls tended to do, not that I'd ever had it done to me, but I'd seen it done a lot. As long as she wasn't doing that, or crying, God forbid, I was good and didn't care.

"I'm lucky to still have my dick after you," I muttered as I got between her and Faith. I didn't want her anywhere near my baby. My baby was not a rough girl like Vanessa.

"This is what happens when boys are around," Allison

sneered and rolled her eyes at all of us.

"No kidding!" Jennifer snapped and yanked herself away from Jeff. "No boys allowed!"

"Hey," Shane said, "if it's Girls Night Out, and no boys allowed, what's this asshole doing with you?"
Jeff and Shane didn't like this frosty-haired douche hanging out with their girls anymore than I did. Jeff looked ready to put him down. He squared up to the guy and demanded to know why he was there.

I caught a glare from Faith for smiling at it all but couldn't stop. It was funny. Especially when Shane took a step towards the guy and said, "Maybe he thinks he's a girl!"

"Maybe he's mackin' on our women!" Jeff threw in.

He was edging towards Faith's cousin Tad as the sky continued to dump snow on us faster and faster.

"Mike," Faith pleaded with me from around her cousin. "Stop this!"

"Stop this? I'm not doing anything!" I laughed. It was the wrong thing to say according to her face.

"Everywhere you go is a fist fight!" Jennifer yelled at me as Jeff squared up to a very shocked and frightened Tad.

"I'm gonna knock that lip gloss right off your mouth, boy!"

Jeff was losing his temper and tensed to lunge at the guy who was stupid enough to answer.

"I'm not wearing any lip gloss!" he spat in a panic.
I looked from his mouth, to Faith's, to Jennifer's, then to Allison's.

"Look," I said and pointed at Allison.

"What?" Jeff asked.

He didn't get it but Shane did. He got it real quick and Allison was his girl. He was a blur towards Tad, But Tad was pretty fast himself and stayed out of his reach. Shane was so great in a fistfight, I thought to myself but he couldn't catch up with this dude at all. He had proven how good he was in the fight against the football team at Sand Creek and I was looking forward to watching him pound the guy who had the balls to get in the backseat with my woman, even if he was her cousin.

Shane finally got a hold of him by his coat and got two hard hits on his mouth, fast. By the way he was cracking knuckles on Tad, it looked like he had healed up completely and had gas in the tank! I shook my head and hooted to see Tad trying to protect his face and not even throwing any punches. I roared with laughter until I saw the look of horror on Faith's face.

"Come on," I grabbed Jeff, "help me stop this killing."

He reluctantly helped me hold onto Shane and keep him from going after the guy, who was now running circles around the Buick and crying and trying to get in.

"She let me borrow her lipgloss because my lips were chapped!" Tad screeched as he slid around in the snow and ran towards the bonfire to get away from Shane.

"Awww Shane, you made him cry for cryin' out loud," Jeff said and tried to sound like he cared but he too was cracking up. It was funny.

"COPS!" We heard Allison yell and we all broke apart.

I grabbed Faith by the hand and pulled her across the snowy asphalt towards her car with me, and Jeff followed. Shane grabbed Allison and yanked her towards Jennifer's car. Tad, the crying cousin stood there wiping his face in the snow until Faith yelled at him to come with us, which set me growling.

But I didn't have time to fight about it. Shane and I did not need more run-ins with the cops. I shuttled Faith around the front of the car fast and into the front passenger seat. Jeff had my door open and the seat forward and shoved Tad into the back and piled in fast behind him.

"Where we going?" Jennifer shouted at us across the parking lot as kids all around the bonfire scrambled to get their snow-covered cars started and get out of there before the cops started arresting people.

"Pizza Hut!" Jeff called back to her as I started the little car and got us out of there.

Chapter Twenty

Pizza Hut was packed but they wanted our rowdy group out of the waiting area fast so they opened up the back room they used for private parties like at Christmas time. They put us in a round booth all crammed in tight with an extra chair for Tad, all alone on the outside. Faith and I sat in the middle, tight against each other, even though she wasn't speaking to me yet, and she wasn't wasn't looking at me either.

I made sure to press my leg up against hers and when she didn't move away, I knew it was going to be okay. She was my girl. All mine and I put my hand on top of her jeans and held it there, her thigh soft and supple in tight Jordache jeans under my hand.

Everyone else was pink-cheeked and chatty and excited about the cops and the bonfire and the snow and finding each other. Jeff and Jennifer and Allison and Shane were chatting and cuddling and being cute in the booth. Poor Tad all on his own and Faith and I quiet; me smiling, my face burning from the warmth of the restaurant and my hand on top of Faith's leg, so close to heaven.

I began to squeeze her leg gently. I squeezed it on every other word I said to the waitress.

"We need at least two pitchers of Pepsi and some breadsticks to start us off, right guys?" I asked everyone as they looked at their menus and nodded and said, yes, that sounded good as they pulled cash from their purses and pockets to make sure they had enough. Faith and I, and Tad too, were the only ones not scrambling for cash.

Everything would be fine. I squeezed my girl's leg and began to rub it just a little. I looked at her to see how she liked it but she was looking everywhere but at me and all I could see of her face was her cute little nose and her long eyelashes. So, I rubbed her higher on her thigh. She shifted a little. But she didn't take my hand away.

The pitchers of Pepsi came and Allison and Jennifer filled the red plastic glasses and passed them to everyone. The waitress forgot a glass for Tad and was summoned back. Jeff and Shane grinned behind their straws at it all and Faith looked miffed. I made sure when the breadsticks came that Tad got the first one. By the time they came to the middle of the table there were only three left. I made sure Faith got one and gave the other two to Allison and Shane.

I squeezed Faith's leg as if to say, hey see, I'm nice! She dipped her breadstick in sauce and asked me if I wanted a bite. Of course I did! I let her feed me while my hand never left her leg. By the time the pizzas came, my hand was rubbing the inside of her thigh. The heat on my fingers was intense. I squeezed and rubbed and rubbed and squeezed and ate with my broken arm. Faith shifted a little and then pressed her leg harder into mine as she spread them open.

I rubbed closer and closer to what we guys called Nirvana. My fingers sought her heat but I didn't go there. I went close but not all the way. She squirmed every time I got close. She squirmed until she bumped my fingers just a little.

I wanted to touch her there. But not with everyone around. I ate countless slices of pizza. We ordered two more pans! And two more pitchers as well!

Tad kept checking his watch.

"Who wears a watch on a Friday night?" Jeff asked and laughed but only Allison and Jennifer laughed with him.

I was with Tad; keeping an eye on the time. I was ready to go but it had nothing to do with curfew or any of the things punks like him worried about.

"Faith?" I asked her.

We hadn't talked the entire time and I hoped she would answer me.

"What?" she asked as she dabbed her lips with her napkin and looked up at me with her big eyes.

"When you gotta be home?"

"I don't know. Why?"

"Well." And here I was stuck. This was opening me up for rejection right here, in front of the whole table and the waitress to boot.

"Mom and Garret went dancing," she piped up, her voice going up on the end of it.
I looked over at her, my hand still between her legs, on the inside softness of her thigh.

"Is that right?" I asked, wondering where this was going.

"Yes, over in Brookworth at the new Marriott Gardens Plaza."

"Oh. Nice."

"Yeah, they won't be back till tomorrow."

"Ok kids, we gotta bail, here's $25 for me and Faith and some tip, let us up!" I said to Allison who was right next to me. Shane, a true brother if there ever was one was already up out of the booth and pulling his woman out too, so Faith and I could slide out and go.

"We're out too!" Shane said and threw a twenty on the table. "Get the rest," he said to Jeff and Tad and started helping Allison get her coat on.

Shane and I had places to go and things to do. Where he did his things, I had no idea. It was not my worry. I was thankful I had a clean, warm, private and quiet apartment to take my girl to and she didn't have to be home until early tomorrow.

"Hey! What about me?" Tad whined as I held the door open for Faith and felt a cold blast of wind and snow gust in on us.
He was not my concern.

Bleacher Girl was.

Chapter Twenty-One

I needed a smoke but we were in Faith's car with me behind the wheel driving us carefully through the deep snow. The car's little tires made muffled munching sounds as the treads gripped the snowy road on our way home. I drove careful. Girls tended to get scared in the snow. It was everything I could do to not run through the gears and absolutely blast us across town to my apartment as fast as possible. That car could have handled the snow. We would have been fine. What's wrong with sliding a little? Sliding was fun. At least to me. But she might not have liked it. My mind was going one hundred miles an hour as it were. But I needed to be careful.

Girls were sensitive. They scared easy. They were fragile. At least Faith was. And I wanted to keep her that way. Fragile was okay with me as long as I kept her safe. Fragile was ok as long as it didn't mean untouchable. Because I wanted to touch her as many times as I could tonight, and we were going to have all night. I shivered as these thoughts skated around and around in my brain as I slid the little car up against the curb in front of my apartment house, nice and tight and killed the little engine. I ran around to her side of the car, opened the door and pulled her out.

We kissed as soon as we got into my apartment, as soon as the door was shut and the bolts all thrown. Her hands in my hair, my hands all over her body, under that puffer coat. She was warm and soft and she squealed when I touched her with my cold hands under her sweater. We left the lights off. We left the blinds open and the moonlight came through, reflected off the falling snow.

We kissed in my hall. We kissed in my bedroom. We kissed standing up as Faith rubbed herself against me.

"You got me so," she trailed off as she rubbed against me as

I chased her tongue with my lips. I needed it back in my mouth.

"I got you what, baby?" I asked her as I tried to get a grip on her and pull her back closer to me.

"So, you know, at the pizza place, rubbing me, got me so," she said and kissed my neck.

She pulled me down to her height and kissed me behind my ear and drove me wild.

"How'd I do that?" I asked her playfully.

"You know. Rubbin' me," she whispered in my ear. Her voice was husky and I pulled back from her a little to look at her. She shocked me.

"You're not mad at me, baby?" I asked her as she nibbled my ear, her small hands on the side of my face made me ripple in trembles all over.

"No. About what?" she asked and rubbed her lips across mine and licked my top lip and sent my eyes rolling back into my head in pleasure.

I shivered again as she danced her fingertips across my scalp and through my hair.

"I love your hair so much, Mike."

"Ahhh, I love you loving my hair."

"I want to rub my boobs on it."

"You what?" I pulled away from her and laughed.

"It's so soft," she sighed.

"I got something else you can rub your boobs on," I said to her.

She walked right into that one. It was that easy and I couldn't stop smiling.

"Oh yeah?" she asked, still touching my hair.

"Yeah, baby," I told her and ground up against her. "And it's not soft!"

"Oh Mike!"

She squealed my favorite words in the world and I would do everything I could to get her to say them again and again. We had all night and I grinned like the big bad wolf himself as I looked her. She looked delicious and I wanted to eat every inch of her. She had no idea the thoughts that howled and thumped in my brain, rabid and wild. She smiled up at me with her eyes wide and sparkling and her little girl charm turned me on even more; turned me into a beast and I leapt on her.

"Oh Mike!"

The first one squealed out and all I'd done is push her down on her back on my bed.

"Put your hands above your head," I told her.

"Is this a stick-up?" she giggled and raised her hands above her head and rested them on the pile of pillows.

"Something's sticking up," I growled in her ear as I lowered myself down on top of her.

"Oh Mike!" She squirmed under me and squeaked.

The second 'oh Mike'. I was gonna lose count but I was never going to get tired of hearing it.

I smiled to myself as I lifted her sweater up over her jijggling tits and dove in face first between them. She was so warm and soft and there was so much of her to explore. I wanted to kiss every inch of her. The deeper I dove, the better she smelled. Cotton, soap, sweet perfume, sweat, everything good in the world resided right there between those two big soft boobs. I squeezed them from the sides and smashed them against my face.

"Oh Mike your beard is making me crazy!"
I paused in my tasting her cleavage to smile again.

"You know where you'd really like it?"

"Where?" she asked but I think she knew where because here she slowly spread her legs apart.

"Right here!" I grabbed her by the waist of her jeans, right above the zipper.

"Oh my!" she gasped.

"Oh my what?" I asked her and looked her in the eyes.

"You aren't ever scared of anything. You're the bravest

person I know."

"Scared of what, baby?" I asked her because I wanted to hear all the ways she thought I was brave. It turned me on to hear her praise me.

"You're never scared to do what you want," she told me and she licked her lips.

"Never. I do what needs done."

"And you say it."

"Say what, baby?" I asked her as I lowered myself on top of her and pinned her wrists down on the pillows and made her gasp. I smiled at her and came close to her face.

"You say whatever you want. You're never scared to say anything, everything."

That wasn't all the way true. Right now I was on fire with passion for her and I wanted to tell her that but didn't know how to say it so she would feel the power of it. I was also scared of letting her know all the ways I burned for her. I was scared of giving her all my power to hold and I squeezed her wrists twice at my lack of words to say.

But I could show her my passion for her. I could show her how I burned for her. And I did with her pinned on her back. I loved kissing her that way. I loved how she wiggled under me in frustration of not being able to get her arms free and not being able to touch me.

She was going to kill me if I kept going this slow but I wanted to make sure she was ready for me before I took her clothes off. I was so ready to go, I wouldn't be able to hold off once she was naked and oh I needed her naked now.

I let go of her wrists and yanked her sweater up the rest of the way up over her head fast. Her hair crackled and flew from static and I tossed the sweater across the room as blue sparks flew from it. She lay below me, busting out of the bottom of her white cotton bra. I yanked at the middle of it but couldn't get the front clasp to open. I smacked at her hands playfully when she tried to help and then I pulled the whole thing over her head against her protests and then the whole thing ripped in two. I threw it as well and she tried to sit up and see what happened to it.

"Grrrrrr!" I pinned her back down by her wrists and stared at her beautiful naked breasts. Her nipples hardened quick in the open air.

I kicked the radiator without letting her go and smiled as it began to clink and hiss. I didn't want my girl too cold. But those hard nipples were looking delicious. I licked my lips and began to suck one as Faith bucked in pleasure underneath me.

I held on as long as I could about taking her jeans off but I could smell her. The crotch of her jeans was hot and damp under my fingers and I realized she has soaked through her panties and had gone on to soak through the denim of her jeans too. She had to be soaked and slick and ready and I couldn't wait to find out. Once her jeans and panties were pulled off, I spread her legs wide, unzipped my jeans and pulled them down to my knees and plunged deep into her. Feeling her naked under me, soft breasts with their hard nipples pressing against me, I couldn't hold on long at all.

"Mike, oh Mike," she panted and wrapped her legs around me and sent me over the edge and I lost my control.

But I had a lot of lead left in my pencil and was ready to go again immediately. I flipped her over on her on her belly and wound her hair around my fist and pulled.

"What are you doing?" she demanded and the tremble in her voice drove me crazy, I barely heard her for the blood pounding in my ears.

"Mike, you're scaring me!"
I froze. I heard that.

"You want me to stop?" I asked and caught my breath and started to let go of her hair. I stopped moving inside her and gritted my teeth to hold on to myself as I slowly pulled out.

"No. You can do it. I like it, I think."

She said it in such a small voice. I couldn't pull her hair after hearing that small voice even if she said it was ok. Even if it turned me on, even if it woke up some wolf inside me, I couldn't do it. I unwound her hair and I straightened it out over her bare back. I rubbed her small back lightly and then I squeezed her ass that was up in the air with both of my hands as the wolf in me panted and waited to get what he wanted.

"We do it like this then, ok?" I whispered up near her ear as I slowly entered her again.

She nodded her answer with her cheek against the pillow and I began long, slow strokes inside her till she was saying "Oh Mike," over and over.

"Oh Faith, Faith, Faith," I chanted as sweat soaked my hair.

The pressure built up in her which made it build up in me till I was whispering her name over and over on ever pump. This time we both let go at the same time.

We took a breather and made a pitcher of cherry kool-aid and each chugged a glass in the kitchen. Faith wrapped herself up in the sheet and I threw on my shorts, to not be weird. Then we tried to do it on the broken kitchen table. The wobbly table threw me off my rhythm so I picked her up and set on the counter under the tin pie cabinets. We banged so hard against them, the old flower sifter broke off and a cloud of white flour exploded in a soft puff around us like it was snowing inside. Faith didn't complain about slamming into the cabinet but I knew that soft skin would have a bruise the next day and I felt bad and I kissed her there on her bare back before I carried her back to bed and lay down next to her. But we weren't there long.

"I'm hungry," she said with her face tucked into my chest, her breath tickled the hair I had there.

Back to the kitchen we went and I watched her eat a bowl of Froot Loops. She made them look really good but they were the last of the cereal in the house so I told her I wasn't hungry. But I was. But I ignored it and instead I feasted on her kisses in the hall as I pushed her against the wall.

This time; the energy, the passion, doubled. Every bit of it was more intense than all the other times. I felt desperate to bring her to the edge. I felt desperate to give her everything I had as I rose up on my toes, my knees against the wall, her legs wrapped around me, and me holding her up off the floor.

I knew it was worth the effort by the way the sweat ran down the sides of her face. I held nothing back. I buried my face in her neck. I pumped her hard, maybe too hard because she let out a whimper. When she did that, I paused to look at her, to make sure she was going to be ok. She stared back into my eyes with her own uncertain ones.

It was that look; innocence, love, passion, all of it hit me right in the heart and I lost control and let go of everything in me. As she cried my name, I heard the weakness in her voice. She scratched my back with her nails, the frantic things she couldn't say, as I held her against the wall with her legs wrapped around me.

She cried out my name on every thrust; her voice broke until she was hoarse and panting double-time. I laughed once, under my breath but it wasn't funny. I felt her clench on me every pump and then she wailed my name again. It shook the window panes, I swear.

"Ok baby?" I whispered to her as she flung all that beautiful hair around.

"Yes, Mike, yes!" she panted and gripped my shoulders frantically where she hung on to me, clung to me.

I pumped her deeper till she shuddered once more.
I lost track how many times we did it that night. But that time against the wall left her completely shattered. She fell apart in my arms. I was left breathing hard from the exertion and from the feeling that I'd gotten rid of something horrible inside that had needed to come out; something that had nothing to do with sex. Like I had shed some horrible greasy smelling old coat that took something dark from around my heart as it left.

Before that last time was over, I let go many things I didn't even know I had inside of me. Dark things. Things that flew out of me like bats.

I carried her to the bed and brought her a clean towel and a glass of kool-aid and tucked her in tight under all the blankets and quilts, right up close to the radiator. I crawled in close to her and held in my arms, naked and soft all over. Every inch of her felt so soft. She was so beautiful with her face relaxed in bliss and exhaustion. I wrapped my arms around her tight and held her close, her head tucked under my chin. I couldn't stop kissing her hair.

"You're so lucky to have your own place," she told me.

I didn't have anything to say to that. It didn't feel like luck. It felt kind of desperate, me living here alone and so young. It was small but it was better than the couch at my parents. It was warm and I was thankful for that because I had slept in my car a few times in my life when I needed to get away from home, before I moved out, and there was nothing colder than sleeping in a car. The radiators here worked overtime and sometimes it got so hot I'd strip down to my shorts but I never complained. I'd crack a window and smoke a cigarette and stare off into the tree-tops or down at the yard but I never complained about too much heat.

"I haven't been feeling lucky lately," I said and laughed but it wasn't funny.

"Why so?"

"Wrecked my car. Broke my arm. Failing school. Lost a couple of jobs."

I stopped there. I was starting to sound really pathetic and weak.

"It's ok. I'll be ok. I'll find another car. And I'll get more time at the tire plant."

I shrugged it all off. I kept thinking about the money from mom and dad that would be coming in every month and how much of a relief it was and I hated it. It made me hate them more than I already did.

"You have so much to take care of on your own."
She reached over and began to stroke my arm above the cast and it felt amazing to just be touched by her.

"Yup."

"Will you be able to do it all?"
Stroke up. Stroke down.

"Sure. I always do."

She stopped touching me. She looked really concerned, like she pitied me. That made me smile a huge one, a real one. She didn't need to pity me. I'd been through much worse.

"Babe, I'll be fine. I've been on my own a while."

"I'll help you with your school. Let me help you."

"That's ok. I can do it on my own."

I knew immediately it was the wrong thing to say. It was so wrong, she instantly had tears popping up and dripping down the sides of her face and into her hair from where she flopped over on her back.

"Oh baby, I can do it on my own but I could really use your help. That'd be great. I'd love your help. I'd probably fuck it all up without your help. Honey, will you help me catch up with my school work?"

I was on top of her so fast and had my good arm around her and I used the fingers on my broken arm to gently wipe the tears off her face.

"Oh Bleacher Girl, my sweet girl, I'm such an idiot."

"No you're not."

She looked up at me with those big blue eyes. But she had stopped crying. Thank God for that. I never liked girls crying but when it usually happened, we were usually parked in front of their place and it was because I'd just broken up with them. Then I could scoot them out of my car and get away and go back to my apartment, which I always made sure that they never knew where I lived.

I didn't want to get away from Faith. And I never wanted to

make her cry again ever.

"I am the biggest idiot, baby."
I kissed her forehead.

"You're very smart. You live on your own and you're just a kid."

"I don't feel like a kid."

I sat and thought about that for a little while.
I didn't feel like a kid. I felt like a man who still had to go to school. And I was lucky I was still allowed at school, at any school, with all the trouble I'd been in and bad grades I got. I sighed with thinking about school and how far behind I was.

"I feel like a man. A man on my own," I told her.

"Why do you live on your own? When did you move here?"
I chose to answer her last question because it was easiest.

"I moved out on my seventeenth birthday last March. My gift to me." I smiled at her again but she didn't smile back.

I wanted to reach over and grab a smoke off the TV tray but I had a rule that I never smoked in bed and I especially didn't want to smoke near Faith all her delicate skin and beautiful hair. I always worried about setting the place on fire.

"But why would you move out? What do your mom and dad have to say about it?"

She asked two questions again but now both of them were unpleasant. I guess they weren't so difficult to answer because the truth was the truth was the truth as they say. But it wasn't the kind of thing I wanted to tell Faith. So I didn't say anything and hoped she fell asleep or even better, maybe she'd want to have sex again.

"Mike," she nudged me and ducked out from under my chin.

"Huh?"

"Why?" she asked, and then she kissed my chin.
That was what got me talking. That gentle kiss on my chin, on the stubble growing there.

"I moved out to get away from my parents. They're not

good people. I was done being a part of it. I needed to not be there anymore. I couldn't live there anymore. I don't care what they think about anything anymore."

"Why not?"

"It was a bad place to be. There wasn't room for me."

"Is your house small?"

"This is my house."

That came out meaner than I ever wanted to talk to Faith. I squeezed her shoulders and tried it again. I glanced at her to make sure I hadn't made her cry again. She was ok. She looked a little shocked but she wasn't crying.

"This is my house," I said softer.

"Oh."

"That house on Robin Court, is their house. It was never my house."

"What do you mean?"

"Well. Um it's complicated. I really need a smoke."

"Ok. Have one."

"I don't smoke in bed."

"Where do you smoke?"

"The kitchen."

I could have gone again, could have had sex again, and would have rather done that than talk. I had a lot of gas in the tank. I was seventeen. Faith was eighteen but she was a girl. Girls weren't like us guys, I thought to myself and smiled as I helped her wrap up in a blanket so she could follow me into the kitchen, so I could smoke, so I could answer her questions. Girls liked to talk. Maybe it was time to tell someone. She was the best someone I knew to tell.

I slipped on my shorts and led her out in my little hall and over into the kitchen. We kept the lights off and I took her to one of the chairs next to the radiator that was clinking hard and fast and kicking out a furious heat while I cracked the window open an inch and sat on the back of the chair next to it. But it felt too tall so I got down and began to pace the room as I smoked.

"What did you want to know?" I asked her in the dim light of the kitchen as I filled a pot with water and set it on the burner and turned up the flame.

"Why did you move out?" she asked quietly.

"Ah yes, that," I said with the cigarette clinched between my lips as I pulled 2 mugs down from the cabinet.
I had one girl mug that had purple flowers and the other mug said Hudson Grain on it, that'd be for me.

"Well like I said, that house wasn't big enough for me. I had Mom and Dennis upstairs in their room. And Dad and Linda downstairs in the basement. There was no place for me to go," I told her as I pulled the tin of cocoa powder out of the cabinet and the sugar bowl too and began to scoop them into the mugs.

"Is it ok if I make this without milk? I don't feel like heating it. It's a pain to do and not scorch it."

"Sure, Mike, any way you want, baby."

Baby. It sent warm chills through me. I felt my ears heat up along with other things. She was too cute there naked and pink faced all wrapped up in my gray blanket.

"Didn't you have a bedroom upstairs?"

"Nope."

"Only one bedroom in your house?"

"No," I said as I turned to look at the pot of water to see if it was boiling yet.

"Then why couldn't you have your own room? Were there other kids?"

"No," I said and smiled with my back turned to her. "I wish there had been other kids. If there had been, I might have stayed," I said as I thought about it and blew out a stream of smoke into the warm room.

"Why?"

"To take care of them. Make sure they didn't get hurt."

I turned and looked at her to make sure she was warm, to

make sure she really wanted to hear this. She looked beautiful and pure. Her cheeks shone pink in the dark room and her eyes were huge with curiosity.

"What if they were brats?" she asked and giggled.

"No," I shook my head slowly, "kids aren't really ever brats. Kids are just kids."

She stared at me a while before she asked her next question.

"What was in that room that you couldn't sleep in it?"

"Mom's stuff," I said and shrugged and turned back to the pot.

"What kind of stuff?"

"Oh you know, mom crap. Sewing machine. Old dining room chairs. Laundry baskets full of stuff. Old phones. Broken record player. Christmas stuff. The tree and things like that. Just a lot of crap. Some phone books and puzzles and Dennis' Harley, just the body, not the wheels."

"Wow."

"The other bedroom was where Dennis was trying to grow pot but it never grew. He didn't know what he was doing. I tried to help him. I told him those red lights wouldn't grow anything. Made him mad."

"Growing pot?"

"Yeh and marigolds. He thought marigolds would get him high."

"Did any of it grow?"

"No. He grew mold. That's it. I used to have this cough all the time. Mom thought I was smoking too much. But it was all the mold." I smiled at the memory of how stupid I was. Looking back, it felt bad and it felt good too.

"Water's boiling."

I poured the water into the two cups and started stirring it.

"No, no sit down, I'll bring it to you," I told her and took her the flowery cup. "Be careful," I told her and watched her lower her eyes and then blow on it.

She was so beautiful. So perfect. She never swore. She never got mad at me. She was 'oh Mike' about everything. Well. She did get mad at me but she never yelled. And she never stayed mad. And she never looked hideous or acted like a bitch.

I'd never had a girl back to my place. I didn't want them to know where I lived. It was easier that way. A man could have some peace and quiet that way. In the car was good enough. But now here she was in my apartment with her hair in tangles, fuzzed and frizzed, and standing up all messed up and looking sexy wrapped in my blanket. My bed was going to have all her smells in it. This was getting serious and I was scared, to be honest.

We drank our cocoa in silence and then she asked another question.

"So what pushed you out? What made you leave?"
I sipped the hot cocoa and glanced out the window to see the snow still coming down in large wet flakes as I thought back to last Spring.

"Hmmm, let me think," I told her and reached over the table for the pack of smokes.
She waited while I lit another one and got it going. She held her cocoa with two hands and watched me.

"Well," I finally said, "let's see. I was getting bad hurt constantly. Dennis was always beating on me while Mom watched. He threw me off the deck and broke my arm. This arm as a matter of fact," I said and held up my cast. "It's been broke three times now. The other two times by family. But before that, Dad kicked the shit, sorry, crap, out of me several times too. My Mom slapped me around all the time. Then she'd get tired of hitting me and have Dennis whale on me." I shrugged.

"Why?"
"Why?"
"Yes why? Why in the world would anyone hit you?"
"I don't know. I was a bad kid I guess."
"What'd you do?"

"Everything. I was dating girls nonstop one right after the next," I said without thinking and then looked at her to see how she reacted to that.

She looked a little hurt but she also looked interested so I continued.

"And I wrecked a couple of cars. And I got in a few fights. A scrape with the cops. I threw a chair at a coach."

"Why?"

I sipped my cocoa and thought about it.

"I was mad."

"What'd he do?"

"Nothing. Cut me from the team."

"That made you mad enough to throw a chair at him? I can see that, I guess."

"Naww," I sighed. "I wasn't really mad at him. I was mad at my dad, and at my mom too."

It looked different now, months away from it, as I looked back on it. I saw it in my mind like a bad movie with a horrible ending, but I wouldn't have taken any of it back. None of it. I shut my eyes to figure out what to tell her and how to say it.

"I smashed up my car," I finally said. Everything bad started with smashing up that car. "It was a '67 Mustang that barely ran. An old man hit me head on. He'd had a stroke and couldn't help it. That was the beginning," I told her. I shut my eyes and continued,

"And dad was taking me to and from practice. It was good for a couple of weeks. He'd never done anything like that. But then he showed up one night and I could smell it soon as I opened the door. He was drunk as hell. I asked him to let me drive. But of course he wouldn't. And he wanted to drive around and talk to me about stuff."

Here I stopped talking. I drank my cocoa but it suddenly tasted fake. Flat. Horrible. I dumped it down the sink and rinsed the cup. I took Faith's cup from her and did the same.

"What happened?" she asked.

She was behind me now as I rinsed the cups. Her hand on

my shoulder, one arm around my waist. She smelled like me and her combined and I set the cups down and breathed it in.

"Dad wanted to know how to get Mom back. I didn't know what to say. And then the next thing I remember he was driving faster and faster on the curves around Hodson Park and we hit a tree. I went through the windshield."

"Oh my God!"

"Yeh." I nodded my head. It was a lot of noise and light and cold air and pain all over. I could remember all of it like it was yesterday. I flew through the windshield because Dad had cut the belt on that side years ago when it had gotten stuck. I didn't tell Faith any of that but as I remembered it, a shudder ran through me and she squeezed me tight. Two windshields in a row; my own and then Dad's. No wonder my nose was so jacked and big.

"I got kicked off the team for missing practices because I was in the hospital getting my nose worked on. I had to have it done twice. That's how messed up it was. It was shattered. And then I got kicked out of school because I threw the chair at him. I'm lucky it didn't hit him or he would have seen me in jail, I'm sure. I haven't seen him since."

Here I gulped. It was all horrible. She'd probably never talk to me again after this. That coach was the only teacher I'd liked, ever and here I was telling Faith how I'd thrown a chair at him like some spoiled pyscho. I waited for her to move away from me but she still had her arm around my waist, her face pressed against my back.

"Then what happened?"

"I got kicked out of school and started up at my new school. And then Dennis threw me off the deck and broke my arm. He called the cops on me after he threw me."

"Is that why you moved out? Wrestling, school, mom's boyfriend?" she asked quietly.

"Yes, and all the other."

"The no bedroom? You poor thing, sleeping on the couch."

"Yes, that and all the ER visits for concussions and broken bones. It all added up. The worst were getting clobbered while I slept on the couch. Mom did those. Well, Dennis did too. Linda, Dad's girlfriend never hit me. But she was creepy."
Faith didn't say anything.

So I continued.

"I had the job at Kahmir's and I was doing odd jobs for my Grandma who lived out on the edge of town near route 48 over by the drive-in," I explained to Faith but she didn't seem like she understood.

"I did odd jobs for her and she always paid me too much," I continued.

Faith nodded. She looked sleepy so I wrapped it up quick.

"I asked to move in with her. She said it was a bad idea. She gave me the money for the deposit on the apartment. She's the one who gave me the idea to move out. She made me feel like she didn't want me."

That last part sounded pathetic. I hoped Faith wasn't disgusted by it.

"Do you still see her? Do you still work for her?" she asked and sounded hopeful.

"No. She had a stroke. She's in a home kinda by you, over in Sand Creek."

This was all a big bummer. I didn't want to talk about it anymore. It was too many problems that I just wanted to go away. And most of them had gone away, because I had moved away from them. Or so I thought. Now I had new problems that were all on me, caused by me. The totaled car. My broken arm. School. Jobs. It was too much.

Faith noticed the change in me and she held my hand and took me back to bed where she pushed me in first, up against the radiator and then she climbed in and nearly got on top of me.

"I love you, a bushel and a peck, a bushel and a peck and hug around the neck," she sang to me and kissed my cheek.

"What's that?" I asked her.

"A song my dad used to sing to me. My real dad," she said and she fell asleep.

Her real dad. I was gonna need to hear that story sometime and sometime soon.

I was getting in too deep with her.

If this ever ended, it was gonna hurt. A lot.

Chapter Twenty-Two

"You should definitely hurt her before she hurts you," Jeff told me as we chucked our garbage out the window of his mom's Buick wagon on the Hodson blacktop on our way out to Hodson Valley Cemetery to drink beer.

"That's dumb," I told him from where I sat in the back seat alone.

"It's not. It's being a man."

"He's right." Shane turned around and said to me.

"How's that being a man?"

"You don't let anyone hurt you. That's being a man." I sat and thought about it in the back seat as the cold wind ripped through the open windows.

"You're so whipped, man and just for a cheap piece of ass." I looked up at Jeff and saw him in the rearview mirror as he said it. I didn't say anything. I glared at him silently.

"Look at you! You think you're a badass and you're dating this girl you think is so perfect, pfft," Jeff continued.

"She is."

"What'd you say?" he asked and laughed. "She's not perfect or pure. She's a fucking whore."

"Watch it," Shane warned him.

"He knows I'm kidding. I'm just giving him shit because he thinks this girl is the hottest thing ever and he's whipped."

"Maybe I am whipped. But she's beautiful."

"There's other girls just as hot who are probably better in the sack too."

"No, there's not."

"You saying she's the best in the sack? She suck your dick

whenever you want or has she sucked it at all? I bet she's frigid as fuck!" Jeff barked out the words like you hear guys doing in ninth grade when they're trying to act loud and tough.

"Leave him alone," Shane warned him as he tossed his cigarette and rolled up the window.

"I'm just saying, she's not the only piece of ass and she's not the best piece of ass either and you can tell by looking at her that she don't like to put out because if she did, half the county would have had her by now with tits like she's got. If she liked to put out she would have been titty fucked by every guy," Jeff trailed off and shut up when he glanced in the mirror and saw me.

I wasn't saying a thing. I was calm. I was popping my knuckles and planning on bouncing his head around a few times, but I was calm and quiet. Everything he said, every little insult against Faith was another check off for a reason to kick his ass as soon as we had some beers at the cemetery. I'd let him think all was forgiven, and then I was taking him down a few pegs. Teach him to keep his mouth shut about Faith.

"I'd watch what you say," Shane warned Jeff as if he could read my thoughts as I sat in the dark.

"It's true though. She's not the hottest chick in town. It's not like she has some magical pussy or something."
Click, click, went the dial on my silent anger.

"It's not like she's hotter than Jennifer or Allison for that matter."

Click click, more anger ramping up. I swallowed hard and then I noticed Shane stiffening in his seat.
I felt the tension roll off Shane on that one.

"She's way hotter than Jennifer and she's way hotter than any girl you've ever been with," I said quietly.

I didn't say anything about Allison, because I thought she was a skinny skank, but if Shane liked her, I'd keep my mouth shut.

"How do you know?" Jeff demanded and the car swerved on the snowy blacktop before he jerked it back into the middle of the lane.

"He's dated them all, that's how he knows!" Shane laughed and turned to look back at me.

I smiled back at him but not because what he said was funny. I smiled back because I knew I was gonna pound the snot out of Jeff before the night even got started. Jeff was giving me tons of grief because I didn't want to go out. I wanted to go find Faith. I still didn't have a car either and I wanted to pick up a car rag from the Thrifty Lube and possibly punch Adam a few times while I was there. Maybe shove him down into the oil hole.

But I'd come out for Boys Night. A real Boys Night. No chance of the girls finding us. We didn't even tell them where we were going, which was Hodson Cemetery on the edge of town. Kids came out here to drink all the time but they did it a lot less after Halloween, when it got really cold and two feet of snow on the ground.

We came because it was the Tuesday before Thanksgiving and no school the next day. We always did something wild the Tuesday before Thanksgiving and ever since we could drive, we came out here to drink, no matter the weather.

When we rolled up to the iron gates there was more than two feet of snow and untouched drifts over the old graves. We were going to make snow men all over the cemetery but we ended up quitting after making only two because we got tired of it and just wanted to drink. We were doing shots of Jack right out of the bottle and chugging beers in between. It was nice to get away from town, just us guys. It was nice until it wasn't.

"When was the last time you got some?"

I started it with my smart-ass question. And then I chucked a snowball hard at Jeff with my left arm and still thunked him a good one in the shoulder.

"Hey man!" he started to protest but Shane, the good man he was, was fast on the follow-up and he hit him with one too.

"Hey! Fuck you guys! I'm not kissing and telling." No grin

on Jeff's face which was telling in itself. It wasn't funny to him that he wasn't getting any.

"Because there's nothing to tell!" Shane laughed and while Jeff was busy glaring at Shane, I walloped him again with another snowball. A slushy one. In the side of the head.

"Dick!" he yelled at me with hate in his face and I tucked my chin down and charged him.

I hit him running and he was too stupid to get out of the way. I hit him full blast with my shoulder right in his gut and knocked the air out of him. He coughed out an oof just before his feet went out from under him and he landed on his back. We hit the thick frozen snow with a crunch and I wasted no time tenderizing his face for him. I used my casted arm and probably shouldn't have, but honestly I forgot I had it on.

"You think you're so goddamn smart, you fat little prick!" I yelled down at him as I jacked his face two more times before he got his hands on the front of my coat.

He grabbed me hard and flipped me off him and onto my back fast. He thumped me a solid one in the mouth before I was even completely on the ground! I'd have to give him credit for being fast with his hits because he followed that one up with a blinding hook to the side of my head that rattled what little brains I had in there.

But that didn't bother me. I'd been straddled and beat in the face and head by Dennis many times while Mom and Dad and even Linda watched and laughed. The only difference now was Jeff wasn't near as mean or drunk as Dennis. And Jeff didn't weigh near as much as Dennis, even if he was a lot heavier built and taller than me.

They both hit the same; great haymaking clobbers to the side of my head and I bet Jeff was also like Dennis in that he would never stop hitting. Not for a long time. I smiled up at him after one of his eye-rattling bangs to my noggin' because I had a plan to stop him; a plan that hadn't worked on Dennis because Dennis had been too heavy for me to lift. I was only sixteen the last time Dennis had straddled me and beat my face to a pulp. Back then I had lay helpless on my back in the living room while everyone watched. I had tried unsuccessfully to toss Dennis off me head first into the tv set.

If I could have lifted him off me, I could have shoved his fat head right into the tv. I had rolled my eyes up and seen it and wanted to do it so badly. I even pictured his head going through the thick green glass. I had never wanted to do something so bad in my life, but he had been too heavy then. But that was months ago. I was bigger now. And Jeff was lighter than Dennis even if he was still heavier than me. Instead of a tv by our heads, there was a tombstone. A gritty, rough, gray and black chiseled tombstone.

I grabbed Jeff by the front of his coat and he stopped punching me and looked confused. I used those few seconds to quickly rocket my arms straight into the black night and hoist him off me. I rammed his head into the granite stone with a crunch and a huge bloody smile on my face. The collision ended with a grinding thud and then I threw him off me and jumped to my feet. I wiped the blood from my nose and lips and onto my hand, careful to not let it drip on my suede coat and careful to not get too much of it on my cast, and I flung the drops into the snow. They landed in perfect circles that shone black in the moonlight. I stared at them and rubbed my aching broken arm and worried I'd hurt it worse and I didn't notice Jeff getting up.

I didn't see him get up and I didn't see what he was doing. But I felt it. And I heard Shane yell. In panic and fear.

I could feel Jeff socking me hard in the back. Right above my kidneys. The ache brought back bad memories from when I was little and Dad had booted me hard there and nearly ruptured one. I was only seven or eight and I had spilled a full glass of beer I was bringing him while he sat on the couch. I tripped in my footed pajamas and threw the beer all over the place, all over Dad. When I was mopping it up with a towel, he stomped me on the back. When

I didn't stop crying for over an hour and when I peed blood, Mom took me to the ER. I missed a lot of school after that. I almost couldn't do wrestling years later because of that.

Shane and Jeff always knew I protected that area of my body and they did too, our whole childhood. But now Jeff was purposely rabbit punching me there. He hit me there in the back again and again and as I spun in the snow and tried to get away from him, he followed me as best he could.

"Fucking asshole! Kidney punches are off limits on Mike!" Shane screamed as he launched himself into us.
Shane entering the whole mess only spurred Jeff to flail more frantically at pummeling me in the back.

"Watch out!" Shane shrieked as Jeff struck him hard under the chin.

I watched in horror as Shane raised his hands to shield himself from the blows of Jeff's fists raining down on him. His wet sneakers blurred as they tried to keep traction on the slippery snow but it was no good and he went down hard on one of the snowmen. The dark night exploded with feathers and screams as something snapped from underneath him. I thought I'd go deaf with Shane's pealing screams for help.

I didn't understand what had happened. All I knew was I didn't think Shane would ever stop shrieking.

Chapter Twenty-Three

I stood there confused.

"What happened? Here, bro, take it," I said to him and offered him my good hand.

But his eyes widened in watery terror and his mouth stretched wide and instead of taking my hand, he grabbed the sleeves of my cowhide coat and yanked me to the side just as Jeff drove his shoulder into my lower back.

I landed face first into the snowman next to Shane. I had just a second to see the stick fingers and arms of the branches we had shoved into the snowman to make his arms. They were pointing at me like dull spears and I fell right on top of them with part of my chest. I was going to get skewered.

I fell hard but most of the impact was softened by the snowman, I heard the brittle crunch of the limbs and thought of those giant pretzel sticks you could buy by the bag at Tolly's. They were so tasty. Just thinking about them made me think I could taste the salt and then realized it was blood and snot from my nose dripping onto my lips.

"Damn!" I groaned. I checked my broken arm to see if I had hurt it worse but it only slightly ached. The palm of my left hand felt firey and raw. It was the one I had landed on. It was ok. But my chest hurt. I used my good hand and felt my ribs where the stick had jabbed me hard. Then I rolled over to see Shane who was now eerily quiet.

Breath puffed out of him in steamy white clouds as feathers still drifted around him.

"You gonna be ok?" I asked him and looked for Jeff.
Jeff was sitting hunched over on top of a squatty little grave stone twenty feet or so in front of us. He was very close to his parked

station wagon and that made my guts clench in worry.

"I'm ok but I either peed up the back of my shirt or I'm bleeding from something that hurts back there."

Shane opened his eyes and looked at me then looked away.

"Let me look."

"Do it," he said and gritted his teeth and rolled over on his side.

The back of his black down jacket was shiny in spots and covered in feathers in other spots. A broken stick was crushed into the snow below him.

"I don't see much blood. But you landed on a stick. I think it jabbed you."

"You sure I'm not bleeding out?"

"I'm sure."

"Blood would look black on the snow. I read that in a novel."

"No blood on the snow, dude. There's some I think on your coat. But it's not drippin' or nothing."

"Cool."

He rolled over on his hands and knees and pushed himself up to his feet, breathing hard, clouds of vapor swirling all around us.

I smiled up at him as I lay there on my back.

"What's so funny?" he asked down at me.

We were keeping our voices quiet as if we were scared to alert Jeff to where we were and send him into another rage.

"I think I landed on one too."

I couldn't stop smiling. But hey, if I was hurt, I was in good company because he was too and really, it didn't feel too bad.

"Dude."

I nodded my head.

"Can you get up?"

"Yes, but I gotta piss like mad."

"Does your back feel wet?"

"No. I landed on my chest."

"Sit up a little."

I pushed up slow to a sitting position so Shane could see the front of my coat. He leaned over to get a closer inspection and I hurried him along. I couldn't see Jeff from here and I didn't like Shane having his back to him.

"I good?" I asked him and began patting my chest where it hurt.

"Looks good to me. There's a dent in your coat over your tit but no hole."

I looked down and rubbed the dent in my coat for a long time, my finger exploring the tough cowhide, but didn't find a hole. Then I really smiled at Shane and he offered me a hand and helped me up.

"What about your kidneys?" he asked.

Soon as he said it, I became aware of the thudding in my lower back where Jeff had pummeled me again and again.

"I'll be fine," I said quietly as we both took a step toward Jeff.

He turned to look at us and it shocked us both to see his face red and covered in tears. I thought maybe he was sorry but I didn't think it very long.

"I'm going home. You're not welcome in my car, either one of you."

That's all he said and he got up and started walking to his car. I had thoughts of tackling him and taking his keys and leaving HIM out here in the blizzard, way out in the country in the middle of the night. But the thudding in my back grew stronger and I felt too tired to deal with it. I *did* have the strength to say,

"Take Shane. He's bleeding. Just take him, I'll walk."

"Mike, no," Shane froze in his tracks and said to me.

"Go with him and send someone, anyone back for me," I said to him quietly. And then I added, "*After* you go to the hospital. Don't try to find someone to come get me till after you go to the hospital. Also, don't take your coat off til you get to the hospital."

"Why?"

"In case it's helping stop the bleeding. You don't want to pull that off here and have blood gush out of it before you're at the ER."

Surprisingly, Jeff agreed Shane could go with him. I didn't even ask a second time if I could, I didn't want to sound like I was begging. I didn't want to give myself a second chance to get in another fight with him. I was just praying they'd get to town soon and Shane would be able to find someone to send to get me before I froze to death. I didn't know how I would be able to walk on the icy, snowy, blacktop in the dark, in the blasting wind, ten miles to my apartment back in town. I couldn't imagine doing it, so I didn't think about it. I waited till I saw their red tail lights fade into the black snowy night and then I started out, pigeon footed, trudging on the side of the road.

I kept waiting to see a cop car. I was certain Shane would go to the ER and tell them I needed help and that a cop car would come. I kept looking far off for the red and blue lights as I trudged along, my sneakers soaked and slipping and sliding. My feet were soaked and freezing. My wet jeans clung to my legs from my ankles up to my knees. Luckily my cast was dry inside the huge cowhide coat. But that arm ached a long hollow hurt deep inside from punching Jeff and from all the rough treatment. I hoped I jacked his face a bad one with it. But for now it hurt and I was so cold. I wished I had a hat. Gloves would be nice. My hair was full of snowflakes that kept melting and running down the back of my neck. My eyelashes were thick with the fluffy flakes.

Still, I trudged. I was hot and sweaty and yet I was cold and freezing. I didn't feel tired though. I wasn't sad either. Every once in a while, I felt a panic at never getting home. I felt a panic that maybe I was going the wrong way. The sky was dotted with flakes flying down fast and straight and I couldn't tell east from west in the dark. Still, I kept looking ahead for the cop lights and listening for the cop car that would come and save me.

After walking for what must have been two miles or more

and nearly an hour, I began to pray for anyone to come by. Any car or truck or any vehicle at all. Santa Claus or the devil, whichever one was fine, but for someone to come by and not run me over but pick me up and give me a lift. Even if it was a lift to the very edge of town right by the Golden Glaze all night bakery. I could sit on a stool and drink coffee after coffee and eat twelve warm donuts right out of the fryer. They were much better at Golden Glaze than Kahmir's. And his roaches. Hell, I didn't even care if they had roaches there. Just warmth. Just anyone pick me up.

I trudged in a jerky uneven rhythm due to the fact that my right leg was hurting a lot from the shin up to my hip. All of it was tight and pulling and it was hard to lift that foot. Shin splints. I hadn't had those since wrestling. I also had trouble trudging along from the pounding Jeff had given me in my back near my kidneys. They hurt and I hoped I wouldn't be peeing blood again like I did as a kid.

I trudged this way in a strange staticky silence with my hands cupped over my ears to keep them from freezing off. Maybe that was why I didn't hear the car munching its way through the thick ice and snow towards me at 30 mph. Maybe I had closed my eyes and that was why I didn't see the shaky headlights cutting through the snowflakes and the dark until they were nearly right on top of me.

Not a cop car.
Weak, shaky headlights and a small four-cylinder engine grinding evenly down the road; the sound of a small, reliable car.
Faith.

The window creaked down halfway as she came to a stop.

"Mike!" her lips at the open window and then the door coming open.

"No, no no, don't get out of the car, it's cold!"

Seeing her get out of the car panicked me for some irrational reason. I was very scared the car would disappear and we would both be stranded out here in this blizzard, far from home. I grabbed her by her forearms and pushed her gently back down on the seat.

"I don't think I can get it turned around pointed back towards town without stalling it or getting it stuck. I want you to drive!" she yelled at me but I didn't answer.

I trotted around the back of the car. It was so warm inside; the frost and snow on the hatchback glass had melted and run down the sides of the metal frame. I ran to the passenger door and got in the blessedly hot car and kicked off my flooded and frozen shoes. But I didn't stop there. I stripped off my soaked jeans and coat and tossed them into the back seat along with my socks and shoes. My undershorts and Adidas t-shirt were still dry and I was happy to sit there with the heat blasting me from the vents in the little car as Faith drove us back to town and away from the cold, black countryside.

"What are you doing?" she asked after I stripped.

"I'm frozen but thank God you're here. I'm warming up. I'll be fine now." I said and promptly fell asleep with my head to the side of the seat and my face pointing at Faith. I couldn't keep my eyes open one more minute, the heat felt that good on my eyelids. I know I had a smile on my face.

Chapter Twenty-Four

I needed to see my Grandma as soon as possible. It was the Wednesday before Thanksgiving and I found myself on the city bus, sitting right smack in the middle of the seat at the very back of the bus, heading clear over to Sand Creek on the special holiday route which would drop me off by the mall. I didn't know how I'd get home. I didn't have a schedule or any idea when it would pick back up and didn't have the balls to ask the big huge dude spilling over the edge of his seat, driving the bus. I got off with the rest of the shoppers who didn't have a car or didn't want to drive in the blizzard twenty miles to the Sand Creek Mall.

Grandma lived in Pale Rose Nursing Home two blocks behind the mall. This was where she went after her stroke. I'd called her a few times but had only visited a handful of times since last March. I brushed the wrinkles out of my newly washed Levi's as I walked fast and noticed they were getting short on me. Lots of white socks showing down there at my ankles where my good Nikes gleamed bright blue and dry against all the snow on the sidewalk. My feet would be wet and freezing by the time this trip was over but that'd be ok. I needed to see Grandma because tomorrow was Thanksgiving and I needed a recipe to make her famous Snicker cake to take to Faith's. I always loved that Snicker cake so much. It was amazing. I think that Snicker cake was the best memory of my whole childhood.

No puppies. No Easter baskets. Not really any birthday parties. Christmas was usually Mom and Dad hungover and looking like hell. I did like to get up at 5am and sit on the floor of the living room in my Hot Wheels pajamas and stare at the tree and all the twinkling lights and the ornaments I wasn't allowed to touch. I always got great gifts, not that they were great but I liked everything no matter what. But I also always got a smack and if I didn't get a smack or a flick to the ear, there was the tension all morning and afternoon of waiting for one.

Mostly, I wanted it to snow on Christmas and not be muddy and I wanted a friend to play with in the neighborhood. But Christmas was a time of kids being with all their family, doing family things. No one but the kids who had it worse than me liked to come out and play. Everyone else stayed inside with their happy parents and Christmas records and movies and good food and toys. Me, I loved it when Grandma came over and her and I'd do a ridiculously hard puzzle all day and she'd feed me her Snicker cake till I was stuffed while Mom and Dad drank with Linda and Dennis.

I needed that recipe for the Snicker cake. I couldn't wait to feed Faith her first bite of it and see the reaction on her face. I couldn't wait to see her again. She was my angel. My angel who rescued me out on the Hodson Blacktop in the snow. When she dropped me off at my apartment, she made me promise that I'd stay in town, stay away from Jeff, and most importantly that I'd come over Thursday at 11 in the morning to start the Thanksgiving festivities with her family. I knew then I needed the Snicker cake. This was the first time I was ever going to go to a girlfriend's family for a holiday. This was the first family I ever wanted to spend a holiday with, all because of Faith. This was why I took the bus clear over to Faith's town, to see my Grandma.

"Grandma!" I exclaimed when I saw her in her wheelchair the near the gas fireplace in the sitting room of the nursing home.

"Mike!"

She held her arms up to me. She had on a quilted flannel purple jacket over a purple blouse, on top of purple slacks and fuzzy purple house shoes. Grandma still loved her purple. She looked healthy if not a little heavier.

"How are you Grandma? Are they treating you ok?" I asked and checked out the rest of her.

Her hair was curled in blinding white curls tight to her head like a helmet and she smelled like powder and soap like she always had when I was a kid. Her hands shook a little but she seemed ok and happy.

"I'm good Mike and I'm much better now you're here! What happened to your arm and your face?"

"Oh nothing much, just life. A little fight with a friend, I tore up my car, broke my arm. I'll be fine."
I watched her as she slid a rubber-band around a deck of cards and put them into her jacket pocket and then she reached out for another hug.

"I'm so glad you came by. I miss you. I wish you'd be more careful. What brings you by?"

"Awww Grandma I miss you too. I'm doing the best I can but you know me, I don't have the best luck. Hey, it's Thanksgiving tomorrow, do you have plans?"

It suddenly hit me that I could ask Grandma to come to dinner at Faith's. How I'd get her there would be another issue, but it'd be ok with them if I showed up with her. That's what Thanksgiving was all about. Family.

"We're having a big dinner here tomorrow at the home, Mike, you know, with all the old people who live here." She spoke about them as if she wasn't one of them and it made me laugh a little.

"Awww that's sweet Grandma. Are you making your famous Snicker cake?" I asked and smiled and pulled up a chair to sit as close to her as I could

"No, I believe the staff is making the dinner, but that would be good. I wish I could make it for you, it'd be great."

"It would be, Grandma. Do you think I could have the recipe? Do you think I could make it?"

"You gonna make it for your folks?"

"No. For my girlfriend and her family."

Grandma's whole face lit up pink at that and she wanted to hear all about it. And she wanted to meet Faith as soon as possible, too. She wanted me to promise that I'd bring her by as soon as possible.

"Well that might not be for a while, Grandma. I don't have a car right now and I need to work a lot and I have a lot of school work to do so I don't get kicked out of school and get kicked out of my apartment. I'm having a lot of bad luck and I'm behind on everything lately."

"You do look banged up Mike. Your folks aren't still hitting you are they, honey?"

My nose was swollen and one eye was a little purple from the swats Jeff had given me the night before but I didn't think I looked too bad. My chest had a small blue bruise where I had landed on the stick from the snowman and that hurt more than my nose.

Grandma's eyes probably saw all the past bruises my parents had given me when she looked at my banged-up face. I assured her I was still living on my own and not in the line of fire from my folks. I told her all about the court case with Mom and Dad and I told her about wrecking my car and losing my job at Kahmir's and at the Thrifty Lube.

"You sure do have bad luck with crashing cars, Mike."

"I know, Grandma and I really need one."

Grandma reminded me the holidays were a time when places were short and that I should pick one that would pay the most and the one I would enjoy the most and log the most hours there. She was sure Kahmir would take me back because really, I'd only quit because of all the bugs.

I told her about the tire factory and her eyes really danced. Grandpa worked there for a while before he got on at the railroad, she told me. She said I should make myself useful there as much as I could over the holidays because that was good experience to have, better than cooking donuts. And she told me to also get caught up on my school work.

"I would but I gotta get a vehicle first. I can't walk to work, it's too far."

"What kind of vehicle are you looking for?"

"Something cheap and reliable."

"What's your heart set on?" she asked and her eyes sparkled.

"A truck."

"A truck," she echoed.

"A truck," I said again and sighed.

"Push me down to the game room," she told me and smiled.

"What for?"

"You'll see."

Chapter Twenty-Five

Pink slip and grocery list in hand I sat in the warm cab of the little truck as the engine quietly rumbled and the windshield wipers swish-knocked back and forth and cleared the fluffy snow off the windshield. I had a new truck. Well not brand new but new to me. Grandma's man-friend John had to give up his drivers license but still had his truck at the old folks home. They let him start it every week to make sure that it would but they wouldn't let him drive it on account he had so much wrong with his health and his eyes.

"Pay me after Christmas," he said when he gave me the keys to it. "That is if you even want it. It's small and it's stick shift and it's old. It only seats two."

"Two is all I need," I said and smiled at him, the biggest smile I'd had in a long time.

"I know THAT look!" he said and whistled at me as he tossed me the keys.

The little white Toyota truck was beautiful. It sat high above big knobby snow tires and looked like it couldn't wait to go crawling through all that snow. A truck. I'd wanted a truck and now here I had one with a cozy little cab just big enough for Faith and me. No one else. Just us two.

This was going to be the best Thanksgiving ever, I thought to myself as I drove the truck slowly in 4-wheel drive through the deep snow in the dark night towards Tolly's to pick up groceries to make the Snicker cake for tomorrow. It was all going to be perfect. I smiled the entire time the checker bagged my groceries. I smiled on into the night as I made the snicker cake and cleaned up all the sticky mess it made. I smiled in the shower and when I got into my bed in my own quiet apartment, I still had a small grin on my face.

I had no idea how perfect it was actually going to be but the next day when I saw the tight orange blouse Faith had on when she answered the door, I knew it was going to be as perfect as anything could be. My God she was stacked, and my God she looked cold enough to cut glass! That was all I could think when she answered the door and took the foil covered Snicker cake.

"Come see my new truck!" I said to her.

"Oh Mike it's too cold!" she laughed and turned to take the cake into the house.

Don't I know it! I thought to myself as I watched her hips sway back and forth in her brown corduroy mini skirt as she went through the living room and on into the kitchen at the back of the house.

This was going to be the most perfect Thanksgiving ever. The whole family could fight and scream and throw mashed potatoes at each other and do vodka shots for all I cared but I had a new truck and I had a sweet beautiful girlfriend built like a million dollars and nothing could take the smile off my face right now. Nothing, except maybe Tad.

"What's he doing here?" I asked a lot louder than I probably should have when I saw him in the kitchen with her mom. He froze in the middle of peeling plastic wrap off a cheeseball and a plate of crackers. He smirked at me and made a weird face like a duck and rolled his eyes. I hated that guy. He looked like a panty sniffer.

"What happened to your face?" he sneered right back at me and I ignored him.

"Tad always comes over for Thanksgiving," Faith said and waved it off like it was nothing.

I wanted to ask why but I didn't. I came from a jacked-up family where anything was liable to happen especially at the holidays and people you never knew were liable to show up and claim to be a cousin or something. Men who weren't relatives but you had to call them "uncle" and things like that, so I understood weird family stuff went down on holidays. It was a given and I let it drop. I let it drop because all I cared about was being close to Faith and getting to hold her later.

Her body was going to kill me. I was in actual pain by the time we sat down later that afternoon for a combination of lunch and dinner. I had spent the afternoon helping Faith arrange the table with the linens and the plates and silverware. And I'd spent a lot of time sneaking in kisses and trying to feel her up and touch her tits. She was a package and I couldn't wait to get her in my truck later and get that blouse off!

Meanwhile I had to explain my face to her parents. And then I had to explain my broken arm. I tried to tell them it was nothing but they were the prying type of parents and wanted details. Of course, I couldn't tell them about Hodson Cemetery and the drinking and the fight and the reason why we had the fight, which was because Jeff had called their daughter a whore.

But I did tell them a partial truth which was that we made a bunch of snowmen and then I started a snowball fight which led to a stupid fistfight. And then I had to tell them about the car wreck but I left out the part about the carton of cigarettes sliding off the seat along with the six-pack of beer. Parents like Faith's were not the kind of parents you talked about drinking and smoking with. They would not want a guy like me, one who drank and smoked and wrecked his car, around their daughter. I told them I slid through the red light on the ice and got T-boned by the dry-cleaner truck and left it at that.

I was thankful to sit down and have stuff to focus on. Like the blessing. I'd never said a blessing of any sort. I'd seen it on tv like the Waltons, and Little House on the Prairie but had never seen a family actually do it. But now this one, we were all supposed to say what we were thankful for.

My throat dried up when Faith's mom told me to go first. I didn't know what to say I was thankful for. I was thankful no one was doing shots. I was thankful no one was chain smoking and no one was cussing or fighting or smacking me in the head. I was thankful Faith's stepdad had a shirt on. I was thankful neither one of her parents had their live-in girlfriend or boyfriend over. I was thankful that she was my girl and that they thought I was good enough to be here even with my bruised face and swollen nose. I thought all these things but my throat couldn't get any words out.

"How about I go first?" Faith asked her mom and stepdad and then smiled at me.

"Go ahead honey," her mom said.

"I'm thankful for Mike," she started with and then flashed me another one of her beautiful smiles before she continued on and said, "and for having my casts off and being done with marching band. Garrett, you want to go next?"

"Sure, honey. Well. I'm thankful the turkey turned out better this year than last when I tried to fry it."

Here he paused and Faith and her mom laughed and Tad rolled his eyes.

"And I'm thankful we added one more to our table this year." Here Garrett nodded at me and I felt a little uncomfortable. I couldn't figure out if he was being phony or if he meant it and I decided either way, I didn't like it. It sounded stupid and I looked to Faith to see what she thought and it looked like she thought it was just as stupid as I did.

"Tad, you go next," Faith's mom tipped her glass of wine towards Tad, the frosted haired cousin.

He shut his eyes and cleared his throat a couple of times as if he were about to say the most important stuff anyone ever heard but I was too busy panicking about what to say when it was my turn to really listen. He blabbered on about being thankful for family and good health and wonderful food and for the turkey not being fried to a gristle again this year and then he was passing it off to me.

"Your turn, Mike," he simpered at me with his shiny face.

"Well," I started out and put my napkin in my lap and wiped my sweaty hands on it before diving in and getting it over with. "I'm thankful for Faith."

I stopped there. No one said anything.

"She's my girl and I love her," I said and smiled at her. I couldn't take my eyes off her. She was the most precious thing I'd ever known and I didn't know how I had lucked into meeting her at that Haunted House but I was thankful.

"Anything else, Mike?" her mom asked me.

"And I love her."

"I think you said that," Tad mumbled and I ignored him. I reached out and took a hold of Faith's hand. I heard Tad snicker and I made a note to lay one upside his head later.

"Oh I'm just going to cry," Faith's mom gushed and got up from the table and grabbed a paper napkin and dabbed her eyes.

"That was very sweet, Mike. We all love Faith very much," Garrett said.

"And we love you too," Faith's mom choked out and then came over and kissed me on the top of my head. I grinned at Tad when she did and then I winked at him when Faith planted a wet one on my cheek. He turned red and looked furious as he snapped open his cloth napkin so hard that it flew across the table and landed in the corn. It was all I could do to not laugh but Faith squeezed my hand a hard one and I wanted to keep on her good side for obvious reasons, so I kept quiet.

**

"Come on Faith, just one kiss. You don't want the only kiss I get all day to be from your mom!"

We were washing all the pots and pans after Faith's mom washed all the dishes and silverware, and I was trying to get her fool around.

"Mike! You have to wait until we get the dishes done!" She kept slapping at my hands as I kept trying to wrap my arms around her from behind while she sudsed up the pans.

"You wash, I'll touch," I whispered in her ear.

"Mike…."

"I'll just hold you 'til you get several washed for me to dry. I'm needy let me hold you."

Any time I wanted my Mom to let me sit on her lap when I was small, she would hold me a little while and then push me off and say I was being too needy. Sometimes Mom would ask if I was feeling needy and if I said yes, she would pull me up on her lap and hold me a little. She stopped doing that when I was about seven because I stopped feeling needy. At least for her.

"Needy," Faith giggled and with that I wrapped my arms high around her waist and squeezed her tight.

"Needy-needy," I repeated in her ear and kissed her neck and it made her wiggle her butt up against me as she scoured the pan.

She smelled amazing. Cinnamon and apples. That scent would be the death of me. Not cigarettes. Not aqua-net. Not cheap booze or stale cooking.
Yummy cinnamon and apples.

I squeezed her "apples" that were so soft and full and heavy and she jumped and yanked her hands out of the soapy water and smacked my fingers, soaking the front of her own blouse.

"MIKE! You got my shirt all wet!"

"You did that! And hopefully that's not all that's getting wet!"

"Mike!" she squealed and I rubbed my palms across her nipples.

"Here, I'm drying them off for you!" I told her as I continued to rub them.
***

We fooled around kissing and rubbing against each other in the kitchen even though Tad kept walking in and out of the door for who knows what every five minutes. I got sick of him interrupting and the fourth or fifth time he did, right when I had both my hands on the back of Faith's ass, I got him. I didn't even pause in kissing Faith long and deep. I heard the door open, opened my eyes, kept rubbing her tongue with mine, and reached over to the wicker basket on the little cart that had the toaster on it, and I took a hold of the rubber grapes and whipped them at his face hard!

"Oh!" Faith cried out because I jerked a little and took my tongue away. She looked around when Tad screeched and rubbed his face and ran out of the room.

"Oh that will teach him! I think he has a crush on me," she told me when we watched the door swing shut and stay shut.

"What?" I wanted her lips back on mine, sucking my tongue, and I have to admit I was also thinking about her sucking something else, but what she said stunned me.

I held her at arm's length away from me and stared at her confused.

"What did you just say?"

"He has some sort of crush on me." She shook her head as she said it and shrugged.

Then she tucked her hair behind her ears and placed her little hands on my shoulders again, ready for more kissing. But I needed to hear more about this crush. And I needed to get it out of her without scaring her or worse, making her mad at me.

"Why do you think he has a crush on you?" I asked and resisted adding that I thought he was gay.

"You'll get mad. I don't want to talk about it," she said and started kissing my lips with these tiny little smooches, each one turning me on more and more.

I had to think for a moment. I had to get it out of her somehow without screwing up my chances of getting some, yet I needed to know. Because I needed to know how hard to grind that guy's shiny face against the curb out front.

"Oh honey," I said as she kissed my neck and really poured on the heat and came onto me hard.

"What?" she asked and giggled.

"That's just silly, you're just being silly, baby."

"Silly?"

"Yes, baby."

"Why do you say that?"

She paused from kissing my neck but now she was rubbing my stomach and every time she ran her palms over my stomach in a circle, a hundred butterflies flew. My balls tingled and pulled up tight. I didn't want her to stop rubbing me like this. She'd never really touched me much at all, ever, it was always me touching her, exploring her. I wanted her to explore me. Touch me.

"Why am I being silly, Mike?" she asked.

Here, I needed to tread lightly or I'd be going home with the bluest balls ever.

"He's your cousin, baby. Why would a cousin crush on another cousin?"

"I don't know. Maybe I'm wrong."

She stopped caressing my stomach. But her hands were still there. And her chin was tucked down into her chest. She wouldn't look up at me.

"Baby tell me. Tell me what's wrong."

"He saw me naked," she said into my chest.

My hand went to the back of her head and began stroking all that long silky hair real slow.

"Why'd he see you naked baby? Are you sure?" I made sure to ask real quiet.

I didn't want to start yelling and swearing. Not at my Bleacher Girl. Not in her house. Not on our first holiday together.

"Yes, I'm sure. I had just got out of the shower and he opened the bathroom door."

I almost choked on my own spit. I had to calm down. I squeezed her shoulder once, hard. I had so many thoughts in my head but the only ones boiling up to the top were, *kill him, kill him now*. But what I said to Faith was, "Doesn't that door have a lock on it?"

"It does, but it's broke."

I kissed the top of her head and gave her a hug and pulled her close to me.

"Is there anything else you want to tell me?"

"He stares at me a lot."

"What about when he saw you naked? Did he get out? Or did he just stare? Or did he cover his eyes?" I was hoping he covered his eyes. I was hoping he was queer. He did have frosted hair.

The image of my naked baby standing there wet and cold while her pervert cousin stared at her was making me see red and start to tremble with pure rage. I held my breath while I waited on her to answer.

"I screamed so loud; Garrett came running down the hall."

"Did your stepdad come in too?" This was getting worse by the second. My head spun I was so angry.

"No. He grabbed Tad as I wrapped the shower curtain around me."

And here the cousin in question came back into the kitchen. His face was contorted in mid-sneer as if he were getting ready to bitch at me about hitting him in the face with the rubber grapes but when he saw the look on my face, he backed out of the doorway fast. I let him go. For now.

"Kids! We're going to watch the football game!" Faith's mom called to us from down the hall and at her voice, Faith started to pull away from me.

"Wait. What else has he done?"
I grabbed her wrist and wouldn't let go.

"He just watches me."

"Do what?"

"I don't know. Whatever. He stares at me."
She shrugged and tried to pull away but I wouldn't let her go.

"Did you tell your parents?"

"No."

"When does he leave?"

"Sunday."

"What the fuck is wrong with this guy? He's your cousin for

cryin' out loud!"

I was getting loud and didn't care. I was mad. I was ready to take him out back and straighten him out. Right then. I didn't care if I ruined the holiday.

"He's not really my cousin though."

"What's that mean?" I held on to her still even though she kept trying to pull away.

"He's Garrett's nephew, yes. But Garrett isn't my dad. So, Tad isn't my cousin, not by blood."

MOTHER -------. I couldn't say it or even think it in the presence of Faith. But I was done foolin' around with this whole mess.

"Mike. No."

She knew it too.

"Oh yes."

I was rigid with anger and I let go of her and now she was grabbing my wrist and holding on to me!

"He's leaving in a few days."

How many hours of him staring at her and peeping at her would that be? One more minute was too much in my book. I'd fix it so he'd have a hard time seeing at all. I was ready. He was good as dead.

"Faith! The game is going to start! We're in the basement!" her mom called to us from the basement stairs.

"Come on Mike we have to go."

"Go ahead. Save me a seat. I have to use the restroom. Freshen up."

I flashed her a big smile and I sent her on her way to the basement with a big bowl of Bugles and a six pack of 7-Up. Then I went out in the hall to find Tad. He wasn't too far away. Nope. Not at all. He was waiting for Faith. He was lurking in the doorway of the family room, waiting for her to walk past to the basement stairs in the hall.

I watched her go past and there he popped out. But there I was waiting across the hall in the dining room and I cut him off.

"Hi Tad," I said up to him. He was a head taller than me. Never stopped me before. Wouldn't be stopping me now.

"Hi. Hey. Are you leaving?" he asked me.

"Oh no. I'm going to step outside for a smoke. Slip on your shoes and come with me."

"I don't smoke. It's disgusting."

"I don't care."

"No thanks."

"Fine."

I grabbed him by the back of his belt with one hand and grabbed a fist full of his shirt with my broken arm and hoisted him right off the ground in his socked feet and carried him that way to the back door of the kitchen.

"Stop it! You asshole!" he hissed at me.
And then he smacked my hand.

That was it. That was the invite I was waiting for and I smiled as I grabbed him by the back of his pointed head and bounced his forehead off the frame of the back door. Just a quick, light bounce. Just enough to wake him up.
He started wailing and yowling.

"Shut your trap or I will!"

I grabbed the doorknob and threw it open and hoisted the frosted haired dickhead out onto the back porch. Once out there in the cold air, I kicked him on down the steps and onto the brick patio. Steam puffed out of his mouth and nose in a panicked burst into the dark night air. It was still snowing those tiny flakes that fall fast and add up faster. The ones that look like perfect flakes like kids cut out of paper in art class when they're small.

I shoved him down onto his butt where he landed with an 'oof' and held his hands in front of his face.

"Why are you here for Thanksgiving? Don't you have your own family?" I asked him and then said, "Wait. I don't care. You're leaving tomorrow morning, got it?"

"I can't."

His nasal voice irritated me so much it was all I could do to pause and listen to him and not just beat the hell out of him.

"Why not?"

"My plane ticket is for Sunday."

"Between now and Sunday, you make sure you're never alone with Faith. Don't even look at her. As a matter of fact, stay in your room and stay away from her. You so much as touch her, whether on purpose or accident, I'll get on a plane too. Come visit you."

"What for?" he asked. His voice shook and he sounded like Mickey Mouse.

"Nothing much. Just shake your hand."

"Shake my hand?"

"Sure," I said and smiled. I was picturing this getting before a judge in the future and I didn't want anything on record of me threatening him. Oh no.

"I don't understand."

"I know you don't. So, I'm going to teach it to you right now, real slow."

I took out my cigarettes and lit one. I offered one down to him but he scowled at me and bared his teeth. I put them back in my shirt pocket, lit mine and began to roll up my sleeves.

I'd give myself till I got done smoking this after dinner grit and maybe that would be time enough to calm down just enough so I didn't kill him. This would be worth police but I didn't really want police. This was for Faith's safety, but if I was locked up, I wasn't being a good boyfriend to her.

"What are you doing?" he whined up at me, still sitting there, squinting up in the snow.

"Smoking a cigarette."

I studied him where he sat almost Indian style on the snowy patio in his khaki pants and topsider shoes and his expensive checked shirt and sweater vest and his frosted hair. He was taller than me and probably had longer reach than me but he didn't look like he knew how to fight except maybe with his fingernails.

"Let me up."

I shrugged.

"I'm not keeping you down there. I'm actually hoping you'll get up soon."

"Why?"

"Well, we can fight on the ground but it'll be an unfair advantage to me because the ground is where I like to fight." I smiled at him a great big wide one and watched the fear widen his eyes.

With that I flicked my cigarette butt off into the snow.

Chapter Twenty-Six

"What have you been doing?" Faith hissed at me from where she sat on a huge overstuffed brown loveseat with a blanket over her bare legs in her mini-skirt.

"Using the bathroom, like I told you."
She looked at me like she didn't believe me.

"Let me see your hands!" she demanded in a whisper as I sat down and pulled the blanket over my legs too. I wasn't cold but I wanted to be as near her as I could get.

"What for? I used the soap! I'm not gross!" I laughed quietly. But she took my hands anyway and felt them and then sniffed them which made me laugh loud, so loud her mom asked what was so funny.

"Oh they're just young and in love, Rebekkah," Faith's step-dad said as he stuffed his face with popcorn.

"Where's Tad?" her mom asked us.
I shrugged my shoulders and smiled at her and popped open a 7-Up and handed it to Faith and then opened one up for myself.

"Dunno," I said and drank my pop and put a Bugle on each fingertip and watched the opening of the game.

"What'd you do to him?" Faith hissed at me again and poked me in the ribs so hard I jumped.

"Nothing baby. I went outside, had a smoke and took a leak. That's all, I swear!"

I waited for Tad to come down into the family room and watch the game. As a matter of fact, I hoped he would. I couldn't wait to laugh right in his face. But he never showed up. Maybe he was going to start doing what I told him to do, right away; stay away from Faith.

We watched the football game and I didn't pay attention to any of it. I had Faith next to me under a warm blanket with her bare legs against me and her body warm and soft pressed against my side. I had my arm draped over her shoulder and she had her hand under the blanket stroking my leg through the first half of the game. I was in heaven. Absolute heaven.

We all ran upstairs to get a piece of snicker cake during halftime and I had to walk off my hard-on. I made the excuse I was going out back for a smoke. I did go and I did have a smoke and I did laugh at the yellow spots on the snow on the brick patio all around where Tad had been sitting. I laughed and I kicked fresh snow off the steps to cover the mess and the struggle.
Tad still hadn't returned. Maybe he changed in to his pajamas and he didn't want me to see him. Maybe he was trying to figure out how to sneak his pee-soaked clothes into the washer. Hopefully he showered. I should have locked him out there in the backyard. That would have been funny. Soaked in pee and locked out in the snow!

It didn't matter. I went back inside to Faith handing me a piece of snicker cake on a plate and a glass of whole milk. Her parents were already back down in the basement.

"Is there whipped cream, baby?" I asked her.
**

We didn't make it back downstairs to watch the rest of the game. We spent the rest of the evening on the velour couch in front of the gas fireplace in the living room, necking and watching it snow out front. Faith covered us up with a soft yarn blanket and she used the blanket to hide the fact that her hands were all over me! She had never been like this and I lay back and shut my eyes and smiled and let her do what she wanted to me.

It was her house with her parents nearby so I kept my hands on top of her clothes. But Faith had my flannel shirt unbuttoned and my undershirt pulled up as she ran her hands all over my chest. I let her be the boss and next I knew, she had me pushed onto my back on the couch and she was on top of me! I couldn't have told her no if I wanted to. Whatever she wanted, I was hers.

We kissed for a very long time, slow and deep and we didn't take it further. I could have done this forever and I would have. I was throbbing in my pants but it wouldn't have been the first time I'd had a hard-on without being able to satisfy it. There would always be later on, alone at home if I still felt like it. I would have been happy to kiss her all night and nothing more. But we got interrupted.

"Faith!"

Her mom sounded shocked but not mad to find her daughter on top of me in front of the gas fireplace with it roaring loud and turned up on high. I thought of my giant boner and hoped I wouldn't be required to stand up for a little while. That was not something you wanted a mom to see, even if she was a looker like Faith's mom was.

"Mawwwwhm! Can't you knock or something?"

"Knock knock honey!" her mom said and knocked on the wooden table behind the couch. "The game is over and it's late."

That was my cue to go home. Even if I had never been to a girl's house before and had never made out on someone's couch, I knew from tv and what scant common sense I had that this was my cue to get out.

This had been the most perfect Thanksgiving I'd ever had in my life and I was ok with it being time for me to go home. I'd never had a holiday like it in my life and probably never would ever again. I felt happy with the idea of kissing her goodnight and heading home in the snow in my new truck.

"Hop up baby," I whispered to my girl and kissed her lips one last time.

"Awww," she said and kissed me back and pressed those boobs into me, making me groan.

"Sorry Mike," her mom said.

"No worries. It's late. I had the best Thanksgiving ever."

I wanted to say, it's not your fault your daughter is giving me blue balls, but I knew better.

"No, sorry Mike, but we don't think you should drive home. The roads are really bad out there."

"Oh," I said from under Faith who was beaming a huge, hot smile down at me.

"Faith, you should get up off me," I urged her and made her smile even more.

"But you're staying here, silly."

"I don't think that's what your mom means."

I looked over at her mom who was now standing in front of the large picture window and looking out at the road and all the bright white snow.

"That is exactly what I mean. That is, if it's ok with your parents."

At this, I gently pushed Faith up off me and I sat up and pulled at the knees of my jeans and tried to straighten them out, and then pulled at my fly and tried to give my dick some breathing room in there before I stood up. I was thankful her mom had her back to me still.

"My parents?"

"Yes, do you need to call them?" she asked as she turned around from the window.

"No, ma'am," I said and smiled and looked at Faith.

I needed her to help me out here. She had never told them I lived on my own and I didn't know if this needed to be kept a secret or not. Either way, I wasn't into secrets at all even if they were from parents.

"Mike lives on his own."

It was Faith who offered this info up with a little feisty smile while she looked over at me.

"By himself?" Her mom sounded like she was real close to hysterical over this information.

"Yes. By himself."

"For how long? How old are you? Oh my God!"

She went from hands on her hips to hands in the air to

hands covering her mouth.

"I'm seventeen. I've been on my own since last March."

I stood up and pulled my flannel shirt down over the front of my jeans. I needed my coat and shoes. I needed to warm up the truck. I needed to be ready to be told I could never see Faith again and I needed to be ready for Faith to agree with her parents and for her to cut me out of her life just as I was really getting comfy being in it.

I shook my head as I left the room and tried to tune out Faith and her mom's raised voices as I went in search of my coat and shoes where I had left them in the kitchen near the back door. But they weren't there.

"What are you looking for, Mike?"
It was Garrett, the step-dad.

"Um. My shoes and coat."

"I put them away in the closet. Where you going? I thought you were staying over? Do I need to talk to your parents?"
I almost laughed. The idea of him talking to my parents was pretty funny. Faith's folks were a whole other world away from my family. They could never meet. They could never talk. That'd be bad.

"Mike?" he asked me because I was standing there chuckling.

"Oh. No, Mr. Miller, you don't need to call them. I um, I haven't lived with them in a while. I'm on my own."

"He's on his own, honey."
Faith's mom looked like she was about to hit the panic switch and start shrieking or something that moms do. I didn't need that.

"Listen. It's ok. It was my grandma's idea. And I've recently been to court for it. The judge knows. And my parents pay me child support and I have a job at the tire factory and I'm getting another job as soon as I can find one. I'm going to school, though I'm not doing so hot there right now. But I got things under control."

I was drowning here. I'd never met parents before and I'd

never known parents I wanted to meet before and here I was failing big time with the first parents that I actually liked. Luckily for me, Faith was there. She put her arm around me and squeezed me tight.

"Mike's a man, Mom, Garrett."

Ooof. I didn't want her telling them that. There was no way they were going to let their little baby see a man. Nope. I'd be getting my things and getting out before the guns came out. But it wasn't like that.

"He's responsible. He's a good man," Faith said and stood on tiptoe and hugged me and planted a wet kiss on my cheek. I touched the hot spot she left behind. I was speechless. I was a good man. I'd never felt so tall in my life.

"Well," her parents said together with Garrett's arm around Faith's mom's shoulders.

They were standing just like Faith and I, with their arms around each other, and I didn't know whether to laugh or say something smart, so I just shut up.

"I guess it's ok then, but I don't understand why you don't live with your family," Faith's mom said weakly and looked from her husband to me and back to Faith.

"It's a long story and I promise it's for the best that I'm not there."

"That doesn't sound good." Now her mom looked very worried and like she was going to cry.

"It's ok, Mrs. Miller. I'm perfectly safe and well fed, you don't need to worry about me."

"But a boy needs his mom, his family."

"Well, maybe someday I'll have one."

That did it. That won her over. That nearly made her cry and she began to fan her eyes as if that would stop the tears. Meanwhile Garrett was silent and waited for his wife to decide what to do.

"Ok. I guess it's fine. Don't stay up too late. And hopefully neither one of you will get sick," her mom finally said.

"Get sick?" I asked confused.

"Yes, Tad is sick. He's been in his room ever since dinner!" her mom exclaimed.

I laughed to myself as I watched her parents go down the hall arm and arm.

"Now what?" I asked Faith. I felt like panting. I was ready to let loose.

"You can sleep on the couch down in the basement or you can sleep on the couch upstairs by the fireplace."

Oh that was a mood killer. I was crushed that sleeping with her in her room was not an option. I understood. I did. She was a good girl in her parents' house. I got it. It was going to be a long night on a couch alone and my balls were tingling like mad. But I got it.

"I'll take the couch in the basement," I told her and flashed her a smile.

"Cool. That one folds out into a bed."

I tried to smile again but just wasn't feeling it.

"Cool."

"I love you Mike."

"I love you too, baby."

"This was the best Thanksgiving ever!" she said and wrapped her arms around my neck.

"I know," I said down to her, smiling once again.

Even if we couldn't sleep together. Even if I had a tack driver in my shorts that wasn't going to get any relief, I was happier than I could ever remember and when she kissed me goodnight, I walked two inches off the ground as I went down into the basement to fold out the couch to sleep alone.

I lay there thinking about Faith. Faith and her beautiful body. That tight orange shirt. How hard it was to not stare at her tits as she helped serve dinner. Her long shiny hair. Her beautiful dark blue eyes. I loved her little pink lips. I loved her small hands. I loved everything about her. I loved how she cried out my name over and over. I loved how new sex was to her.

I lay there with a hard-on in my shorts that was going to keep me awake all night. There was no way I could beat off on that fold out couch in their fancy basement no matter how badly I needed to do it. It would be my luck that someone would come down and see me in the middle of it. Someone like her pervert cousin, Tad. Or worse, her mom! My GOD! That would be awkward. And now I was even harder thinking about her mom seeing me with my dick in my hand.

I was becoming a perv myself!
I got up out of the warm bed and went to the bathroom to try to pee and with plans of splashing my face with cold water to snap me out of my horniness. I was in there, eye-balling the hand lotion and thinking of taking care of business when I heard someone padding softly down the steps.

"Mike?"
It was Faith.

I opened the door as slow and quiet as I could and almost died when I saw her.

Light green Ziggy nightshirt on and nothing else. She had so much on top that the front of her nightie rode up high and I could see the triangle of cotton that was the front of her panties. Ugh. She was killing me.

"Hey honey, what's the matter?" I asked and tried to look innocent as I came out of the bathroom. There was no hiding anything that was going on in my boxers and I hoped she didn't see it.

"I can't sleep," she said and yawned and I watched her breasts swell and rise under that thin cloth that clung to her. I watched the hem of the t-shirt rise and her panties peek out.

I couldn't help but lick my lips. Everything about her looked delicious. She too was looking at me standing there in my boxers with every ounce of my attention poking through the thin cloth of my shorts and she came to me with her arms out.

I embraced her from the side, one arm around her back so as to not poke her. I was trying to be good. I was trying to not get thrown out of this house. She wasn't helping. Not at all.

"Mike," she whined.

She was not having this side hug business at all. She wrapped both her arms around me and pulled close to me. She pressed her big warm tits against my chest and my hard-on pressed into her stomach. There was no hiding it. That thin nightie was worse than if she had been naked. It teased me as she pressed up against me through it. I ran my hands over her back and her butt.

"Mike," she said and something sounded wrong. She sounded worried.

"What baby?" I asked and I waited to hear what she had to say and I worried she was going to complain about me poking her in the belly.

"Mike, I'm having a hard time sleeping. I feel restless. Are you having a hard time sleeping too?"

"I'm having a hard everything," I told her and kissed the top of her head.

"Mike, do you think I'm sexy? I feel fat. I feel bloated. I feel crampy and moody. My boobs hurt. They feel angry and sore." she said and rubbed against me.

"They feel angry?" I asked and laughed quietly as she pressed up tight against me.

Her tits didn't feel like anything but wonderful. They were so soft and plump and warm it felt like they were melting against me. I wanted to squeeze them and kiss her nipples right then but I held back when I heard her say they hurt.

"You're very sexy, baby. Maybe it's going to be your time of the month." I had to clear my throat to get any words out. She was taking my breath away.

"What's sexy about me?"

"How sweet you are, Faith."

"Sweet? People always say I'm sweet. And cute."

I looked down at her and saw her pulling a pouty face like a little kid.

"What's wrong with that?" I asked her.

"I'm tired of being called sweet and cute. It's like I'm a puppy."

"I like puppies. I always wanted a puppy," I said down to her and smiled.

"But am I sexy?"

"Yes," I whispered in her hair right where it parted. "And your boobs are like puppies," I chuckled and I held one in each hand and they were like holding a fat little puppy with a soft warm belly. When she didn't answer, I repeated myself, "You're very sexy and very cute. You're so sexy you're killing me."

I held my breath and prayed she didn't say, ok, and turn and go back up the stairs. I was praying that she would hold me like this all night. I might pass out from having a hard-on for so long, but that was ok. That'd be fine. Just as long as she held me all night. But she stepped away from me. My bare chest immediately missed her warmth, her softness.

She stepped back from me and looked up at me and said, "Do you know what I like about you?"

This reminded me of the time in my apartment when she suddenly got very mad at me and I didn't want to answer. Besides, I couldn't possibly imagine her liking anything about me but finally I asked her, "What, baby? What do you like about me?"

"I like how big your nose is," she said and I had to interrupt her.

"What? It's not so big is it? I've seen guys with bigger ones." I reached up and felt it. It was tender from taking a pounding from that jackass, Jeff.

"I like it. It's manly. It looks like a man's nose," she said and put both her hands on my waist and pulled me this way and that so I was slowly doing the twist.

"I also like your smile," she said up to me and made me

smile even bigger than I was. "You're always so happy."

"I am. It's true. Life can be going completely in the ditch and yet, I'm still smiling."

She was right. I could be catching a beating from Dennis as a kid, but if Mom had Swanson's pot pies in the oven, I felt like the luckiest kid in the world knowing she was making me two of them and would give them to me on the tv tray with a huge glass of milk. Sometimes it was powdered milk, but I didn't care. It made me happy, because it came from her.

"But my favorite thing about you are your eyes."

"My eyes?" She bumped me right out of my memory and she shocked me.

I had plain brown eyes. One looked larger than the other on account of I got rammed in the corner of the eye with a stick by Dustin Collins that little red-headed punk down the street when we were eight and I had scar tissue built up behind my eye. Made it stick out a little further than the other one.

"Really?" I asked.

"Yes. I love your eyes. Sweet puppy dog eyes."

She reached up and ran her fingers lightly across my forehead and the scar above my eyebrow and then she touched my hair. I had to shake off a shiver. Her touch made me wild. I couldn't help but smile at her. I was being as patient as I could with her but I wanted to grab her and hold her tight.

"They're just brown," I told her.

I was done talking about me. I wanted her in my arms and I reached for her but she stopped me.

"They're beautiful. They're so deep. I feel like I fall into them. They make me melt."

"I hope that translates into me turning you on a lot, baby," I said and laughed and winked. I tried to take her into my arms again but she pushed me back once more and my hopes for getting lucky fell.

She stepped back from me on her tiny socked feet and held

up one finger as if to say wait.

This made me grin like the devil himself. She was making me wait for something and whatever she had was always worth waiting for.

She took a hold of the hem of her t-shirt and slowly lifted it above her head and dropped it on the floor. I held my breath looking at her body. I could see her little ribs on her side and I gulped. Her breasts swelled well past them and were heavy and round compared to her little frame. She shivered and her nipples hardened. I watched goosebumps prickle her arms in the dim light of the table lamp. After what felt like forever, she held her arms out to me and I took her in my own. I squeezed my girl to me tight and then tighter still. Then we both sighed and I put her down on the fold-out bed and covered us both up.

Chapter Twenty-Seven

The best Thanksgiving in my life fizzled out into cold reality the next day as soon as I came in the front door of the apartment building.

"Hi Mike! Been looking for you!"

"Hi Molly."

I could not say the same back to her. Wew. She did not look good. She had a bandana wrapped around her head and all her hair pulled up in it. She was breathing hard and had her sleeves rolled up to her elbows and her shirt looked soaked. She smelled bad like wet leaves or toilet or something decayed.

"I bet you were with your family all day yesterday," she panted and wiped the sweat off her forehead with the tail of her shirt and let a big roll of her dimpled belly out for me to see.

"Somethin' like that," I said and grimaced and started to go up the stairs.

"I don't suppose you have time to help me. My sink backed up yesterday morning."

"Oh." That would explain why she was such a mess.

"Toilet backed up too."

"Oh," I said. That explained even more and was not going to be fun. I stopped going up the stairs.

"What else is going on?" I asked her.

She looked like she had a lot going on. I was scared to hear what else but with Molly and with Doris as well, and with people in general, there was always something else and it was best that I hear it all before I went into that apartment and got stuck.

"Well," she took a huge breath and her whole body heaved and grew larger until she let it out and said, "I can't get the dryer to dry my clothes either. So, I hung them all over my apartment because Doris is out. I couldn't ask her. And you were out. I didn't want to bother you but I did knock on your door several times yesterday and last night too. I'm sorry I bothered you on Thanksgiving."

"That's ok. I wasn't home," I replied, just a little confused, and came back down the stairs.

"Did you travel far? To see family?" she asked as I came down to the entryway and followed her into her apartment.

"No, why do ask?" I asked her as she shut her door behind me and closed me into her place that had clothing hanging literally everywhere.

"You look tired is all. You don't have to help me."

"I'm good. Let's start with the sink."

I spent all morning and afternoon and evening working in Molly's apartment. I cleaned out her sink pipes and I unclogged the toilet too. But I also had to clean out the pipes in her bathroom sink and the radiator as well.

"I think something is rusting somewhere and maybe the main pipe for the building is crumbling or something. Something big somewhere in this building is falling apart," I told her as I scrubbed my hands with soap for the tenth time that day.

"That sounds bad."

"It IS bad. It could be tree roots or a busted pipe, I'm not sure. But the way everything is draining slow, in my apartment too, I bet it's something big and important. Can you tell Doris when she gets back?"

"She's not gonna like that."

"Be worse to let it go till it gets real bad."

"I don't know, Mike."

Molly was quite a few years older than me but she was like a lot of people; she'd rather ignore a big problem and hoped it went away rather than face it. Being older didn't mean you were better at solving problems and facing things.

"Big problems never go away, Molly. They just get bigger.

Best to fix it while it's still small, before it makes a big mess is what I always say."

"That takes courage."

"Not really. You're gonna have to face it whatever it is, eventually."

She looked like she didn't agree or didn't understand that at all so I let it drop. Like I said, most people are like that. I never understood why. Face it and be over it already.

I scrubbed her sink out for her but I told her the toilet was all her. Then I fixed the dryer in the laundry room. The hose to the vent that went outside was clogged full of lint. I used Molly's vacuum to suck it all out and then reattached it.

"Hey, you got any pantyhose I can have?" I asked her as I looked at the hose from the washing machine that dropped into the drain in the floor.

"Why?" she asked, aghast.

"Not for me. We can use the toe of it and a rubber-band on the end of the water hose to help keep the drain from clogging from lint."

I put the toe of a pair of her stockings on the rubber drain hose on the washer and as I did it, I asked myself, how long till THIS clogs up? You think you're doing something smart but are you really? I didn't know. I was a seventeen-year-old kid trying to take care of a hundred-year-old house that was chopped up into apartments. What did I know? It felt like a bandaid on the Titanic for a moment. Maybe I was just tired.

"Hey Mike," Molly caught me as I was finally going up to my own apartment.

I wanted to take a shower and rest and eat something. Last night had been wonderful with Faith but I was starting to drag with exhaustion.

"Yes?" I asked and hoped she didn't have one more thing for me to do for her.

"I got one of your letters in my mailbox the other day."

"Oh ok."

I took the mail from her and saw that she had opened it.

"Sorry. I opened it before I saw it was yours."

"That's ok."

"You're having a hard time in school."

Oh no. She had read it too.

I pulled the letter out. My grades for typing, PE, and Geology were in there, all F's and a letter telling me I was going to fail to graduate and have to do another semester in the summer. I had until Christmas to get my grades up to D's. Three weeks to catch up and stay caught up.

Or I could drop out right now. Take my GED and be done. But I didn't want to be a drop-out. I could hear my parents making fun of me loud and clear in my imagination. I was going to have to fix it. I'd already let it get big and now it was almost too big to fix.

I gulped.

"Why don't you get some help with your studies?"

"They're not that hard."

"If they're not that hard, why are you failing?"

"Good question."

Molly's comments were making me cranky but she was right.

"I could help you."

That was the last thing I wanted; to spend my evenings with mouth breathing Molly and her apartment full of problems. No thank you.

"That's ok," I said and smiled at her as polite as I could.

I couldn't imagine her being good at school. She lived in this run-down old apartment house and that didn't exactly scream success to me.

"It's not really studying I need to do, it's just homework. Worksheets, papers, things like that."

"You working too much to do it?" she asked.

"Naw, just you know, I have a girlfriend."

"So do your homework with her. She's in school, right?"

Things looked brighter for a moment as I imagined Faith helping me with geology and rock cleavages. I almost laughed. But then I thought of typing homework. And PE. How would I improve my grade in any of those? Those would have to be done at school, which would mean more days spent staying after school instead of working and instead of seeing Faith.

"She wouldn't want to do that. I don't think she COULD do that if she wanted to."

I started up the stairs. I really needed away from Molly and her heavy breathing and her prying into my life. Didn't I help her out a ton today? Wasn't that enough?

"You should ask her!" she called up the stairs to me as I took them two by two and then before I shut the door, "I owe you, Mike!"

I didn't want any repayment from her. I wanted her to keep her door shut when I came in the building and stop reading my mail and stop trying to help me. I was fine on my own.

Chapter Twenty-Eight

"Faith?"

"Yes Mike?"

She sounded hopeful and that made me happy and feel like a bum all at the same time because I had nothing happy to tell her.

"Faith. I need your help with something and also, I can't go out."

No answer. Silence. Here it comes. She was either going to yell or she was going to cry. Which one did I want? I couldn't remember which one was the best. Staci Whippley yelled when I had to cancel our date to the ice rink and she called me a liar. And let's face it, I was a liar. I lied about why I couldn't go. I wasn't sick and she knew it but I also couldn't tell her I couldn't ice skate.

What kind of a guy can't ice skate? She had yelled. Screeched as a matter of fact. She screeched so loud you could hear it over the phone which Mom and Dennis did hear and did laugh. Mom tried to take the phone from me but luckily Staci had told me to go to hell and she had hung up by the time Mom got the phone away from me.

Yelling ended things quicker than crying. But I didn't want a quick ending and I didn't want crying either.

What did I want? I wanted her to understand. And I wanted her to say she would help me.

"Baby. I'm working nights at the tire factory now on Fridays, Saturdays, and Sundays. I go in at 4 and get off at 12:30. I guess I could pick you up at 1am or you could come over," I trailed off at how horrible that sounded. Good girls like Faith did not wait all night to see their guy. They didn't come over at 1am. That was not what a good girl like Faith would do and it put me in a hard place. Mr. White the 2nd shift foreman himself called me that afternoon to ask if I could start coming in regularly on Fridays, Saturdays, and

Sundays to work the evening shift and I could not turn it down. I needed the income and I hoped Faith would not be mad that I couldn't see her tonight as I'd be going in to work in a couple of hours.

"No. I understand. You need to work. That's ok. I'm not feeling so good to be honest, so it's good for me to stay home, stay in. But what do you need help with?"
I took a huge breath and let it out long and slow.

"I'm failing school."

More silence. Now would she break up with me because I was such a failure? Amanda Kemper laughed in my face when I asked her out in 10th grade when she saw my remedial math book under my arm. How could I have known she was into brainy guys? I was smart. Smart enough to help her jump her car a couple weeks later when it was too cold to turn over. But that still didn't change her mind about dating me; she still said I was too stupid. That one hurt for a while. Till the next pretty face came along. Oh I could not take the silence from Faith and I could not sit here and think of all the girls in my past who thought I was stupid.

"How can I help?" she finally asked and I heaved a sigh of relief.

"Um. I don't know. But I need help. I need a typewriter."

"My mom has one. But when can you come over?"

"Tomorrow afternoon a couple hours before I go to work?"

"Sure!" Here she perked up.

"But are you sick?"

"No. I just don't feel good."

"Isn't that sick?"

"No. I just feel a little woozy and tired. Mom is really keeping a sharp eye on me but I don't have fever, so you can come over."

"Did you get sick from Tad?" I asked and grinned at the thought of him hiding in his room until his flight home on Sunday.

"No! He's better!" she sounded excited about it and I found

my grin hardening into a scowl.

"Is he bugging you?" I asked a little too harshly.

"No, he's on his way to the airport. Garrett's taking him. He got an early flight home. So do you want to come over tomorrow and I'll help you study?"

"Yes, it's a date!" I said like a doof and smiled into the phone. I really wasn't so good with the whole phone thing. It was hard to be cool on the phone. I was still smiling that evening when I went to the tire factory to work my first late shift.

The next afternoon Faith looked radiant even if she said she didn't feel good. Her cheeks were rosy and full and she glowed. She seemed sure of herself and confident like a grown woman. Her body curved in delicious shapes in her red sweater with her ponytail pulled up high when she answered the door. I followed her and watched her hips sway in her faded, tight jeans as she took me down into the basement.

We both paused and looked at the couch, the squeaky bed now folded up and made back into the family couch. But just the other night it had been our bed together for the night and oh what a night it had been. We'd only had sex once because Faith had fallen asleep with her face against my chest right after, but it had been beautiful. She had slept, naked against me in my arms all night and I had lain awake, wanting her but mostly just loving everything about her.

Now we smiled at each other and then she took me to a little room behind the basement family room.

"Here's the office. My mom likes to write sometimes, so this is her typewriter. She said you could use it as much as you like." Faith sat down on an old metal office chair and flipped on the typewriter which began its powerful little electrical hum immediately.

"You have your practice books?"

"Yep," I told her and patted my backpack.

I worked on my typing practice for half an hour and then it was on to reading Geology on the couch in the family room. Faith read most of it to me. It was much more interesting hearing her read it and definitely more interesting than hearing the teacher read it. Also, I was able to follow her a million times better than reading it myself. She kept my attention. We didn't even fool around. She was all business.

"You can't fail Mike! We both have to graduate at the same time!"

She was very hung up on that. Even though we went to different schools, it was her thing. I didn't get it but I didn't press it. I would have been fine with dropping out if I didn't come from such a long line of losers in my family and if I didn't have such a big chip on my shoulder about being different from them.

Faith's mom brought us turkey sandwiches and leftovers and glasses of milk while I worked on a drawing of South Dakota's rocks and a cross section of all the land formations there. Faith helped color it while I ate a second helping of snicker cake. By the time we carried the dishes upstairs, it was time for me to warm the truck up and clean the snow off and head to work. Just before I put it in reverse, Faith waved at me to stop.

"I packed you a lunch!" she said with excitement sparkling in her big eyes.

"Aw, thanks honey. It's almost like we're married!" It just popped out. I looked at her to see how she took it.

"Oh Mike!" she laughed and shut her eyes and blushed.

"Goodbye dear!" I called to her as she wrapped her coat around her middle and shuffled back to the porch.

"Bye Mike! Don't hurt your arm at work!"

"I won't!" I laughed and promised her and rolled slow down the drive.

I didn't hurt my broken arm but I did get the cast filthy black from the tires. They moved me from cleaning and sweeping to helping pull tires from molds all night and load them on a hand-truck. It was boring but easy and kind of fun and paid $2 more an hour than the normal $10.50.

I was going to make almost $100 a night for work! I would be working 4 to midnight tomorrow and then off all week till Friday where I'd do it all over again; Friday, Saturday, Sunday. I'd be making almost $300 a week plus $250 a month from Mom and Dad. I'd be able to put away most of it into my savings because rent would be free again for all the work I did in Molly's apartment.

My money problems were gone. With Faith helping me catch up on school, those problems would soon be gone too. Just last week it seemed everything was against me but I had faced and it had all worked out okay. Maybe I could even work things out with my parents. Maybe now that I didn't live with them, we could come to some sort of understanding; one of them being not hitting me. Maybe not though. Them having to pay me $250 a month wasn't gonna help things between us. Maybe I could slip it back to them and the judge not ever find out and then that way we could be family again. I could ask Grandma what she thought. I needed to get over there and pay her friend for the truck.

Things were going so well that I was on a cloud when I rolled up to my apartment at 1am and ran right into Jeff and Shane standing on the front porch.

"Well, well, well," was all I said as I looked at them standing on the top step.

"Hey Mike," only Shane spoke to me.

"What's this all about?" I asked and the two of them moved out of the way so I could unlock the front door. Doris kept the front door locked because she said with Christmas coming, she was worried about break-ins, and she also said she kept seeing an unsavory looking guy in a black car loitering around across the street every day.

"Can we come up?" Shane asked.

I looked at Jeff. He had a stupid hang-dog expression on his face as the cold night dumped tiny flakes of snow on him and stacked up on his wool coat.

"Is this asshole gonna jump me?" I asked Shane but never took my eyes off Jeff. I was bouncing on the balls of my feet ready to spring.

"We're here to talk."
Jeff said it so quiet, his voice was lost in the dark night.

"All right. But I'm tired and I'm not putting up with any of your psycho bullshit in my house."

I opened the door for them both to go in ahead of me. I was polite. And I wanted Jeff in front of me.
As we passed through the entryway, Molly's door creaked open an inch. I saw her huge eyes blink in the light of the wall lamps and I nodded at her once and then winked and smiled to let her know everything was ok. She was one of those neighbors who knew everything that went on at the apartment. She was one of those neighbors who would call the police at the sound of any trouble at all.

Jeff and Shane followed me up to my apartment and after I got it unlocked and opened, they followed me and stood quiet while I dumped my pockets out in the China bowl on the little table inside my door. Keys, change, rubber bands, pocket knife, all went into the bowl. Then I kicked off my work boots and went into the kitchen.

I didn't want them in my bedroom. I didn't want them in the room that was touched so much by Faith recently. They had no business in there.

"Dude, I've never seen your place before," Shane said as he sat at the now fixed kitchen table. "It's really nice," he added as he looked around the kitchen after I snapped the light on.

"Thanks. You guys care if I make dinner? I'm hungry."

"No. Go ahead," Jeff said and drew a long stare from me.

"You left me in the cold way out in the middle of fuckin' nowhere after you jacked me in the kidneys. Why am I asking your permission for anything?" I shook my head at him and couldn't help but laugh at how crazy this whole scene was.

"I know. I'm sorry."

He stood up from the table. I didn't know if he was going to hug me or offer me his hand or what but I wasn't ready for any of that.

"I'm sorry I punched you in your kidneys."

"Hmm," I said and turned my back to him to pull bread and butter and cheese from the fridge.

"That was fucked up of me. I'm sorry dude."

"I know. I heard you."

"We done?"

"We are not done," I told him.

We were not done. I didn't care that he'd taken cheap shots on me in my kidneys. I could get over that. I couldn't get over what he said about Faith; calling her a whore and all the other things he said. I didn't want to talk about it though because I was dead tired and didn't have the patience for it. I wanted to eat my cheese toasty, wash up in the sink, and go to bed.

"I said sorry I hit you there, bro," Jeff said and began to pace the room.

"Yup. You did."

I took the skillet off the heat and flipped my sandwich onto a plate and cut it in half.

"I left you out there on your own in the blizzard."

I didn't have anything to say about that. If he didn't stop talking about it, I was gonna be mad about it all over again.

"He got home all right," Shane said.

"How did you get home?"

"Faith."

Here I glared at him.

"Oh."

"Oh," I repeated and nodded my head.

"Fuck. I'm glad she knew to come get you." He sighed and sat down backwards in my one of my kitchen chairs.

"How did she know to come get you?" he asked after a minute.

"I told her. I called her," Shane admitted and we both looked at him.

Shane looked really uncertain and nervous about everything and kept tapping an unlit cigarette against the table and flipping it in his fingers.

"Thanks for calling her, man. How's your back where that stick stabbed you?" I asked him and shot a glare at Jeff.

"Fine. Just a couple of stitches. Nothing big."

"I'm real sorry about that too. I already told you and I feel horrible about that and you, Mike. I feel bad your girl had to drive out in that blizzard to get you."

I kept standing by the counter to put distance between me and Jeff. I poured a glass of milk and ate my sandwich while I watched it snow past the window and I tried to think about calm things.

"I shouldn't have said all that shit about her. She's not a whore. I'm sorry man."

"It's over with. It's past. No worries. Forgiven."
That's all it took. I wanted him to apologize for that, for saying all the things he said about Faith.

"Are you sure?"

"Yep. Never speak of it again. We done now."

"Thanks man, you're a solid friend. I've been an asshole lately. I got a lot on my mind."

He got up and came over and now he hugged me as much as I'd let him which was a clap on the back. And then he collapsed back into the chair.

"Jennifer's the whore," he said and put his forehead on top of his arm on the back of the chair.

"What?" Shane and I both asked at once.

"She's pregnant."

"Dude!" we both yelled at the same time.

"No way!" Shane gasped.

"She says it's mine but there's no way. We haven't done it in months and then I didn't even finish. So it can't be mine. She's the whore. She's steppin' out on me with everyone. I heard she's been shackin' up with one of Derek Charles' friends."

"Where'd you hear that? They're at Sand Creek, they could be doing everyone and anyone and we wouldn't know. How do you know this?"

Shane asked him all this, which was good because I didn't care and couldn't muster the energy to pretend. I never worried about Faith cheating on me with anyone at her school. It never crossed my mind. After she got her casts off her leg and arm, and I stopped worrying about how she got around school, I stopped thinking about her and other guys. Maybe I needed to ask her sometime if guys bugged her at school.

"It's all over school."

"Our school?" Shane asked and sounded doubtful.

"Yes. Our school. Dude, you had to have heard about it. Everyone is talking about it."

"I haven't heard anything," Shane shrugged.

"The girls in home-ec were talking all about it."

"Did you say home-ec?" I asked.

"I got put in home-ec because Mr. Larry in shop said I was a dumbass and kicked me out of auto."

I frowned at him and looked him up and down but didn't ask for more details. Mr. Larry was probably correct.

"I pick up all kinds of good gossip in home-ec from the girls in there. Some of them are pretty hot too, just sayin'. But they were talking about this couple who got busted having sex in the Santa House behind Sears."

"In the what?" Shane and I both asked at the same time.

"Santa's House. The one that looks like a cookie or something. They get it out right around Thanksgiving. Police busted them. Arrested them both. Girls in home-ec said it was some couple from Sand Creek; a football guy named Troy and a girl from the band whose dad owns the Buick dealership, Kerner's Corner Buick.

That's her. Jennifer Kerner. How embarrassing was that? To hear about my supposed girlfriend from a bunch of girls in home-ec." Jeff rubbed his face and shook his head back and forth as he told us this. I rubbed my face too but for a different reason.

"I'm too tired for this," I told them and sat down and lit a cigarette.

"That's funny though," Shane said.

"You all right?" Jeff asked him. "Because I'm not finding any of it funny. Not at all."

"I'm thinking."
Shane stared out across my little kitchen at the blank wall above the stove.

"Why is that funny?" I asked him after a minute.

"Because Allison told me she got a ride home the other day from school because she missed the bus and Jennifer wasn't there. She got a ride from a guy on the Sand Creek football team. From one of the dudes in the Homecoming Dance fight! She told me she recognized him in the car and was scared the whole ride home."

"Why is that funny?" I asked him. "Did she shack up with him or something?"

"No," he snapped and then he paused and got quiet.

I could have sworn I could see the gears in his brain trying to put something together. "And it's not funny at all. As a matter of fact, I have half a mind to go find him and kick his ass for messing with my girl. She was really scared he was going to try something." Shane's face turned red and purple with anger as he sat and thought about it more.

"It is funny though," Jeff piped up. "It's funny," he said and took a smoke from my pack and I tossed him my lighter. "It's funny and weird because Jennifer wasn't there to give her a ride because she was off with that football guy in the Santa House. And what's a Sand Creek guy doing hooking up with our girls? It's too much coincidence; both of them off with Sand Creek football guys at the same time and they're not football girls, they're band girls."

"Faith's a band girl. Or she was," I mused but I didn't think she was anything like Allison and Jennifer. Not at all.
It was as if Jeff read my mind.

"There's band girls and then there's marching band girls and then there's BAND GIRLS," Jeff said and waved his hand through the smoke that hung in the air.

"What the fuck does that mean?"

"Well, there's good girl band girls, like your Faith, shy girls who want to be involved in school things. Then there's girls who do ALL the bands, the symphony, the jazz bands and the marching band because they're serious music nerds. Then there's the girls who want to go to all the football games on the pep bus with the team so they do only marching band. That's Allison and Jennifer. I'm not saying they're in it just to score football players, but a lot of them try to. But the football jocks never shack up with them, maybe a blowie on the bus but not much else."

"I don't think Allison is like that, but true, you're right," Shane agreed and I realized how much more they knew about high school than I ever did. I also realized how much more they cared about it, and I never did. All I knew was, I was glad Faith was out of band. I conjured an image of her on a packed bus loaded with jocks and no one there to protect her on the dark ride home and I didn't like it one bit.

"So what?" I snapped, and ground out my smoke in the ashtray.

"So Jennifer is shagging a football player who's above her class, in the Santa House, and now she's pregnant. And then Allison is getting rides home from one of them too?"

"Pregnant. Wow. What's that dude's name?" I asked.

"Troy Lannerman," Shane said out of the side of his mouth to me as if scared to speak it around Jeff.

"Troy fuckin' Lannerman, tight end," Jeff grumbled.

"You know what position he plays?" Shane asked.

"Naw, but whatever, those guys are all dicks."

"Maybe they're not out of our girls' league."

Shane looked hurt to hear he and his woman were in a lower league or class or whatever they called it. I didn't care. Faith was beautiful inside and out and while I knew she was perfect and I wasn't, I didn't waste time worrying about it.

"Dude. They are. Jennifer and Allison are hot but in a Pizza Hut slut sort of way. Not in a football and college bound rich girl sort of way. And Faith? Faith is way the hell out of your league but you always score whoever you set your sights on so it doesn't matter that you're a short dude who's built like a bag of cable with a beaten-up mug with a big-ass, smashed-up nose," Jeff laughed and shook his head at me.

"Who gives a shit? I'm tired. Can you guys get out? I need to crash."
I stood up and tried to shoo them towards the door.

"This whole thing is fishy and that baby isn't mine," Jeff said with a jab of his finger at me and Shane as he started to go towards the door.

"These football guys are doing this shit to find out stuff about Mike or get to him. I'm telling you, dude," Shane said in a far-off voice.

He was still sitting and still looked like he was trying to figure out the most difficult problem in the world.

"I'm telling you," Shane continued when Jeff nor I said anything, "this is to get to Mike. They're not done with him. I expect we'll be jumped again before Christmas, both of us, me too, because I fought those assholes off too."

"True, you did, but I don't care what they want. They can fuck off. I kicked their ass once, I'll gladly do it again, but right now I need sleep."

"They're planning something, I'm telling both of you, you better keep a watch out for anyone lurking or stalking you," Jeff warned us.

And with that, I shoved the two of them out the door but

before I could get it shut Jeff came back and said, "I love you, bro, and I'm sorry. I'll make it up to you. I owe you!"

His words had a weird echo to them as if I'd heard the exact same thing recently but couldn't remember where and it gave me a chill but I wrote it off as being tired.

"Sure, sure, whatever."

Chapter Twenty-Nine

Jeff and Shane were talking crazy and I pushed it all to the back of my mind, or I tried to. But there was too much to shove back there. JENNIFER WAS PREGNANT was the first thing that kept falling out of the pile at the back of my mind and disrupting my thoughts as I brushed my teeth and got ready for bed.

Jennifer was pregnant and Jeff didn't think it was his. He was probably right if they hadn't done it in months and he didn't finish, as he said. My God, imagine telling your best buddies you didn't finish? How embarrassing. But if it were true, then it was definitely not his. Couldn't be. And then the fact she got arrested having sex in the Santa House with some football player. That was hilarious because it was in the Santa House. But it wasn't funny that it was some football guy and now here she was putting the heat on Jeff that she was pregnant with HIS baby. I wondered what he'd do about that. What a mess that was.

Jennifer Pregnant. I heard it in my head over and over as I tried to fall asleep. Imagine telling your parents your girlfriend was pregnant but that it wasn't yours. That'd be embarrassing. More embarrassing than just telling them you knocked up your girl and she was pregnant. Jeff's parents would want to know how. How. How funny was that? My parents wouldn't want to know how. They'd know how. I'd been careless is what they would tell me if I shared something like that with them. Not that I ever would. They'd be last on the list to know that.

The silence in the apartment ticked on after my thoughts stopped. I could hear the fridge compressor kick on, on the other side of the wall. The water in the kitchen sink dripped; ploop! My heart beat sped up and began to hammer. I broke out in a sweat and felt nauseous all over. My feet tangled in the blankets as I kicked at them to get them off me. Even my legs felt sweaty.

I had to sit up on the side of the bed and lean all the way over and try to slow down my breathing. I couldn't get enough air. It was too hot in here. I was going to have a heart attack. Something was wrong. I was going to die right here alone in this apartment and Doris would find me, all because of the thought pounding its way through my brain, waiting for me to acknowledge it.

I managed to get up and pace around the apartment. I stumbled to the kitchen and got a glass of water and yanked up the window to let a blast of frosty air in the room. The snowflakes sizzled on the hot radiator as they blew in.

Had I been careless? Had we been careless? I had never asked if she was on birth control. I just assumed she was and I'd never used a condom with her. I had them with me but I wanted to feel her completely. I didn't want that between me and her. I'd always used a condom with all the other girls I'd ever been with. I could open the wrapper with my teeth and get it on fast without even taking my eyes off the girl under me.

What had Faith said about being sick the day before? Was she pregnant sick? She had said her tits hurt at Thanksgiving, didn't she? That's why I didn't squeeze them right there and then. I had told her she was going to get her period soon probably which was why her boobs hurt. But then she had said she felt woozy. Woozy. The word lay there like a pile of letters waiting to be sorted. Woozy.

What if she was pregnant? She was so good, she wouldn't even think about it, I bet. I mean, she wasn't stupid. But she was Faith. She was a good girl. She was my good girl.
It would be ok. Maybe I was going to be a dad too. I smiled and rinsed my glass and went back to bed. Now I was cold and I snuggled down in all the blankets. I couldn't wait to talk to Faith in the morning. I couldn't wait to tell her maybe she was pregnant, maybe we were going to have a baby!

Up by 9 and calling Faith while running my fingers through my hair and buttoning my jeans, the phone tucked under my jaw. I was scampering around the place, making my bed, picking up, dumping the ash tray, pulling on my work boots and hoping Faith would answer the phone and not her folks.

"Faith!" I nearly shouted in the phone after she answered.

"Hi Mike!" It was her mom. It wasn't her.

"Oh Mrs. Miller, can I talk to Faith?"

"She can't come to the phone right now, Mike. She's a little sick again this morning."

"Does she have a cold?"

"No, she's got an upset tummy. She said she feels woozy." There was that word again. My own tummy did a loop-de-loop at hearing that. She had to be pregnant.

"Oh. Will you tell her I called?"

"Yes. I'll let her know. Hope you don't get it either after being here yesterday."

There was no way I was going to get it. Not this tummy problem. Her mom had no clue at all. But I knew. And I needed to talk to someone right now. Shane or Jeff or someone. Someone I could trust. I was bursting at the seams with the amazing news. I was going to be a dad!

I ran down the stairs to head out to clear off the truck.

"Mike!"

It was Doris. The clitoris.

"I'm sorry Doris, I can't fix anything right now!"

"Can you shovel the walk real fast? We don't want anyone to slip and fall."

All my excitement slowed down to a shuddering stop in my brain. It wasn't like I was going to get to go see Faith and I didn't know who else to talk to about all my worries and all my hopes. I sure couldn't go talk to my mom about any of it.

"Sure, I guess," I said and held back my frustration.

"Mike, you're the nicest tenant ever!"

"I know, Doris, I know."

I shoveled the walk-way that went all the way around the entire house and then I did a good portion of the sidewalk for about half of our street. I could see Molly and Doris watching me from the bay window in Molly's apartment downstairs. They looked warm in huge flannel shirts and turtlenecks sitting at the table drinking steaming mugs of something hot and I waved to them from the walkway.

When I got done shoveling, I found the bag of salt Doris had left out on the porch and I scattered that on the porch and the steps and all over the walks. By the time I got inside my fingers and face were frozen. I wanted to call Faith right away and see how she was.

"Mike, come have a cup of hot cocoa with us," Molly called to me when I came back inside.

They knew I had something on my mind. They tried to get it out of me but I was tight lipped and a little tense. I tried to work my charm with them but it didn't get them to stop trying to figure out what was on my mind.

"The rent is taken care of for December and January, Mike, but I hope that if things come up you can still help fix them," Doris told me over her cup full of marshmallows and cocoa as I sat with them at the table.

"Sure, sure."

"Is the rent what's worrying you?" Doris asked and I noticed Molly's eyes widen as she waited for my answer.

"Naw. I have a good job. I'm good. I need to go see my Grandma is all."

"Why's that bothering you?"

"Well, I'd like her to come here for Christmas but I don't think she can get up all the stairs."

"You can tell us Mike," Doris urged me but I wasn't feeling it.

"Yeh, Mike, you can confide in us. We're looking out for you."

"You, literally," Doris said and pointed at Molly and then snorted and nearly choked laughing.

They were close to thirty years old but sometimes they acted much younger than me. Maybe this was why they were still single and never dated anyone. Maybe they were still in the 'boys are icky' phase of life.

"I'm just looking out for the building is all," Molly said and sounded mad.

"What are you guys talking about?" I asked.

"Molly called the cops this morning."

"You did? Why?"

"That black car again! Didn't you see that black car out there when you were shoveling?"

"No. I didn't notice. I didn't see the cops either. Did they come?"

"No. They never showed up. And that's worrisome! I'm going to call back and complain!"

Maybe THIS was why Molly was still single. She was a little intense and not in a good way. Her eyes bugged out and didn't seem like they were going to go back in any time soon.

"What was the black car doing?" I asked her and helped myself to more tiny marshmallows.

"He's been parking out there a lot and just sitting."

"Hmmm." I didn't see the problem.

"He comes every morning around 9 or 10 and just sits for an hour or so."

"Is he waiting to pick someone up?"

"No. No one ever gets in."

Her eyes looked huge like she was frightened about it all.

"Have you called the cops before?" I asked her and helped myself to a stack of Oreos and dunked one in my cocoa.

"No." She wiped her lips with a paper napkin and then folded it as small as it would go.

"Does he sell drugs?" I asked her and this got Doris'

attention.

"Oh no, I hope not!" Doris said and now she looked as panicked as Molly.

"I don't know. Maybe he does. I have no idea but he shouldn't be there every day, just sitting across from the house!"

"Why today? What made you call today?" I asked her.

"He's scary looking. And today he rolled down his window and he watched you."

"He watched me?" I asked and I couldn't help but laugh. I could not imagine some guy watching me. How weird.

"It's not funny!"

"It sounds funny, sorry. Why was he watching me?"

"I don't know. But he looks mean!"

"Oh yeah? What's he look like?" I asked her as I ate another cookie.

"I don't know. Let me think."

"Is he young or old?"

"Hmmm he's kinda young."

"Ok. And what's his hair like?"

"Brown."

"Hmm."

"Molly," Doris told her in a weird soothing voice that creeped me out, "close your eyes and think about him. What do you remember?"

"He had thick eyebrows."

"Anything else?" Doris asked.

"No," Molly answered with her eyes still shut. I could see them moving from side to side under her eyelids.

"Color of jacket or was he smoking or anything like that?"

"No, I don't know. He wasn't smoking."
She popped her eyes open and she stared at us.

"But he definitely rolled down his window as soon as he saw Mike come out. And he watched him the whole time."

"And you didn't notice him, Mike?" Doris asked me.

"Nope. What kind of car was it?" I asked Molly.

"A black one."

That was no help.

"Small or large? Or foreign?"

"Small I guess, because it only had two doors so it had to be small, I think. But it had a long front."

She shrugged.

"I don't think it's a big deal. Maybe it was the truant officer from school, checking up on me. Was he fat?" I asked.

"No not really and I don't think he was that old. I've seen that guy, the truant officer, and it wasn't him. He's like sixty and this guy was not that old."

"Hmmm," I said out loud but what I thought was, Derek Charles. Or Adam. Or any of the Sand Creek football team because it seemed they had it out for me probably. Who knew? Could have been the motorbike kid I borrowed that 2-stroke bike from for all I knew.

"Probably just casin' the place to rob it because it's the holiday season. Let's make sure all the doors are locked," Doris said as I got up to leave.

"Yeah, I'll keep an eye out too. Probably just some guy from school or something."

I couldn't think it about it now, I had much bigger concerns. I had poor little Bleacher Girl who wasn't feeling so hot. I had to take care of her for one and possibly a baby too. We hadn't been careful and we had done it more times than I could count. I needed to talk to her right away.

But when I called her again that afternoon, I still didn't get to talk to her.

"She's still not feeling good at all Mike. I'm pretty certain it's a bug or something she ate or she has the flu," her mom told me.

"I need to come see her. Just for five minutes."

It was Saturday afternoon and it'd only been a day since I saw her but it felt like forever. I really needed to talk to her in person.

"Mike, the flu is very contagious, I can't let you do that."

"Ok. But if she gets worse, please call me and let me know!"

"I will. I'm sure she'll be fine."

I was sure she would be too but I was dying to see her. But if that couldn't happen, then I'd go see Shane and Jeff and see what was happening with Jennifer. I was excited as hell at the idea of Faith having my baby, but I couldn't wrap my mind around it. I couldn't believe that it could be true. I needed my friends. I needed to see how Jeff was handling his situation; I needed to know if Faith had said anything to Jennifer.

But I had no idea where Jeff could be and I didn't want to show up at his house so I went to McDonalds to see if Shane was working. He might know where Jeff was. Shane was working but he wouldn't be off for two hours and by then I'd be on my way to the tire factory for the night.

"Where's Jeff? Any idea?"

"No, but we're going drinking later. He's meeting me here. You in?"

"Nah, I can't. I gotta work till midnight."

"What'd you want him for?" Shane looked at me suspiciously.

"Aw nothing. Thought I'd see how he was handling his problem, you know, with Jennifer."

"Aw yeah, that," Shane said and bugged his eyes out at me. "That's pretty messed up."

"Well, maybe I'll catch you guys another time."

"Sure. We'll be around late. We could stop by your place again."

"Nah. That's all right. I need to sleep after work."

Working at the tire factory was a lot different than flipping burgers at McDonalds. I spent the entire night flipping rubber tires out of their molds and onto the cart again just like last night. It never ended. I started when the whistle blew and didn't look up or stop until it blew again for break. Then was back at it 30 minutes later. I didn't think about much, I just popped those tires out of their molds and flipped them onto the cart. Someone would come by and take the cart away as soon as I filled it, and bring me an empty one. I paused here and there to drink water from the water fountain right behind me but I didn't do that too much because I didn't have but one break to go pee.

"You sure work hard, Mike," the night foreman Mr. White told me.

Everyone called him Whitey but I was too scared of him to call him that. He was a busy and rigid man who walked the entire long assembly line and kept tabs on all of it with his clipboard. He ran a very tight ship, was what the other guys said, and I wanted to make sure I didn't let him down.

"Thank you, Mr. White," was all I said to him and went back to flipping till the whistle blew at midnight to end my shift.

"Maybe you can do overtime for me next week Mike and pull some shifts on Tuesday and Wednesday?" he asked me as I clocked out.

"I don't know Mr. White, I have a lot of homework to do."

"You in college?"

"No sir, I'm in high school."

He looked shocked at that and stepped back from me and looked me up and down.

"You do look young but I thought you were out of school by the way you fill carts so fast."

"No sir."

"Well be careful driving home and see you tomorrow night."

**

I did do homework the next day but it was on my own. Faith still wasn't feeling good but I did get to talk to her at least.

"Faith? Are you ok?"

I was so glad she picked up the phone and not her mom.

"I'm fine but I just don't feel so hot in the morning."

Her voice sounded weak, watery. Like she'd just got done puking or something. I wanted to ask if that was what it was but couldn't find a nice way to do it.

"Faith, I gotta talk to you. Can I come over?"

"No Mike, Mom won't let you come in and won't let me leave the house. She's being really weird and super strict with me. She's at the store getting me 7-up and crackers right now or else I couldn't even talk on the phone."

"Can I run over there right now? It's important. "

"No, Mike, by the time you got here, she'd be back."

"Ugh," I sighed.

"What is it you want to talk about?"

"I can't say it here. I have to say it there, to your face."
She was silent after that, so silent it was a solid silence like a thick white hunk of plastic between us.

"Are you breaking up with me?" she asked and I heard her gasping and sobbing hard.

"No baby, no. Never. Of course not!"
I squeezed the phone so hard I heard the green handset crack a little.

More sobbing from her end and no talking. Now hiccupping and crying loudly too.

"I promise Faith, I cross my heart and promise! No, I'm not breaking up with you! I love you!"

"I love you too," she squeaked.

I was frantic. This was wrong that I couldn't see her. She had no idea she was pregnant or if she did, she was so scared, she didn't want me to know. I bet she didn't want me to know. Maybe she knew she was pregnant and she thought if I knew, I'd break up with her. Maybe that's where that thought came from. This was why we needed to talk face to face. She needed to see me to know for sure I loved her and I was there for her and the baby.

"Mike, I have to go. Mom is back."

"Ok, but I," I started to say I had something important to tell her but she had hung up already.

I stared at the handset for a second before it made the dial tone sound at me.

"You hung up," I said to a dead line.

After I shook off the feeling of abandonment from Faith hanging up on me, I decided to do school work on my own. I did homework all morning in the kitchen, reading my geology book and coloring in past due maps and graphs and even wrote a short paper. I worked till noon then ate an egg sandwich and decided I needed to get out of the apartment. I needed to talk to Grandma about my dilemma with Faith, but I needed to talk to Grandma here and not in the nursing home. But I didn't know if I could make it work so I went downstairs, all those stairs.

"Hi Molly."

"Hi Mike, wow this is a surprise," she said and blushed so bright her freckles disappeared. "You want to come in?"

"No, but I wanted to ask a favor."

"Sure. I owe you one or two or," she said and giggled and snorted and I thought something shot out of her nose.

My God, no wonder she was single. She was sort of a mess. I looked away and let her wipe her nose on the back of her hand.

"I want my grandma to come over for dinner, but I don't think I can get her upstairs to my place."

"Oh! You want to use my place?"

"Well, I don't know about that. Isn't this little unit across from you vacant? Do you think Doris would let me use it for a day?"

"Oh. Well maybe."

She looked very disappointed.

"Maybe if Grandma can get up the porch steps ok, the next time she comes over we could have dinner with you?"

Her face brightened and she nodded her head vigorously.

"Sure, sure, I'd love that!"

"Do you know where Doris is? I tried her apartment, but

she's not there."

"I think she's out buying a Christmas tree. But I could ask her for you if I see her later."

I knew then that Molly would sit by her big bay window watching for Doris to return and that she would set it all up for me. Now I just had to ask Grandma.

When I called Grandma, she sounded like she didn't feel good either. Maybe something was going around after all. But she said she would love to come over Monday afternoon for an early dinner if I could come get her in my truck.

"Grandma, I need to pay your friend Richard for the truck when I come by."

"Don't worry about it, Mike," she said and started coughing hard.
When she finally stopped, I asked her why.

"He's not here anymore. It's yours."

"Where'd he go?"

"He died the day after Thanksgiving."

"Oh. I'm so sorry Grandma."

"Don't be Mike. That's why he gave you the truck. He knew he was going. He gave away everything he had before he went. That truck was the last thing he had."

"I know. He said that. Wow. Can I give his kids money for it?"

"No. Richard wouldn't have wanted that. He'd want you to have a good time in it with your girlfriend. By the way, will I be meeting her Monday night too?"

There was an idea. I hadn't even thought of that so I did now and then I said, "Not this time Grandma. But she is the reason I want you to come to dinner, besides, you know, having dinner with you."

"This sounds good, Mike. I'll be ready."

Chapter Thirty

Grandma was ready when I pulled up to the nursing home Monday after school. She had on a purple and green pantsuit when I picked her and helped get her in the truck. I folded her walker up and placed it gently in the bed of the truck and came around and got in.

"Oh," she inhaled and let out a big sigh after she got situated in the truck. "Smells like Richard in here," she said and shut her eyes.

"Was he your special friend, Grandma?"

"He was. I miss him. No one left to play poker with me, or help me cheat the other old folks."
She opened her eyes and smiled at me as the sun lit up her gray eyes.

"Thanks for picking me up, Mikey. I miss our visits. You used to come see me all the time before I had the stroke."

"I been busy. Sorry Grandma."

I put the truck in gear and gently nosed the truck out of the drive of the old folk's home and drove us slowly over the icy ruts in the street to take her to my place. Doris had let me set up the little one room unit downstairs which was even smaller than my place, for the day, so I could have Grandma over for dinner. On the menu; spaghetti and garlic bread and iced tea and decaf coffee. The place didn't seem too small because all I had set up in there was a little table and chairs in front of the galley kitchen.

"I wish you could come up and see my place Grandma. It's bigger than this but there's too many stairs for you to do."

"I'm sure it's lovely. You've done so good for yourself. It's too bad you had to move out at such a young age but your parent's ain't worth a poop."

Grandma was always honest about how things were at home. I spent a good portion of my childhood trying to convince her things were just fine at home but around age 10 I stopped trying. She knew. She saw it all; the bruises, the tore up house, the motorcycle taken apart in what should have been my bedroom, me sleeping on the couch. She saw the hundreds of beer cans, the ashtrays piled with cigarette butts. She saw it all and probably much more than my kid eyes even saw while I lived there.

It felt good to hear Grandma say she thought I was doing good on my own. I couldn't remember my parents ever complimenting me about anything. Maybe Dad did a couple of times when I did some hard take-downs in a wrestling meet. But he was mostly just glad I didn't get my ass beat in front of him. Oh no, couldn't stand seeing another kid take me down but he had no problem watching Dennis whale on me for years. That never seemed to bother him at all. I never understood how a dad could watch another man beat on his son.

My emotions must have played across my face as the memory rippled across the back of my eyes because Grandma said, "Mike, your childhood was bad but it made you who you are. Since you didn't have a choice about how you were raised, you should be proud how you turned out to be despite it."

Grandma reached across the little rickety table and took my hand in hers. I was surprised how hot her hand was and how strong. She gave mine a hard squeeze and I gave her a gentle one back and felt how loose her skin was and smiled. It reminded me of the time she came the hospital after I had my tonsils out in kindergarten and how she held my hand all night when I was too scared to sleep there alone.

I remembered vomiting when Mom and Dad and Dennis and Linda came in reeking of cigarettes and how the nuns of the hospital had kicked them out. Grandma had showed up then. And she stayed with me and fed me jello and soup and sang to me till I finally fell asleep. She was there in the morning when I woke up too. And she was here now.

We ate spaghetti and made small talk and then she dug in when I stood up to get her more coffee.

"So who's this girl?" she asked and grabbed my hand and pulled me gently back down into my seat.

"Her name is Faith."

"Yes. A lovely name. You told me that so far."

"She's beautiful. She's the most beautiful girl I ever saw."

"I bet she is," Grandma said and her whole face lit up.

"Do you have a picture?" she asked me.

"I do. Upstairs. Should I run up and get it?"

"Yes. Let's see her."

I ran upstairs and flashed Molly a thumbs up and a huge smile as I saw her crack open her door and peek out.
I grabbed the framed photos Faith had given me from Homecoming. The pictures we had taken before the fight. Before jail.

Me and Faith in front of her parent's house. My arm around her tight. My face split open in a huge toothy smile, my eyes wide and dancing. Faith's eyes on my face, smiling up at me sweetly. All that golden hair piled up on top of her head with long sexy strands everywhere. That wonderful body of hers filling out her pink cloud of a dress. Us at the dance standing in front of the fake gazebo. Both of our faces pink from dancing. Faith standing on a white crate so she was tall enough to almost be eye to eye with me. Her cleavage popping out of the top of that dress from dancing so much. She was so beautiful. I never got the chance to kiss her and hold her in my car because of the fight that happened. I never even knew how she got home. All of that was stolen from me by Derek Charles and his football goon friends.

I handed the photos to Grandma one at a time as I stood behind her shoulder and watched her as she slowly looked at each one carefully and then placed them gently on the table.

When she was done, I took them and stacked them on a little table by the door of the tiny apartment and came back to the table.

"What do you think?" I asked her and smiled bigger and bigger because I knew Grandma loved her.

"She's lovely Mike. I can't wait to meet her."

"Isn't she lovely?" I asked. I couldn't stop shaking my head and smiling.

"She is. She is perfect for you, sweetheart. But I can't help and feel like there's something you're not telling me."
Here she folded her hands and placed them on the table and waited for me to tell her everything and I did.

"Grandma, Faith isn't like other girls. She's innocent, you see?"

"She's a virgin. A good girl." Grandma nodded her head to show me she understood and approved.

"Well. She was."
I looked down. This was hard for me to tell her. I didn't want her to think less of Faith because of what I had done to her. She could think bad things about me but just not about Faith. It was all my fault and I said it now.

"It's all my fault, Grandma. She's pregnant."

"Oh!" Grandma lurched back a little from the table and I thought her teeth were going to fall out on the table for a moment.

"I'm really happy about it, though."

"How does she feel about it?"

"She doesn't know."
Here I slumped and looked down at the shiny wood floor.

"Why doesn't she know? How does she not know and you do? Shouldn't the woman know first?"

"Well. I'm pretty certain she's pregnant. She's sick every morning. Then she gets better in the afternoon. Her body is a little different too. Like. She's tender, do you know what I mean?"
Grandma's eyes got huge.

"Michael!"

"I know!"

I got up and paced the room and then began to clear the table and stack the dishes in the sink. I'd have to wash them later; the soap was upstairs in my apartment and so was the wash cloth.

"Michael, you're only seventeen!" Grandma almost yelled and then she started coughing hard.

"I know Grandma, but I'm ready. If she's pregnant, I'm ready to take care of them both."

"Michael! You're too young!"

"I got this Grandma. It'll be fine. I'm a little scared because I know even though Faith is older than me, she's eighteen already, but she seems younger than me, you know what I mean?"

"Michael, my God have you told your parents?"

"No. They have no say in it. I don't want them near Faith ever, much less our baby. I need to talk to Faith. I don't think she even knows."

"How could this girl not know? Is she right in the head??"

"She's innocent. I'm telling you, she's pure. If she suspects anything, she's not telling me. And her mom thinks she has the flu so she won't let me see her. And I need to see her. If she's pregnant, that's my baby. I need to provide for my baby. Now."

Here Grandma frowned and slit her eyes as if she had heard the most ridiculous thing in the world ever and maybe she had. Then she started nodding her head just a little.

"Faith knows. Trust me. And her mom knows. That mom knows. Trust me. She just doesn't want to face it. And maybe Faith doesn't want to either."

I thought about that for a little bit. Maybe so.

"What do I do?"

"You go in the afternoon, when she's feeling better. You show up. Give them that smile, and go on in. You got this Mike. And I'll be here to help you. A great grandbaby," Grandma said and smiled as she looked out the window at the late afternoon pink sunset on the snow.

"A baby."

"What will you do?" she asked and didn't take her eyes of the snow.

It was as if she were holding her breath while she waited for me to answer. I looked at it too as I spoke.

"Marry her. Work hard. Get a better place. Take care of my baby and my wife," I said it in spurts as if I'd just sprinted a mile. What a great feeling it was.

"Come by the old folks home before you go see her," Grandma told me when I pulled up in the U-drive of the Nursing Home to drop her off after our lunch together.

"What for?" I asked, curious, as two staff-members came to the truck to help Grandma get out safely.

"Got something for you."

Chapter Thirty-One

I went to see Grandma right after school Tuesday like I promised before heading over to see Faith.

"Mike. I can't get out of bed."

"What's the matter? Should I get someone?" Grandma was tucked up in bed with the covers up to her chin. I could see she didn't have her teeth in. She shook and trembled like she had a fever.

"You have fever? A cold?"

"No," she whispered. "That's not it. I'm just not having a good one."

"Should I get the nurse?"

"No. I don't need her. She'll bring me something when it's time. Get the box off my night stand."

Her eyes went to the little table next to the head of her bed. There was a battered old fat square silver colored box on the corner.

"Take it. For your girl."

I walked slowly around the foot of the bed, past the hissing vaporizer that sat on a plastic chair, to the night stand.

"Mike." Grandma reached out and took a hold of my arm. Her hand was cold today and felt wooden; completely different from yesterday.

"Yes Grandma?"

"Open it." She shook my arm hard, twice so I opened the box.

Inside it, tucked into the satin inside were two rings welded together. One had several tiny diamonds that sparkled every color of the rainbow as the light hit them from the window. The other one had one diamond. It wasn't very large but it was pretty.

"That's for your girl. I haven't worn them since Pop died."

"Wow Grandma. Thank you."

I couldn't catch my breath. It was really happening. I hadn't even thought of a ring. There were a hundred unnamed things I hadn't thought about but they'd rear their heads when the time came, of that, I was sure. And I would take care of them as they came in their own due time like I did everything else in my life.

"You like them?"

"Yes. They're beautiful."

I couldn't stop looking at them. I took them out and put them on the tip of my finger and turned them to catch the light.

"Congratulations, boy." Grandma smiled a gummy smile at me and held my gaze.

"I'm not even sure she's pregnant."

"Oh she's pregnant. I can feel it." She smiled again, briefly.

We were quiet a while then Grandma shut her eyes and sighed and let go of my hand but I still held on to hers and I gave it a squeeze and she opened her eyes.

"One more thing," she said and smacked her wet lips a couple of times and then swallowed.

She tried to sit up but then gave up but she fixed me with her tired eyes.

"There's a fat envelope in my top drawer under my underwear. Get it. Take it with you too."

"Ok."

Her hand let go of mine and dropped back on top of the starched white blanket and she immediately started snoring with her mouth wide open.

I found the fat envelope in her top drawer under her underwear and I tucked it in the waistband of my pants, under my winter sweater. I shoved the old square ring box in the front pocket of my cowhide coat and stepped quietly out into the hall.

"Nurse, something is wrong with my Grandma."

"Did she fall?" The nurse looked panicked.

"No, she fell asleep."

Here the nurse relaxed and sat back down at her desk. She didn't look concerned.

"She's completely different than yesterday, I think something is wrong with her," I told her and willed her to get up.

"Are you Mike?"

"Yes."

I felt like a 5 yr old kid talking to a teacher. That was the affect this nurse had on me. I had all my hopes on keeping my grandma safe on this woman in a white uniform.

"She's pretty sick," the nurse said to me.

"Well can you check on her?"

"Sure."

I didn't leave till the nurse checked on her and until she assured me that she was fine. Then she told me what was wrong with her. A lot. And all of it to do with her heart. Not good. And that was why she couldn't do the steps at my apartment. That's why she used a wheelchair now. Her heart.

All that news hit me hard and I went home to the apartment on autopilot. I walked up to the porch in a daze and only came out of it when I realized the front door was locked and I didn't have my key out and had actually left my keys in the truck.

"Shoot," I whispered to myself and turned around to go back to the truck.

That's when the black car burned rubber and fishtailed down the road as fast as it could go on the icy ruts. I tried to watch it go and see what make it was but was distracted by Molly pounding on the glass of her bay window.

"That's the car!" she yelled at me through the thick wavery old glass. She sounded and even looked like she was underwater. Some deranged mermaid dressed in an oversized neon pink sweatshirt over lime green stretch pants.

"What?"

"That's the car," she said in a normal volume after I got my keys out of the truck and came inside. "That's the car that's always out there, lurking!"

"Did you call the police again?"

"No. They won't come. I've already tried."

"What kind of car was that?" I looked to where it had sped off down the road, throwing ice and slush as it went, trying to remember what it looked like.

"A black one," she said and shrugged.

"I know it was a black one but what kind was it?"

"A Buick?" she asked and sounded hopeful.

"No, Buicks aren't black unless they're Grand Nationals. That wasn't a Grand National. And it was too curvy."

We were both quiet.

"It's wasn't maroon, was it?" I asked her.

"Maroon? No. It was black. Why?"

"I know someone with a maroon Regal."

"Mike!" Doris called down from the second-floor landing.

"Hey!"

"Your phone is ringing!"

"Oh man!"

I hustled it up the first flight of stairs, zoomed past Doris and told her thanks.

"It's been ringing all day!"

"Sorry!"

"That's ok! You can't help it every sound travels through the vents!"

I could hear the phone ringing as I flew up the stairs to the 3rd floor. It had to be Faith. Finally, Faith was calling me. I skidded down the hall, unlocked my door and ran in and grabbed the phone off the tv tray.

"MIKE! It's Shane! We have to talk!"

"Bro what's up?"

"Me and Jeff are picking you up in 10, ok?"

"I guess. I'm kinda busy."

I felt the hard lump in my coat pocket and then patted the

fat envelope still stuffed in my pants.

"It's important."

So is this, I thought as I pulled the square box out and sat it on top of my dresser along with the envelope.

"Ok. But I can't be out long."

I got important things to do, I almost said but then I realized I wasn't sure if I was going to talk to Jeff and Shane about the things I needed to do. I needed to hear from Jeff what he and Jennifer were going to do first, even though he was sure it wasn't his baby.

"Where we going? And don't tell me it's the cemetery." I said when they picked me up and I got in the back of Jeff's mom's Century wagon.

What I said made them both groan.

"Cuz I don't feel like walking home from there again!" I said and laughed and reached over the seat and pounded Jeff a solid one or two on his chest and then I took out a smoke and lit it.

I felt like a king, but if I was going to be a dad, I'd have to quit smoking. I looked at it for a moment and thought about that. That'd be fine, I decided. I'd do anything for my kid, but for right now, I was smoking.

"Real funny, bro." Jeff brought me back to the here and the now.

Shane chuckled next to him and then Jeff turned and shot me a worried look.

"Naw, for real, where are we going? I'm kinda hungry."

"What's new? You're always hungry or horny!" Shane forced a laugh back at me over the seat and Jeff and I managed a couple laughs back at him but they fell flat.

But he wasn't wrong; I was kinda horny thinking about Faith being pregnant. Mmm. She would look good pregnant. Pregnant women were beautiful.

"What's that word in that shampoo commercial with the naked chick in the shower?" I asked.

"Lustrous," Shane offered up and looked back at me,

curious.

"Yeh, I think that's it, lustrous. Faith is lustrous." I was thinking out loud as I sat in the backseat alone.

"You're LUST-trous!" Shane hooted and laughed for real this time.

"Listen, guys, this is serious." Jeff brought me out of my horny daydream from where I was slouched in the backseat with what could be one of my last cigarettes.

He sounded like someone had just died as he pulled away slowly onto the icy rutted road. As I got comfortable for the ride, I glanced out the window and glimpsed a black car parked across the street from the apartment. I hoped Doris had the front door to the apartment house locked. I felt my keys in my pants pocket and was glad I locked my door all the time now ever since Mom had let herself in. The rings Grandma gave me were in the silver box on my dresser and the stuffed envelope was in my top drawer. I hadn't even opened that yet. It could be anything. But I was sure it was valuable, whatever it was.

"So what's the plan?" I asked as we headed down the ramp that would take us on up to the county highway towards Sand Creek.

"Jennifer is indeed knocked up," Shane told me and I looked at Jeff who was gripping the wheel hard and staring straight ahead.

"For sure?" I asked him.
He nodded.

"With child, my friend," Shane told me and the corners of his lips twitched.

"This is funny to you?" I asked him and I too almost laughed.

"It is. A little."

"Dude. This is so not funny. It's not mine."

"Are you going to tell her that?" I asked him.

"Like she'd listen to me. She would just scream at me."

"Well. Are you getting married or what?" I asked him.

His loud bark of laughter bounced off the roof of the car and sat me back in my seat.

"Hell no!" he yelled and laughed some more. He sounded out of his mind and I was a little scared about him driving us if it was icy on the road.

"Then what are you doing about it?" I asked him.

"Mike. It's almost 1988. Get with the times. I think I'm going to get her an abortion. Maybe."

"Really?"
I couldn't wrap my mind around it. People really did that? I didn't think normal people did that. Didn't they just get married?

"I'm not ready to be a dad, man."

"Why not?"

"Dude. I'm only eighteen. You're only seventeen!" Jeff yanked the wheel as his voice broke on the words and I wondered why we always let him drive as he swerved the car.

"I'm ready for it. If that happened to me, that is," I said quietly and both of them jerked around to face me.

"The road! Watch the road!" I hollered and pointed out the windshield.

"Here, pull off here," Shane pointed to the off ramp.

"What's here?" Jeff asked as I moved to look out the window.

"This is where that new hamburger place, Patty's is, and down the road there is the place you can get an abortion. Planned Parenthood," Shane said.

"Sounds creepy, planned something but it ain't parenthood, it's the opposite of it," I said from the backseat as we pulled into the burger stand.

"I can't eat supper at a time like this."
Jeff had turned off the car in one of the slots but he had his head on his hands on the wheel.

"Come on man, it's not even your kid," Shane said to him and patted his arm.

"You know what I'd do?" I said from the backseat as I lit another smoke and cranked down my window halfway and cold air blasted into the car.

"What?" Jeff asked and turned around. He looked hopeful.

"I'd go talk to that dude she shacked up with in Santa's house. What's his name?"

"Troy. Troy Lannerman," Shane offered up.

"Fucking Troy Lannerman," Jeff echoed and his head went back down on the steering wheel.

"That guy," I said and took a drag of my cigarette and then was interrupted by the carhop on the speaker.

"Yeh, we'll take three cheeseburgers, three orders of chili, and three vanilla shakes, and three small cokes," I yelled at the little brown speaker.

"Oh, that sounds good," Shane said while rubbing his chin and he and Jeff both nodded their heads as the carhop read it back and told us the total.

"How much do you think this is gonna cost?" Jeff asked.

"She said on the speaker, we all put in $6," I told him as I dug ones out of my wallet.

"Naw, the abortion."

"Don't talk about that, we're getting ready to eat." Shane looked pale every time Jeff said abortion.

"Talk to that Linnerman," I told Jeff as I passed him my ones when carhop brought the food to his window.

"Lannerman," Shane corrected me.

"Yeh, whatever, football asshole guy," I said and something clicked in my head.

"Did you guys get a look at that black car out in front of my place?" I asked them as we all shoved food in our faces.

"What for? Didn't you just buy the truck?" Shane asked.

"Naw, yeh, but not for that. I mean it's always out there casing the apartment."

"Really?"

"Yeh, who do we know who has a car like that?"

"What kind of car is it?" Shane asked.

Jeff was eating dumbly and not paying attention.

"I don't know. Maybe an Olds. Maybe a Buick. Maybe a Riviera?"

"Those don't come in black," Shane corrected me.

"You're right. What was it? I know that car! It's gonna drive me crazy. They're stalking me!"

"Who is?" Jeff asked with his mouth full.

"I think it's a Sand Creek football boy." I really did. It had to be. Who else had it out for me?

"Probably right. We kicked their asses and it didn't set well with 'em," Shane said and took the lid off his shake and drained it.

"And you want me to go talk to this guy? This football player and tell him he's the dad?"

"We'll go with you. No need to be afraid."

"Where do we find him?" Shane asked.

"Kerner's Corner. He waxes cars at Jennifer's dad's lot."

"Jesus wept," Shane whistled. "Is that how they met?"

"Dude, probably. Maybe this is good news to him. Maybe he's trying to marry into the business. Who knows? Let's go find him and tell him the good news." I patted Jeff on the shoulder twice and then chucked my trash out the window.

Some went in the can and some bounced back out on the drive. I didn't care either way. I needed to help Jeff with his mess and then I needed to man up and help Faith.

To help Faith, I had to find her and to find her, I had to get away from these two nugget heads.

"What are we doing way out here anyway?" I asked as we pulled away from the burger joint.

"I thought I wanted to go by here," Jeff said as we slowly cruised past the purple and white Planned Parenthood building.

"What for?"

"To see about getting an abortion for Jennifer."

"What?" I asked and laughed.

"I was going to take care of it for her," he snapped at me.

"An abortion isn't something you get to-go or carry-out. She has to go there." I was upping my volume right back at him.

"I know that, shithead, but I was going to go ahead of time and see how much it was!"

Jeff yanked the wheel across the lane in time with his explosive yelling and I was ready to bug out and catch a bus back home. He would be a shitty dad with a temper like that. I felt bad for his future kids. They'd be screwed up for sure.

"Guys calm down. What's the plan now?"

"Let's cruise over to Sand Creek and look up that asshole. See if he's working at Jennifer's dad's car lot," Jeff said like it was the smartest idea he ever thought of.

"Dude, take me home. I don't want involved in any more fist fights. I gotta keep my nose clean."

"Really?" Shane asked.

"Yeah or drop me off. I'll grab a bus or something back."

"Dude, that's too far." Jeff turned and looked at me.

"Watch the road, man."

"Dude, we need your help with this. This is important! We need to be there for Jeff! This is a big problem for him!" Shane bore his eyes into me as he smacked the back of his hand into his palm at the end of every accusation.

"Yeah man, I'd be there for you!" Jeff gave me a quick look before getting his eyes back on the road.

"Maybe I got my own big problem to handle. You guys ever think of that? At least you guys have family to go to for help. I got no one."

But that wasn't true and I felt bad for thinking it. I had Grandma. But Grandma wasn't doing so great. Maybe my first thing to do would be to go see how she was doing.

"Bro, you got us!" they both said to me now.

"Jeff, seriously you should go to your parents. Your dad is a good guy. Tell your dad about him and Jennifer and all of it," I told him. I wished I could go to my dad for help but that's now how it worked in my family.

"Dude. No. I could never tell my parents the shit I do."

"You only did it, what? Once?" I asked him, trying to help him but he wasn't having it.

"Fuck you."

"No, for real though."

"Once."

"All boys screw girls. It's nothing new. Tell your dad. He's not an asshole like mine."

"Wait. Are you saying what I think you're saying?" Shane asked.

His face shined red and he had a toothy smile I didn't like one bit.

"I'm not saying a thing," was all I offered up.
I sat back far against the back seat, away from them and pulled a cigarette out.

"Bleacher Girl," Shane breathed and whistled long and low.

"What?" Jeff asked and looked from Shane to back to me to back to the road as he pulled out onto the county blacktop to take us back to town.

"Mike impregnated Bleacher Girl. That's so fuckin' hot, man," he said and leaned around his seat and grinned at me before pulling out his own smoke and lighting it.

"Fuckin' A no way!" Jeff yelled and smacked the steering wheel.

They were quiet for a little while and all I could hear was the heat blasting out of the vents, trying to keep up with the freezing air blowing in the windows we'd cracked open to let the smoke out.

"Damn. You're the king," Jeff said and finally turned around and looked at me once before he faced the road and settled back in his seat.

I was thankful the two of them were silent and left me to my thoughts for just a minute or two.

"Shoot dude, should I turn around and we both go check out the abortion place? I know you, of all people, will want to do what's right for her, Mike."

"Naw man. That's ok. I need to talk to Faith. I'd never want her to do that. To my baby," I said quietly.

I scooted closer to the door and rubbed my head as I watched the empty frozen fields whip past the window. I couldn't wait to get back home. I was going to jump right in my truck and head over to see Faith.

"What will you do?" Jeff asked.

"Take care of it. Be a dad." I shrugged at him when he turned around to glance at me.

"But you're only seventeen, man." He sounded so sad, so worried.

"It's ok. I'm almost done with school. I can go full time at the tire place and rake in the dough. We'll be ok. Maybe Doris can set us up with a bigger apartment and my rent is almost always free because I fix things. We'll be fine. It'll be fantastic," I said and felt my face burn hot with how corny I sounded.

"Fuck," Jeff sighed.

"Dude. You're the oldest seventeen-year-old I know, you're like a forty-year-old man," Shane leaned around the seat and said to me. His face darkened into a seriousness I hadn't seen since we knocked in the heads of the Sand Creek Football Team.

"Thanks." I shrugged.

"For real and you're the luckiest bastard there ever was."

"That's funny!" I laughed as I thought about all the crap I'd been through recently.

"No really. Look," he said and pulled himself around to face me more before ticking off on his fingers, "You got Bleacher Girl, the most beautiful girl I have ever laid eyes on ever. For real. I mean that." Here, Shane took a deep breath and sighed. "And," he went on, "You've knocked her up. Which means you've scored with the hottest girl ever AND those tiddies are gonna get even bigger, you old dog!" he yelled the end and reached back and tried to swat me on the shoulder one.

"Shut up!" I yelled back but smiled.

Faith was the most beautiful girl ever and I was the luckiest dog in the world. Shane was right, I was a dog next to her. And a pregnant Faith would be even more beautiful. And he was right. Her body was going to full on pop in all my favorite spots. I couldn't wait. And at the end of it, a baby. My baby. I was happy. I was happy but first I had to find her. I had to make sure it was all true. But first I needed to check on Grandma. Then I could run over to see Faith.

Chapter Thirty-Two

"Did you give her the rings?" was the first thing Grandma asked me when I found her in the nursing home.

I went to see Grandma first thing after a horrible day at my retread school. I had turned in all my homework and re-did a failing Geography test, only to be given more homework and a quiz to study for. It all seemed stupid in comparison to what was going on in my real life. I stuffed all the papers in my Trapper Keeper and threw that in the passenger seat the of the truck and headed to Sand Creek to see Grandma.

She was out of her bed and looking much better. I found her sitting in a wheelchair next to the fireplace in the front room of the home, staring at the gas logs and shuffling her old deck of cards mindlessly. She sparked to life when she saw me come down the hall.

"Not yet. I got 'em in my pocket. I'm going there after visiting you. I wanted to make sure you were better."

"I'm good, Mike, I'm good," she said and pulled a Kleenex out of the neck of her sweater and blew her nose.

"I'm glad to see you're better. What was wrong?"

"Just old people troubles. Lots and lots of old people troubles," she said and laughed and coughed hard and for a little bit. She pulled a Kleenex from the neck of her sweater and blew her nose and wiped her eyes and then said, "Nothing too bad. Now tell me your plans and when do I get to meet this girl?"

"I'm going to go ask her right after I leave here. I'm so nervous. Do you think she'll say yes?"

"Only one way to find out; ask her!"

"What if she says no?"

That question sat like ice right in my heart. What if she laughed and said no?

"Honey, first of all make sure she's pregnant. Then ask her to marry you."

I thought about that for a little while and didn't like it.

"No Grandma, I want to marry her even if she's not pregnant. I want her to be my wife. I want to start a family with her right away. I want to be a dad more than anything I've ever wanted ever."

"Is that what she wants?" Grandma asked me and then with a shaky hand she pointed at the Styrofoam cup of tea sitting on the table nearby. I handed it to her and helped her get a drink.

"I don't know. Isn't that what girls want? To get married? To have babies?"

"You're old-fashioned Mike. You want a family bad; I can see it in your eyes," she said and reached out and touched my face with the back of the knuckles of her hand that was still curled in from the stroke.

"You need to shave too, I see," she said and laughed.

I touched my face and felt my beard. I'd been so busy I hadn't shaved in a week. Maybe I needed to shower and clean up before I asked Faith such an important question. I couldn't go over there looking like a bum!

"You look good, honey. Your beard matches your beautiful brown eyes. It is amazing how the eyes are made beautiful by who is behind them. You've turned out to be quite a handsome man." And here she reached out and touched my face again and I smiled at her and blushed.

"I want this more than anything," I confessed to her.

"What's that?" she asked, her voice a hoarse whisper and I handed her the tea again.

"Wife. Baby. All of it. I want to be a dad. I'd be the best dad in the world."

"I never seen a seventeen-year-old kid so excited about

being a dad. Most of them want to be baseball players or astronauts."

"No one ever really does that," I dismissed what she said. I didn't have time to have foolish kid dreams. I had to be focused on reality. I was flying without a net. I had one chance to set my course for manhood and go the right way. Dreams of being rock stars and racecar drivers was not part of it. I didn't have time for that foolishness.

"You want to be a dad that bad?"

"I do. I didn't know that's what I wanted in life but now I know. Now I want to do good in school and get a decent job and go be the best dad ever."

I gulped. It all sounded dumb and it probably was. Being a dad was easy. It was simple. But it was supposed to come after college and careers. No one ever told you *how* you were supposed to wait that long. How were the girls supposed to wait that long for us boys to be ready? I was ready now. Faith was ready. If she wasn't, I would help her be ready. She'd be a great mom. Not a mom who smoked and drank and had hangovers. Not a mom who hit and cussed. A good mom.

"I can do this."

"You want to be the dad you always wished you had. You think if you're a good dad, it'll make up for the bad childhood you had."

"No. I want to be a dad because I like kids."

"Where have you been around kids?" she asked and then laughed a small laugh like a bell.

"I don't know. School?"

"If you like kids so much, go and volunteer at an orphanage or something but don't rush into this. You're hung up on this because your dad wasn't worth shit."

"Grandma!" I couldn't believe she'd say such a thing about her own son.

I looked around to see if anyone had heard. A nurse in lime

green scrubs walked past on white sneakers that sighed on every step as she went but she didn't look our way because she had a Walkman strapped to her with music blasting out of the orange headphones.

"Mike," Grandma whispered and reached over to me with her shaky hand while her other hand lay tight and curled in her lap.

"Yes, Grandma, you ok?"

She had tears in her eyes and was trembling.

"Mike, I have to tell you something about your dad while I still have time."

Grandma's eyes filled with tears as she squeezed my hand. She sniffed and pulled another tissue out of the neck of her sweater.

"Your dad is a horrible man, Mike," she choked out and then waved at me to not interrupt.

"He's a drunk and a real sonuvabitch. Now let me finish. He thinks he's the smartest man there ever was because he got on at that casting plant. Oh he talks a big game but when they found out he was too stupid to actually build anything, I mean look at that motorcycle that's been taken apart for years that he had, IN THE HOUSE. My God."

"Grandma that's Dennis' bike. Not Dad's. And Dad never worked at Warner's Casting. That was also Dennis. You're confused."

Grandma's eyes pinched tight on the word 'confused' and I saw that I made her mad. But only for a second.

"Mike," she patted my hand. "I'm not confused."

I was dumbfounded. I wanted to understand her but my mind wasn't keeping up with her words. She must have sensed that for when she spoke again, she did it real slow.

"Mike, my Lonnie and your mom got married in 1969 and the man you call Dad, my boy Lonnie, went back to Vietnam. While he was over there in Nam, I worried about him every day and every night," Grandma said and cleared her throat here several times and looked away from me as the tears rolled down the wrinkles in her cheeks.

"Grandma, it's ok," I patted her hand. I wanted to hug her but she waved me back into my seat.

"Gimme a sip of tea."

I did and after a bit she continued.

"My poor boy Lonnie got her letter while stationed over there. I didn't hear about it till years later. I had no idea. Well, I had some ideas because you don't look like him and you don't look like her either. But I never said anything. My boy told me though when they split up."

I knew what she was going to say, but I couldn't put it all together and I wanted her to stop before the pieces met up. I stood up and paced the room. I stood in front of the gas fireplace and felt the waves of heat roll off it and onto my shins under my jeans and I walked back to my seat to get away from it.

"Your mom wrote your dad in Nam and told him she was pregnant. But she told him that he wasn't the dad. She had shacked up with Dennis soon as your dad went back to Nam. Dennis is your dad. But then Dennis got sent up to Browerton County Prison for writing bad checks and he was gone when you were born."

"I don't get it. Why isn't Dennis my dad then?"

"He IS your dad. But when your mom had you, he was in prison. She sent a telegram to the man who raised you, Lonnie, and asked him to come home right away. She said it was an emergency. They let him come home for a bit and he's been your dad ever since."

"He is my dad."

I looked at her and waited for her to agree. My mind buzzed in confusion.

"He tried to be. But he did a piss poor job especially after your mom brought in Dennis."

"None of this makes sense."

"Your mom wanted to go back to Dennis when he got out of prison. Dennis wouldn't claim you though so she stayed with your dad and he let Dennis move in."

"What kind of man does that?"

"I'm not proud of him. All he ever tried to do was be your dad but your mom wanted Dennis back and Dennis really was your father."

"No he's not." The whole mess of my childhood ran around in my head. Mom. Dad. Dennis. Even Linda, Dad's girlfriend, who he never really loved, all of them in that house, sitting around the kitchen table chain-smoking off their hangovers. It was all a mess while I tried to grow up in the middle of it. I hated them all.

"Neither of them are my dad."

"Mike, don't be mad."

But it was too late. I was already boiling and I stood up and ducked out from under her grasp on my arm. Her dry fingernails barely scraped across the sleeve of my coat.

"I'm sorry Mike."

I heard the heartache in her voice. None of it was her fault. And just like that, the anger was gone. I couldn't be angry at her, not at Grandma who had tried so many times to help me have a normal childhood.

"It's ok. It's not your fault. It's HER fault."
Grandma opened her mouth to say something but then stopped and shut it again.
She had snot running off the end of her nose and I saw it tremble in the light of the gas fireplace. I grabbed a Kleenex box off the mantle and handed it to her.

"I have to go Grandma." I tried to sound normal. I tried to not sound extremely mad and as upset as I felt. I hoped I sounded like a man with a lot of things to do, because that's what I was.

I couldn't stand being in there any longer. I needed to stretch my legs and drive off into the dark and go see Faith. I didn't need to think about which one of those men were my dad and which was trying to act like my dad. One of them bought me toys and gave me rides sometimes and the other one was always ready to pound me or blister my ass or throw me off the deck while the other one watched. And no one, fake dad, real mom, no one, stopped him from whalin' on me all those years because he was my real dad. I was his son. I came from him.

It was a lot to swallow. It was hard to keep it down.
Faith would never want me now if she knew who my family really was.
Now I was crying.

"Michael, don't cry. None of it's your fault."
Grandma tried to reach for me. She tried to roll the wheelchair towards me but I backed away and she couldn't do it with her one good hand.

"I need to tell Faith. I need to see if she's ok. She hasn't been feeling well. I need to see if she'll still have me after she finds out what my family is like. She has to know. I can't marry her unless she knows everything. She has to see them. See what I come from."

"Don't lose those papers I gave you, Mike! And don't underestimate Faith! I haven't met her but I know she loves you for you and not who you come from! Don't push her away!"

"I won't Grandma!" I called to her over my shoulder as I hustled my way down the long hall and out the door of the nursing home and out to my truck.

I couldn't wait to see Faith. I had a hundred things to talk to her about and I was certain I would be able to tell as soon as I saw her, if she was pregnant or not.

**

Chapter Thirty-Three

"I'm sorry, she went where?" I asked Faith's stepdad Garrett when he told me Faith wasn't home.

I shook my head in confusion at what he said.

"She went ice-skating with her friends over at the arena over at Hammond Park."

"But I thought she wasn't feeling good?"

"No, she's fine. Never better," Garrett told me.

I thought about asking him more about her. I thought about whether I should ask him for her hand in marriage. I rubbed my palms on my jeans several times and couldn't get them dry.

"Mike? Is something wrong?"

I touched the lump in my coat pocket that was the ring box.

"No. Why?"

"You don't look so good."

I rubbed my face and felt my beard and how heavy it was. I probably looked like a bum in my old Levis and the big suede cattle coat and my whiskery face.

"I'm good. I'm fine. What happened to Faith's real dad?"

It just popped out. It popped out so randomly I surprised myself.

"Mike, you should talk to Faith about that."

"I will. I should. I will do that. But where is he?"

"Mike, he passed away when she was two."

"Oh."

"It's ok, you don't have to feel so bad about asking about it. Talk to Faith about it. I would rather she tell you. It's her story, not mine."

"Ok. I will. Um. Who'd she go skating with?" I asked before stepping off the porch.

"Jennifer and Allison."
Jennifer and Allison.
**

I saw them first in the crowd of bright colored ski jackets when I got to the ice arena.
Jennifer and Allison, shrieking, their hair huge, white skates, pom poms on their toes, flying around the rink together, holding hands, going faster and faster.

And then I saw Faith. Awkward. Toes pointed out, ugly brown rented skates, blades glinting in the light of the flames of the huge fireplace as she scraped across the ice, jerkily. She couldn't hear me call to her from where I stood at the end of the rink. No one could. Joan Jett blared over loudspeakers at a crackling level before it was lost into the cold dark night. Under that commotion were the squeals and yells of 100's of teens skating and sliding and scratching by. Girls trundled past in awkward clusters and some went by on their own, gliding and turning and spinning easily. Boys crouched and zoomed fast, their faces red. A handful of kids scritched and scratched around at a lurching rhythm, randomly falling and flailing across the ice.

Jennifer and Allison. Two speed demons, their eyes magnified with thick smudges of eyeliner; their hair crimped and sprayed huge. They clung to one another's hands as their skates cut the ice as they flew past.

Jennifer didn't look pregnant. But did pregnancy even have a look that early on? Especially under that puffy ski jacket? I didn't think so. She looked like the same hard-faced girl she always was.

Then I looked at Faith, now down at the far end of the rink. Her hair fanned out across the back of her pink puffy jacket where it swayed to and fro as her legs worked hard to keep her from falling. Her arms windmilled out for balance, waving ridiculous lime green mittens out in front of her. She shouldn't be on the ice. Not if she was pregnant. Not safe. I needed to get out there but you had to pay for a ticket to get through the steel turnstyle and there was a huge line of pink faced Sand Creek kids in their Sand Creek jackets slowly going through. I didn't have time to wait for that.

I gripped the top of the boards as I watched her take the curve on the opposite side of the rink of me. Then I lost sight of her as a cluster of girls went in front of her like an ice barge made out of winter jackets and huge hair. Then I lost her in the spiraling figure skaters, the zig zagging hockey boys zipping past playing tag or keep away, or being general assholes. Then there she was. Her mittens high in the air in front of her like Frankenstein. I smiled. She was trying so hard to go. One leg was doing ok. The other leg didn't know how to go and kept holding her back. Maybe it was the leg she had broken when she fell on the bleachers. I wondered if the gold chain was around her ankle under her socks.

She pressed her lips together in determination.

Allison and Jennifer lapped her, their faces red and maniacal. They were the ones who asked her to come skate and they weren't even helping her. They saw me as they came down the straightaway and into the curve where I stood. Their faces turned sour at the same time and then they broke out into laughter and skated faster. But my eyes were back on Faith. She was almost halfway down the straightaway coming towards the curve where I stood. I hopped up and down on the balls of my feet. I smiled and ran my hands through my hair, trying absently to make sure it looked cool.

She was beautiful. She was too beautiful for me. She was trying to smile but then she'd nearly fall and then she'd frown. I was ready to leap over the boards. She needed to get off the ice. Her ankles were giving out and it looked like it hurt. That was it. I was going over the boards and going to go get her in my sneakers.

I put my palms on the boards and bounced easily to the top of the wall and would have made it except,

"Hey dickwad!"

The hand on my jacket jerked me back to dry ground and spun me around. I didn't care who it was. I jacked them in the face immediately, no time for second thoughts. And I was glad I did it too. Derek Charles and all his football buddies were with him. Soon as I saw it was him, I jabbed him another one right in the nose.

"Don't ever touch me again!" I snarled at him and punched him on every word.

I wasn't sure he heard me over the Quiet Riot now blasting out of the speakers, or over all the punches, so I racked his head back with another power punch below his eye. I saw him sway on feet and I let him go and went back to jumping over the wall.

Now Faith had seen what I did. Ugh. I didn't want her to see me in another fight. She'd think I was too immature to settle down with. But she had seen me and she had stopped skating. Her ankles wobbled weakly as she let her blades follow the deep ruts of other skaters.

I never took my eyes off of her as I hopped over the wall. But I shoved off too hard. Pain shot up through my broken arm as I pushed off on it. Things only got worse when my sneakers slapped the ice hard and the soles of my shoes slipped. My legs pistoned for traction and found none, and I fell hard on my face to the laughter of kids on both sides of the wall. I wasted no time pressing up onto my good arm and both knees and had to act fast to save my bare fingers from the blades of kids flying by. A glob of blood was already congealing on the cold ice from my nose. Busted it again.

But no time to waste because I felt Grandma's silver ring box pop out of my coat pocket. I saw it glide across a smooth spot on the ice a foot in front of me. I quieted my panic and crawled to it and grabbed it up just before a swarm of hockey guys flew past. Their digging and cutting blades sent flakes of snow into my face. I shoved the little box into the front pocket of my jeans this time and got up on one knee and saw Faith still coming to me but even slower now.

"Faith!"

"Mike!" she yelled but her yell ended in a startled shriek as Jennifer and Allison each hooked one of her arms and carried her off past me in a blur of pink coat and hair and screaming.

I stood there, helpless on the slippery ice while kids flew past me and I watched Faith get pulled against her will around the rink. The tips of her blades caught in the ice and slowed her down with little jerks and yanks but Jennifer and Allison pulled her harder. I watched as she went away from me and headed into the curve. As they rounded the turn, without warning, Jennifer let go of her grip on Faith's arm. It took Allison a minute to realize the game was over and then she too let go and sling-shotted Faith into the boards of the wall. The world around me blurred red with rage as I watched Faith slump onto the ice and fall over on her side.

Hatred boiled inside me, followed by pure cold fear and I struggled to slip and slide my way to her but not before the group of fast boys in hockey skates got to her. I watched, sick to my stomach, as they gently picked her up and took her to the wall. Then one in a bright hockey jersey pulled on the wall and it opened and he helped Faith up a step and then she disappeared, all except her pom-pom hat. The boys were clumped around her still when I got there, out of breath. As I slid into the wall, I held out my hand to the one in the bright jersey who had helped Faith off the ice and onto the bench.

"Thanks man, I owe you," I said to him as I shook his hand.

"No prob bro, this your girl?"

"Yeah man," I said and my feet slid out from under me as I tried to make it closer to the wall.
This time I didn't land on my broken arm. I landed on my side.

"Ooof you forgot your skates!" one of them said down to me and then two of them hoisted me back on my feet.

"Mike, oh my gosh Mike, I'm so glad you're here!" Faith cried and stood up and reached out to me.

"Faith are you ok?"

"I'm fine. I crashed into the wall is all. No big deal."

"Faith I saw it. I saw them fling you into the wall."

"Oh they were just trying to get me to go faster."

"No Faith. They weren't. Are you all right?"

"I'm fine," she hiccupped.

"Are you sure?"

"I think so."

"What about the baby?" I tried to say it quietly.

No one said anything; not me, not the boys in hockey skates, and not Faith.

"The baby?" she finally asked.

"Are you pregnant?" I asked close to her ear as I could so she could hear me over the loud music and over all the kids skating and screaming as they flew by.

"I ... I don't know.. Maybe."

Maybe.

A shiver ran through me that had nothing to do with the cold.

"I think one of my friends is," she said to me.

"They're not your friends. They wouldn't try to hurt you like that if they were. They wouldn't have thrown you into the wall like that."

"Why would they do that to me?" she asked as tears dripped down her face.

"Because they're bitches," one of the hockey dudes said and a couple of them laughed.

"You're right." Faith's voice was small but then she said, "Where are they?"

"Right there," I pointed to the two of them as they zoomed past.

"YO!" the guy in the jersey yelled and both Jennifer and Allison looked over.

"Get over here! Get over here!" they all yelled and it disgusted me to see that the two girls smiled and turned and came right over, tossing their hair and trying to look cute as they came.

"You threw me into the wall and that wasn't nice!" Faith said to them, her breath whispery with emotion. She wiped her tears with the back of her mitten.

"We were just playing!" Allison smirked.

"I didn't do anything!" Jennifer snapped.

"You did too!" Faith sounded outraged and angrier than I'd ever heard her.

"Let 'em go, who needs 'em? Let 'em rot! They don't exist!" I spat the words in their made-up faces and then to Faith I said, much quieter, "I love you, come 'ere," and took her hand and pulled her to me where we stood in the little penalty box surrounded by the hockey players.

"Mike I'm glad you're here."

"Me too," I said and smiled and felt the eyes of the dudes around us, watching our every move.

"Why did you come?"

"I think he came for this," a kid with red hair, wearing a red St. Thomas hoodie said and handed me Grandma's silver ring box.

"Oh man, it fell out again! Thanks!" I told him as I took the ring box and started to put it in my coat pocket once more.

"Bro, no offense, but I think it'd be safer with her," he told me and smiled and I saw he was missing a front tooth.

"Mike, what is that?"
I looked down at her and her eyes were huge in the bright light of the ice arena.

"Faith," I started to say and my voice trembled and I couldn't speak. I was shaking all over.

"Get on your knee," one of the hockey guys whispered out of the side of his mouth and then several others echoed it.
Faith sat down on the little bench and I looked around at all the faces of all the guys around me, guys I didn't know, a couple of them smiling and missing teeth, several with busted noses, and I realized they were ok fellas. Then I looked back at Faith and got down on one knee.

"Faith," I took her hand in mine, "I love you more than anything. And I know we're really young but I'm ready for forever, if you're ready for forever with me," I said and as I did, I opened the box and took out the two rings that were soldered together.

Then I looked up into her face, to see that her cheeks were shiny with tears and she was smiling down at me.

"Oh Mike," she gushed and then she nodded her head a hundred tiny nods as she blinked back the tears

"Yes?" I asked because I wasn't sure.

She nodded it more, several fast nods and then she said, "Yes!" and covered her mouth with her hand and cried.
I pulled her green mitten off and slipped those rings on her hand FAST and she looked at them a moment and then clinched her fingers in a fist because they were too big for her.

"Oh Mike," she started to say but I stood up and pulled her up with me and took her face in my hands and I kissed her long and deep as the hockey players cheered behind us.
I helped her get over the back wall of the ice rink and got her out of there as the hockey guys cheered us all the way to the car.

"I need to tell your folks," I told her in the truck.

"We need to tell them."

"We."
I grabbed her hand and put it over the stick shift and had her help me shift gears as we drove away.
**

But when we got to Faith's house, I didn't want to go in.

"Faith, we need to talk first."

"About what?"

"I have things I need to ask you. We should go to my place."

"Ask me here. I want to show Mom and Garrett the rings and tell them the news!" She held her hand up and admired the rings while I waited impatiently.

"Please Faith."
She stopped looking at the wedding rings and took my hands in her own small ones and stared into my eyes. She had me mesmerized. All I could think of was getting her naked and making love to her

all night in my bed. She made me weak.

"Mike. You're so handsome," she said without warning and smiled and I could see that she was blushing in the dark.

"Faith, please, stop," I begged her when she reached out and touched my hair.

"I love you, Mike."

"I love you too, baby. But we have some things to talk about."

"Like what?"

"Like the whole, are you pregnant, thing."

"Would you change your mind and not want to marry me if I wasn't?"

"No." I didn't even have to think about it. I'd want to marry her even if she wasn't pregnant. She was the one.

"I think I am. Pregnant."

"Tell me."

"I missed my period the week before Thanksgiving. And then I didn't feel good that day. And now I wake up really early and so hungry but feel so sick to my tummy."

"How do you feel now, after falling on the ice?"

"I'm ok. I think."

"We should go to the doctor."

"I can take a home test."

"I mean to see if you're ok from falling. To see if baby is ok," I said and reached for her tummy but it was under her winter coat.

"I feel fine. Nothing hurts. And I don't know if I'm pregnant yet. We need to find out."

"You want to take one right now that we buy one at the drugstore?" I asked her as I turned the truck back on.

"Sure! Yes!"

"You stay in the truck," I told her after I parked at the drugstore. "I'll run in and buy it. No one needs to see you buying that. They don't know me here, no one will care."

"K."

"Jennifer is pregnant too," she told me when I got back in the cab.

"So I heard." I started to light a cigarette and then thought better of it and stuck it behind my ear.

"She's going to get an abortion," Faith said in a small voice.

I was concentrating on getting the truck down the icy road without bumping along too hard in four-wheel drive and couldn't look at her. But I did grab her knee and then I said, "That's not what I want. Is that what you want?"

"No."

"Me either. I want this baby," I said and looked at her and saw her smile.

"Me too."

"Oh man, sorry babe, gotta pull over, ambulance coming." I barely made it out of the way for the orange and white ambulance barreling down the road.

"Wow, he was bookin'!" I exclaimed and checked the mirrors after he went past and I started to pull back out into the lane.

"They go by all the time because the nursing home is just a couple blocks that way."
Her words echoed in my head over and over. The nursing home. Grandma.

I looked across the cab of the truck. Faith. The pregnancy test.

Faith smiled at me and my choice was made as we continued on to her house where we ran right downstairs to the family room without her mom or step-dad hearing us. I sat on the couch and waited while she went in the bathroom. I heard the toilet flush and thought to myself, no going back, no matter what that test says.

"Mike?"
The wings of my future thudded against the wall of my heart as I stood up to go to her but my voice betrayed nothing.

"Yes honey?"

"Come in here, I can't watch."

I let myself into the small bathroom to see Faith sitting on the toilet seat, her head in her hands and her hair spilled in front of her face.

"Where is it? What do I do?"

"It's there. On the counter."

"What do I do?" I asked and glanced at the little white stick.

"Watch it. Tell me what it does."

"Ok. What's it supposed to do?"

"Two lines in the window means pregnant."

"K."

I leaned over and looked at the stick in question and the little square window.

"What's it doing?" she asked with her head still in her hands and her hair in front of her face.

"One blue line so far and I don't know what else it's doing."

"Is there another line?"

I strained to see it better without touching it. It looked like there was a shadow of a line there but it wasn't as strong as the first bright blue line. That one was clear. That one there was no doubt. Whatever that one meant, that first line, it was certain. The next one was a ghost of a line.

"I see liquid moving," I told her.

"That's my pee."

"What?" I asked and laughed once.

"My pee. I had to pee on it. Where's the pee?"

"Where's the pee? Well, it's in there. It's moving across the little window. Your pee is on the move."

Now I was laughing harder.

"Now what's happening? What's so funny?"

"You peeing on this dipstick, that's what's funny!"

"What's it doing? Is there a second line?"

"Let me look at it better."

I picked up the stick and squinted. The second blue line looked like it was turning a little red. Red? How could that be?

"I'm not sure what's going on," I told her as I held it right up to my eyes.

"MIKE!"

"What? What's wrong?" I asked as I dropped the whole works on the floor.

"Mike! You're not supposed to move it!"

"Well heck! Now I dropped it!"

I scrambled to pick it up and put it back on the counter but I looked at it first.

"Honey," I said to Faith and couldn't get another word out.

"What is it? What does it say?" she asked and slowly got up off the toilet and came over to me.

"It says your new name is Mom," I whispered with my arm around her and my mouth in her hair, kissing her a hundred times.

"Oh Mike, I'm gonna faint."

I squeezed her to me tight.

"Faint later, baby, we gotta tell your parents right now."

**

"Mr. and Mrs. Miller?"

"Hey kids," Faith's step-dad smiled at us from where he sat reading the TV Guide and holding the remote as he sat in the recliner in the living room while Faith's mom untucked her socked feet from under where she sat on the couch.

Mrs. Miller sat up on the edge of the cushion and her face tensed. I braced for yelling, for cursing, for just a second and then I remembered this wasn't my family. Faith's family didn't do things like that.

"Come in, sit down," she said and held her hand out to Faith and then waved me over too.

And that's when the tears started.

**

I went from being a guy who moved out to get away from

his own parents, and a guy who never ever met any girl's parents, to being a guy who asked a girl's parents if they were okay with me marrying her.

I stood there dumbly, hands in pockets with Faith's step-dad and watched as Faith and her mom both hugged each other and cried.

"Are you sure?" her mom asked a hundred times.

"We're sure! We took the test just now downstairs! And besides, I'd marry Mike even if I wasn't pregnant!"

"But my little baby can't be having a baby! Oh my gosh I'm going to be a grandma! I can't be a grandma! Have you ever seen such a young grandma?" Mrs. Miller asked and fluffed out her big feathered hair.

"Grandma, I should go tell my Grandma. She lives in the nursing home just a couple blocks away. She's who I got the rings from."

"They're beautiful, so beautiful. Honey, aren't they beautiful?" Faith's mom gushed over the rings on Faith's hand and called to her husband, but he was digging in a buffet cabinet full of drawers.

"What are you looking for?" she asked him.

"Cigars. I know we have cigars in here from when we went to England."

"Cigars are nasty, honey. No one wants a cigar."

"Mike and I are gonna have a cigar."

"Um… I really need to go see my Grandma and Faith should come too. I need to tell her the big news. She's who gave me the rings."

"The rings are beautiful, sweetie, but you'll have to get them sized. They're huge on her! She's gonna lose one!"

"What's that?" I asked.

"They're too big, she can't keep them on her finger!"

"But I don't want to take them off." Faith sounded upset. She looked from me to her mom and back to me.

"Oh it's just for a little bit," her mom assured her and started to take them off.

"Not yet." Faith balled her hand into a fist to keep the rings on and pulled away from her mom.

"This is so much to grasp," her mom sighed and sat down on the couch while her husband still dug in the cabinets for cigars. I pulled Faith towards the door and helped her with her coat then called to her parents.

"We're gonna go tell my family the news now."

"Well, be back in a couple of hours for a special dinner!" her mom called to us as we left to go to the nursing home.

But Grandma wasn't there. Her room was empty. Her quilt gone. Photos of her and Grandpa and her knickknacks were cleared off the dresser.

"I'm sorry, Mrs. Kilo passed away this afternoon," the nurse at the desk told me.

"Where is she?" I asked as Faith squeezed my hand.

"I imagine the hospital still, and then after that, wherever her services will be."

"What happened?" I asked. I felt like all the air had been sucked out of me.

"Mrs. Kilo had several heart problems the past six months and it finally took her. I'm so very sorry."
The nurse didn't look sorry. She looked like she wished I'd leave.

"If I hadn't come by, would I have even known?" I asked and couldn't help but raise my voice.

"Sir, we called her son, who was listed as next of kin."

"My dad," I said and pushed away from the counter and brought Faith with me.

"Mike, I'm so sorry."
I squeezed her hand in reply. I couldn't speak. I pulled her gently out the door and held open the truck door for her.

"Where are we going now?" she asked.

"My parents."

I stared straight ahead and drove us out of Sand Creek and onto the blacktop that would take us to my hometown and my parents' house. All of my parents; my dad and my real dad. Which was which, I didn't know anymore.

But when we got there, neither man was there; just Mom and Linda sat at the table, smoking cigarettes when I let myself in. I held Faith's hand and wouldn't let her come in any further.

The house reeked of cigarettes, stale beer, wet laundry. The stained white carpet was piled with dirt, mail, beer cans, cigarette butts, and random things like silverware and plates crusted in food. Things were strewn all over the floor and piled deeper near the walls. The old couch sagged in the middle and had an assortment of work boots stacked in front of it.

Mom and Linda froze where they sat at the old brown and yellow flowered kitchen table. Both women had their greasy hair pulled back in rubberbands and both wore old slacks and sweaters with white socks and natty house-slippers. Two of them. Almost exactly the same. I'd never noticed it before.

"Mike?" Mom asked in her sharp voice. "Who you got with you? You hear about Grandma?"

"Yes."

"Well shut the door, come in."

"Nah, we're leaving."

The look on Faith's face told me she was disgusted by it all. For me, it was time to go but she wasn't having it. She pulled away from me and stepped towards my mom. I wanted to jump in front of her, protect her; she was carrying my baby and I didn't want my mom anywhere near her.

"No Mike," she whispered.

Faith stepped around me and walked right up to my mom. Her long honey hair swished back and forth over the back of her pink puffy coat as she held out her hand to my mom.

"Hi, I'm Faith."

Her little voice sounded like the tinkling of an angel's bells in our cruddy, smelly, little house. Those four walls had never ever heard such a voice. This was a house full of cussing and yelling, doors slamming, and suffering and crying.

I glanced over Faith's shoulder at the dented brass knob of the kitchen door and remembered Dennis kicking it shut when I was four as I was standing on the other side of it. I had caught that doorknob in my mouth with my front teeth and I had almost swallowed them. It hit me so hard I had fallen on my butt on the back deck and sat and cried and cried. When Dennis opened the door and saw me, blood spilling out my mouth, my eyes dazed and crying, he had laughed. He had held his belly and laughed and laughed.

I had a busted mouth or nose my entire childhood. My arms were in casts so much, but I never stopped playing, I never missed PE, I never rested. I looked over at the old flowered couch and could count on one hand how many times I stayed home sick on it. Chicken pox was one. Stomach flu a couple times the other. Otherwise, I went. Snot nosed and coughing, I was the kid the teachers would let sleep in a corner of the room covered by spare blankets when I was too sick to sit at my desk.
I would never let my baby into this house again. This would be his first and last time here as a little tiny dumplin' in Faith's tummy.

"Well hello," I heard my mom say and then she peeked around Faith to look at me.

She had a smirk on her face as if something was hilarious and only her and I knew what it was. She shook her head and chuckled as she ground out her cigarette butt in the overflowing ashtray.

"What brings you by?" Mom asked me and then she looked Faith up and down and said, "News of Grandma? News that the old woman finally cashed her chips in?"

"Yes. I just found out. I came by for that and we have some news of our own." I stepped even with Faith and took her hand.

"Oh, and what's that? You knock up little Missy here and

are looking for more handouts?"

"No. We don't need anything from you. I wanted Faith to see where I came from. That's all. So she can know me better."

"Is that right?" Now mom's voice was loud like how she always blasted it when I was young. She reminded me of a cartoon elephant trumpeting out her nose. It was the voice she used when she was ready to start chasing me and hitting me.

I ignored her now. She wasn't hitting me now. I glared at her once and she bared her yellow teeth at me between her cracked lips.

"This is my house, Faith. Well, it was my house," I corrected myself before saying, "This is my mom, and that's my dad's girlfriend, Linda. That is the man that's not really my dad but he called himself my dad. My real dad is Mom's boyfriend Dennis. But neither one of them did much to raise me besides kick me around and cuss at me. These are the people I come from. This house, these people, this is the reason I moved out on my own."

"Oh you're so perfect and good and we treated poor Mike so bad!" Mom mocked and lit another cigarette.

Linda sat next to her and lit another one too. She looked high and out of it. Her eyes were huge and out of focus. She was always high on something. She never stepped in when they were all having a go hitting me. But I couldn't blame her. Maybe she was more trapped than I was as a kid.

"It was a mistake coming here, let's go."

"Don't go, it's just getting good. So, you know about Dennis, he's your real dad. Did he tell you? Or did your dad tell you?" Mom asked and took a long drag on her cigarette and blew it out her nose.

As I looked at her, at how disgusting she looked, I wondered how I ever smoked and I knew I never would again.

"Grandma told me the other day. Where is Dad? And where's Dennis?" I felt jumpy with Dennis not in sight. It would be just like him to hit me from behind when I wasn't looking.

"Your dad is at work. Dennis, I'm not sure. He's out."

"Hmph."

"So, when's the baby due?" My mom asked Faith in a sweet voice that made me sick.

"We don't know yet. We just found out," Faith answered her and held up her hand to show my mom the rings.

"Get your hands off her now!"

Mom had grabbed Faith by the wrist fast as a trap and I wasn't having it. I was ready to knock her out.
But Mom didn't let her go. Not immediately. She pulled Faith's hand closer to her face and examined the rings.

"I know those rings! Those are your grandma's rings! I should have had those! How did you get those?"
I shoved my mom down into her seat as soon as she let go of Faith.

"Grandma gave them to me."
I made sure she wasn't going to get up again then I said to Faith, "Let's go."
And I pulled her out of there quickly but gently, watching for Dennis the entire way.

"That's my mom. That's my house. That was the couch I slept on all my life. All of that is why I moved out. Part of it at least. Now you know where I come from, kinda. I don't even know where I come from because I just now found out my dad isn't my dad. So, if you don't want to marry me, I guess I'll understand."
Everything felt horrible suddenly.

"Mike, I know who you are. I didn't need to see any of that to know who you were. You aren't them," Faith said and shivered and wrapped her arms around my neck and kissed me on the mouth.

"Mmm," was all I could say back.

"Mmm, what?" she asked.

"I just wanted you to see that so you know who I am. So you can decide now if you could love someone like me who comes from such a horrible place."

"I do."

Her voice was tiny and I needed her to know how much I loved her.

"Faith."

"Yes?"

"I love you so much."

"I know."

She looked up at me with those huge dark blue eyes. I could look into them forever. I could disappear in them. They were full of our future together. They were full of everything good which was all her.

"Faith, you're perfect, you're beautiful and sweet, and such a good girl. I love you so much, I don't deserve you."

"Are you trying to break up with me?" she asked and her lip curled into a tiny smile as she asked.

"No, baby. I just want you to know how much I love you."

"Mike, I was teasing you. I know how much you love me. I'm bad at saying it back because I'm not as good expressing myself like you are," she said to me and I had to interrupt her.

"Faith, you're perfect at expressing yourself."

"I don't think I've ever told you how much I love you, Mike."

"That's ok, baby."

"No, it's not."

She put her little hands on the front of my coat and then walked them up over my shoulders and wrapped them behind my neck where her fingers immediately began to play with my hair and drive me crazy. I had to roll my shoulders and pop my neck to get the chills to settle some.

"Mike, I love you so much. You make me so," she trailed off and blushed and tried to let go of me and back away but I wasn't having it. I clamped my arms around her waist and held her tight.

"So what?" I asked her and we both laughed a little.

"You know what you do to me," she said and smiled.

I did. I knew all right. Which was why we were in this

predicament. The best predicament of my life. Faith was going to have my baby. I was going to be the best dad the world had ever seen. I'd have my own family. We would have so many kids. The holidays would be wonderful. And summer vacations. Beaches and hotels. Sunday dinners. First days of school. Little League games. Sunday School and church. We'd get a dog. I'd work hard. Faith would cook and teach the kids to be sweet. It was going to be the best thing to ever happen to me.

"Let's go home," I told her and opened the door of the pick-up. I wanted to get her out of there before my dad or Dennis showed up and ruined everything.

That was the last thing I needed; Dennis coming home and trying to rough me up in front of Faith. I never wanted her to see that sort of thing ever.

"My mom's making a big dinner for us!" Faith said when I got in the cab.

"No, I meant our home, my apartment."

Her eyes grew round and huge when I said it and when she smiled, I put the truck in gear and roared away from the dingy little house with thoughts of never returning to it ever again. I didn't care which one was my dad; Dennis or Dad. I hoped to see neither again.

Chapter Thirty-Four

We saw Molly in the hall as soon as we came in the front door of the apartment house. She was agitated and her hair was coming out of a ponytail on the side of her head. She was dressed in head-to-toe neon colors. A huge sweatshirt hanging off one of her plump shoulders added to how chaotic she looked.

"Molly?" I asked and couldn't help but flash the woman a huge uncertain smile. She was so unpredictable, who knew what she was doing? Maybe aerobics or some dance video in her pink Reebok sneakers.

"Mike! The black car came back and a guy came in the apartment!"

"Holy crap no way!"

"He's crazy looking and he kicked in your door!"

"My door?"

"I called the police! They're on their way! You should come in here! Be safe!"

"Faith, get in there! Molly! Lock the door! Barricade it! This is my future wife! The mother of my baby! Don't let anyone get in!"

"Oh my God Mike! Get in here!" Molly reached for me but I pushed Faith into her arms and I pulled the door shut behind them with a bang.

Then I ran up the stairs, hard, and as I went, I realized I hadn't seen Faith's face one last time. Nor had I told her I loved her. Nor had I kissed her.

I pushed all that out of my head. I had a good idea who was in the black car that kept casing the place. I could hear him tearing apart my apartment before I rounded the stairs to the third floor. Luckily, the door to my apartment was smashed open all the way and I could see what was going on before entering. Drawers from my dresser were broken against the far wall where they had been thrown full blast. Plaster and splintered wood covered the floor in sharp pieces and crumbling chunks. As I walked up to the door quietly, I watched my tv as it flew across the room, smashed in a crash, and joined the broken dresser pieces on the hardwood floor. Dennis stood with his back to me, stooped over and heaving hard, catching his breath after wrecking my little apartment. Me and Faith's future home together. I saw red for a second but I didn't move as he froze and slowly turned to face me.

"There you are. Son," he heaved and smiled and cleared his throat.

"Hi Dad. I'm home," I gritted my teeth and answered him and stepped into my apartment and swung the door shut behind me.

"You find what you're looking for?" I asked him.

"I did, somewhat," he answered with a toothy smile and then reached over to the empty dresser that was still standing, albeit with holes where the drawers had been.

He pulled a fat envelope off the top of the dresser and held it up.

"I read this," he told me and squeezed his eyes into squints as he smirked at me from where he stood on top of all my clothes that he'd dumped out of the drawers.

"Oh really? I didn't know you could read." I threw a smirk right back at him and took out a cigarette.

"Light?" he asked and held out his zippo to me and flicked the flame.

There was no way I was going to let him get near me, much less with a burning zippo. I stepped back from him, almost into my entryway.

"No?" he asked and cocked his head.

I didn't answer. I watched him as he held the zippo in one hand and the fat envelope from Grandma in the other. Then his eyes bugged out and his greasy, whiskery face broke into a vulgar grin as he brought the flame to the envelope and lit it on fire.

I stepped back into the entryway and calmly walked into my kitchen. There was no use in fighting him. Not with my hands at least. He was twice as big as me and he was going to burn it if that's what he wanted. I didn't even know what it was, though I had a good idea.

He could burn it but I didn't have to watch. That took some of his power away. I stood in front of the windows and opened one to listen to the cars outside. Then I lit a cigarette and stood by the kitchen table as cold air swirled around my pantlegs.

"That was your grandma's Will, you little prick. You got no right to any of that anyway. You're not her kin," he said from behind me.

I ignored him and kept smoking, thinking about how it was probably going to be my last smoke and that I'd better enjoy it while I could.

"Anything in that Will belongs to your daddy who isn't your daddy, you little asshole. Besides, you're taking enough money from your parents as it is."

I still didn't turn around and I still didn't say anything. Instead, I crushed the half-smoked cigarette out in the ashtray on the kitchen table.

"This whole place is gonna be an ashtray in a little while. You better get out before your whole mousehole of an apartment goes up," he taunted from behind me and still I didn't turn around.

I eyed the table leg that I had tried to glue back together. It looked like it was on crooked. It'd be something I'd need to fix before Faith moved in. I stared at it till my eyes watered. I stared at it till I heard the apartment door open.

"Mike, is everything all right?"

"Who's this? Your bitch girlfriend?" Dennis asked and laughed. "She's got some big ol' tiddies on her! Damn son! Look at you getting' some big tiddies!" he roared as he leered at Faith.

I saw red. I felt red. I buzzed all over with hate. I kicked the table leg hard and broke it off with a hollow "chonk" and grabbed it, choked up on it, spun on the worn soles of my Nike shoes, and hit Dennis square in the face and knocked his teeth out. They sounded like someone throwing a handful of river pebbles when they hit the old white refrigerator. He fell on the floor, conveniently in front of them.

"Oh my God, Mike! Your apartment is on fire!" Faith shrieked from the entryway.

"Shit! Get out of here Faith!"

I shoed her out the door of the apartment, then I came back in and hoisted up Dennis over my shoulders. I glanced back at the little apartment. My home. My clothes. My bed where Faith and I had made love all night. All of it was on fire. Then I carried Dennis down the three flights of stairs as the firetrucks rolled up.

Chapter Thirty-Five

I got an award at the end of that school year.
I joked with Faith that they really just wanted me out of their school
so they pushed me along and gave me an award so that I would
never return. But it was a real award, according to the principal. An
adversity award, he called it. The school said I faced more adult
problems in one school year than most of their students do in four
years there. That was saying a lot because it was a rough school full
of rough kids who came from a lot of problems. Me, I thought I had
less problems than most of them because I was able to move out
and away from my problems.

But still, it was my first award. I had trophies for wrestling
and even one for track. But the last award I could remember being
given had been in second grade for being a good citizen for carrying
Kenny the Howler Kimmel to the school nurse after he got hit by a
car on his bike two blocks from school. It probably wasn't the safest
choice considering he had a broken arm and hip, and he had
howled the entire way, earning him the nickname, but I didn't
know better when I was eight to not move an injured person.

I lost the award and the picture Dad had taken of me getting
it when Dennis burned my apartment up.

I lost everything and what a way to start a new life with
soon to be new wife and new baby, with nothing. But I guess it was
ok.

New life. New stuff. New old stuff. So many people chipped
in stuff to help us get started. The guys at work. Jeff and Shane and
their folks. Faith's folks. Doris. Molly. And I shopped around for
things with my own money.

Faith got an award from my high school too which was now her high school. Highest GPA. She also helped tutor about twenty kids and helped them graduate. Yep. My high school. She had to transfer because she was pregnant and didn't want to be at her old school. I told her she really just wanted to be with me, and that she just wanted to be at my graduation with me too. And you know what? I think it was the truth. Her smile told me I was correct. Her being at the same graduation as me was the only reason I went. We even got to sit close to each other because our last names were close together.

We had spent that winter semester holding hands in the hallway every day, walking to classes together. I never missed a single class except to go to all of Faith's doctor appointments. Other than that, it was class every single day. And then work at the tire factory every night and not just weekends. Faith spent the nights at her house where she still lived with her parents.

I spent them at Grandma's little old white brick house out near the drive-in theater, down the road from the tire factory. It took all winter to clean that place out and paint it all but I got it wife-ready and more importantly, baby ready. I slept on a mattress in the front room for a long time. But I got us furniture. I had the whole house filled with what we needed by that June when we graduated high school. Jeff and Shane helped out too and Jeff even got on at the tire factory with me at nights. We were all growing up. Or maybe we weren't.

"Dude, there you go. Look at her," I whispered to Shane as the boombox played the song Faith had picked out for her bridesmaids to walk down the aisle to. It was some classical slow serious song that I had laughed at before. But now, now it was making me emotional and I was trying to distract myself from the dust in my eyes by getting Shane and Jeff to check out the bridesmaids.

"There you go," I said again as the girl with the huge head full of brown curls came through the lace curtains at the end of the aisle carrying a bouquet of pink flowers.

We were at Mint Falls, on the little lookout across from it, close friends and family gathered all around on white chairs for our little ceremony. It was a beautiful sunny day and the falls danced and laughed as the water hit the rocks.

"She looks, interesting," Shane whispered back to me.

"She's tall," I said and smiled and nodded at him, my face hot from nerves and excitement.

"She is. I like tall."

"Tall is good," Jeff agreed.

"Oh but look at this one," I whispered as another girl came through the curtains.
This one wasn't so tall. But what she lacked in height, she made up for with a lot of red hair and even more freckles that clashed with her pink satin dress.

"This one looks like a handful," I said out of the side of my mouth and leaned over to Jeff to see that he was blinking fast and staring at her as she came down the white carpet that had been rolled out on the stone path.

"Wow," was all he said.

"She drives a Camaro," I told him and when he looked at me I couldn't help but smile a huge one at him.

"She have a date?" Jeff asked.

"You, if you play your cards right."

"Nice," both of them said at once.

"Jinx, you owe me a coke," Shane whispered.

"Oh wow boys, look at this one. I like this one the best," I whistled softly and I stood up as straight as I could in my black tuxedo and I held my breath as I felt my eyes dance at the beautiful sight of her. This one made me smile. This one lit me up in all the right places. I could look at this one forever and never get tired of seeing her.

Faith, in all white lace and beads and satin gown with her veil in front of her face and down her shoulders looked glorious.

Her mom and stepdad held her elbow on either side of her as they came through the curtains. When Faith came through all the way, and I saw all of her, she took my breath away.

"Oh I like this one a lot," I told the boys as I caught a glimpse of her pink face under the veil.

"She looks like work," Shane chuckled.

"She looks like a handful," Jeff added.

She looked like more than a handful. She was glowing, she was radiant, she was eight months pregnant and shaped like a basketball. A beautiful basketball. My basketball.

"Wowee," I whispered to her as her step-dad brought her all the way up to me.

I saw her smile under the veil. I saw the tears clinging to her eyelashes and bobbing just like the sparkly little earrings that bobbed on her ears as her head trembled. I saw nothing else till the preacher said, Kiss the bride, and then I shut my eyes and kissed my beautiful Bleacher Girl. My Faith.

**

That little basketball held on all through July, making me wait to meet my baby. I worked six nights a week with Jeff pulling tires out of molds for hours on end where we both talked about doing something else, even if it meant going to school some more, while I waited on the arrival of my child.

"I can't do more school. I hate school. I'm looking at the pipefitters," I told him.

"What is that? Sounds like a baseball team or something. Minor league."

"No, dummy. Plumbers, Pipefitters."

"Hmmm does it pay good?"

"Yes. Better than here."

"They need more than one?"

"Yes."

"Count me in."

"Cool. I got a family to feed. I need to make more than here.

And this is boring as heck. I'm about to fall asleep."

"I don't have a family to feed," Jeff grumbled and kept pulling tires and stacking them.

"I know."

"That baby wasn't even mine. That Troy Lannerman lost his marbles when he found out she got rid of that baby."

"You didn't pay for the abortion, did you?"

"Nah. She wouldn't talk to me. Her parents probably did. Or she did herself. Or who knows, maybe she hooked some other guy into it," Jeff shrugged.

"How do you know it wasn't yours?"

The idea of a girl aborting my baby would have made me feel awful. But I didn't tell Jeff this. This was too much to explain over the noise of the tire machines. I wouldn't have told him anyway.

"Not sure, I guess. But the way he lost his mind at the car lot, smashing all them windshields, he must have been pretty certain that that baby was his," Jeff shook his head slowly and trailed off.

I knew all about smashing windshields and how it made you feel a little better sometimes. But I wouldn't have to worry about Dennis or his windshield for a long time. He got sent up for arson and that was a third strike for him, so he'd be away a long time.

I sat and thought about this as we pulled the rubber tires out one after another. That's how this job was; you could zone out and think of other things while doing it. That's why it took me a moment to realize Mr. White, the late shift foreman was calling my name.

"Mike! Hospital! Baby's on its way! Get out of here!"

"Baby on its way!" the guys on the line all cheered and pulled out cigars and unwrapped them right there on the assembly line.

"Have a cigar, Mike!"

"Can't! Baby! Wife! Gotta go!"

I clocked out and ran out to the truck. Wouldn't be long and we'd be driving everywhere in Faith's little hatchback with a baby in the back but right now I couldn't believe I was finally going to be a dad; I was finally going to meet my child. Girl? Boy? I had no idea. I just hoped Faith would be alright.

But as I pulled out of the tire factory I heard the ding-ding of the train lights and then I saw the grain train. After sitting the longest five minute of my life I went around the back of the Thunderbird Bowling Alley, past the carpet mill and under a viaduct that went under the train, instead of over it, and on my way to St. Mary's.

I found a much smaller, much paler Faith in the bed when I skidded into the room on my worn-out work boots.

"Where is he? She? Baby? Is the baby ok? Are you ok?" I asked her as I ran to her side and kissed her sweaty forehead.

"Do we need to push or breathe or do I need to get ice chips or hot water?" I asked her and glanced all around.
Faith looked different. She looked flat. The basketball was gone.

"Mike, the nurse has the baby. She'll be right back."

"She? I have a daughter?"

"I'm talking about the nurse, silly," Faith said and smiled up at me.

Her eyes had purple rings under them and she looked exhausted.

"So, it's a boy? I have a son? Or is it a girl? Why didn't you wait for me?" I asked and was nearly shouting it.

"I tried! But it happened so fast! You'll see!" Faith laughed.

"There's Dad," the nurse called from the hall as she wheeled in a clear little bassinette.

I could see a tiny pink fist waving around up in the air, free from the tight white blankets. A wee scrunched up red face with dark eyes blinked up at me, looked up at me with interest, and I could not look away.

"Say hello to your son, Mr. Kilo, he came fast and early and will need to be observed."

"A son. A son," I breathed in and out fast. "Is he ok?"

"He'll be fine," the nurse crooned down at my boy as she picked him and handed him to me.

He was warm and heavier than he looked and he fit right up next to my chest. I could feel him squirming under all the tight blankets. I would never let him go.

"He'll be ok?" I asked again and gulped.

"He'll be just fine," the nurse said one more time.

"We did it, you did it, Faith."

I looked from my son to my beautiful wife whose golden honey hair spilled all around her shining face on the white pillow and then I kissed my boy.

"I love you son, you'll be fine, you'll be fine," I told him and kissed him again.

I'd kiss him every day of his life until he got big enough to make me stop, I loved him that much. I felt more complete than I ever had my whole life. I felt ten feet tall.

"He'll be fine," Faith echoed from the bed as she reached out for us.

"He's gonna be a lot of work, this one, but he'll be so worth it."

THE END

Bleacher Girl

Shirley Johnson

www.ingramcontent.com/pod-product-compliance
Lightning Source LLC
Chambersburg PA
CBHW020910200626
46814CB00001BA/261